GA_ _LEN
F_

Duke

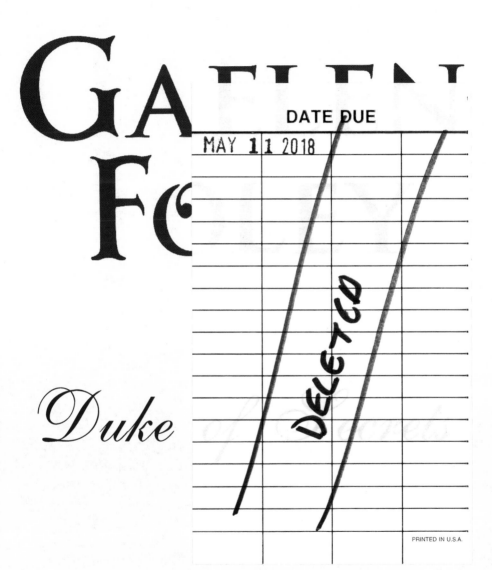

MOONLIGHT SQUARE, BOOK 2

Also by Gaelen Foley

Ascension Trilogy
The Pirate Prince
Princess
Prince Charming

Knight Miscellany
The Duke
Lord of Fire
Lord of Ice
Lady of Desire
Devil Takes a Bride
One Night of Sin
His Wicked Kiss

The Spice Trilogy
Her Only Desire
Her Secret Fantasy
Her Every Pleasure

The Inferno Club
My Wicked Marquess
My Dangerous Duke
My Irresistible Earl
My Ruthless Prince
My Scandalous Viscount
My Notorious Gentleman
Secrets of a Scoundrel

Age of Heroes
Paladin's Prize

Moonlight Square
One Moonlit Night
Duke of Scandal

Anthologies
Royal Weddings
Royal Bridesmaids

Gryphon Chronicles
(Writing as E.G. Foley)
The Lost Heir
Jake & the Giant
The Dark Portal
The Gingerbread Wars
Rise of Allies
Secrets of the Deep

50 States of Fear
(Writing as E.G. Foley)
The Haunted Plantation
Leader of the Pack
Bringing Home Bigfoot
Dork and the Deathray

Credits and Copyright

Table of Contents

Chapter 1 – The Forbidden Man...1

Chapter 2 – Cat and Mouse...18

Chapter 3 – Intruder Unmasked...35

Chapter 4 – In the Dark...56

Chapter 5 – Bonfire Night..70

Chapter 6 – Drawn In..85

Chapter 7 – Traveling Companions 97

Chapter 8 – Owlswick..112

Chapter 9 – All the Dark Corners...124

Chapter 10 – Ghosts..138

Chapter 11 – A Change of Plans...151

Chapter 12 – First Snow 165

Chapter 13 – Destined 179

Chapter 14 – Origins...191

Chapter 15 – The Past Catches Up 206

Chapter 16 – Angels & Demons..217

Chapter 17 – Coming Home...232

Chapter 18 – Wild at Heart..244

Chapter 19 – Blood Ties 254

Chapter 20 – The Duke's Revenge..267

Chapter 21 – Unleashed 279

Epilogue – Snowfall..297

About the Author

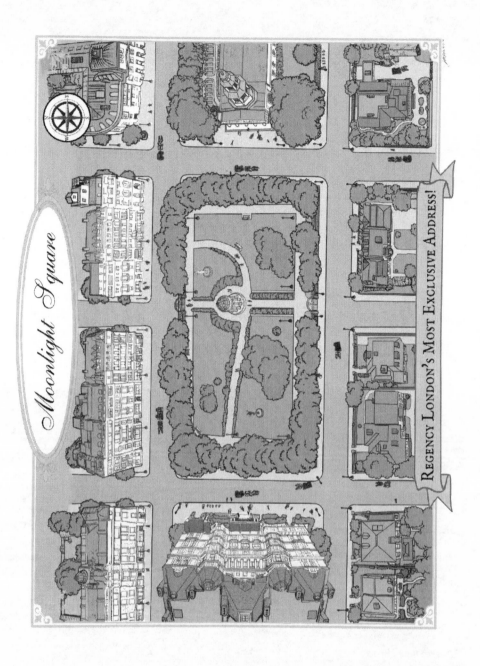

Moonlight Square

REGENCY LONDON'S MOST EXCLUSIVE ADDRESS!

CHAPTER 1

The Forbidden Man

A single moonbeam, ghostly and pale, slanted through her window, piercing the blue-black darkness of her chamber to illuminate the clock face. Quarter till midnight, it read.

Almost time to go.

Lady Serena Parker sat tensely on the edge of her bed, waiting. No sound but the mantel clock's steady tick-tock filled the heavy stillness in her room. Her pulse, however, beat at a quicker pace, considering her illicit intentions.

Dry-mouthed, she took a sip of tangy white wine to settle her nerves, then rechecked the lacings of her half-boots.

All the while, the large, fluffy family cat perched on the windowsill, posted as her lookout. Wesley's striped tail twitched as he peered out through the glass.

But even with the feline's keen night vision, not even the tabby could see the duke's corner mansion on the opposite side of Moonlight Square from the bedroom window.

The autumn leaves still clinging to the plane trees in the garden park blocked the view of Rivenwood House, as Serena herself had confirmed, many times.

Now and then, her family's London townhouse creaked around her in the autumn wind gusts of this chill October eve.

But inside her room, it still smelled of summer, thanks to the flowers sent by suitors who had only grown more ardent now that she was no longer seen in the company of her unlikely former favorite, the bookish

Lord Tobias Guilfoyle.

The thought of her quirky ex-beau gave her a pang; Serena took another shaky sip of wine.

Alas, Toby had proved a coward, caving in to his parents' disapproval of their match after certain revelations had emerged.

As for the rest of her suitors, they were all the same. They bored her. Toby might've been quirky and rather hapless, the dear, rumpled thing, but at least he was an interesting person.

Anyway, larger matters than marriage obsessed her now. How could she take the slightest interest in love when her entire world had been turned upside down by the awful things Toby had uncovered about her family while researching information for his book?

She needed answers—by God, she deserved them—and that was why she was fully dressed and prepared to leave the house as midnight approached.

On the face of it, she knew her plan this night was rather mad, but she had suffered in darkness and ignorance long enough. Her mother's cruel, heartless, *stubborn* refusal to divulge basic truths about Serena's origins left her no choice but to seek the answers on her own.

The clock bonged once, nearly making her jump.

Quarter to twelve now. She got up restlessly and paced over to join Wesley by the window.

Glancing out, she watched the moon-silvered treetops half stripped of leaves sway and toss in the wind, but they still blocked her view of Rivenwood House on the opposite corner of the square.

Drumming her fingers silently on the white window sash, Serena supposed she was nervous but not afraid. On the contrary, she felt sharply focused, maybe even a little excited at the prospect of the night's dubious adventure. Eager to go.

She just wanted to make sure she gave the revelers at the duke's mansion enough time to throng into the party and have a few drinks.

Midnight should be late enough, she trusted, considering all London had been waiting for this night with bated breath.

It was the first time the intensely mysterious Azrael Chambers, Duke of Rivenwood, had ever opened up his house to Society.

Given the reclusive, pale-haired nobleman's peculiar mystique and his family's dark, almost spooky reputation, reportedly counting among their ancestors the infamous John Dee, occult master and court astrologer to Good Queen Bess, it was no surprise—to her, at least—that with

Hallowe'en approaching, His Grace had chosen to summon the ton to a masquerade ball.

Serena, too, had received one of the coveted invitations.

No doubt the enigmatic loner had only sent it to mock her, however, considering the cat-and-mouse game they had played for the past few months, without even having a proper introduction.

They were neighbors in Moonlight Square, of course, but they'd never met properly, for he was a man who famously kept to himself, and — more importantly — her mother had always forbidden her to talk to him.

Until recently, Serena couldn't fathom why. She knew her parents were acquainted with him somehow, for she had a faint childhood memory of the young duke visiting their country house in Buckinghamshire once, some thirteen years ago.

He could not have been any older than twenty-one, the same age she was now, having just attained his majority.

Why he'd come, she did not know, but he'd left again in less than half an hour and never returned.

She remembered the day well, not only because he'd made quite an impression on her eight-year-old imagination, but also because she'd found her mother crying after he was gone.

An affectionate child, she'd run over and hugged the countess, asking what was wrong, but Mama had said it was all right — she was crying because she was happy.

None of it made any sense.

Serena knew it was all tied together, though, and was determined to get to the bottom of it tonight.

Yet...what His Grace must think of her after all the times he had caught her staring at him over the past few months, she shuddered to wonder. He must find her very strange, indeed — though that was the pot calling the kettle black, eccentric as he was.

She couldn't help it. She had become slightly obsessed with the man, now about thirty-four, and it wasn't just because of his wary, elusive magnetism, or the beautiful bone structure of his sharp-angled, high-cheek-boned face. Or his ice-blue, almost silvery eyes. Or his sensitive, unsmiling mouth. Or his elegant, understated way of moving.

Though she had certainly noticed all these, watching him so closely.

Indeed, he had a fascinating, otherworldly appeal, but it was not romantic interest that drove her.

It was the knowledge, finally divulged by her old childhood nurse, that the current Duke of Rivenwood alone might possess the answers to all her burning questions.

And so, for months now, Serena had stood back in a state of uncertainty, continually weighing in her mind whether it was worth the risk to try to approach the intimidating stranger and ask him outright what he knew about these dark family secrets.

Secrets that her parents, the Earl and Countess of Dunhaven, had once shared, it seemed, with his father, the previous Duke of Rivenwood.

Ultimately, Serena had decided against trying to involve her intriguing neighbor for a variety of reasons. First, she was not supposed to talk to that man, ever.

Of course, after Mama had proved such a liar and a fraud, Serena no longer felt entirely bound to obey, but there were other reasons, too.

For example, secondly, in order simply to explain the context of her questions, she'd have to confide in His Grace about some very embarrassing truths, and there was no telling how he would react.

She did not want her secrets used against her or, worse, exposed to all the world.

But thirdly, and most worrisome of all, the dreadful rumors that Toby had accidently uncovered in his research concerned not just Serena's parents, but Azrael's, too.

And therein lay the rub.

Everybody knew that Azrael had witnessed his father's murder as a boy.

The previous Duke of Rivenwood had been stabbed to death by a homeless vagrant whom father and son had caught poaching in the woods at one of their estates when they had gone out walking together.

Indeed, it was widely thought this tragic incident explained why the son had grown up so strange and withdrawn, preferring the company of animals to people.

The whole ton knew, moreover, that the topic of his father's death was taboo with the present duke; one mentioned it in front of him at one's own peril.

And since this was precisely the subject Serena would need to broach with him to get the answers she craved, she had no idea how to surmount this obstacle.

It didn't seem worth it to go opening up that particular Pandora's box. God only knew what it might get her.

Her old childhood nurse had made it very clear, after all, that while the Rivenwood men might look like beautiful fallen angels, shining and pale, they could be extremely dangerous.

"Even your mother was afraid of his sire," old Mrs. Hopkins had warned—and that was saying something, for the haughty Mariah, Lady Dunhaven, wasn't afraid of much.

Her Ladyship knew well that her striking beauty gave her great power in the world—even more so when she had been Serena's age.

Back then, she could have anyone or anything she wanted, and had apparently been wild enough to indulge in that privilege as she pleased.

Of course, now the reformed countess spent most days with her head buried in her Bible, but back then, well, Serena now knew, thanks to Toby, that Mama had been a hellion.

And whatever unpleasant pursuits she'd been involved in, the previous Duke of Rivenwood had been the ringleader.

Which was why Mrs. Hopkins' ominous words still rang in Serena's ears: *"Stay away from that one, milady. He's likely just as bad as his father, the wicked heir to an evil family."*

"Well, that makes two of us," Serena had nearly replied.

But if the current Rivenwood was as evil as the last one was reputed to have been, then she was wise to hesitate about approaching him.

So for five months now, she'd hung back, growing more desperate by the day.

And then, suddenly, out of the blue, the invitation to his masquerade ball had arrived.

She'd been elated. Here was the perfect opportunity to get inside his house and have a discreet look around, maybe even find a few clues that might lead to the answers she craved without having to speak to him directly.

Instead of simply accepting the invitation, therefore, she had seized upon a more devious strategy and sent back her regrets. She had a simple ruse in mind that would allow her to move about in that enemy territory much more freely.

Oh, she'd be there, all right—she just didn't want *him* to know that. Since everyone would be in costume, she figured she had an excellent chance of getting away with it, too. It was a risky plan, but perhaps she had a dash of her mother's youthful wickedness in her...

Wesley, meanwhile, was watching her intently.

She bent down to whisper, "You're not going to tell on me, are you?"

The cat responded with a meow.

"Shh, you'll wake Cousin Tamsin." She petted the tabby's head, and he purred before she prowled away again.

It was now five minutes to the hour. Serena glanced down at herself, considering any last-minute wardrobe changes, but no.

She had selected her clothing carefully for this mission, donning the plainest beige walking dress she could scrounge out of her wardrobe. She had purposely chosen something that would allow ease of movement, plus help her blend in.

The latter wasn't easy, considering her taste for bold colors and jewel tones. Demure whites and pastels were deemed more suitable for unmarried young ladies, but with her wavy black hair, pale skin, and brownish, olive-green eyes, just like Mama's, those sweet, limpid shades made her look like a sickly ghost.

Admittedly, she was vain enough to refuse to wear what did not look well on her. She was especially fond of red. But to Mama's amusement, Serena merely snapped her fingers at those who disapproved—like Toby's dam.

Ah well, her mother had always let her get away with everything.

Now at least Serena knew why.

At last, the mantel clock began to sigh out its soft chimes, though not loudly enough to wake her timid chaperone.

Mousy Cousin Tamsin was their spinster kinswoman on her mother's side. She had remained in Town with Serena on Mama's orders after Parliament's closing and the end of the Season, when the rest of the family had migrated to the country, as usual, to spend the autumn and winter at Dunhaven Manor.

Presently, Cousin Tamsin was fast asleep in her chamber down the hallway.

Serena's heart skipped a beat as she stalked over silently to her dressing table. Just for a moment, she stared at her reflection in the moonlit mirror.

Are you sure you want to do this?

It was brazen, reckless, sneaking into a ball hosted by a man of dubious reputation—a man she suspected was as keenly aware of her as she was of him.

But she had no choice. After all these months, the need to know the truth about her family and own origins was driving her quite mad.

And so with that, she lifted the waiting half-mask of beaded black satin and lace from her dressing table, fitted it over the upper half of her face, and, with trembling fingers, tied the ribbons behind her head.

Next, she swept the black velvet domino around her shoulders, fastening the large button loop between her collarbones. With the cloak secured, she lifted the hood and draped it over her head.

Hmm. She gazed at her reflection, transformed into some sort of mysterious lady of shadows.

Well, it would've been a dreadfully dull costume if she were attending this masked ball in earnest, she thought, but since her sole intention was to blend in and avoid being noticed, the disguise suited her task perfectly.

She paused to toss back the rest of the wine in her glass, needing its liquid courage for what she was attempting. She reminded herself that she did not intend to engage His Grace of Rivenwood tonight—or anyone else, for that matter.

No one would even know she was there. She just wanted to slip in, have a discreet look around inside the Rivenwoods' secretive abode, and finally, perhaps, seize upon some clue that would lead her toward the truth, or at least point her in the right direction about what her parents had got up to in their youth in his father's fast-living set.

Serena set the empty wineglass on her dressing table, noting the smudge on the rim from her rouged lips. She did not normally wear cosmetics, but tonight she had dusted her face with pearlescent powder and daubed her lips with scarlet stain, the better to disguise her identity.

Satisfied with her eerie transformation, she decided it was time to go.

"Goodbye, Wesley," she whispered, bending to give the cat a scratch under the chin. "I won't be long."

She pivoted, her cloak swirling around her. Before leaving, she silently retrieved her invitation to the masked ball from the top drawer.

She slipped it into her pocket, just in case His Grace's servants stopped her at the door.

Certainly they would be surprised to see her, considering her negative RSVP, but if it came to it, she would simply give them her blithest Society-belle smile, giggle, and say she'd changed her mind.

She wondered if the duke would gloat if that happened—but it wouldn't, she vowed, marching over to the door of her chamber, her pulse racing, her step resolute.

She sidled out into the hallway, then glided down the staircase, meeting no one on the way.

The servants were all abed by now, and with her parents and two blockhead younger brothers gone to the country, the rest of the house was empty.

Stealing back toward the kitchens, it was an easy matter to slip out of the townhouse through the rear door. She pulled it closed with a soft click behind her, and finally exhaled.

At once, she pressed on. Striding swiftly through the garden, she exited through the gate without a sound, then hurried down the cobbled mews, smelled the stables as she passed.

She turned a corner at the edge of the stone wall, and the night pooled, dark as ink, as she traversed the narrow passage between the buildings.

Such darkness was a little unnerving—perhaps all the more so because of all Toby's peasant legends about how "the Veil" thinned at this dead time of year, allowing spirits to roam the earth, culminating on All Hallows' Eve. Ah, but he was the folklorist and she was the down-to-earth, sensible one, who'd always laughed at his fairy stories and superstitious tales, teasing him for his overactive imagination.

A pang of missing her longtime suitor made her wince, for they had been great friends before they courted, but she mentally shoved it off. At least now she wouldn't have to listen to Toby's fey nonsense for the rest of her life, she thought with a huff as she hurried along.

A few seconds later, she burst out onto Moonlight Square proper.

Lanterns burned outside the stately rows of large, elegant terrace houses, flickering over their tidy front doors and matching white pillared porticoes.

Likewise, quaint black streetlamps cast golden circles of illumination at regular intervals along the cobbled streets of their aristocratic neighborhood.

Still, she found the night eerie.

Dead leaves whisked down the street, whirling past her feet. Above, billowy, dark clouds played hide-and-seek with the moon, while just a few stars peeked out impishly. It was cold—nearly cold enough for a flurry, she thought, glancing at the sky through the eyeholes of her mask.

She shivered and hurried on, pulling her thin domino more tightly around her. Crossing the street, she headed for the tall wrought-iron gate surrounding the dark, quiet park in the center of the square.

The genteel garden park at the heart of Moonlight Square was generally kept open to the public during the day, but at night, only residents had access. Each family had been given a key.

Serena pulled hers out of her pocket and, ever so quietly, unlocked the cold metal gate, then stepped through it onto the graveled path. Cutting through the park reduced her chances of being seen on the way to the duke's party.

Heart racing, the wind rippling through the folds of her long cloak, she pulled the gate shut behind her. The lock clicked back into place. She dropped the key into her pocket again and moved on.

With her black domino flowing out behind her, she strode down the shadowed path that wound through the park's sculpted acres. The gravel and dead fallen leaves crunched softly beneath her anxious strides.

She tried not to think about the history of their pleasant garden park, how, a century ago, it had served as a public hanging ground. If any place in London were likely to be haunted on a night such as this...

She gulped, scowled at herself for letting Toby's ghost tales unsettle her, and pressed on, more jittery with every step closer to her destination. But she knew she could easily pass through the party unnoticed.

The duke would be preoccupied with his two hundred guests, and even if he looked right at her, how could he guess who she was with her face masked?

This was no time to lose her nerve. She'd never get a chance like this again.

She focused on the more pleasant details of the night to calm her fears: the earthy smell of autumn from the leaves that piled here and there beneath the big trees, the homey scent of fireplaces burning to ward off the night's encroaching frost.

Halfway through the park, Serena passed the gazebo where Toby had sat her down that dreadful day five months ago and explained, with tender difficulty, the painful things he'd learned about her family. Like a fool, she'd assumed that the reason he had asked her to meet him there was because he'd finally worked up his nerve to propose. And she'd been prepared to accept!

What a rude awakening, she thought.

Instead, he had shaken her world to its foundations with the news that: one, her parents had been involved in some very dark things when they were young; two, she'd once had a sister who had died before Serena was born; and three, the man she'd called Papa all her life wasn't her real father.

She still felt dizzy from it all, just looking at the gazebo. The quaint structure gleamed an ethereal pearl white in the full moon's glow.

Seeing it now only made her all the more determined to find the answers to the whirlwind of questions that had sent her till-then-orderly life spinning, for her mother refused to talk about it.

Well, too bad, Serena thought.

These mysteries and lies had already cost her not only the match she'd expected to make, but had also wrecked her once-close bond with her mother, upended her whole understanding of her place in the world, and robbed her of her peace of mind.

If Papa was not her real father, then who the devil was?

It seemed a simple question, and she had a right to know, but Mama would not give her an answer. She had shut down like Serena had never seen her do before.

No doubt she had her reasons, but her silence was cruel—and had left Serena no choice.

Tonight, she was determined to learn something, anything, that would help her start putting all the scattered puzzle pieces of her life back together—on her own, since nobody would tell her the truth.

Upon reaching the far side of the garden park, she let herself out through the opposite gate, then took a few wary steps across the pavement, staring up somberly at the five-story mansion across the street.

Unlike the joined terrace houses lining the streets of Moonlight Square, the giant houses on the corners stood alone, every one of them owned by a duke.

Rivenwood House loomed, a great square block with muffled music pouring out the open front door. Orange light gleamed in the windows, revealing the silhouettes of countless guests.

Seeing the place, Serena deigned not to try her luck at the front door, but padded down the alleyway nearby and sneaked onto the ground through the back gate. Heart thumping at her trespass, she kept her stare fixed on the back of the mansion as she walked down the grassy, silvered path through the duke's gardens.

The closer she got to the house, the more people she encountered. Now she could hear the orchestra playing inside. She glimpsed masked couples whirling about through the large upper windows of what was obviously the ballroom.

It was brighter closer to the house, the night lit by burning torches and a smoky bonfire, where servants were roasting chestnuts for guests who wanted this old-fashioned autumnal treat. She moved at a casual stroll to avoid calling attention to herself, passing like a shadow among shadows in her black cloak.

Costumed guests mingled here and there, some gentlemen smoking near the fanciful stone fountain, a group of ladies laughing together beneath the barren trellis.

Then she came to an open section of the grass where an odd choice of garden features had been erected. Serena arched a brow at the makeshift ruins of a faux stone circle like a miniature Stonehenge, a few of the boulders picturesquely toppled.

The strange sight, so out of place in one of London's most fashionable neighborhoods, reminded her afresh of Toby's words about the Rivenwoods' occult preoccupation.

She must always remember she was dealing with no ordinary man. *Stay on your guard.*

With this inner warning, she forced herself to slow her pace to an idle saunter, her pulse hammering away so loudly she thought it might rattle his windows in their casements as she approached his house.

Determined to brazen it out, she glided up the outdoor stairs to the flagstone terrace off the back of the house. Here more guests in various costumes clustered, leaning against the carved stone balustrade. The music grew louder, the laughter, the incessant chatter of voices.

She lifted a glass of wine smoothly off the tray of a liveried footman posted near the French doors leading into the house. She took a sip as she stepped over the threshold, strolling into his house as though she had every right to be there.

It took a moment for her eyes to adjust to the light. As she blinked rapidly behind her mask, her immediate impression was surprise at the medieval-inspired, neo-gothic décor.

The effect was slightly disorienting, for the inside of the house did not match the outside at all.

The famous architect Beau Nash had designed Moonlight Square along neoclassical lines, with grand Greco-Roman symmetry, smooth and regal Palladian features.

Indeed, the exclusive neighborhood had rules on acceptable paint colors and such, but these only applied to the homes' exteriors. Inside, residents could do as they liked with their homes, and Rivenwood certainly had, sparing no details in the rich, faux-medieval style.

From the fluted pillars and pointed arches to the plaster-beamed ceilings, ornate wood carvings, rich red and dark blue draperies, and the gargoyles peering down from the corners here and there, it was like walking into an old castle or a small medieval church.

The contrast was decidedly confusing, and yet, once she started getting used to it, she decided that she liked it.

He was certainly *different*.

The neo-gothic space had been decorated with simple charm well suited to the occasion of a Hallowe'en ball. Small flowers and garlands of mossy forest greenery were strung up and twined about everywhere.

On shelves and tables sat small flickering lanterns made from hollowed-out turnips, like the ones children carried from door to door on All Hallows' Eve when they went begging for treats, warning of tricks if they were not rewarded.

The whole effect turned the Rivenwood mansion into a medieval fairyland, and Serena walked through the place with a fleeting sense of wonder. It made her feel as though magical things might happen here...

She fought to stay focused on her task, however. She had come not to fall under Azrael's enchantment, but to seek information.

Clear, simple facts.

Proceeding forward through the house, she came to the lofty entrance hall. All the houses had them, but Azrael's had been transmogrified into a long, narrow great hall that belonged in a castle, with a vaulted ceiling two stories high.

Ornately carved wooden galleries above overlooked the crowded space, and at the far end, opposite the front doors, an Ecclesiastical Gothic screen with double pillars and pointed arches framed a grand staircase softened by a red carpet runner.

Halfway up, a landing split the staircase, and it continued up in both directions. Serena gathered that the ballroom was up there somewhere.

But in the "great hall" where she stood, the dark oak-paneled walls were hung with knight helmets, a few antique shields arranged with crossed swords, and old, tattered banners and ancient battle pennants— though she doubted they were authentic.

Everything within these walls seemed fanciful, and *that* intrigued her all the more about the master of this place. She secretly adored people with imagination. Nonconformists. Those who didn't play by the rules.

She spotted him just then standing by the wall: the enigma, tall and tense, looking uneasy at his own party, though his smile was polite.

Even surrounded by people, Azrael had a solitary air about him. What a strange being he was, she mused. *In* the world, but not *of* it.

Well, how could he be normal, when his sire named him after the blasted archangel of death? she mused. *Terrible thing to do to a child.*

Yet it seemed to suit him somehow.

His long, smooth, flax-blond hair was pulled back in a simple queue. He wore formal black-and-white evening attire. An antiqued gold half-mask in a vaguely Roman style obscured the upper half of his patrician face.

Pity, that. She loved his almost Nordic-looking cheekbones, high forehead, fine nose, and the crisp line of his jaw. But even these did not compare to his mesmerizing pale eyes.

She had so relished the disconcerted flicker she had often seen in their silver depths when, once again, the duke caught her watching him over these past months. She sensed that he did not know *what* to make of her, and that suited her very well indeed.

At least it made them equal, for she certainly didn't know what to make of *him*.

Why she felt so drawn to this strange man, this mysterious presence who had first shown up when she was a child, she could not say.

Perhaps there was a droplet of pity amid her wariness of him. He always seemed so alone.

Even now, from the moment she saw him, she felt the pull of his familiar fascination. Goblet in hand, he was exchanging pleasantries with some of his guests when he happened to look over and see her—as though he'd felt her stare.

Serena froze. She almost relaxed when his gaze glided past her, but then it came rushing right back, landing on her with an owl's swiftness.

Her pulse jolted. She gulped and, at once, turned away, ducking her head to let the loose draping hood of her cloak hide her face completely.

Wobbly-kneed, she moved on, resisting the urge to flee with undue haste, for that would only draw his further attention.

Instead, she wove on through the crowd with measured paces, telling herself he couldn't have recognized her. She'd only imagined it, surely. She took one more glance over her shoulder at him before stepping into the next room.

He was gazing after her, unreadable behind his tarnished gold mask.

She stepped out of his line of view into what proved to be a dining room. The offerings of a feast were laid out on the vast oak table and massive sideboard.

The ham and puddings, tartlets and cakes, fruits and cheeses all looked and smelled delicious, but her stomach was in knots.

Worried their keen-eyed host might grow curious and come after her, she pressed on through the far doorway into the next crowded room to put more distance between them. She passed through a large sitting room, where people dressed as all manner of things were playing cards or engrossed in conversation.

Everyone seemed to be having a good time. At least his first social event looked like a success—even if he *had* waited until October, when much of Society had long since left Town for the countryside.

It was a start, anyway, she thought in amusement, calming down again. Holding an acceptable Society gathering probably wasn't easy for bachelors, she supposed.

Local gossip had it that Azrael's one known actual friend, the newlywed king of the rakehells, Jason, the Duke of Netherford, had suggested he hold the party. His fellow duke—also a resident of Moonlight Square—had reportedly helped him prepare for it, along with his bride, Felicity.

Serena was not an intimate acquaintance of the new Duchess of Netherford, but she and Felicity were friendly enough.

Personally, she had thought the girl was mad for marrying Netherford when she'd first heard about it. He was known to be a *very* bad boy. But in the end, Serena had to give Felicity credit. It hadn't taken her very long to bring the rogue to heel.

In any case, Felicity was obviously here somewhere tonight, so Serena stayed on her guard, careful to avoid running into her friend, lest she recognize her.

Drifting on, observing everything around her, Serena peered into the next room and felt her pulse quicken with excitement as she arrived at the duke's library. Surely this was the best place to start her search for answers in earnest.

Better still, the room was empty at the moment. She quickly shut the door and glanced around, eager to get to work.

Where to begin?

From the rich, dark rug to the painted coffered ceiling, the library was a beautiful room in same fanciful neo-gothic style as the rest of the house. Oaken bookshelves with pointed arches. Heavy, medieval-inspired furniture. A dark wooden mantelpiece, ornately carved, and stained glass insets in the windows.

She strode toward the shelves, unsure what exactly she was looking for—hopefully, she'd know it when she saw it—when, suddenly, a full-length portrait on the wall caught her eye.

She stopped and turned to face the man in the portrait. *My, my. Are you the reason no one's in here? Have you chased everyone away, Your Grace?*

To be sure, that haughty, gray-eyed stare could've turned the Thames to ice.

The grand personage in the portrait was Azrael's murdered father.

"Even your mother was afraid of him."

She took a step closer, gazing up boldly at the portrait. *Well, you don't scare me,* she thought.

He'd been a handsome man. The late duke had the same pale silver-blue eyes, champagne-blond hair, and sharp, patrician features as his son. He was portrayed in court dress, a ceremonial cape of some sort flung over one shoulder.

An array of jeweled badges, brooches, and the insignias of various knightly orders were displayed across the duke's chest. She studied them carefully. Some looked familiar, some didn't. It was hard to say.

In the lower corner of the portrait she saw what she assumed was their family crest: a black leopard rampant on a red shield.

Then she noticed something in the peculiar background of the painting.

The late duke was shown standing in a Renaissance-looking setting, but through the velvet-curtained window behind him could be seen the pyramids of Egypt, of all things.

Furrowing her brow, Serena assumed the duke must've visited it on Grand Tour as a lad.

Well, I can see why someone would want to murder you, anyway, she thought. He looked every bit the cruel, unpleasant man her nurse had described.

She did her best to shake off the paralyzing hold of the elder Rivenwood's icy gaze, irked at herself. Lud, she was acting as superstitious as Toby now.

Get on with it. Determined to be thorough, she began speedily scanning the bookshelves. For the most part, the collection seemed fairly typical. Standard classics of philosophy and literature, dusty tomes in several different languages—Latin, Greek, even a few in Hebrew, along with the usual French, German, and Italian, though most were in English.

She noted volumes of poetry and large leather-bound folios with colored prints of fine engravings; books full of architectural drawings; informational volumes about various topics, such as *Improvements to Rural Properties Explained*; and, of course, no shortage of diverse histories.

Suddenly, Serena spotted a book whose gilt title stamped upon the brown leather-bound spine gave her a jolt of recognition.

A Collection of Old English Folklore, Volume One, by Lord Tobias Guilfoyle.

She pulled it out with no small measure of amazement. *What is this doing here?*

Toby's first literary work had been published just last year. Which meant that only the current duke could've added it to the family collection.

And it wasn't as though her former suitor's debut book had been some great popular success.

Toby had told her that only about a thousand copies had sold, according to his publisher. Azrael must've deliberately sought it out for some reason.

Hmm. Glancing around again, Serena considered the various odds and ends on display about the bookshelves more closely: small statues, curiosities from foreign lands, a dried piece of coral, a few fossils of insects and leaves.

There was a lacquered Chinese puzzle box. An impressive geode split open to reveal glistening purple amethyst crystals inside—but no telltale evidence anywhere of whatever dark business the late duke had got her parents tangled up in before she was born.

She shook her head in frustration. *I'm getting nowhere. Blast it, this whole effort is probably daft.*

But having come this far, she wasn't leaving empty-handed. Glancing over with a frown to make sure the door was still closed, she grew even more brazen and began searching the big oak desk in the middle of the library. Quickly, she sifted through the few items sitting out on the desktop, then tested the drawers, rifling about inside the ones that would open.

Nothing.

Impatience welled up in her. *How much longer can I do this? I'm going to get caught. I should get out of here.*

It was then she noticed something *else* odd in this altogether eccentric house.

The brass sphinx statue on the corner of the large oak desk was lined up precisely with the pyramids in the background of the duke's portrait.

Why a sphinx should be included in a gothic-style house, she could no more guess than unfortunate travelers could answer the sphinx's riddles in ancient legends of the mythic beast.

Intrigued, she tried to pick the statue up in order to inspect it more closely, but to her surprise, it wouldn't budge.

It was attached to the corner of the desk.

Knitting her brow, she fingered the statue in confusion and promptly discovered that the head could bow, bending at the neck like a lever—and then she gasped.

For when the sphinx's head moved, a bank of bookshelves across from her popped away from the wall, revealing a dark, door-like opening.

A secret passage!

She drew in her breath and stared at the gaping black opening, her eyes wide, her heart thumping.

I knew it. She bit her lip, staring into the tunnel's beckoning darkness. Instinct made her absolutely certain that whatever it was she had come here to find, it was that way, somewhere in there.

Dare I?

Suddenly, she heard voices in the corridor approaching the other side of the library door. She glanced swiftly over her shoulder, then ahead again at the secret passage.

Ignoring her misgivings, Serena paused to lift one of the hollowed-out turnip lamps off the nearest bookshelf.

Lantern in hand, she hesitated only for a moment at the threshold, then swallowed hard and stepped through into darkness.

The sphinx lifted its head again as Serena pulled the bookcase-door shut behind her, and disappeared into the walls of Rivenwood House.

CHAPTER 2

Cat and Mouse

Why in the hell did I ever let Netherford talk me into this?

Azrael Chambers, the Duke of Rivenwood, was not used to so much noise inside his house. Normally, it was as quiet as a graveyard, and that was how he liked it. He was not accustomed, moreover, to so many people pressing in on all sides of him.

It made him intensely uncomfortable, but this was his own fault.

He was the one who had invited this throng of strangers into his home. Indeed, he had spared no expense.

Alas, at the end of the day, there was no bloody point in any of it, since the one person he was most interested in meeting hadn't bothered to come.

Or, more bluntly, rejected him.

Eh, it served him right. He had no business being interested in Dunhaven's daughter in the first place.

His little Staring Girl, who'd watched him like some predatory species on the hunt for the past five months.

God only knew why. He could not figure that girl out.

Meanwhile, a bizarre cast of creatures peopled his house in a dizzying array of showy costumes—strange animals, devils and gods, a large chess piece, numerous ghosts.

He sipped his drink, feeling out of place, but it rather amused him to think that, for once, he was the normal one.

A jolly medieval knight traipsed by with a papier-mâché horse molded around his waist. The knight could not control his mount, and knocked a glass vase off a low table in the drawing room when he swung about to greet an acquaintance.

The poor knight was mortified, but Azrael brushed off the mishap while his servant fetched a dustpan and broom.

"Not at all," he said in answer to the guest's profuse apologies, then he gestured to his annoyed butler, Grimsley, to bring the fellow another drink.

Azrael also indulged. Savoring a lemon macaroon, furthermore, saved him the trouble of having to think up another topic of conversation.

Frankly, this was agony for him.

It was not just that he did not really *know* any of these people, but his full understanding that he could *never* know them.

Or, at least, they could never know *him*.

Not really.

It was also their morbid curiosity about him. He could feel it swirling around him: the prying, the probing, the pools of hushed gossip gathering in the corners of his house here and there.

But let them talk. He was used to it. It did not signify.

Of course he knew his family's reputation ranged into the shadowy side of life. Half from defiance about it, Azrael had opted, sardonically, to play right into the ton's expectations with his spooky, Hallowe'en-themed masquerade.

It seemed fitting, after all.

Still, he couldn't help wondering as he studied the crowd how many of these people had known his father. Had crossed to the other side of the street whenever they'd seen the previous duke coming.

Not that he could blame them.

The mad bastard had terrified him, too.

Which was precisely why Azrael wasn't sure it had been wise of him, opening up his house to this invasion.

Considering that the one soul he had hoped to lure in hadn't deigned to come, it was all for nothing, and he feared he was drawing too much attention to himself with this.

There was always the danger that those he specifically *hadn't* invited would be tempted to drop by. Just to keep an eye on him, as they had all his life, ever since he was orphaned.

The rogues' gallery of his father's corrupt minions.

Meanwhile, to add to his annoyance, his damned mask was digging into his cheekbones and probably leaving grooves in his forehead.

As if he needed it to camouflage himself. Not he, no. On the contrary, Azrael had long since mastered the art of hiding in plain view, concealing himself behind his many layers of carefully cultivated eccentricity.

It was the only way he'd managed to survive his damned childhood.

"Your Grace, what a pleasant evening! Thank you so much for inviting us," an older couple greeted him.

Azrael smiled politely and nodded in answer, but went blank on their names. Damn it. He knew they lived down the street. Nice people. The ones with that whole pack of red-haired daughters. Viscount…something.

Made uneasy by *his* uneasiness, the middle-aged couple awkwardly hurried on before he could recall their names, and he floundered, standing there alone.

The cloud of talking and laughter, chitchat and life throbbed around him, while the orchestra he'd hired sawed away at their violins in the ballroom upstairs. The air was close and stifling, the great hall a stew of smells from the paint and powder of so many different costumes, and the greasy spiced pomade that allowed the more imaginative among his guests to sculpt their hair into weird and whimsical shapes.

His throat felt constricted, but the cool draft wafting in through the open door touched his cheek in reassurance.

It carried in the alluring smell of autumn leaves, a hint of winter, maybe even a whisper of snow, mixed in with the smoky scent of the bonfire, all of it tempting him to escape outdoors.

Back out into solitude and freedom and darkness.

He would much rather have been out walking his cat by moonlight.

It was then that Azrael spotted, with some relief, his singular new friend sauntering toward him—the great instigator, former king of the rakehells—Jason, the Duke of Netherford, and he couldn't help but smile.

The large, dark-haired rogue was aptly dressed as Julius Caesar in Roman regalia, complete with a bay leaf crown. He processed through the crowd in his robes like he had been born to the role of emperor, smiling at all his subjects, as it were.

People gladly stepped out of the towering fellow's way, as usual, while his celestial young bride followed him.

Felicity looked charming, arrayed as a swashbuckling lady pirate with an eye patch and cutlass. The golden-haired duchess paused to exchange greetings with some friends while Jason came over to him.

"Still alive, I see," Caesar greeted him.

"Barely," Azrael drawled.

Jason flashed a grin, his dark eyes twinkling with amusement and whiskey. "Well? What do you think?" He held up his arms at his sides.

"I think that you look fit to be stabbed to death by thirty of your peers."

Jason flashed a scowl of mock indignation. "Et tu, Brutus?"

Azrael wryly offered his glass, and Jason clinked his own against it with a chuckle.

"It all seems to be going smoothly enough," Azrael admitted as Felicity joined them, smiling at him as she took her husband's arm.

"Well done, Your Grace! I do believe your masked ball will be remembered as the event of the year," she declared. "And if anyone disagrees, I shall make him walk the plank."

Azrael bowed to her in amusement. "Thank you, captain."

Then Jason elbowed him. "Spot any interesting quarry here tonight?"

"Miss Burns threatened to come," Azrael answered discreetly.

"Did she, indeed? I should probably hide, then," said Netherford.

"Humph," said Felicity, propping a hand on her waist and giving her husband a skeptical look.

Jason shrugged, more than happy to pass along his expensive ex-mistress to the next man.

Apparently, the voluptuous songstress Bianca Burns only accepted dukes for her protectors. She had set her greedy cap at Azrael after Jason had sent her packing. But in truth, for all her talent and curvy fame, the diva did not interest Azrael as much as the girl who had just crept by in the black domino.

Who was that? he wondered. He looked around in lingering curiosity. She had vanished, but a small, persistent uncertainty about her niggled at the back of his mind.

He could have sworn it was Staring Girl, even though she had RSVPed that she would not attend. Might she have changed her mind?

Hope flickered, but he was probably mistaken, seeing her everywhere, that one he could not have.

The one he continually insisted to himself he did not want.

It probably wasn't Lady Serena, anyway. He'd only *hoped* for a moment that it was, because then all his efforts this night would not have gone to waste.

The more he thought about it, though, the unknown lady, whoever she was, had certainly gone sneaking past him in a most suspicious fashion.

God, maybe his enemies—Lord Stiver and the rest of Father's henchmen—had sent some woman in to spy on him.

He wouldn't put it past them.

When he looked over and found Jason and Felicity swept up in their own private world once again, the formerly womanizing duke adjusting his pirate girl's eye patch for her with a tender little motion, Azrael turned away, abashed by their intimacy, so alien to him.

Leaving the newlyweds to linger in their portable paradise for two, he decided to track down the girl in the black domino.

He was suddenly as wary as he was intrigued about her, but figured he'd better investigate now, for once the very determined Bianca Burns arrived, she'd be on him like a leech and he wouldn't get the chance.

Azrael stepped up onto one of the stairs and looked around the crowded great hall, but the girl in black was long gone from this room.

Careful not to get drawn into conversation again, he jumped back down, then prowled through the crush of guests, nodding here and there politely, feeling increasingly restless.

What if it was *Lady Serena?* he thought, his pulse quickening at the possibility. What if she *had* come? What might that signify, then?

Did she like playing games?

The thought made his stomach tauten with excitement.

He wasn't even sure why he'd first suspected it was she. The pert angle of her chin beneath her black half-mask, perhaps, the alluring plumpness of her lips, the graceful stealth with which she moved? Or perhaps the sable lock of hair falling over her shoulder.

The more he thought about it, aye, the more he suspected that it truly might be his Staring Girl and not some spy sent by his father's former devotees. But why would she do such a thing?

Why refuse his invitation, then sneak into his home? Just to be more of a pest than usual?

A smile tugged at his lips as he considered the possibility. And if it was her, what exactly was the luscious little minx up to?

Determined to find out, Azrael wandered through the various rooms where the party was underway, pausing only to answer a question from a servant.

There was no sign of the lady in the dining room, the entrance hall, the sitting room. Perhaps she had gone up to the ballroom, he thought, though he had not seen her ascend the staircase.

He went up anyway and made a circuit of the state rooms on the upper floor. The ballroom was packed, the music room noisy, the drawing room a clamor of laughter and activity with various silly games in progress, but still, he saw no sign of her.

Had he missed her or was she hiding from him, he wondered, keeping away when she saw him coming?

If so, well then, Azrael thought, it probably was Serena.

God knew they had been at this all Season.

And he'd enjoyed it, even though he knew he shouldn't.

His pulse ticked with anticipation. Brow furrowed, a half-smile dancing on his lips, he went back down the steps, scanning the entrance hall from the landing as he descended. He walked through the rooms on the ground floor one more time.

But there *was* one room he had not checked.

Brimming with curiosity, he walked back to the library and stepped inside.

It was empty.

He gave his father's portrait a cold glance, then looked around, rested his hands on his waist with a sigh, and almost left—when suddenly, a dire thought occurred to him.

His stare homed in on the sphinx.

Oh, God no…

His gaze swept across the desk and he saw a book lying there. Certain he had not left any book lying on the desk, he fairly leaped across the room to pick it up.

His eyes narrowed when he read the title: *A Collection of English Folklore*, by Lord Tobias Guilfoyle.

"Damn it! I knew it," he whispered. At once, he threw the book down and ran.

He could not be absolutely certain that the mechanism that opened the tunnel had been triggered, but if there was *any chance* that meddling little minx had found her way into the secret passage, she was in more danger than she knew.

A curse on his lips, Azrael flew out the library door—and promptly barreled into a curvaceous blonde strutting down the corridor.

"Rivenwood, darling!" Bianca Burns melted against him with a breathy laugh, laying her white-gloved hands on his chest.

Whether his more respectable guests recognized the famous songstress or not, he knew it was she, her famous face concealed by a jeweled white satin half-mask.

Her voluptuous body was arrayed in the highly unlikely disguise of a scantily clad angel in white, with a plunging décolletage and white feathered wings.

She was indeed made to take a man straight to heaven, but Azrael had no time for this.

"Miss Burns, you must excuse me." He tried to step past her, but she swept in front of him, giggling. "I have to go check on something a-at once."

"But I only just got here!" she said playfully.

"Sorry—it's a bit of an emergency. If you'd...make yourself comfortable, I-I'll be right back!"

He ran.

"Rivenwood! What's wrong? Can I help?"

He waited not a heartbeat more to answer her questions, and pounded up the nearby backstairs, taking them two at a time.

"Rivenwood!" Bianca followed, but he paid her no mind.

He might be wrong about this. He hoped to God he was.

Perhaps no one had entered the secret passage.

But if so, he had to get there first.

Especially if it was Serena who had ventured in—and really, who else would dare?

One hand on the newel post, Azrael swung around the quarter landing and vaulted up the next flight of stairs, racing faster.

For only *he* knew what waited for the unsuspecting trespasser on the other end of that tunnel.

Serena ventured on through the darkness. Up, up the secret passage went, winding through the house, concealed behind the mansion walls.

Sometimes it ascended on cramped, narrow ladders, sometimes on ramps. Other times it rose on twisting wrought-iron stairs that were such a tight squeeze she had to be careful not to bump her head.

Serena followed the route in fascination, the tiny glow from her turnip lantern flickering in the pitch blackness. All the while she wondered where it led and why on earth Azrael should have this in his house.

But maybe it hadn't come from the current duke. Maybe it had come from his steely-eyed father.

There were small, half-sized doors along the way leading to various rooms throughout the mansion. Since the house was full of guests, Serena did not dare venture out. She was taking enough risks just being here.

She moved on, lifting the hem of her domino to avoid tripping when she had to climb again.

The passage continued on its wandering course past the ballroom; a peek through the eyeholes confirmed it. She slid the small rectangle of wood aside and found herself peering out from the wall behind the orchestra. *Well, that explains why the music got so loud.*

You're enjoying this too much, her better sense accused her.

She slid the spyhole shut and moved on.

After coming to a corner, where she had to climb another cobwebby ladder, she had now, by her best estimate, reached the third floor. It was much quieter up here, probably around the bedrooms.

Having reached the private quarters of the house, perhaps now she could really begin searching for clues about the previous duke's nefarious club.

At that moment, the passage ended abruptly at one of those small doors cut into the interior wall. *Looks like I've come to the end.*

She leaned forward, putting her ear up against it. She heard nothing, but when she glanced around for a spyhole, there wasn't one. Though she couldn't confirm it visually, she felt confident the room was empty because it was so very quiet on the other side.

Well, nothing ventured, nothing gained. Quite ready to escape the cramped, lightless secret passage, she cautiously opened the door.

Only more darkness waited beyond.

Lifting her turnip lamp ahead of her, she climbed through the miniature doorway into what appeared to be a massive piece of wooden furniture—possibly a large cabinet or wardrobe.

It must've been set there against the wall to help conceal the tunnel's entrance to this room. Once again, she listened for all she was worth, and, hearing nothing, decided to venture out.

Gathering her nerve, she slowly pushed the wardrobe door open.

The room beyond was pitch-dark, and as she climbed out, the first thing she noticed was the sharp, acrid smell of the room. Her eyes watered; she wrinkled her nose.

God, what on earth is that? It smelled like ammonia salts. Or Wesley's litterbox, times ten.

Two large, arched windows on the exterior wall let in just enough moonlight to show her the outline of a few large plants. Gracious, they were potted palm trees that almost touched the ceiling. She shook her head.

This place just keeps getting stranger.

Holding up her lantern, she surveyed the room, befuddled. *Where am I, some sort of guestroom, conservatory?*

There was a bed, but no other furniture, save a large leather trunk pushed up against the wall near the door.

The feeble glow of her lantern barely picked it out. *Hmm.* The trunk instantly drew her. Maybe there were secrets of some sort hidden inside.

As she crossed the chamber toward the leather trunk, she saw but barely registered other odds and ends in the room: a rope hammock like a fisherman's net hung up in the corner, a fat log standing in the middle of the room for no apparent reason, and what looked like large dog toys strewn about at random. A leather ball, a bulky twist of rawhide.

She had no idea what to make of it, but dismissed these details as irrelevant, eager to find the information she had come for. Reaching the trunk, she set her lantern down and eagerly lifted the lid.

She peered inside, only to be disappointed. The trunk held nothing but some folded blankets, what appeared to be a leash, a variety of brushes, and a few more...

Animal toys.

A gasp of belated understanding escaped her—and at that very moment, a low growl arose from somewhere behind her.

Behind her and *above.*

Oh, God. Serena froze, petrified by the menacing, throaty rumble at her back. She could sense something right behind her.

Something large.

But it didn't sound like a guard dog. Not the least because it was up by the ceiling.

Pulse thumping, she turned around slowly and lifted her gaze to the rafters.

She gasped but bit back a shriek to find a jet-black leopard balancing on the open beams that crisscrossed the vaulted ceiling.

Utter shock gripped her. Pinned against the wall, she was paralyzed with fear. *A leopard? He has a leopard?*

Its eyes were golden-green, its fangs pearly white as it warned her with another monstrous hiss.

Serena shrank down in disbelief.

Why *does he have a leopard?*

She saw its big white claws gripping the beam, the annoyed whip of the tail thrashing behind it. Most of its shadowy shape was nigh invisible in the darkness, but it looked huge.

More than that, it looked hungry.

With a gulp, Serena began edging toward the door. "N-nice kitty…"

It dawned on her that the big cat must've been reclining on top of the wardrobe where she had come out, for she hadn't even seen it.

Oh God, I hope he's tame.

"There's a g-good kitty," she whispered weakly, not taking her eyes off the beast glaring down at her as she edged toward the door.

Her movements were ginger and agonizingly slow so as not to provoke the beautiful monster into attacking. And though outwardly she was silent, inwardly, Serena was screaming her bloody head off.

Why *does he have a leopard?*

Of course, she had seen his coat of arms in the library, but she was beyond rational thought.

She bit back a half-hysterical shriek when the beast pounced down from the ceiling to the floor, landing lightly before her.

Oh. My. God. It's going to eat me.

The door was in reach now, but would she make it? She was all but hyperventilating. A bead of sweat ran down her cheek as she held the animal's stare.

"Nice beastie…I'll just be on my way…"

The leopard stood as tall as her hip, wiry and beautiful and deadly, an elegant creature made for stealth. Its long whiskers twitched as it leaned forward as though to sniff her.

Serena jerked away and the cat complained with a low yowl.

"Sorry to bother you," she said as her fingers wrapped around the doorknob. "I'll be going now."

She kicked a nearby toy toward the big cat to distract it, then flung the door open and threw herself out, whirling into the hallway beyond and slamming the door with a shriek just as the cat leaped.

Big paws thumped against the other side of the door.

A whispered stream of terrified curses poured from Serena's lips as she paused in the hallway, trying to collect herself. Her whole body shaking, she had to cover her mouth with her hand to keep from screaming after the fact.

It was only then, as she stood there, knees knocking, that she noticed the sign on the door: *Beware! Danger! DO NOT ENTER.*

"Now you tell me," she whispered, trying to bring herself under control. "I daresay." Clutching her chest, she strove to will her heartbeat back to normal and, still quivering, glanced around, trying to get her bearings.

She found herself in an upper hallway. Thankfully, it was empty except for her.

That'll teach you, her better sense chided. She swallowed hard and decided perhaps it was wise to abort her mission while she was still in one piece. *I think I've had enough for tonight.*

If the Duke of Rivenwood kept a wild animal locked up in his house, Lord only knew what other traps might still await the unsuspecting snooper.

Aye, she thought, blowing out a steadying breath, maybe there was a *reason* why he only had the one friend. Clearly, the man was not fit for human company.

Never mind him, she thought. The more important question was, *How do I get out of here?*

She certainly couldn't go back the way she'd come. Her whole body still filled with the pins-and-needles aftermath of panic, she stood there clenching and unclenching her hands a few times, then winced as it dawned on her she'd left her turnip lantern in the cat's room.

Perfect. Now she had left evidence of her trespass behind. Tiny as the flame was, enclosed inside a vegetable, she was not concerned about it burning the house down, even if the big cat investigated.

The creature might singe its whiskers, but one puff of breath would blow the flame out.

Finally regrouping, she focused on escaping Rivenwood House without further incident. Obviously, she'd have to find a staircase. She glanced in both directions down the hallway, trying to decide which way to go.

It looked like the top of a staircase to her right, so she headed toward it with a huff, still shaking her head—a pet leopard!

She had taken only a few steps down the hallway when she heard footsteps pounding up the same stairwell she'd intended to go down.

Oh, God, what now? Someone was coming. *I can't be seen up here. Hide!*

She glanced around wildly, but the hallway itself offered no concealment. It had nothing but a carpet runner, a pier table under a mirror, and a fauteuil beside it. Her only choice was to risk entering another one of these godforsaken chambers. But really, how many of them could contain wild beasts?

The footsteps were growing louder, nearing the top of the steps.

Hide! Panicking, Serena picked a room at random across the hall and a few doors down from the cat room. Opening it, she swept a darkened bedchamber with an anxious glance, trying to ascertain if it was beast-free.

"Rivenwood! Where on earth are you going?" a woman called from the direction of the stairwell.

Serena gasped. Not just anyone was coming. *The duke!*

"Bianca—please, as I said, I'll be right with you. I have to check on something right away."

Egads. He sounded slightly frantic, Serena thought, whisking into the bedchamber. Pulling the door shut silently behind her, she held her breath and listened through the door as the Duke of Rivenwood himself apparently came running into the hallway.

The footsteps stopped at, she believed, the cat room.

"Stay back, Bianca!" A door creaked open, then she heard him say, "Raja? Are you all right in here, boy?"

Serena stood motionless as the cat door clicked shut again. *My God, he went in there with that thing?*

"Rivenwood!" this *Bianca* complained. It sounded like the woman had come up into the hallway. She knocked on the cat room door. "What's going on? What are you doing in there?"

"Stay out!" he barked, his voice muffled.

Serena heard the lady huff at his curt command.

"Rudesby!" Bianca muttered. "You invite me here and then ignore me? You're worse than Netherford."

Ohh. Serena's eyebrows rose as she realized then who Bianca was—that scandalous theater woman.

Certain ladies of Moonlight Square kept everyone apprised of the latest gossip. Most knew by now that the reformed rakehell Netherford had been the diva's keeper before the clever Felicity had brought her duke to heel.

After a moment, Serena heard the door open again, and Azrael apparently emerged from the beast's quarters unscathed. "Sorry about that."

"Rivenwood, what on earth?" Bianca demanded.

"Just checking on my cat, dear."

"Oh, may I see him? I have a cat myself."

"Er, not right now. He's a bit riled up with all the people here."

"Why does the door say Danger, Your Grace?"

"Uh, it's a long story."

"Well, never mind then. I think you *know* I didn't come here to talk."

There was a moment of silence on the other side of the door. Serena frowned, suspicious about what was going on out there.

The moment passed.

"What is it, Rivenwood? You still seem distracted." Bianca sounded slightly breathless as the duke's heavy footfalls moved past the door where Serena was hiding.

"It's probably nothing," he answered. "I could've sworn we had an intruder here tonight who'd somehow wandered up this way. Perhaps you should go back downstairs whilst I check more of these rooms."

Oh no! Serena's eyes widened. Realizing she wasn't in the clear yet, she spun around silently and scanned the bedchamber for a hiding place.

At once, she stole off to the far end of the room even as she heard the duke begin opening and closing several doors out in the hallway.

But she was in luck. The bedchamber she had chosen at random had a balcony through a dainty pair of French doors. She hurried toward it, but it immediately occurred to her that if Rivenwood checked out there, she'd be caught red-handed. *No. Too obvious.* As was the wardrobe—and the adjoining dressing room, for that matter.

Hurry! At her wit's end, she simply concealed herself by stepping behind the voluminous drapes that framed the balcony doorway. *Oh, this is the most ridiculous situation.*

How her two oversized little brothers would have laughed at her antics if they could see her right now.

At least her hiding spot concealed her well enough. So much fabric cascaded down the lintel and pooled on the floor that she easily disappeared behind it by flattening herself against the wall.

She had barely got out of sight when the door banged open across the dark chamber.

Serena held her breath, waiting, while a few stealthy footfalls prowled into the room.

"What do you mean, an intruder?" Bianca asked in alarm, following him in. "A burglar? Shall I fetch some footmen to assist you?"

"No need," Azrael said quietly.

Serena heard the wardrobe doors open, then close. She listened on the razor's edge of suspense, heart thumping, as he crossed to search the dressing room she had rejected as her hiding spot.

"It doesn't look like anyone's in here to me," Bianca said.

"No," he murmured. "It doesn't *look* that way. And yet...I have a sense about such things."

He sounded close.

"Well, I don't see anyone." Relief must've made the songbird bold. "Just you and me and this big, empty bed," she added coyly.

The duke's answer was a low, self-conscious laugh. "How terribly convenient."

"I think you purposely made up this whole intruder story to lure me up here," the woman teased. "You crafty fellow."

It sounded as though she had slipped her arms around him, but he must have evaded her. "Let me go and check the balcony."

Serena held her breath and prayed for invisibility, fearing he'd hear her pulse pounding; she glimpsed him when he stepped up to the French doors, lifted the latch, and stepped outside.

Across the room, she heard Bianca shut the bedroom door to the hallway. *Her* plans were clear enough.

Satisfied there was no one hiding on the balcony, Rivenwood returned. Serena caught a brief glimpse of his puzzled frown as he stepped past her again, returning to the chamber.

Holding her breath, Serena stayed stock-still.

"Happy now?" Bianca drawled.

"I suppose."

"Good. Because I've just taken off my halo."

Serena frowned, hearing a rustle of fabric as the woman sashayed up to him.

"And now that I have you alone, my dear duke, I should like to ask you a rather impertinent question."

"Yes?" he asked drily.

"What exactly did Netherford tell you about me and my various fields of expertise?"

He laughed uncomfortably. "Nothing, Miss Burns. I'm sure he is far too much of a gentleman to repeat whatever he might have done with any lady."

"Oh, please!" She laughed. "Netherford is anything *but* a gentleman. And I'm no lady—much to your delight. So why don't you begin by telling me exactly what you like? Or better yet, show me."

Scandalized, Serena stared at the swath of fabric hanging right in front of her nose while the duke hesitated. "What about my guests?"

"Oh, they won't miss you, so long as your staff keeps them in liquor. Besides, this won't take long. But I guarantee I'll send you back to the party with a smile on your face."

Serena nearly choked, hearing this. *Oh, Lord, they're not really going to do this now, are they?*

She squeezed her eyes shut, mortified at the sound of a low, needy male groan.

"You're a very determined woman," the duke whispered hoarsely.

"Darling, you have no idea."

More kissing sounds. Stuck behind the curtain, Serena shook her head and rolled her eyes. *Unbelievable.*

Heavy breathing now.

"Come, sit down and let me give you a small demonstration of all the ways that I can please you, Your Grace."

"I'm not sure this is the best idea..."

"You think too much. You need to let go."

Oh, leave him alone, Serena thought in annoyance. *You only want his money, anyway.*

"You really don't have to do this," he said, while Serena heard them move to a nearby piece of furniture.

"Hush, you need this so badly. I can tell."

Serena did not hear any further argument from His Grace. She bit her lip, thinking. Perhaps if they grew absorbed enough in their activities, she could escape unnoticed—slip right out onto the balcony, somehow manage to climb down, and run home.

The French doors were only a foot away, and she had no desire to stand here as a silent witness to their tryst. When Azrael groaned with pleasure, she grew positively *desperate* to get out of there.

Ever so cautiously, she peeked out from behind the curtain to ascertain the couple's whereabouts.

She was in luck. The wing chair where a very wicked angel knelt before him was angled away from Serena, facing the door.

Serena doubted they would notice her, absorbed as they were in their pleasures, the white-clad harlot with her head buried in the duke's lap.

She did not even want to *think* about what that was all about.

What mattered was that if she was extremely discreet, she believed she could tiptoe out of the room without being noticed. Sliding out from behind the curtain, she reached for the latch on the French door, and lifted it silently, her heart thumping.

As she moved clear of the curtain, she hated herself for it, but she was not immune to the shocking feelings that stirred to life in her body in response to what was going on over there.

Well, she was only human—besides, she thought, the Duke of Rivenwood was a beautiful man and had long fascinated her.

Despite his initial reluctance before Miss Burns' aggressive pursuit, he had obviously let himself be persuaded by her determined efforts to impress him. The woman had untied his cravat and parted the top of his white shirt. His hands rested atop her blond hair as she pleasured him with deep, open-mouthed kisses and stroking hands.

Wide-eyed, Serena shuddered and turned away, stepping out into the cool night air. Later she would worry about trying to scrub that indecent image out of her mind. For now, she closed the balcony door behind her again without a sound—not that they'd have heard.

At once, she stepped out of sight, past the frame of the glass-paned doors to lean against the stone wall, her knees shaking, her belly quivering with her unwanted awareness of the man in the other room.

What a harlot that woman was! She decided that the proper response was blistering disapproval.

Any twinge of jealousy was utterly absurd. She took a deep breath and shook her head to clear it, then looked around to orient herself.

Since Rivenwood House was on the corner, the balcony overlooked the side garden, and, thankfully, there was no one in sight down there.

Somehow she'd have to climb down. She dared not stay here and hope to outwait them. What if they came outside for a breath of cool night air when they were done? They would find her at once.

Unsure how much time she had to escape, she peered over the edge of the balcony to judge her prospects of climbing down. To her surprise, it didn't look too bad.

She studied her possible route in the moonlight. First, she'd have to go over the balcony railing, then inch along that ledge there for a few feet, she thought.

At that point, she could begin climbing down on the ivy-covered trellis she spotted affixed to the house. It looked sturdy enough to hold her weight. Of course, one wrong step, and it would be a long way down.

She shrugged with dismay, seeing no other choice, then hitched up her skirts in the most unladylike fashion and slung her leg over the blasted rail, berating herself all the while for ever thinking this whole misadventure might be a good idea.

Unfortunately, the trellis was not as strong as it looked.

As Serena soon learned.

The hard way.

CHAPTER 3

Intruder Unmasked

*A*t a sudden yelp from outside, Azrael flicked his eyes open. *Damn it, I knew it!* He clutched Bianca's shoulders to stop her, pushing her back slightly.

"No more," he croaked, tearing off his mask. *Oh, please tell me that isn't who I think it is, and that she didn't just see us doing this.*

"What is it?" Bianca panted, her wet lips glistening.

"Didn't you hear that?" he rasped, suddenly disgusted with himself for giving in, when he knew full well her narcissistic motives. Pressing his would-be mistress aside, Azrael stood, quickly buttoning his black trousers. "Somebody's out there."

"What?"

He didn't answer, his heart pounding with sickening guilt to think that his virginal, one-time betrothed may have just witnessed him being fellated by this smug, overpriced whore.

Furious at himself for letting his guard down and not listening to his instincts, Azrael strode out onto the balcony, frightened over what sort of trouble his fair intruder may have got herself into out there, if it was indeed she.

Shaking off his lust as best he could—though the interruption had put quite a damper on his desire—he planted feverish hands on the cool wooden railing and anxiously searched the silvered night, glancing around below.

To his relief, he saw her then—dangling some twenty-five feet above the ground, with one hand on the trellis and the other on the ledge.

Like a little black kitty-cat stuck in a tree.

He arched a brow in wry relief while she sent him a frantic glance. There was no mistaking her identity now—it was the one and only Staring Girl.

The black domino in which he had spotted her earlier cascaded down her slim body, but at least she'd the sense to pull up her satin mask before attempting the climb. It rested atop her pretty head.

"Good evening, Lady Serena," he greeted her, his tone pleasant but sardonic, masking his rush of exhilaration to find his one coveted guest had come after all.

Better still, he would now relish their first verbal exchange. Provided she didn't die, of course. "Nice night for a climb?"

"Oh, God, don't just stand there, help me—please!"

Bianca stepped out onto the balcony and gasped with embarrassment when she saw Serena. "What is the meaning of this?"

"I wasn't spying on you, I swear!" the girl wrenched out. "I only wanted to leave! Please—I'm going to fall!"

Just for a heartbeat, Azrael smiled at her in satisfaction, the ravishing Miss Burns already forgotten.

He couldn't take his eyes off his errant intruder.

"Goodness me, I thought you declined my invitation," he taunted softly, leaving her there for a moment to contemplate the error of her ways.

She was positioned safely enough for the moment, one foot braced.

"I changed my mind, all right?" she cried, frantic. "I-I brought my invitation. It's in my pocket—though it may have fallen out. Are you going to just stand there while I fall to my death?"

"Ah, I see," he said. "So you'd like to come back in?"

Horrid man! Serena glared at him, clinging by her fingernails to the ledge and the surprisingly rickety trellis.

"That would be nice!" she retorted, cursing the handsome face peering over the rail at her in mild amusement.

When the wooden trellis rung let out another treacherous crack under her right foot, though, she shrieked again. "Help me, for the love of God—I'm going to die!"

At once, he whipped the untied cravat off his wide shoulders and peeled off his coat. "Now, now, I won't have you splattering my garden with your blood. Hang on, dear thing. I'll be there in a trice."

"Should I go and call for a servant?" the singer asked anxiously.

"I don't need a servant, but yes, do please see yourself out, Miss Burns," said the duke.

Lean and long-legged, he was already climbing over the railing, his pale hair shining in the moonlight.

"Y-you want me to leave?" Miss Burns said, recovering from her astonishment after a beat.

Azrael all but ignored her.

His silvery stare was fixed on Serena, who, for her part, was only half listening to the lovers' exchange. Hanging on to her grip was infinitely more important at the moment.

But she did hear him say: "This young lady and I need to have a little talk."

"Oh. I'll wait for your downstairs, then," the diva said uncertainly.

"That won't be necessary."

"I beg your pardon?"

Azrael didn't look back, making his way with agile steps along the ledge toward Serena. He held her stare as he approached; she willed him to save her while a bead of sweat ran down the side of her face.

"Your talents are prodigious, Miss Burns, but I fear we'd never suit."

"Oh really?" she exclaimed with an indignant scoff.

"Goodnight, Miss Burns," he said. "Do enjoy the party."

"Well! I never." She flounced back inside, banging her fake wings on the doorframe.

Impatiently, she had to step sideways in order to fit through the opening. Serena almost laughed, but more with hysteria at her own imminent demise than with any real humor at the haughty star's indignation.

"Look at all the trouble you've caused tonight," Azrael said softly when they both heard a door slam from somewhere inside a moment later.

She realized he was teasing her again, but Serena's arms and shoulders were screaming, her fingers threatening to slip. "You needn't have sent her packing on my account," she said through gritted teeth. "Just rescue me, and I'll be on my way."

He laughed as he lowered himself along the ledge. "Oh, you don't ask for much, do you?"

"You think this is funny?" she cried, hanging on for dear life.

"A little. But then, I'm told I have a slightly twisted sense of humor."

Reaching her at last, he crouched down gracefully on the ledge with a sort of careless stealth. Stretching out one arm, he secured himself by gripping a vertical post of the balcony railing. With the other, he reached down toward her. "Take my hand."

"I dare not let go," she uttered, torn.

"Very well. I'll take hold of you then. With your permission, of course?"

"Yes, yes—just hurry!" This was no time for his exquisite manners. Serena whimpered with fear as he curled his strong, warm fingers around her wrist.

"How much did you see back there?" His Grace inquired, perhaps to distract her from the terror of her doom as he began to pull her up.

"I wasn't spying!" she insisted again, mortified, as he lifted her weight with one hand, balancing precariously.

"Hold still! Don't fight me. You're only making this more difficult." His grip was iron around her wrist, his long, graceful fingers strong and sure.

He braced himself with one knee on the ledge, shifted his weight, and then, with compact, sinewy strength packed into his lean, elegant form, he pulled her right up to his warm, hard body, and turned at once to help her scramble onto the ledge.

Serena clawed onto the cold, solid surface, hugging the side of his house, and panting with relief, but still frightened.

"Easy," Azrael murmured, his hand on the small of her back, steadying her. "Do you need a rest for a moment, or can you crawl back to the balcony now?"

She took a shaky breath and nodded. "I-I'm fine. I'd rather go."

"Get rid of the cloak first," he ordered quietly. "You can't afford to trip."

"But everyone will see me if I don't have a costu—"

"Do it."

Too shaken to argue, Serena unfastened the button at her collarbones while he shielded her from the precipice with his outstretched arm.

She let him pull the domino off her from behind. He cast it to the ground, and it floated away like some dark phantom that Toby would've liked to add to his folklore book.

"Good. Now, make your way to the railing, you silly-headed widgeon," he added with a fervor that finally betrayed his real concern about the danger in which she'd placed herself.

Though she frowned at the insult, she could see how he'd view her that way at the moment. He must think her quite an idiot.

Nevertheless, she swallowed hard and obeyed, crawling along the ledge on all fours, already feeling mortified.

Azrael freely kept his hand on her hip the whole time, a much too familiar, almost possessive touch, but she supposed he was merely providing a firm counterweight to keep her as close to the wall as possible.

She was too scared to protest at the contact, under the circumstances, though she cringed to consider the intimate view of her backside he now had as he came along behind her.

At last, she gripped the upright bars of the banister around the balcony. Slowly, she stood, keenly aware of the duke's hand sliding oh-so-helpfully over various parts of her body as she straightened up, inch by inch.

When she climbed back over the railing to safety, she feared that she bared far more than her ankles to his watchful eyes in the process.

Once she'd reached the enclosure of the balcony, she turned with a heart full of worry to see if *he* needed any help.

But the man had the preternatural grace of that blasted leopard.

His eyes gleamed and the moonlight sculpted his patrician features as he followed her with ease.

Serena stood by awkwardly, her mumbled offer of help clearly unneeded. In the next heartbeat, he swung his leg over the railing and vaulted back lightly onto the balcony.

She swallowed hard as she wondered what the consequences of her actions might turn out to be. Plummeting to her death didn't sound so bad all of a sudden, compared to facing the wrath of the Duke of Rivenwood alone and in private.

A wave of chilling worry washed through her to recall all her nurse's dire warnings about him and his line.

Well, he had her now. She was in his clutches. He had rescued her, but now what?

Serena held her breath as she gazed up at him, wide-eyed and shaken.

He rested his hands on his waist for a moment and assessed her with a guarded stare. "Are you hurt?"

She shook her head. "N-no. Thank you."

He arched a brow. "You might not wish to thank me *quite* yet, my lady."

She gulped. But when he saw her shiver with the aftermath of her brush with death, he frowned, picked up the tailcoat he had cast off, and whisked it around her shoulders.

"There. Now, come inside, and tell me what the hell you think you're doing."

"Are you...angry?" she ventured as she followed him with reluctant steps into the dark bedchamber.

"Hmm." He went and lit a branch of candles, not answering her question, but as the light rose, he passed a wary glance across her face. "Still pale," he remarked. "Let me get you a drink. You look like you could use a sip of something strong."

Serena stood uncertainly a safe distance away while he carried the light over to a small cabinet, where he took out a crystal decanter and began to pour.

The few candles' glow revealed a large canopy bed nearby swathed with ruby velvet curtains with large gold tassels. Beyond their reach lurked the shadowed hollows of the dressing room alcove, as well as the dark recesses of the high vaulted ceiling above them.

Serena's heart pounded. "I-I really don't think I should be in here...alone with you, Your Grace."

A low laugh escaped him as he glanced over his shoulder at her.

"Oh, *now* you realize that? Sit," he ordered, gesturing at the wing chair he himself had lately left.

"Not there." She folded her arms across her chest.

"Well, you're welcome to lie on the bed if you prefer. I might prefer that myself."

Her scowl deepened at his insinuating quip, but she supposed he felt free enough to say such things to her, after what she'd already witnessed—and interrupted.

Anyway, she *did* rather need to sit down after her ordeal. Her knees were still knocking. First the leopard, and then a fall that could've broken her legs, if not her neck.

Overconfidence. She shook her head, but harrumphed and gave in. "I suppose the chair will do."

As she lowered herself gingerly onto the armchair, the echo of his groans still whispered through her mind, along with questions about how that woman had wrung such intoxicating sounds from him in the first place. *I wonder how it's done.*

Eyeing him from across the room while he finished pouring her drink and corked the decanter, she tried to block out any other feelings toward the man except for wariness.

It wasn't easy. For weeks now, her curiosity about him had been intense.

And the speculative way Azrael looked at her as he turned and brought her the glass made her wonder if the feeling weren't mutual.

He crouched slowly before her, and she noted the breadth of his shoulders, tapering down to the trim line of where his waistcoat hugged his lean middle. She beheld the sweeping curve of his neck and throat, the jut of his Adam's apple, and the tantalizing glimpse of his bare chest, thanks to the state of undress in which that woman had left him.

She licked her lips and lowered her gaze, annoyed at how he mesmerized her.

"Take this." His voice was husky as he pressed the cup into her grasp.

His long, warm fingers brushed her hands as she accepted the drink from him, mute with confused desire, her stomach half knots, half butterflies, her gratitude all jumbled up with fear.

Glancing down into the cup for a second, she hoped he had not put anything in it that would harm her.

"Go on, drink it," he urged softly, giving her arm a kindly caress. "You're trembling."

She looked at him, taking in his earnest gaze. She was shocked by his air of solicitude. *Very well.* Shrugging off her mistrust, she took a cautious sip and discovered it was brandy.

The fiery spirits made her eyes water as it spilled its heat down her throat.

Studying her, Azrael rested a knee on the floor, his pose a dangerous reminder of the one Bianca Burns had taken before him a short while ago.

Unfulfilled desire still smoldered in his ice-blue eyes. She knew what it was, for she had observed it in many of her suitors before. Those males had been easy to deny.

But they were not the Duke of Rivenwood.

Sensing the hunger in him, she helped herself to another, larger swallow of brandy. It burned all the way down to her belly, but after a moment, it somehow began to restore her temporarily absent courage.

A mysterious smile curved his lips as he watched the color return to her cheeks. "That's better," he whispered.

Serena rested the cup on her lap, unsure what he meant to do with her, for his pose, though casual, was also sufficient to make sure that she stayed in the chair. Having captured her, he clearly did not intend to let her escape.

Her embarrassment began deepening by the moment to have been found in such a situation. Considering she had broken into his house and watched him cavorting with that woman, she began to wish the earth would open up and swallow her.

"Now then," he said. "Tell me what you are doing here, and do not waste my time with lies."

Serena floundered, not knowing where to begin.

He waited, but only for a moment, and when his eyes narrowed with impatience, he reminded her of that leopard again. "Was this your brilliant idea, or did someone put you up to it?"

"Put me up to it?" The question startled her. "I-I came of my own volition, of course. Why would you think otherwise?"

"Obviously I have enemies," he murmured, his expression unreadable. "Why the hell else would I have a secret passage in my house? The question is, which are you—friend or foe?"

Serena shrugged. "Neither. We are not even acquainted."

"Then why are you here? Explain yourself," he ordered, hemming her in when she longed to rise from the chair and walk away. "If you were an ordinary young woman, I'd assume it was avarice that brought you. That perhaps you merely wished to see the house over which you would have been the lady."

She drew back at this, furrowing her brow. "Pardon?"

"Oh, come, don't play innocent. Well?" He paused, looking around at the room, then at her again, a hint of defiance in his glance. "You might as well give me your opinion, then. Do you like the neo-gothic style or hate it?"

Serena knitted her brow, unable to make a shred of sense of his words. She suspected he was only changing the subject to try to throw off her equilibrium. It was working.

"I-I like it well, Your Grace. But why on earth should I have been the lady of your house?"

He stared blankly at her. "Because of our childhood betrothal, of course. Isn't that why you're here?"

"*What?*" Serena could've fallen out of her chair.

He tilted his head, searching her face in confusion. "I assumed you must've recently found out about it. Isn't that why you've been stalking me all Season?"

"I—" Routed, she turned red and had to defend herself against the humiliating charge before she could even process the questions exploding through her mind. "I have not been *stalking* you!" she cried.

"Of course you have," he said in amusement. "There's no point in lying, darling. I didn't mind it, really. *My* only question was whether you were sorry to miss out on becoming the Duchess of Rivenwood or thanking your lucky stars to have escaped that fate."

"I-I..." She stared at him, flabbergasted, and now even Azrael was starting to look puzzled.

"What's this?" he murmured, more to himself than to her. "Is it possible you truly didn't know?"

"I have no idea what you are talking about!" she exclaimed, at a loss.

He blinked. "Our parents—well, your mother and my legal guardian—pledged us to each other shortly after you were born, Lady Serena. I was but a boy myself."

Serena choked with astonishment.

Azrael frowned, drawing back a bit.

"I don't understand," he said, eyeing her with newfound suspicion. "If you didn't know about this, then what *are* you doing sneaking around inside my bloody house? And why the deuce have you been staring at me everywhere for months?"

"Because I needed information!" she burst out. "And I was told you were the only person in the world who could help me."

At last she'd found her tongue, but she was still beet-red at his blunt questions.

Azrael furrowed his brow, visibly on his guard now. "What sort of information?"

She hesitated, routed by this new revelation. She was to have been Azrael's bride?

God, how many more lies of her mother's would yet emerge?

"Were we really engaged?" she asked incredulously, still barely able to absorb it.

"Of course. I do not lie." He paused, scrutinizing her through narrowed eyes. "Do you?"

She shook her head. "No. I despise liars."

"Me too. Though sometimes...a little deception is necessary," he admitted.

"Yes," she forced out with a chastened look. After all, her incursion into his house had hardly been the most transparent example of honesty. "I truly am—sorry about this, Your Grace."

He arched a brow at her, but shrugged off her apology. Looking away, he flicked a glance down at her cup. "Maybe you'd better finish that drink. You look like you could use it. For that matter, so could I."

He rose and gave her some breathing room as he crossed to get himself a glass.

Serena watched him, still filled with lingering astonishment to think this strange man might've been her husband. How on earth had *that* come about?

And why had this supposed engagement been cancelled?

Innumerable questions burned in her mind, but given his famous dislike of speaking about anything to do with his father, it seemed wise to let him swallow a few mouthfuls of spirits before she attempted to ask him anything. She was still wondering how to phrase her opening question when Azrael spoke first.

"You're lucky Raja didn't eat you, you know."

"Raja?"

"My cat."

"Oh yes. We met." She paused. "And, um, why do you have a leopard, Your Grace?"

"Doesn't everyone?" He turned around with a devilish smile that stole her breath.

He drifted over to lean against the bedpost across from her. "He was a gift from some toady of my father's, given to me as a cub because of the leopard on my coat of arms."

"I see. And he gets his own room?"

"Are you jesting? He practically owns the whole house. I'm lucky he lets me live here, too. But that's cats for you."

A cautious smile broke across her face as she thought of Wesley sitting at home on the windowsill. Azrael held her gaze with an almost wistful smile, in return.

"Poor Raja," he softly said. "He usually stays at my country house— I inherited an entire menagerie of exotic animals, I'm afraid—but his ablest keeper fell ill, and none of my other servants are quite comfortable taking care of him. I had no choice but to bring the cat here and look after him myself until he can be returned to the country."

"I see. And is the leopard enjoying Town life, Your Grace?"

He flashed another rare smile. "The Netherfords presented him with a white leather collar made to look like a cravat, so at least he has a proper Town wardrobe now."

Serena grinned.

"It is a shame, though," he added in a softer tone. "He doesn't belong here at all—not in London or England or even this half of the world. But this is the life that he has, so we have to make the best of it. I'm just glad he didn't bite you. Not for your sake, of course," he added with a teasing glance. "I should hate for him to get a taste for human flesh. They do sometimes, in India, I'm told."

A small sound of dismay escaped her, and she drew back with a wince. But apparently she had got the recluse speaking on a topic he was comfortable with, for he continued.

"Everyone thinks it's tigers that are most dangerous, you see, but the local hunters in India claim that leopards are craftier, more intelligent. This makes them considerably more deadly." Azrael watched her, as though assessing her reaction to his words. "Plus, being smaller than tigers, which are enormous, leopards are better at hiding."

"Indeed?" She wasn't entirely sure they were only talking about leopards here.

"Oh yes," he said. "I've heard they can crouch in the rafters of some villager's hut and steal away a small person to eat before anyone even raises the alarm."

Well, she mused, arching a brow, the eccentric didn't disappoint.

"I say, Your Grace, doesn't it worry you to keep a killer like that in your house?"

"I've worked hard to train him *not* to be a killer ever since he was a cub. Still, you're quite lucky. You should not have been snooping," he added, gesturing at her with his glass.

To her relief, his tone was mild, his frown merely chiding; he looked more curious than cross about her trespass.

She attempted the slightest hint of a charming smile and looked up at him through her lashes. "I said I was sorry."

He snorted. "It was your beau's book that gave you away. You left it on my library desk." He took another swallow of his drink, his stare unreadable. "I do wonder what the gentleman would say, though, if he knew where you were right now. In this bedroom. With me."

The frank way he pointed out their situation made her gulp silently.

She would be ruined forever if anyone ever heard about this.

"Come, you remember your suitor, my lady," he said, cynically prodding her for a reaction. "I know there are so many to keep track of, but I refer to the little rumpled chap with the spectacles and curly hair. Your favorite. The folklorist?"

Stiffening, she looked away. "I take it you haven't heard."

"Heard what?"

"He jilted me."

"*What?* No," he said. "Not possible."

She sighed. "It's true."

He leaned toward her with an incredulous look, as though scanning the depths of her eyes for deception. "I don't believe you."

She shrugged with a frown.

He straightened up again, scowling, puzzled. "Pardon, I don't understand. You're one of the most desired young women in the ton. How could *you* have been rejected by th-that skinny-necked worm? Is he blind, mad, or stupid?"

Startled and flattered by his indignation on her behalf, Serena nevertheless turned away with a pang. "Do not speak ill of him in my presence, if you please."

"Really?" Azrael cocked his head. "You still have feelings for this fellow?"

"Not that it's any of your business, but he had no choice but to end our courtship. His parents would've cut him off."

Azrael scoffed and muttered something about a sniveling excuse.

"Lord Toby was a friend long before he became my suitor," she said. "And, the fact is, I owe him."

"For what?" he demanded with a puzzling display of lordly indignation on her behalf.

She paused, realizing he had just given her an opening to broach the subject that had brought her here tonight. "He at least told me the truth when my own flesh and blood gave me only lies." She hesitated. "In fact, Your Grace, that's the real reason I'm here."

"Well," he murmured, "at last she comes to it. Do go on, Lady Serena. You have my full attention."

Pulling over a wooden chair, he twirled it backward and sat down astraddle it. He rested his arms across the chair back, then took another swig of his brandy. "Begin, please. I'm all ears."

Serena debated how to start. "As you know, Lord Toby has a literary hobby as a folklorist. Last year, his publisher released the book you have in your library, *Volume One* of his *Collection of English Folklore*."

"Yes."

"He is fascinated by all the old peasant superstitions from around the British Isles. He collects them, writes them down so they won't be lost. From ghost tales and supposed encounters with supernatural creatures to fairies and bogarts and will-o'-the-wisps."

"Right." He nodded. "I read it."

"Well, he's working on *Volume Two*, to be published next year. For his new book, Toby wished to include a chapter on various legends surrounding the many ancient barrows and burial mounds dotting the countryside."

With those words, Azrael's easy air of curiosity instantly changed to a guarded expression.

Serena forged on. "This past spring, his research on this topic led him to a village in Buckinghamshire called Owlswick. I…think you've heard of it, Your Grace."

His face had darkened at the name. He sat back, as though pulling away from her. "What of it?"

"Toby told me there is a large barrow near this village, which the people there swear holds a curse."

Azrael said nothing.

"He asked the locals of Owlswick what made them so sure this curse was real. The story they told shocked him to the marrow."

"I daresay it would," Azrael murmured, staring at her. "He had better not put any of that into his book."

She glanced at him uncertainly. "He told me he would not, for my sake. Since the tale concerns my family. And yours."

He flicked a wary glance over her. "What else did he tell you?"

"Well, the peasants of Owlswick informed him that many years ago, on regular occasions, there was a wild group of aristocrats who traveled out to certain lesser estates they owned in the vicinity. They'd come thundering in from London and all parts of the country to participate in revels there of…an unsavory nature. Things well beyond the bounds of common decency. And apparently—forgive me—your sire was the ringleader of this group."

He stared at her, unblinking. No sign of denial.

She swallowed hard, unsure what she had expected. Protestations of innocence? Assurances it was all made up? He just sat there, steely-eyed.

"The peasants told Toby there were rumors that your father's coterie of rakehells and wild ladies was a splinter group that broke off from the Hellfire Club after the authorities discovered that dreadful bit of business decades ago, made arrests, and forced it to disband. After all, Owlswick isn't too far from West Wycombe, where all that originally took place."

Azrael studied her in silence.

"Toby said that, even to this day, the peasants were still frightened to speak about the visitors' activities on account of the curse these wayward nobles brought down on themselves."

"Hmm."

"All the mansions they once used as their pleasure grounds have long stood abandoned. Doesn't that seem strange?"

"Very," he said, but his dry tone made her think he was only humoring her.

She continued anyway. "Toby was at least able to coax *some* information out of the villagers, though. He can be very disarming."

"I'm sure," he drawled in a low tone that almost made her wonder if he was a wee bit jealous of her ex-beau.

She shook off the startling question and continued, forcing her attention on the vital topic at hand.

"The villagers told him the decadence that went on at those parties was as scandalous as one can imagine. The people involved already had everything in terms of worldly wealth and power, but it wasn't enough for them. Eventually, they began seeking some sort of control over, um, supernatural forces, as well."

Azrael sighed wearily, rubbing his forehead. "Yes, go on."

"The peasants described the group's activities from that point onward as dabbling in some dark form of witchcraft." She shook her head. "This was all kept hidden, of course, but some of the bolder local farmers would spy on the visitors out of concern for the profane goings-on there. Others from the village would be hired on as temporary servants while the owners were in residence, and they saw things, too. Things that frightened them.

"They gave Toby their firsthand accounts describing what they'd witnessed. Lords and ladies of the ton engaging in…occult rituals, possibly satanic in nature. But they only gave him two names— Dunhaven and Rivenwood."

Azrael said nothing, merely took a drink.

Serena was shocked he hadn't denied any of it. He didn't even look surprised.

"Tell me," he said, "who all have you and the lad spoken to about this?"

She blinked at the question. "Toby only spoke of it to me, and, I believe, to his parents, a little. I confronted my mother about it, but she would tell me nothing, so I eventually tracked down my old childhood nurse to see what she might be able to tell me, but she did not want to speak about it either."

"Anyone else? Friends? Father? Chaperone?"

"No."

"Good," he said. He considered, then took a drink. "So what did our dear Lord Toby make of this wicked story?" he asked after a moment.

"Well, the whole thing spooked him terribly, of course."

"He believed it?"

"Oh, he lives for such tales. All that superstitious talk about witchcraft and devilry, contacting dark spirits and supernatural mayhem. He swallowed it whole, of course. Even some nonsense about blood sacrifice."

"Hmm. And you?"

She scoffed. "To me, it sounds like nothing but a bunch of rich, bored aristocrats with jaded appetites and too much time on their hands attempting to amuse themselves with silly, make-believe magic. Mere entertainment, just another passing novelty until they grew bored of that, too, and moved on to the next idle pleasure."

"Hmm," he said again.

"Unfortunately, Toby learned that these misguided revelers felt compelled to continually increase the risk and daring of their exploits, until finally, they resorted to vandalism, I'm afraid, and broke into the barrow.

"Not only did they open the ancient burial mound, they robbed the dead pagan king inside of his grave goods, and then held some sort of disgusting ritual inside, because the place was supposedly built upon the ley lines, or some such foolishness. They supposedly wanted to harness the site's *mysterious energy*," she said, quoting Toby.

Azrael rested his chin on his forearm, which was propped along the chair back. He did not look the least bit shocked, and his calm about it all disoriented her.

Still, it was a great relief to be able to tell someone about it at last.

Someone who'd understand.

She was just happy that, so far, he hadn't got angry at her for mentioning his father.

"According to the peasants, it was the group's trespass, breaking into the barrow and disturbing the slumber of this ancient clan chieftain that awakened whatever pagan curse, evil spirits or what-have-you, was lurking inside the barrow. They freed it—so the tale goes—and this 'power' they had sought to contact followed them out, soon after which, the group's members all soon discovered they were cursed."

"This part of the story I know," he said with an idle nod. "One man was killed in a duel a few weeks later. Another's ancestral pile burned down about a month after that. Half his servants were killed in the blaze, his wife hideously scarred.

"One's heir murdered his valet," he continued, "and had to flee to the Continent to escape the hangman. But his ship sank in a storm in the Channel before he ever reached Calais. The following year, one of the female members leapt to her death off a Cornish cliff."

"Nor did our families go unscathed," she pointed out. "Your father was murdered, and as it turns out, I once had a..." Her voice faltered as a wave of sorrow crept over her.

"A sister who died," he said in a soft tone.

"Yes!" She drew in her breath and stared at him, shocked. "You knew?"

Azrael shrugged.

"Well, I didn't!" she exclaimed.

Toby's most painful revelation that day had been that, before Serena was born, her parents had had a two-year-old daughter, little Lady Georgette, who had apparently drowned in the ornamental lake at her family's estate near Owlswick.

An estate Serena hadn't even known her parents owned.

Why she had never been told about her dead elder sister, she could not imagine.

But that wasn't even the worst family secret. Merely the saddest.

"I'm sorry for your loss," Azrael said quietly after a moment.

"Well, I'm sorry for *yours*," she countered. "It must have been awful for you, seeing that." The words slipped out before she could stop them.

She bit her lip, knowing she was now on dangerous ground.

But he still seemed placid enough. Silent.

She wondered how much she dare reach out to him on this delicate subject. "They say you were there when it happened, Your Grace," she ventured. "That you saw the whole thing, and you were just a boy."

Before her eyes, he closed down. A deep wariness stole over his finely chiseled features and dropped like a veil behind his eyes.

"Yes, that is what they say. But you didn't come here to talk about me," he said with a bland smile, politely redirecting her, his eyes frosty. "If you already know all this, then why *are* you here, Lady Serena? Perhaps you could get to the point? I have a great many guests downstairs."

She looked away, stung but not surprised by his rebuff. "Because that wasn't *all* Toby told me. I'm afraid there's an even worse secret he revealed. The real reason he rejected me is that... Oh, this is difficult."

Azrael waited.

"Please, you mustn't tell anyone," she whispered.

He shrugged. "Of course not."

She stared at him, struggling. "When Toby returned from Owlswick, he was so troubled by all he'd heard that he decided to ask his parents about it—the Marquess and Marchioness of Chalmers.

"Given the high birth of all the people involved, he figured there must've been rumors circulating in the ton about the group's activities back in those days. He merely wanted confirmation so he could be sure the peasants hadn't made the whole thing up. So he asked his parents if they'd ever heard any whispers about such things back then. And indeed they had."

"Go on."

She lowered her head. "I couldn't believe it when he told me what his mother said. That is, I didn't *want* to believe it. But in my heart, from the second I heard the words, I knew it must be true."

"What did she say?" he murmured, studying her.

Serena floundered, overcome by the need to try to explain, if not justify, her mother's behavior first. "You must understand, Your Grace, my mother was a great beauty in her youth—still is, for her age. Many women have hated her from jealousy and spite. But men? Well—please know, she's changed now. If there were indiscretions, they were in the past.

"Mama is devoted to a life of virtue now. She reads her Bible daily, always goes to church. Back then, however," she said with a wince, "Lady Chalmers said Mama was wild and scandalous. The marchioness said my mother's indiscretions grew even worse after her child died.

"She was apparently so heartsick from losing little Georgette that, according to Lady Chalmers, she went rather mad for a time. At least, when it came to men. My parents' marriage was known to be all but ended after the child drowned. Anyway, it seems I was the end product of that period of her life."

"I see," he said quietly.

She gazed at him in distress, hating the humiliating words that now defined her in a Society where lineage was everything. "And so I'm...illegitimate. Someone's bastard, a by-blow. Not your father's, of course. He died sixteen months before I was born. Toby helped me verify the dates."

She sighed, relieved at least to get the weight of her confession off her chest, here in his church-like house. To be sure, she had never expected to have the Duke of Rivenwood as her confessor.

"So *that* is how I found out that Lord Dunhaven is not my real father. Who is? I have no idea." She shook her head, embarrassed. "My mother won't tell me, if she knows. She won't even admit who all she was involved with back then, possible candidates for my true sire. She's too ashamed. She wants to pretend her past simply doesn't exist. But this is my life and I can't live it as a lie. I need to know who I am."

She stared at him. "That is why I did what I did tonight. I know how bad this looks, my breaking into your house, and I *am* sorry. It's just—since your father was the leader, I thought I might be able to find some clue here of who his followers were back then. For I believe that one of them is likely to be my real father."

He tilted his head, pondering the mystery. "Does Dunhaven know you're not his own?"

"God, no," she said. "That was the one thing Mama begged of me, not to speak of it to him. Of course I haven't. I don't want to hurt Papa. He is a good, simple man, and he worships the ground my mother walks on. You know, I admire them, because somehow, after all that, the loss of a child, their unfaithfulness on both sides, they changed their lives and repaired their marriage."

"That is no small feat," he said softly, nodding.

"I know. I would never take that away from them, either, by revealing my mother's secret. I just want to know for myself who I actually belong to."

He said nothing.

"Anyway," she continued with a sigh, "Lady Chalmers finally saw fit to mention to Toby that while she has no objection to his friendship with me, he'll never have his parents' permission to marry me, given my dubious origins. They do not wish to be allied with such a family, and are concerned I might turn out to be like Mama. Were he to proceed against their will, he would be cut off. So, he ended our courtship."

"So he gave you up for money." Azrael shook his head.

"*Well*, he also believes I might actually be under this same, supposed curse on our families."

Azrael arched a brow.

"I told you he was superstitious."

"And a fool," Azrael murmured, staring meaningfully at her.

Serena blushed but regarded him with skepticism. "You call Toby a fool for rejecting me, yet you claim you and I were once betrothed. I never knew about it, so it must've been you who ended our match. It doesn't sound as though you have much room to criticize, when you apparently jilted me, too."

His lips twisted at her sardonic tone. "Our situation was different."

"How?"

"It's complicated."

"I suspect, with you, most things are."

A soft, rueful laugh escaped him.

"Come now, at least I know that Toby rejected me in order to keep his inheritance. So what's your excuse?"

He frowned.

She started to rise from her chair. "Unless you'd rather get back to your guests? And, of course, the *ravishing* Miss Burns."

"Sit! Very well, if you really want to know, I'll tell you what happened."

"Please do."

"As soon as I turned twenty-one, legally of age to conduct my own affairs, and free at last from being under the thumb of half a dozen guardians and trust officers, I had only one desire: to take control of my own affairs. I immediately set out to erase all vestiges of the life my father and his henchmen had mapped out for me. Our arranged marriage was a key part of that. No offense was intended, I assure you."

"None taken." She studied him. "You know, I remember you coming to our country house once when I was a child."

"Yes, that was when I had your parents sign the documents dissolving our betrothal."

She searched her memory more intently. "Did I not physically barrel into you while chasing about the house after my brothers?"

He started laughing. "You did. Little apple-cheeked terror, running around giving orders like the wee fairy queen."

"Yes, I often got scolded for that!" She chuckled. "As it happens, you made a deep impression on me, Your Grace. On my imagination."

"Nonsense," he mumbled, looking embarrassed but pleased.

"It's true. How could I forget you? So somber and elegant, with your long, pale hair spun from moonbeams," she teased.

He laughed at her, looking slightly sheepish at her description. "I was skinny as a rail back then."

"Well, I was a brat," she said cheerfully. Enjoying his mild discomfiture, she pressed her luck. "Oh, yes, I remember you quite well. I was sure you were some fey prince from an elven kingdom in the forest, who had just ventured out into the human world on some noble but highly dangerous mission."

"Story of my life," Azrael drawled, and took a drink.

"Well!" she said, blushing a bit herself. "After I made such a frightening first impression on my future spouse, I can see why you didn't see fit to wait for me to grow up."

"Oh, I didn't end the match because I could see you were going to be a handful," he told her, "but to deny my jailers their victory. And believe me, your parents were all too happy to sign the papers, too. They no longer wanted me for your husband either. For, by then, you see, they'd extricated themselves from the group. They dreaded being drawn back in all because of some old agreement they had signed while they were still, shall we say, in darkness."

So that's why I've been forbidden to talk to you.

"Your mother actually cried and hugged me after I *set her daughter free*, as she put it. So, be glad you escaped it," he said, toasting her with his glass.

She studied him for a long moment, mystified. "Do you ever wonder how it might've been, Your Grace?"

Her frank question startled him, she saw.

His eyes flickered with wary calculation. "It doesn't really matter, so why think about it? Beautiful as you've become, I could never marry the bride those devils had picked out for me."

"Ah." She hid a twinge of disappointment at his blunt words. "And why is that?"

"Because." He leaned toward her, lowering his voice, as if some unseen presence in the chamber might hear them. "These are deeply evil men, Serena. And my father was the worst of them all. I shall deny it beyond this room, but you, of all people, have a right to know."

Her eyebrows rose, but he wasn't finished.

"Between you and me"—he paused, his eyes flashing like silvery blades—"he got what he deserved."

Oh my God, she thought as stunned suspicion flooded through her mind. *You're the one who killed him.*

CHAPTER 4

In the Dark

*A*zrael wasn't sure which part of what he'd just said had upset his fair intruder, but plainly something had.

She had stiffened slightly, drawing back from him just a bit. Her dewy lips parted, and her captivating hazel eyes grew even more guarded as she stared at him in the candlelight.

He could not say why, but God's truth, that almost feline wariness in her delighted him. If he was of the moon, as she had so fancifully claimed, then Lady Serena, with her raven hair and sparkling eyes, was of the night itself—darkness and comets and stars—drawing him out with her mysterious allure.

He couldn't believe he'd had to give her up. He was a greater fool than Lord Tobias Guilfoyle. But this was the first time they'd ever actually spoken, and he was shocked at how instantly he felt at home with her.

Perhaps that was because he'd been aware of her all her life.

Even so, he'd been stunned to see her from afar when she'd first appeared in Society as a debutante. He had noted the flock of admirers around her from the start. And though he knew full well he couldn't have her, that didn't mean he'd never wondered how she'd taste.

"Excuse me," Serena murmured, cooling toward him, rising from the chair abruptly.

She had just enough room to slip by him as she paced off toward the liquor cabinet, setting her empty glass atop it.

She slid his black tail coat off her shoulders. "Thank you for this," she said, her tone awkward, her gaze averted. "I am warm now. Do you wish to put it back on?"

"Not yet. You can set it down if you like." He gestured with his glass toward the bed.

Of which, he gathered, they were both acutely aware.

"As you wish." She nodded, smoothed his coat over her arm, and laid it on the mattress.

He watched her through narrowed eyes, slightly confused by the shift in her attitude. "Are you all right?" he asked. "I know it's been a lot to take in."

"Oh, yes—I'm fine." He couldn't help but notice that she seemed to back away from him.

Her pale, expressive hands clenched and unclenched by her sides, then she smoothed her skirts and marched off around the foot of the bed.

"Are you leaving, then?" he said, holding himself back from the urge to prevent her.

She hesitated, her back to him. Clearly, something else was on her mind.

Azrael watched her in fascination, his gaze following the set of her shoulders and the sweet, supple curve of her back in that dull beige walking dress.

To be sure, the gown she wore tonight was not her usual fare. He was accustomed to seeing her in striking, bold-colored satin.

When she turned slowly and glanced at him again from around the bedpost, he was puzzled by the troubled look in her eyes beneath those lush black lashes.

The girl was eyeing him like most of his servants watched Raja whenever Azrael brought the big cat out on the leash.

What the devil? He frowned. She hadn't seemed nervous around him before. Not like this, anyway.

"Why are you looking at me like that?" he inquired in a low tone, remaining on his chair to let her keep her distance, if that made her feel safer.

"It's just that it's getting late. You need to get back to your guests, I'm sure, and I..." She began to twirl a finger through a lock of ebony hair lying across her shoulder.

"You what, Lady Serena?" he asked, watching her.

"I'm still no closer to the main question that I came here seeking answers for in the first place!"

He heaved a sigh. "Very well. What exactly do you want?"

She took a single step toward him, her gaze imploring, and though she kept the carved oak column of the bedpost between them, she curled her hand around it.

"I want to know who my real father is, of course."

Azrael frowned but could not deny a sympathetic tug at his heart at the lost, plaintive note in her voice.

"Everything Toby said leads me to believe he was one of the men in your father's set years ago, when they were all involved in these unpleasant things. As I told you, I tried to ask my mother. As soon as my conversation with Toby ended that day, I marched straight into the house and confronted her privately, but she wouldn't budge. She refused even to have the conversation with me. She said I had no right to ask her such impertinent questions, and then she stormed out. We've barely spoken since."

Serena leaned her head wearily against the bedpost. "I wish I could ask Papa, but I promised I wouldn't. Besides, I don't have the heart. And I doubt he knows anything, anyway." She dropped her gaze. "In truth, Papa doesn't notice much beyond the sports gazettes."

Azrael could believe it.

The large, burly Earl of Dunhaven, or "Dunny," as most called him, had been involved with his father's group in those days, but he'd always been a follower, happy enough to do the bidding of cleverer, more labyrinthine minds.

A simple man, really. The brawn to those with twisty brains. Easily manipulated.

"Anyway," she continued with a sigh, "Mama's refusal to confess left me no choice but to try questioning my old nurse, Mrs. Hopkins, for information next. She's old now, long since retired, but I managed to hunt her down.

"She did tell me that the previous nurse before her, who'd allowed the accident to happen, had been charged, found guilty, and transported to Australia, even though Georgette's death was an accident. My parents made sure the poor woman was destroyed.

"Unfortunately, Mrs. Hopkins claimed that her memory had grown poor with age when I asked if she could remember which gentlemen used to visit my mother in those days. She said it wasn't a servant's place to notice such things about her mistress, and I suppose that's true.

"So, you see, Your Grace, you are my last hope of ever finding out who my real father might be. I've already exhausted any other options I could think of. Lord Toby already shared with me everything he learned, my mother refuses to even think about the past, I can't ask Papa, and Mrs. Hopkins' memory is fading. It was she, by the way, who suggested that if the answers were to be found anywhere, they would be most likely in your possession," she added. "That is why I did what I did tonight."

Serena paused. "I'm not proud of it, sneaking in like that, trying to deceive you. It was wrong of me. I hope you can forgive me." She slipped around the bedpost and took a step toward him. "But please—if you have any information at all on where I should begin my search, I will not bother you again, I promise."

Azrael gazed at her, torn.

For a man with any chivalry at all in his veins, it was nigh impossible to deny such an innocent damsel anything. Especially a request that, in truth, she had every right to make. She deserved answers, he knew.

But the truth would only bring her misery.

And possibly put her life in danger.

"Please say something," she urged.

His expression sobering, Azrael pushed up from his chair, set his glass aside, and went to her with tender regret. "My lady, you do not truly know what you are asking for."

As he approached, she held her ground, and the candles' glow caught the flecks of gold in her greenish-brown eyes. When he stood before her, searching her face, he could not resist running his fingertips down the curve of her creamy cheek.

Then his stare came to rest on her plump ruby lips. With unsated need still simmering under the surface after Bianca's attentions, the temptation grew too strong.

If things had been different, she might have been his.

"What a splendid rose you have become," he said in a husky voice, running his fingertip along her jaw line until he came to her pert chin. He lifted it with a gentle touch, lowered his head, and kissed her.

She stood very still, as though she knew she ought to pull away, but didn't.

Azrael pressed his lips to hers, closing his eyes at the aching sweetness of her innocence.

When he paused and glanced at her, he saw her inky lashes fanned against her blushing cheeks. Those lips were now slightly parted.

It was more than he could resist; he moved to deepen the kiss.

She stopped him halfheartedly. "What do you think you are about, sir?" she asked in a breathy whisper.

That had not sounded entirely like a rebuke to him, and when her lashes swept upward, he saw lightning in her eyes.

His pulse leaped with want. She made no effort to flee as he gathered her closer.

"That," he whispered, "was my recompense for saving your pretty neck. But this I collect as the price for my *generous* forgiveness for your naughtiness, sneaking into my party."

"But I was invited."

A sensuous smile curved his lips. "Yes, you were." Then he kissed her again, sliding his arm more firmly around her waist and pulling her closer.

The feel of her supple body against his set his blood on fire.

Just a taste, he vowed, though he thrilled to the featherlight touch of her palms landing uncertainly on his chest, as though to temper him, but making no move to push him away.

Azrael kissed her lips apart and indulged for a long moment in the treasure that might've been his, if things were different. Serena allowed it; he could feel her virginal curiosity about his tongue's incursion into her mouth, and he could fairly smell her arousal deepening.

He gripped her in his embrace, but when his hardness began to throb painfully against her soft, flat belly, he fought off the hunger to lay her in that bed, and somehow tore himself away.

Panting, he released her abruptly, before he lost the will. "I think it's time for you to go, my lady."

He stepped away, turning his back on her in an effort to get himself under control. The taste of her lingered on his lips.

Behind him, she was silent for a heartbeat. "But you haven't answered my question yet."

"You don't know what you're asking for. If you want my best advice, let this matter go."

"Let it go?"

He did not turn around, striving to tame his lust, and staring at the floor, acutely aware of her just a few feet away.

"Please, I've only ever had your best interests at heart, Serena. You don't know what you're dealing with. These are dangerous men—tangled up in a sort of secret society. So I suggest you forget what you heard and, for God's sake, don't go stirring up the past.

"I understand how it must've hurt to lose your beau over things beyond your control. But the boy is a coward and a fool. Find another suitor. It won't be difficult for you. One who'll accept you for exactly who you are."

"But that's just it, Your Grace. I don't even know who I am anymore, who I'm supposed to be. Don't you see? My whole life has been a lie! All this time I thought I was Lord Dunhaven's daughter, and now I have no idea who I belong to. Please, won't you help me?"

Drawing on all the ice that ran in his veins as part of his Rivenwood heritage, he lifted his chin and flatly said: "No."

"I see."

He turned around again just in time to see her flinch as though he had struck her.

"Very well." She pivoted toward the door. "Then I shan't trouble you further, Your Grace. I'll see myself out."

"That won't be necessary." He grabbed his coat off the bed, blew out the candles, then joined her near the bedroom door.

He could feel her stewing, and got the impression the headstrong beauty was not used to having anyone, especially males, tell her no.

"What?" he prompted in a low tone.

She huffed. "I can't believe I let you kiss me, and you still won't budge. You tricked me!"

"You liked it," he muttered.

"So what if I did?" She paused, tilting her head with a coy glance. "Would a third kiss be sufficient to get me what I want, Azrael?"

"The price for what you want, darling, would cost you much more than a kiss." He tapped her on the nose. "But we both know *that* is never going to happen."

"So you're really going to leave me in the dark?"

"We are all in the dark, my lady. 'Tis the human condition. Come now. Since we both know you cannot be trusted to wander about the house unchaperoned, I will escort you out personally. I'll take you down the servant stairs," he added as he put his coat back on. "That way, you won't be seen by my other guests."

She gave him a pretty glower, but waited while he opened the door and glanced out into the corridor. "All clear."

Turning to beckon her out, Azrael paused when he saw her mutinous expression by the lamplight coming from the hallway. Her lips were pursed in a tight bow, and veritable flaming arrows shot out at him from her eyes.

"Serena," he said with a sigh.

"How can you do this to me? If you *know* who my real father is—"

"I don't *know*," he interrupted. "The only thing I can tell you with any certainty is that, given your choices, the answer wouldn't please you. The wisest thing you can do is forget what Toby told you and settle your mind on Dunhaven as the only earthly father you need. Trust me, he was the least bad of the lot. Not evil, merely—thick. Now, if you don't mind," he said with an impatient gesture at the doorway, "after you."

"Humph." Serena marched out over the threshold with her nose in the air.

It was bad of him, but he found her righteous indignation amusing under the circumstances. After all, the girl had trespassed in his house and spent the past half-hour with him alone in a darkened bedchamber— and now she wished to play the wronged, virtuous heroine?

Still, he had not exactly been on his best behavior himself.

He winced at the thought of the yelp from her that had interrupted Bianca's audition for the role of his mistress. He scratched his eyebrow awkwardly with one hand as he pulled the door shut with the other.

"Er, my lady, may I say I...I do wish you had not seen me with Miss Burns," he ventured as she marched off ahead of him.

A short, cynical laugh escaped her. "What does it matter? You can do as you please with any woman, I'm sure." She sent him a pointed look as he caught up, walking beside her down the red-carpeted corridor.

"It's not as though we are engaged."

"That's not what I mean. You are innocent."

"Am I? On the contrary, it sounds like I was born with wickedness in my blood. Just like you, my dear duke."

He frowned, perturbed by her words. They were truer than she knew.

Then he shepherded her through a simple service doorway near the end of the corridor. "Just through here," he said none-too-patiently.

"So eager to be rid of me?"

"No, it's just that I have no idea how we'd explain your presence here without your chaperone, never mind a costume. Come along—and mind your step, you little minx." He led her down a creaky wooden staircase, dimly lit by an overhead lantern.

The stairs led down to an unobtrusive side entrance on the ground floor. She watched him undo the locks when they reached the door at the bottom.

"So you really won't help me, then?"

"No!" he exclaimed, exasperated. "How many times must I tell you? Not in this matter. If you had asked for anything else, I should have done it, gladly." He felt bound to this girl in ways he could not explain. "But not this. It's too dangerous. Now, wait here for a moment," he ordered sternly, "and I'll go fetch the cloak you dropped."

She sighed, sounding very put-upon. She did not thank him for this favor, of course. Apparently, the beauty was used to having peers of the realm run and fetch for her.

Azrael harrumphed. Stepping outside, he strode off to collect her domino from the grass beneath the balcony, shaking his head at her impertinence.

Perhaps it was for the best that she had driven him out of the room with all her pestering about things he dared not discuss. Otherwise, he might've been tempted to keep her in there all night.

Ah well. He marched through the cool grass while the wind played with his hair, and fortunately, the indigo night soothed away his annoyance.

He supposed that at least one had to admire the girl's persistence. He felt sorry for her, in truth. He could see that she'd had her world upended by Lord Toby's findings. Still, there was nothing *he* could do.

Then he spotted her lost domino and went to snatch it off the grass.

When he brought it back to her, warily, Serena let him drape it over her shoulders. He resisted the urge to inhale the enticing scent of her hair. Having set her domino in place for her, he stepped back and studied her by the light of a moonbeam while she put her mask on again.

He couldn't help smiling as he watched her. "You didn't fool me, you know," he remarked. "I recognized you at once."

"How?" She propped her hands on her waist.

"I'm not sure." His gaze lingered briefly on those much-too-kissable lips. "I only marvel that you went to such lengths with this ruse. Next time, just come and talk to me."

She shrugged. "What good would it do me?"

Before he could think of an answer, she forced a brisk smile and pulled up her hood.

"Well! At least you needn't worry about me *stalking* you anymore, Your Grace. As I said, I shan't trouble you again. Farewell."

As she pivoted to go, he reached out and captured her wrist. "Come, Serena," he cajoled her. "Let us not part on bad terms. I would help you if I could."

"But you *could*, Azrael," she said, boldly using his first name again, as he had used hers. "You merely choose not to, for reasons of your own. But that is your prerogative, and so be it. You may go back to your life, and I shall go back to mine. Only, do not imagine that we are now friends."

He lifted his chin, stung. "Is that so?"

"They who are not for us are against us."

"I am not *against* you, Serena," he said, but she just pulled away.

"It does not signify, Your Grace. Farewell." Yanking her wrist free of his light hold, she traipsed off alone into the darkness, her black cloak billowing around her.

Azrael's heart sank as he watched her go, his lovely almost-bride.

Aside from being slightly stunned at the way she had just put him in his place, frustration overwhelmed him.

He banged the heel of his fist into the lintel of the doorway and muttered a curse.

All the while, his heart pounded with the familiar litany of his defenses—or excuses—running through his head.

They seemed so inadequate just now. *I keep to myself. I mind my own business. I keep my head down and the bastards leave me alone.*

She has no idea what she's asking of me. I can't risk being drawn back in, or I might prove as bad as he was.

Maybe even worse.

One did not simply shrug off being named after the archangel of death, after all. It was not a name he wanted to live up to.

Letting out a sigh, he leaned against the frame of the open door, half in shadow, half in moonlight.

Trying to help her would've been extremely unwise. He knew that, of course. Blast and damn, though, he hated to disappoint her.

He glanced at the waiting doorway and felt no desire to return to his own party or even to participate anymore. Hell, his whole life was a masquerade, and if he were honest, he was a lifelong expert at playing a role. Wasn't he the boy who, years ago, had convinced his father's twisted cronies that he wasn't quite right in the head?

Too scarred, withdrawn, and unstable after seeing his sire murdered that day in the woods to live up to his dark destiny. They had hoped to groom him to take his father's place one day as the leader of the next generation of Prometheans—but he was damaged goods.

At least he'd taken pains since the age of twelve to make sure that they believed so.

Once he had realized the sort of men who had control of him after his father's death—the trustees of his fortune, headed up by his chief legal guardian, Lord Stiver, his father's right-hand man—Azrael had quickly grasped the danger he was in.

The mysterious man in the woods that day, the so-called vagrant, had driven that point home with his dying breath. *"Don't grow up to be like him, and if you ever need help, go to Dante House on the Strand. My colleagues there will assist you..."*

Meanwhile, by some blessed stroke of luck, in his studies at the time, his old tutor Mr. Foxham had had him reading *Hamlet*.

With the dying agent's warning seared into his mind, Azrael had seized upon the Danish prince's strategy of fooling the villains with a charade of weakness, eccentricity.

And by God, it had worked.

By the time he'd turned fifteen, he had convinced the evil bastards that, sadly, he would never be the great man his father had been, alas.

He wasn't *raving* mad, they concluded, not like King George, for example.

Merely mad around the edges, like the Bard's overcautious Danish prince. Unable to deal with much, certainly not with the occult high darkness they dabbled in.

Obsessive. Withdrawn. High-strung. Too intense.

Ah, these true believers were filled with such regret to have to admit defeat where he was concerned.

They'd had such high hopes and tried with all their might to mold him into the monster his sire had envisioned, the next powerful leader destined to guide their future followers down the left-hand path.

But Azrael had thwarted them at every turn with his wits and his lies.

He remembered staying up late into the night as a lad, somberly designing what his next bout of madness should entail. He had to be convincing, but it was vital not to overdo it. And he remembered crying sometimes into his big old dog's fur, hugging the animal's neck. But for his pets, he was sure he had been the loneliest boy on earth.

Friends? They were but liabilities, as he had cruelly learned. A real friend was someone you told your secrets to, and *his* secrets could get people killed.

Like his poor old tutor.

Mr. Foxham had been his sole accomplice for a time, early on. But the old man had made the fatal mistake of standing up to Lord Stiver once.

The aged scholar had disappeared the very next day and was never heard from again. That happened to a surprising number of people in his guardian's orbit.

After that, Azrael had been more alone than ever, full of aching despair and the futile wish that someone out there would've magically noticed somehow that the duke's heir with his supposedly tragic story was actually a prisoner inside the palace he'd inherited.

No one but the servants ever knew the truth, but of course, they wanted to live, too. He couldn't blame them for turning a blind eye. They were as kind to him as they dared be.

By the time he had attained his majority, his jailers had given up on him for the most part and generally left him alone.

Of course, they still kept an eye on him, watching for any sign of his desire to return to the fold.

Indeed, Lord Stiver still held out some faint hope that Azrael's "madness" could be a portent of an even darker greatness in him than his father had possessed, yet to unfold.

In ancient times, after all, lunacy could signify that one had been touched by the gods, like the oracles and prophets.

They left him alive for that reason, and out of respect for his sire.

Of course, his guardians had been highly displeased when Azrael, immediately upon attaining his majority, had freed himself from the arranged marriage and moved to London as his permanent residence, forsaking his country estates.

Unfortunately, Town life hadn't brought Azrael the happiness he'd hoped for. It seemed he himself was the problem.

Slowly he'd begun to realize it was already too late for him—his untrusting habits and solitary mode of life were already set, too deeply ingrained.

What he'd seen in the woods on that day had cut him off from the rest of humanity, and now he did not know how to scale the walls he had built around himself. He'd been independent of his former masters for over a decade now, but he was still trapped somehow in the solitude that had been his safety for years.

Trapped by his secrets.

With a sigh, he dropped his chin to his chest, wearily pushed away from the lintel, and stepped back inside.

Pulling the door shut, locking it, he returned to his tedious duties as host with a creeping sense of futility.

Maybe, he thought, some people were simply destined to be alone.

Fool! How could you let him kiss you? Angrily, Serena hurried back through the park, casting the gazebo a glare as she passed it, and disregarding the moon as it leered down at her from between the clouds.

Dreadful man. Thank the Lord above she had not been forced to marry such a creature. How dare he take such liberties and then make a mock of her quest?

Her breath clouded as she gusted through the park, refusing to admit how much she had enjoyed Azrael's kiss, but the cold air helped somewhat to cool her simmering temper.

Ordinarily, a night like this would have been eerie enough to unnerve her, but after what she had just been through, really, this was nothing. She couldn't believe she had almost been eaten by a leopard and then nearly fallen to her death—all for naught!

But that wasn't even the worst part. She had risked her reputation and her life, spending the better part of an hour in a bedchamber with a man she'd been warned was evil. A man who might've committed patricide as a mere tender youth!

She was probably lucky he hadn't murdered *her* for some bloody Hallowe'en fun while she was there, she thought with a huff. Well, that was admittedly an exaggeration, because in truth, he hadn't seemed *evil-*evil to her. But he was certainly exasperating.

And selfish, she reminded herself as she trotted along the winding graveled path.

Why wouldn't he help her? It didn't make any sense. He claimed his refusal to get involved was for her own good, but who was he really protecting? Himself, or the members of his father's twisted little club?

But so be it. His refusal changed nothing. Even without Azrael's help, she would not be deterred in her search. Her real father might turn out to be as bad as his, but she at least had to know who the blasted man was.

After all, how could she ever marry without knowing? God forbid she unwittingly fall in love with some fellow she was related to.

Ghastly thought.

She shuddered then quietly let herself out of the wrought-iron gate on the opposite end of the park. After closing it behind her, she glanced both ways up and down the cobbled street to make sure no one was about.

She was fairly sure no one had taken note of her presence at the masked ball; now she just had to make it the rest of the way home and back up to her room. The street was empty, the houses still dark on this end of the square.

Moving stealthily, she padded out of the shadows of the plane trees and dashed across the street.

Once more, she slipped down the passageway between the buildings, turning the corner into the mews.

When she reached the back garden of her family's townhouse, she discreetly removed her disguise on the remote chance she crossed paths with Cousin Tamsin.

Explaining why she was fully dressed in a walking gown at this hour would be tricky enough. If her chaperone caught her sneaking back into the house wearing a Halloween costume, that would be considerably more difficult to explain.

That, Cousin Tamsin would have to report to Mama.

Serena folded up her domino and tucked her black half-mask into its velvet folds. Before returning inside, however, she stood on the garden path for a moment, took a deep breath, and strove to collect her thoughts.

When she looked up at the sky, it was so dark. She could feel the cold of winter creeping in, and her quest tonight had failed spectacularly.

What a waste of time. She had risked life and limb, shared her deepest secrets with someone who obviously didn't care, and made a fool of herself to boot.

Naively, she had fancied there was some kind of inexplicable bond between her and Azrael, but clearly, she was mistaken.

Still stung by his refusal to help her, she let out a sigh. It was difficult not to take it personally, especially after the scoundrel had been brazen enough to kiss her. Perhaps he thought their former betrothal—and she was still shocked at that news!—gave him the right.

He was wrong.

Well, what now? So he wouldn't help her. He had saved her life, though.

That would have to be enough. A fall from that height, after all, could have left her crippled or dead, not to mention banished from Society, because proper young ladies did not sneak into gentlemen's houses.

But having failed to come away with the key information, Serena rubbed her forehead in dismay where her mask had chafed her. Honestly, she did not yet know her next move.

It would help if she could think clearly, but her wits were all muddled up with sensuous memories of his marvelous tongue stroking hers so deeply, and the feel of hard, muscled body holding her close when he'd pulled her up from that ledge. She lifted her fingertips to her mouth, her lips still tingling with warmth and a regrettable hunger for more.

Serena shook herself and looked around, trying to clear her head. The whole row of houses was dark in the back. Even the horses in the stables were fast asleep, and standing there, she felt like the last person left alive on the face of the earth, never mind the house full of revelers on the far end of the square.

She tilted her head back and looked up at the full moon, sitting amid two banks of clouds. The man in the moon seemed to watch her, with his long-fingered, elegant hand propped beneath his silver cheek.

What are you looking at? she thought with a scowl. *Leave me alone.*

Yet her traitorous heart registered a pang that, after all her months of observing Azrael from a distance, becoming to some degree wrapped up in her fascination with him, the lout had turned his back on her.

He was no elven prince, she thought, squaring her shoulders. He was just another dead end in the maze of her search.

All that was left to do now was cross him off her list of possible leads in trying to solve this mystery and move on to the next step.

As soon as she figured out what the blazes that might be.

CHAPTER 5

Bonfire Night

*I*n the days that followed, Azrael found himself going through the motions of his usual routine, but he kept thinking about Lady Serena and sensed that something inside of him had changed.

He wondered continually about the bond and the history they shared—whether they liked it or not.

Or maybe it was all in his imagination. He wandered through a tangled forest of uncertainty, confusion, for days.

Netherford's basic male simplicity came as a relief when Azrael went to the Grand Albion, the huge, stately gentlemen's club that dominated one end of Moonlight Square.

The loud ex-leader of the rakehells still held court there, though his bride had put an end to his infamous womanizing. Fondly, Azrael recalled how he had personally prevented Netherford from being blackballed after the rogue had burned the club's wager book in a fit of temper.

Another club-mate, Gable, Viscount Roland, newly returned from the countryside, passed around cigars as he announced that his wife, Trinny—the eldest of all those red-haired sisters down the street—was expecting a blessed event.

Netherford took care to introduce Azrael to Lord Roland and to their cheerful blond friend, Viscount Sidney. Azrael appreciated the gesture. He was beginning to see that his friend really was a kinder and more perceptive man than he let on with all his brash joviality and bawdy irreverence.

His fellow duke seemed to have decided that Azrael would no longer be permitted to lurk like a ghost around the edges of the club. His one friend was determined to drag him out into the warm glow of the men's general camaraderie.

Before he knew it, he suddenly had two friends, then three. He particularly liked Roland's wry, understated wit, and sunny Sidney's unflappable cheer.

In any case, Azrael joined in the applause as Roland, the proud expectant father, was soundly cheered for his accomplishment. He even accepted a cigar on the viscount's behalf, though he despised the things.

A few nights later, he came upon the Netherfords and the Rolands together at some ball; it seemed the wives were good friends as well.

Watching the two men so unabashedly smitten with their brides, Azrael found himself thinking once more about Serena.

The girl *he* was to have married.

What if he'd made a colossal mistake, calling off the match? Was that even possible, under the circumstances?

Ah, but he had learned the price of her "friendship," and it was too steep for him. What was he to do?

He simply couldn't get involved in her quest. The only way he'd survived all these years was by giving his father's friends a wide berth.

Besides, he didn't have the slightest bloody inkling of who her real father was. A mere twelve-year-old at the time of his sire's death, he had hardly been privy to the details of the group's activities or who was sleeping with whose wife on any given night.

He had no idea how many men might have been involved at that point. Obviously, Lord Stiver, Azrael's head guardian, had succeeded his father as the coven's grandmaster, but there must have been one or two dozen more involved in their ridiculous, horrid rituals. For all he knew, Lady Dunhaven might have lain with any or all of those men.

What business was it of his, anyway? The poor woman. Azrael couldn't blame the countess for wanting to forget and pretend that that part of her life had never taken place.

His own mother had survived by a similar strategy, slowly disappearing into a laudanum fog.

The drug had killed her one night when she took too much, drifting off into a soul-stealing dreamland from which she had never awakened.

Azrael had envied her at the time.

More days passed, in any case. Gray, cold, empty days. Then it was a week past his masked ball.

He worked diligently, trying to forget about what had happened between him and Lady Serena in that room, and what he wished would've happened.

But when the nights descended, his musing about her turned steadily into a craving.

The hunger for even a glimpse of her lured him out into Society again, just as it had for weeks now, if he was honest.

Ever since he had noticed Staring Girl's preoccupation with him, he had been more frequently seen at Society events, all in hopes of glimpsing her—fascinated but wary as some forest animal.

Now, however, when he spotted her at some ball or banquet or rout, all he got from her was a distant, courteous nod. Then she'd turn away.

She might as well have run a sword through his heart.

Why her dismissal of him hurt, why it took him aback, he could not say. They were not even supposed to know each other, after all.

As she had told him flat out, they were not friends.

The change in her attitude toward him stung him nonetheless.

Where she used to lurk and stalk and amuse the hell out of him—as if he didn't notice—now he got no more than a polite nod and a nonchalant smile. The chill was palpable from across a ballroom, especially in the dwindling numbers of the ton present during the cold months.

Azrael felt startled—no, shocked—and oddly bereft when the raven-haired beauty now simply ignored him. He waited, hoping for a change, but Staring Girl had clearly moved on.

She made no effort to come closer, or to contrive to speak to him. Indeed, she seemed completely indifferent to his existence now, while he had been practically obsessing over her.

He felt like such a fool. Anger crept through him as the truth sank in. *So, all she ever wanted from me really* was *information.*

Of course. That was the only reason she had let him kiss her. The eager attention she had paid to him all Season long had been driven by nothing but pure self-interest.

It had never had anything to do with him. Once she saw that the answers she wanted would not be forthcoming, she had all but discarded him.

With as little trust as he already had in humanity, her subtle jilt wrenched his gut. Did it not even matter to her that he was a bloody duke? *He* was the one who'd keep people at arm's length, thank you very much.

Having it done to *him* for once was another experience altogether.

Oh, he was well aware that he was being manipulated—not that he could entirely blame her, given the stakes of her search. He mused upon her naughty cleverness as he watched her one night from across the table at a late, after-theater supper. Always she stayed at a tantalizing distance.

Azrael was sure she was deliberately torturing him to try to change his mind about helping her. What most infuriated him, though, was that he actually found himself considering it. *God, I must be suicidal.*

But it was one thing to live on the outskirts of Society, connected to none.

It was something else again to have tasted the nectar of being open, briefly, with someone who shared one's deepest secrets, and then to be shunned by that person.

Loneliness he could endure. He'd endured it all his life without complaint. But this…this was like being banished to outer darkness after having a brief moment in the sun.

All he could do was watch her hungrily from afar. Perhaps he was the one "stalking" *her* now, but turnabout was fair play, he thought cynically.

He pondered her gowns, the white pearls in her black hair, the way she laughed, the way she wrinkled her nose briefly when someone asked her to dance—as though she really didn't want to, but didn't wish to be rude.

It depended on the fellow. Some she turned down flat. Some she gave polite excuses. A few, very few, she accepted with a warm, genuine smile—the affable Lord Sidney among them.

That smile wrenched Azrael with seething jealousy. He wanted it all to himself.

Ah, but nobody could *not* like Sid. Especially ladies, Azrael supposed, glumly deciding as she danced with the viscount that the chap was a lot better-looking than he was, and ten times as charming.

Bleakly, he couldn't help wondering what reaction *he* might get if he ever took that step of asking her to dance.

But, of course, it was impossible. If he were seen going anywhere near her in public, the news would go rushing back to Stiver and his cronies, and their dark hopes for Azrael to return to the fold would be ignited anew.

She was to have been his queen of the damned, after all, his prize, the perfect lure meant to bind him in their darkness forever.

A man would gladly give his soul for such a woman.

All Azrael knew was that, in hindsight, he'd had no idea how much he'd enjoyed their silent game of cat-and-mouse all Season long until it had abruptly ended.

With a sickening feeling, he began to think their little game might just be the closest thing he had to a true connection with any eligible female.

Pathetic. Just pathetic, he thought for the umpteenth time the next day as he hurled his knife across his own, empty ballroom, practicing, while Raja gnawed contentedly on a large bone nearby.

Azrael narrowed his eyes in satisfaction as his blade bit deep into the target on the other end of the ballroom.

As for his sorry state of affairs when it came to females, well, he had done this to himself. Now he'd merely have to live with his choices.

He supposed he should probably find some other young lady to pursue. But the thought of marriage made him shudder.

No. No more strangers in his home. Especially not on a permanent basis.

A wife would hardly let him use the ballroom of his mansion as a studio for training at arms. Which seemed a great deal more practical to him.

He hurled two more of his throwing knives in rapid succession.

"Ahem, Your Grace, if I may interrupt?"

Azrael immediately tightened his hold on his throwing knife and turned toward the doorway of the ballroom, where his butler waited.

"Yes, Grimsley? What is it?" he asked, chest heaving with his exertions.

"Excellent news, sir," the bald, gloomy fellow intoned, folding his bony hands behind his back. "Your man Jenkins has just sent a note that Lord Tobias Guilfoyle has returned to Town."

"Is that so?" Azrael murmured, taking a step toward his butler, while Raja pricked up his velvety ears and paused in gnawing his treat.

Jenkins was one of Azrael's most discreet, loyal, and intelligent footmen. Perceptive, quick-witted, and literate, the man could've easily gone to work for Bow Street, but Azrael paid much better.

Given his roster of high-placed foes, it profited Azrael to secure the services of such a bold and capable fellow. While the rest of the footmen polished silver and served meals, Jenkins frequently served as an extra set of eyes and ears for Azrael whenever he needed them. Jenkins also kept him apprised of servant gossip from around Moonlight Square and elsewhere.

Servants missed little in a household, after all, and what they didn't know, they could learn. But normally, they only trusted their own kind.

In any case, the day after the masked ball, Azrael had assigned Jenkins to pin down for him the habits and location of Serena's former suitor. He was very keen to have a word with the folklorist regarding his potentially deadly work in progress.

Jenkins's initial report was that Lord Toby was out of town on another research excursion, this time to Cornwall.

Apparently investigating tales of Cornish pixies.

Azrael could only shake his head at this. He'd sent Jenkins back to watch the house, with orders to report to him when the daftling returned.

Apparently, today was the day.

"Did Jenkins say where the lad is now?" Azrael asked, toying with his knife and wiping his forehead with a pass of his arm.

"Yes, Your Grace. Jenkins stayed on his trail when the gentleman went out this morning. Lord Tobias has presently settled in to do a bit of writing, it seems, at his favorite coffeehouse, Killigrew's, in Bury Street, near the British Museum."

"Excellent," Azrael murmured. "Have Paulson ready my carriage. I'll go at once, before we lose him again."

"Very good, sir." His bald, creaky butler bowed out and then went to alert the coachman.

Azrael crouched down on the edge of Raja's pallet, taking hold of the animal's leash.

"Perhaps I should take you with me, eh?" he said while he scratched his magnificent pet behind the ear.

Raja purred loudly, pushing his huge head against Azrael's hand like an oversized housecat.

He smiled, amused at the thought, but, of course, bringing the leopard out to a coffee shop would draw far more attention than he wanted for the occasion.

Besides, he trusted he did not need the leopard's assistance to put the fear of God into this lad, which he fully intended to do today.

For all their sakes.

❖

A short while later, Azrael stepped into the coffeehouse from the quiet side street not far from the British Museum, leaving a vortex of dead leaves swirling behind him on the pavement. He paused to pull the door shut against the day's chill, then glanced around the low-ceilinged coffeehouse.

At once the smells of the place washed over him. Generations of pipe smoke and coffee grinds. He could almost hear the endless hours of political and literary arguments that this place must've heard over the decades.

It was warm and oddly homey, though. A cheerful fire blazed in the wide stone hearth, and the place was certainly quiet enough for the author to get some writing done.

At once, Azrael spotted him. It was easy to do. The place was practically empty.

The gray light of the early November day revealed a curly-headed young man hunched over a round table near the mullioned bow window. The table was piled with books and papers, and the writer seemed to be very much in his own world, a skinny fellow, rumpled and ink-smudged.

He looked at one stack of papers, then scribbled hurriedly on another, pausing every now and then to try to blow the ink dry. In between sips of coffee—Azrael guessed that was what the folklorist was drinking—he sprinkled a pinch of drying sand on his page and hastily blew on it before setting it aside, turning to the next.

And they say I'm odd.

Azrael took off his hat, then drew off his gloves as he slowly approached the scuffed round table where the chap was working. Under his arm, he had tucked his copy of *Volume One*. He took it out now, after stuffing his gloves into his pocket.

As he approached the table, Azrael could see through the window to where Jenkins and his driver Paulson were waiting for him by the carriage. The writer did not appear to have noticed it, blind, deaf, and dumb to the world in his literary absorption.

Lord Tobias Guilfoyle, it seemed, was off somewhere among the fairies.

"I beg your pardon, sir," Azrael greeted him, eyeing the figures and sketches and notes arrayed around the table amid a haphazard collection of pencils, papers, journals, and books.

Lord Toby glanced up at the interruption, still mouthing the phrasing of a sentence to himself, intense concentration behind his smudged spectacles.

"I don't wish to intrude," Azrael said ever so politely and, somehow, without a trace of mirth, "but aren't you the famous author, Lord Tobias Guilfoyle?"

The young man's eyes suddenly widened, and he came fully alert, gasping, jolting backward in his chair so that his coffee splashed on the margin of one of his papers. "Oh God! Have you come to kill me? I-I know who you are! Please! I won't tell anyone, I swear!"

Azrael arched an eyebrow, quite startled. He gave the lad a moment to regroup.

"Er, rather an odd greeting for an admirer of your work. But no. No murders scheduled today, my lord. I merely wondered if you would be so good as to autograph my copy of your book." He laid it gently on the table before him.

Toby stared at the *Collection*, finally recognized it, and then glanced nervously at Azrael, as if he suspected this was a trick.

And a rather transparent one, at that.

Which, of course, it was.

"I particularly enjoyed the chapter on castle ghosts," Azrael said, lifting his chin and hoping the fellow calmed down. Because, really, this was just embarrassing.

"Er, th-thank you," Toby stammered, looking so out of sorts that Azrael picked up the lad's quill pen and handed it to him, then opened the book to the title page.

Toby took the quill, as if only just then remembering what it was used for.

Azrael hid his bemusement as the author dipped the tip into his little inkpot. The pen shook in his hand as he tapped away an excess droplet. Then Toby glanced up at him dazedly. "T-to whom should I make it out, Your Grace?"

"Why, to Rivenwood, of course." Azrael narrowed his eyes. "But as you said, you already know who I am." He sat down slowly in the chair next to Toby. "Indeed, you know much more than that."

Toby gulped. While he bowed his curly head and dutifully jotted down a brief inscription along with his autograph, Azrael searched his brain for what could've possibly attracted a beauty like Serena to this yellow-bellied quiz.

Guilfoyle was an interesting fellow, to be sure, but not your ordinary fare for a smoldering vixen like Serena—or any diamond of the first water, for that matter. He was nothing in particular to look at, disheveled and slightly gawky; he was not especially rich, and, as a younger son, held a mere courtesy title.

He was not even a very practical man, and not at all suited to taking good care of a wife, if he was off halfway across the Realm chasing fairies.

And yet this creature was her favorite.

Damn, but she was an interesting girl. Maybe she had thought she would protect *him*, take care of *him*.

That, at least, Azrael could see.

"Thank you," he said when the author had finished his inscription.

He left the book open so the ink could dry on the signature, and drummed his fingers on the table, pinning the writer in his stare.

"Do you know why I am here?" he asked softly.

Toby managed a grim nod. "I...can imagine."

"I am not going to harm you, so do please relax. Frankly, I am not the one you have to worry about." Azrael scanned Toby's artless face. "I came merely to warn you that if certain tales of Owlswick were to appear in any published edition of *Volume Two*, your life will be forfeit."

"Well, I figured that much out myself!" Toby whispered, leaning closer, and looking rather stricken. "Believe me, I never discussed it with anyone since I came back from that horrible place. There was only one person I told—in strictest privacy!"

"Yes. We have a mutual acquaintance, Lord Toby. Don't worry," Azrael said as fresh terror flooded into the lad's eyes. "I mean her no harm whatsoever."

The relieved slump of Toby's shoulders at this assurance suggested that he believed him, but he still looked spooked.

"So it's true, then?" he whispered, eyeing Azrael warily. "All of it? Satanic rites in the barrow? Contact with demons? The curse?"

Azrael stared coldly at him.

Toby dropped his gaze. "Never mind."

"I shall want to read a copy of the full manuscript before it goes to print. Merely to ensure you haven't said anything foolish."

Toby furrowed his brow, but it seemed he did not dare protest. "If you insist."

"Good. I am glad we understand each other." Azrael paused. "You are a fine writer," he told the lad rather awkwardly, feeling a bit bad about scaring him. "I quite enjoyed your first effort."

"Er, thank you, Your Grace." Toby looked at Azrael like he did not know what to make of him.

The feeling was mutual, to be sure.

"I did not know you and Lady Serena were acquainted." Toby hesitated. "How is she?"

Azrael dropped his gaze to the table, suppressing a wistful sigh. *I wish I knew.*

He just shook his head. Then he frowned, skimming the lad with a probing glance. *What has a fellow like you got that I don't have, that you should have grown so close to her?*

"What is it, Your Grace?" Toby asked, squirming at Azrael's predatory stare.

"Tell me," Azrael said abruptly, "what did she *see* in you?"

Toby lifted his eyebrows. "Dashed if I know." Then he frowned. "Rather personal question, don't you think?"

"Humor me. Given what you know about me and my family, I think it's only fair."

Toby's sigh conceded this.

"Why did you jilt her?" Azrael asked, leaning back in his chair. The ink on his inscription was dry by now, but he still didn't budge. "Fancied you could do better?"

"What? God no."

"Then was it all of this unpleasantness with Owlswick that put you off her as a bride? Or fear of some supposed curse? She said you're superstitious. Or did you simply jilt her to get your parents' money?"

"She told you all this?" Toby exclaimed, coloring.

The lad was clearly embarrassed, but at least he'd calmed down as he realized Azrael had no intention of murdering him there in the coffee shop.

"Well?" Azrael prompted.

Toby took off his glasses and rubbed one of the lenses with his handkerchief. "I suppose it was a combination of all those things. But above all, I couldn't marry Serena because I..." He faltered. "I knew she'd regret it within a fortnight."

Azrael arched a brow.

Toby shook his head. "She doesn't love me."

"She seemed very loyal."

"Loyal, yes. Fiercely so. It's that stubborn streak of hers. But the thing of it is, well, she dotes on me as if I were a child or some helpless lapdog—and maybe, to some degree, I am. But deep down, I know Serena better than she thinks. What a ridiculous match, honestly."

"Yet you courted her."

"Of course I did! Who wouldn't? I was in love with her for years. I never thought she'd actually pick me, though. It was safer to admire from afar, I suppose."

This was an amusing fellow, Azrael decided. In a sea of dandies and coxcombs, his humility was refreshing. "I see."

"Once I realized she was partial to me, believe me, I was terrified. I knew I could never make her happy, not really—look at me."

"And why do you say that?"

"We couldn't be more different. Serena is bold and glamorous and willful and strong, and I, well, I'm none of those things. I'm just a scribbler and a dreamer. But I will always care for her, and I would never put anything in a book that could harm her in any way."

Toby frowned, silent for a moment. "I didn't want to hurt her. I do hope she knows that. It's just, with the doubts I'd been keeping to myself about our alliance, once I discovered all this about her family's past, I knew the time had come to make a choice about whether she and I really had a future together or not. My parents turned out to be completely against it—and at the end of the day, a goddess like Serena does not belong with a bookworm like me."

"Then *how* did you gain such a place of affection in her heart?" Azrael asked in a murmur, leaning closer.

He needed this information.

Toby seemed to search for a response. "Serena doesn't let many people very close to her. Her beauty has made her a target at times. Men would prey on her, and women frequently despise her when they don't even know her. As a result, she's learned to be rather guarded. And she doesn't take any nonsense from anyone, believe me.

"But behind that sophisticated, fashionable exterior, she has a soft, whimsical side that few people ever get to see. Those of us she does take under her wing, she dotes on most tenderly, nurtures and protects."

The words sank into Azrael's love-starved soul as he sat there listening.

"In truth, I think she felt sorry for me, since I can be…I don't know. Not very worldly. But no man wants a wife who sees him, how ever affectionately, as an object of pity."

Azrael nodded, pondering. "Yes, but how did you make her pick you?"

Toby shrugged. "I simply respected her intelligence. She's much cleverer than most of her admirers realize. All they see is that glorious body and beautiful face, not the sharp mind behind it. Although," he added, "her adventurous streak does occasionally overcome her better sense and lead her into trouble."

Azrael's lips twisted as he recalled her dangling off the trellis. "Yes, I noticed that."

"How is she, anyway?" Toby asked with a slight wince. "Not that I flatter myself to imagine she's pining over me. God knows she has no shortage of devotees. But asking as a friend, is she all right?"

Azrael thought about it, then shrugged and shook his head, dismayed to realize he did not know the answer to that question either.

"I dare not approach her myself to ask," Toby said. "I doubt she wants to see me, but I'm worried about her. Dumping all that dark, frightening information on her, and then leaving her to deal with it alone? Not that I had much choice. It would have been unseemly to continue attending her after we'd agreed to end our courtship. If she hates me now, I honestly couldn't blame her, though." He hesitated. "I feel I abandoned her when she needed me most."

As did I, thought Azrael. Chastened by the realization, he lowered his gaze.

"I-I didn't want to," Toby stammered, "but—propriety."

"Right," Azrael murmured. *Fortunately, some of us don't have to bother about such things.*

With that, he reached for his signed book and shut it.

Perhaps it was time to swallow his pride, ignore Serena's claim that they were not friends, and check on the lady himself.

After so keenly disappointing her about helping her find her natural father, it was the least that he could do.

"As well as you know her customs," Azrael said evenly, taking care to keep the emotion out of his voice, "where do you suppose she'll be tonight?"

"Tonight, I've no idea, but I wager I know where she'll be tomorrow evening—at Richmond House, for Their Graces' *essential* Bonfire Night celebration." A wistful sigh escaped the lad. "She always did love the fireworks."

❖

And so, the next night, Azrael dutifully went to the Bonfire Ball — against his better judgment, to be sure.

Loner that he was, he received invitations to most things because of his rank, so even he knew that those who missed a ball hosted by the Duke and Duchess of Richmond did so at their peril.

If, after all, the blasted Battle of Waterloo could break out in the middle of one of Her Grace's soirees, as it so famously had in Brussels, anything might happen.

Thus, any event the Richmonds gave was sure to be a crush.

This rule applied in spades whenever fireworks were involved, as they were every year on the fifth of November, for the duke's majestic palace sat right on the bank of the Thames and had an excellent view of the annual display.

Richmond House, moreover, built with the flowery splendor of the style a hundred years ago, lay just a stone's throw up the road from Parliament, where the misguided Guy Fawkes and company had attempted to overthrow the government back when Shakespeare had been penning his plays.

Well, they continued paying dearly for it to this day, Azrael mused as he sauntered along through the mansion, following the flow of aristocratic guests now pouring out onto crowded Whitehall to view the raucous nighttime parade passing by.

The long, noisy, torch-lit procession of revelers, some in costumes, some with faces blackened with soot to resemble gunpowder, was slowly winding its way from St. James's Park toward the riverbank, carrying their captive, the effigy of poor old Guy, to be tossed upon a raging bonfire.

It was a rough and riotous occasion, which, in itself, quite entertained the crème de la crème. Once a year, even the ladies had a perfectly patriotic excuse to be indecorous, joining in the ruthless chants of *"Burn him, burn him!"*

Azrael presumed this was as close as many of them ever got to mingling with the commoners. An exciting novelty to many of them, no doubt.

Inside Richmond House, the celebrations were lavish but rather more genteel. In the huge dining room, the traditional foods of the occasion were on offer: sausages cooked over a great bonfire carefully tended by servants in the garden; baked potatoes passed around like small, edible grenades in honor of the night; the scrumptious, sticky Parkin cakes flavored with ginger and treacle; mugs of soup to warm the belly while guests stood outside enjoying the festivities.

A German brass band played on the terrace overlooking the green that sloped down to the river, where Bonfire Night would culminate later in an eruption of fireworks.

There would be rockets and stars and spinning wheels with glittering spangles that changed color as they flew. It was sure to be an occasion of dazzling brilliance, and from the terrace of Richmond House, the guests would be able to see everything.

The night was cold, though, and people were well bundled up. Serena had tucked her hands into a small fur muff before stepping outside, Azrael noted.

He still had not managed to procure a moment alone with her so he could ask how she was doing, per Lord Toby's concern about her, and his own.

The problem was, of course, her pesky throng of admirers.

If only she weren't so damn beautiful, but she took after her mother in her irresistible appeal to the male race. She was continuously surrounded by attentive gents—and giving Azrael the coy *you don't exist* treatment, to boot.

They had made brief eye contact, however, so at least the minx knew he was there. She had sent him the barest of nods and the shadow of a smile, the sassy sparks in her eyes outshining any fireworks with ease.

He detected that she seemed distracted, though, and got the feeling she was up to some new mischief once again.

That girl. He shook his head to himself but kept a wary distance, watching for his opportunity to approach her.

He knew he had to be discreet, but his motives were pure.

There would be no keeping her alone in a bedchamber for nearly an hour tonight, alas. He merely wondered how she was, and thought himself a considerate chap for caring enough to ask.

Frankly, he cared to an alarming degree.

Idiot.

When she joined the herd of the Richmonds' guests spilling out onto the crowded avenue to watch the procession, Azrael followed.

He had taken one of the toffee-coated apples on a stick so he wouldn't have to talk much, and savored the sweet and tangy treat as much as any child of six would. But well before he reached the mansion's wide doorway, he realized he needn't have been concerned.

No one could hear himself think in such a clamor, let alone hold much of a conversation. Noise filled the air, along with the stink of burning pitch smoke from the revelers' countless torches.

All the while, the aggressive, military-style drumming of some martial band drove the marchers on, rat-a-tat-tatting as the parade inched by, and the crowd accompanied the rhythm by shouting *"hey!"* along with the beat every few measures.

Azrael just chewed, leaning idly in the doorway. Personally, he had always found it strangely ominous to watch the gleeful mob taking their hay-stuffed prisoner to his execution.

Truth was, he had always felt a little sorry for the Guy, secretly. He had absolutely no doubt that someone with a far more twisty mind had likely put the poor patsy up to his crime in the first place.

Someone like my dear old dad, he mused cynically. He took another thoughtful bite of his toffee apple and chewed it slowly, watching the parade pass, but ever keeping a vigilant eye on the fair, nay, luscious Lady Serena.

All of a sudden, a low, sly, sniveling voice startled Azrael with a question at his ear: "Beautiful, isn't she?"

CHAPTER 6

Drawn In

*I*t was a familiar voice, but one he hadn't heard in a long time. Azrael whipped around to find that his former guardian had come lurking up behind him.

"Lord Stiver," he blurted out.

In fact, it wasn't just the earl but several more of his father's cronies from the old days that he found now subtly surrounding him.

"Your Grace."

They offered him respectful nods as they stepped out onto the few stairs in front of the mansion, hemming him in; Azrael stood on the threshold of the house with his back pressed against the open doorframe.

Neither in nor out.

"Gentlemen." Quickly recovering, Azrael managed a taut smile in answer to their greetings.

But a part of him instantly felt reduced to boyhood once more, standing there holding his candy apple by the stick like the child he once had been when his guardian had ruled his life with an iron fist.

"Come back inside for a moment and talk to us!" Stiver said with what passed for a friendly smile, but, of course, it was more a command than a request. "It's too loud out here, and we see you so rarely. Come, it's been a long time."

Azrael hesitated, but knew that making a fuss would be a bad idea. Best simply to get it over with. He donned a polite smile, gritted his teeth, and followed the bastards back inside, on his guard.

With every step after Lord Stiver—the others flanking their former prisoner, then falling into step behind him, as if to block his exit—Azrael was filled with an ominous sense of dread.

Come back inside, indeed. They'd like that, wouldn't they? Back into the fold.

Damn it, this was why he chose his public excursions carefully. He did his best to avoid running into them, but just as Lord Toby had pointed out, no one who was anyone missed the Richmonds' *essential* Bonfire Ball. These devils especially must feel right at home, he thought, among the drumbeats and flames.

They stopped a short distance into the entrance hall.

There was the lecherous Viscount Jarvis, ginger-haired, mustachioed, and paunchy; the ruddy, foul-tempered Earl of Querrell; and the humorless Baron Falk, bearded, bespectacled, and balding.

They were all in their fifties now, and it dawned on Azrael that any one of them—or even Stiver himself, their ringleader—might be Serena's natural father.

There were other candidates, of course, but as a boy, he had never known who all might be part of his sire's secretive Promethean cell.

He had a vague memory of them even trying to recruit one or more of the royal dukes, the Regent's younger brothers, especially the second-born. Then, when some unfortunate accident undoubtedly befell the hapless Prinny, they'd be in control of the next king.

Stiver, a slim, blue-eyed man with salt-and-pepper hair and an oily surface charm, gave him a smile and an affectionate clap on the shoulder. "It's nice to see you out and about, my boy. It's good for you to be with people. How've you been?"

"Not too poorly. And yourselves?" Azrael endured a few moments' idle chitchat, but he felt his every word assessed, read, scrutinized for deeper meanings, suggestions of what he might be hiding.

He was Hamlet once again.

"How's Raja? I hear you have him in London now," said Stiver.

"He's enduring it," Azrael said.

"Ah. You know, we were so surprised you had that masked ball last week," Stiver said.

"And didn't invite us," the leering Jarvis added in mock reproach.

"Ah, it was a small thing, more aimed at entertaining my neighbors in Moonlight Square." Azrael waved off his gathering with an apologetic smile. "Wasn't sure if it would turn out a disaster, anyway. Next time, I'll be sure to include you. My apologies."

Stiver squeezed his arm with encouragement. "The important thing is, you're trying. I am glad." The earl searched his face with a show of concern.

Too bad Azrael already knew that self-interest animated the bastard's every move.

"You're really changing, aren't you? Coming out of your shell at last. That's excellent, my boy."

"Must be Netherford's influence," Falk remarked. "He's a very sociable chap, by all accounts."

Azrael bit his tongue and curbed the urge to punch any one of them in the face.

With his glass, Stiver gestured toward the door and chuckled unpleasantly. "But I see what captured your attention outside. Your child bride has grown up into a splendid creature, hasn't she? You must be kicking yourself."

"A bit," Azrael admitted. That much was true.

Stiver took a sip of his whiskey. "It's not too late, you know. Especially not for you—Your Grace," he added meaningfully.

As if Serena cared a whit about titles.

The earl elbowed him. "You should go and talk to her."

"Perhaps I will," Azrael murmured, just to be rid of them.

"Do you require an introduction? It can be arranged. Querrell's son knows her."

Already chilled to wonder if they'd been keeping an eye on Serena like they monitored *him*, Azrael masked a jolt of horror to think that the descendants of his father's cronies might already be among the belle's throng of admirers.

But he forced a cool smile, desperate to put himself between them and Serena. "I can manage, thanks."

"Then we won't keep you." Stiver winked at him. "Good hunting, Your Grace."

Jarvis grinned.

"Rivenwood," Falk and Querrell said with slight nods, as though savoring the chance to utter the name of the great one again.

Then they all slithered off deeper into the mansion, while Azrael turned away and took a breath. At once, he headed in the opposite direction, toward the entrance and the noisy street outside.

Bloody hell. His heart was still pounding.

In any case, he returned to the doorway and shivered once as he paused on the threshold. Standing on the top step, he picked Serena out of the crowd again.

He now felt a renewed urgency to go to her and make sure she was all right. He spied his moment to approach her when the procession paused and the drums quieted, as did the chanting.

It was all part of the entertainment as a cheeky fellow dressed as a pope went over to the mob's Catholic prisoner and urged him not to fear death, for it was God's will that he kill his Protestant king and as many peers as possible.

While the crowd laughed, jeered, and booed in response to the player's antics, Azrael walked down the few steps, onto the pavement, and wove through the crowd until he had worked his way up right behind Serena.

She had managed to procure a spot right at the edge of the street.

His aim was merely to address her discreetly, but when he'd ventured close enough to touch her, he heard the nearly shouted conversation she was having with the older matron next to her.

Her words drained the blood from his face.

"Do you remember the previous Duke of Rivenwood, my lady?" she asked much too loudly to be heard above the clamor.

Azrael nearly choked on his toffee apple.

She continued in a friendly tone, as though it were naught but idle chitchat. "I'm trying to learn which gentlemen in the ton were part of His Grace's set when they were young bucks. Papa has been teasing me lately about some of *my* friends, you see, so I thought I'd do some inquiring before he returns to Town for the opening of Parliament in a few days. I figure if I can find out who some of his chums used to be when he was a young man, I can tease him right back! I've heard they were all a bit wild."

Azrael listened in stark horror, gripping the stick of his toffee apple, which he had all but forgotten he was holding.

What in the hell does she think she's doing?

But the answer to that was plain.

Denied his help, the dauntless lady was still trying to find the answers on her own.

Dear God. This was the one possibility he hadn't given much credence to, taking it for granted that he'd made his point on the night of the masked ball. That it was too dangerous. He really hadn't thought she would attempt it.

Obviously, he had been wrong.

I'm going to strangle her. He leaned to get a look at the woman she was talking to, and breathed a sigh of relief. He doubted the plump matron had had anything to do with his father or the group.

Still, this must not continue. *She'll get herself killed.* Then *he* would have to live with knowing that this was his fault.

He was the one who had driven her to it, all because of his strict personal creed of detachment.

His stubborn, selfish will to simply stay out of it all. Good, evil— he'd never wanted any part of the fight. He just wanted to be left alone to live some semblance of a normal life.

All these years, he'd just been trying to survive.

In that instant, he knew he had been wrong to have kept his distance from Serena and her quest, with Hamlet's own over-caution.

Like it or not, it ended *now.*

Damn it, she might already have put herself in danger with her little investigation.

He reached out from behind her and grasped her firmly by the arm. Instantly, he felt her stiffen as he leaned to put his lips beside her ear.

"A word, my lady," he growled.

She glanced over her shoulder at him, and must have seen the wrath in his eyes.

"If you please. *Now.*"

"Humph," she said.

"We need to talk."

"You don't say?" she retorted.

"Follow me," Azrael ordered, and somehow, eyeing him warily, the brat obeyed.

Between the throng of revelers and ball attendees jostling about, they wove their way in single file back through the crush around the entrance of Richmond House.

A short distance into the entrance hall, Azrael glanced around, made sure his father's friends were not watching.

Taking her by the hand, he pulled her into a dimly lit side room off the entrance hall. With most of the guests drawn outside to watch the parade or on the back terrace overlooking the river, watching the few preliminary fireworks that their host had provided, they had the long gallery to themselves for the moment.

It had red walls, high ceilings, and a great many statues.

"What is this, a statuary?" he mumbled—merely thinking aloud.

"Most observant, Your Grace."

Azrael narrowed his eyes at her.

Serena gave him an arch look. "If you weren't such a recluse, you would know the previous Duke of Richmond collected all these plaster casts of great Italian statues in his travels." She folded her arms across her chest. "They're exhibited here to the public. Someone was telling me they even have students come in and receive instruction on them." She glanced around at the otherwise empty room. "Impressive, don't you think?"

"Damned eerie if you ask me," he said, glancing around again at their silent, blank-eyed audience.

Life-sized marble men and women stood frozen in all manner of attitudes around them. The severed heads of alabaster busts on pedestals all seemed to stare at them.

With the uncanny sense that all these tall white silent people posing everywhere around them were eavesdropping on their exchange, Azrael led her deeper into the sculpture gallery, farther out of view from the entrance hall. He stopped in between the tall stone horse and the bronze lion.

"You wanted to speak to me?" Serena asked. "About what?"

"As if you have to ask, you little hellion!" he whispered with a frown. "You cannot be going about asking questions like that. It simply has to stop."

"Have you been spying on me, Your Grace?" she countered in surprise, not the least bit ruffled by his demand.

"Listen to me. You have no idea the hornets' nest you'll be stirring up if you continue."

She feigned a bored yawn.

"Serena! These are dangerous men." He kept his voice low. "If they hear you've been asking questions about them... Why can you not let this matter go?"

"How can I?" She glared at him. "My sister is dead, my real father is unknown to me, my mother's a liar, my whole life up till now has been a fiction, and the one person in the world who could help me *won't*. Beg your pardon, but I will not *let it go*, Azrael, and it's not your place to ask it of me."

"But—"

"If there's danger, that's a risk I'm prepared to take. Because I can't go on like this anymore. I need to know who I am. So, please," she added with great sarcasm, "do not trouble yourself for my safety. I can take care of myself. Good evening."

She pivoted and started to walk away with her chin in the air, and Azrael heaved a sigh.

"Fine. Let me do it for you, then."

She halted, slowly turned back around, and passed a suspicious glance over his face. "What do you mean?"

He lifted his eyes to the distant painted ceiling, shook his head, then looked at her in resignation. "*I'll* do it. I'll find out who your father is for you, if there is an answer to be had. But *you*. Must. Stay out of it."

She took a step toward him, searching his face. "You're really willing to help me?"

He harrumphed but nodded, then took another sulky bite of his toffee apple.

Her face softened, and thus became even lovelier, much to his annoyance. She stepped closer. "Thank you, Azrael."

He growled.

Serena hesitated, watching him. "There's something I've been wondering." She cast a furtive glance about, then whispered, "Do you think this man *knows* I am his daughter?"

"Probably, yes," he said as he chewed.

"Then he's aware of me."

He nodded, swallowed. "*And* most assuredly aware of the fact that you and I were once betrothed. Which is to say that if he sees us together, that will raise some eyebrows." *Frankly, it already has tonight,* he thought.

"Why?"

"Has anyone ever told you that you ask too many questions?"

Despite his open exasperation, her reply was a mischievous smile.

She lifted his toffee apple out of his hand by the stick and helped herself to a languorous lick of the candy coating.

Seduced where he stood, he felt his jaw nearly hit the floor.

He looked at that mouth and could not be angry at her. He just wanted it on him.

"This is good," she said, savoring it.

It took him a beat to regather his wits. "Just promise me that once I get you a name, you will be satisfied. That will have to be enough. You won't try to make contact?"

"I can't promise that. He's my father."

"Trust me, Serena. You don't want any of these men in your life."

She puckered her alabaster brow. "Are they really so bad?"

His gaze softened with tenderness for her naiveté. "You are very sheltered, and there are darker evils in this world than you yet comprehend." Then he took his apple back from her.

She folded her arms across her chest and stood there thinking things over for a moment. "How will you begin?"

Azrael shrugged. "Well, there is much I cannot remember from those days. The memories of my childhood are...sketchy." It was like his mind didn't want to remember.

Indeed, whenever he tried to face his past, he either got a splitting headache or sank into a wave of fatigue so strong it was as though someone had drugged him.

The torpor made the effort seem too strenuous and not worth the bother.

"However," he continued, with a furtive glance around, "if there are answers to be had, they'll be at Owlswick. Our country house there. I suppose that's where I shall start."

"I'm coming with you," she said at once.

"Serena!"

"Why not? Toby said the whole barrow site and all the country houses were abandoned ever since our families started believing in the curse. There'd be no one there to see us. Please, please?" she said prettily, tilting her head.

He frowned, weighing the possibility. "I don't see how I could possibly take you with me."

"I respected her intelligence," Toby had said. By such simple means, even that quiz had won her favor, so maybe...

She moved closer, took hold of his lapels. "Come, Azrael," she said with the skill of a born coquette, "I won't be any trouble, I promise. I'll be good. I'll do whatever you say. Just let me tag along. I want to see the place where my sister died. Surely you understand. Maybe then it'll finally start to sink in."

He held her gaze, torn.

"Please, I know you are a kind man." She gazed up into his eyes.

He scowled as he saw she was awfully good at getting what she wanted.

Azrael looked away, waving his candy apple by the stick with idle indecision, knowing he should refuse.

But the truth was, he'd be grateful to have her along when it came time to face that place again.

He'd always known he'd have to go there sometime. He couldn't put it off forever, but he dreaded the memories that awaited him there.

His wayward kitty-cat would be a most welcome distraction, maddening as she was.

"You'd have to come alone without your chaperone," he warned, his tone stern. "No outsiders. That good lady can have no part in this."

She nodded eagerly. "Very well."

"But, with that caveat, I suppose, if we were both on hand to search for the materials I believe are hidden somewhere on the premises, we could cover more ground that way and get out of there all the faster."

She let out a soft cheer and startled him with a brief hug, then stepped back again before anyone saw, and nodded eagerly. "When can we go?"

"Tomorrow morning," he suggested. "Might as well get it over with."

Before I come to my bloody senses.

"Oh, right, I see." She nodded, turning serious again and hanging on his every word. "Shall I come over to your house?"

"No. Let's not risk your reputation any more than necessary. Just around the block from Moonlight Square, there's a covered passage between the livery stable and the tailor's shop. Do you know the place?"

"Yes, yes, of course."

"I'll pick you up there in my carriage at, let's say, seven tomorrow morning. It'll just be getting light then, so it'll be easier to avoid being seen. The journey there and back will take most of the day, so whatever excuse you give your chaperone will have to be sufficient to explain your absence until about, oh, five or six o'clock in the evening. Will that be possible?"

She nodded rapidly. "I'll think of something."

"Are you sure you want to do this, Serena?" he whispered, leaning closer as he read the apprehension in her eyes.

"Of course. I have only one question." She hesitated, blushing a bit. "Do you mean to make me *barter* for this information in the manner that we, um, discussed at your house?"

Azrael chortled at the question, recalling her *supposedly* reluctant offer to trade kisses for information. "Now there's a fine idea. Very tempting. But no. You have my word you will be safe with me, my dear. I only wonder if you can promise *me* the same, hmm?"

She flashed a mischievous grin. "I promise nothing."

Is she flirting with me? he thought, and warmth flooded his body.

"Anything else I need to know? Should I bring anything?" she asked.

"No. Just don't be late."

"A lady is never late," she said with a pert smile. "She arrives just when she means to." She snatched his candy apple daintily out of his hand, like his own wayward Eve, and took it with her, savoring it as she strutted off in a rustle of satin skirts.

Azrael only then remembered to breathe as he was left standing there among the silent alabaster statues, unable to wipe the idiotic smile off his face.

Oh, my Staring Girl, he thought, *you'll probably be the death of me.*

He would say one thing for Serena Parker, though. She would've made one hell of a duchess.

Azrael did not remain much longer at the ball, but went home to prepare for tomorrow's journey.

He told Grimsley of his plans, and as the butler made arrangements with the coachman and ordered the kitchens to have a hamper of food for two ready to go tomorrow morning, Azrael paid a visit to his wide-awake leopard.

Raja was a nocturnal creature, after all.

He found the cat agitated from all the Guy Fawkes noise outside across the city—the fireworks, the drums.

For all he knew, Raja could even hear the crowds' distant yelling, though for humans, that was now out of earshot.

The fearsome black beast was half hiding under the bed, his yellow eyes gleaming. He let out a grumpy growl of displeasure when Azrael stepped in to visit him.

"Oh, you poor thing." He shut the door behind him and went over to the animal. "There, there, boy. It's all right. Come, now. That's no way to behave, you big baby. Come out from under there."

"Rrrriiirrr," the leopard replied.

Azrael frowned. "Hmm. Very well, then. A bribe it is."

He sent word to the kitchens to send a nice slab of raw mutton for the beast.

Soon, having distracted the leopard from his fear with a few bites of red meat, he put Raja on his leash and brought him down to the ballroom for some exercise.

He would've liked to walk him outside as he sometimes did late at night, but that would not have been a good idea with all the noisy festivities still in progress.

As usual, spending a bit of time together seemed to help both man and beast. For Azrael, the pleasant distraction of his lovable, deadly pet kept his mind off the horrors he would have to revisit tomorrow.

He played with the big cat for a while, wrestled with him a bit, and threw his rawhide toy across the ballroom a few times for him to chase.

Raja enjoyed chasing things, and pounced on his toy with glee, but, of course, the kingly beast had far too much self-respect ever to bring it back like some lowly trained dog.

Leopards didn't fetch. They did like to climb, though.

"Hey! Get down from there, you nonesuch," Azrael ordered when the leopard unsheathed his huge white claws and started climbing one of the fluted wooden pillars in the ballroom.

He seemed to be pretending that his rawhide toy was his kill, and he was dragging it up into some jungle tree. His claws left big scar marks on the wood finish, but Azrael didn't care.

Indeed, watching the leopard's antics, Azrael always felt equal parts happy and sad.

He had inherited the menagerie of animals at one of his country houses and never really knew what to do with them. It seemed cruel to keep them all in cages, but sending them back out into the wild, half domesticated and defenseless, surely would be worse.

He merely directed his servants to give them the most humane care possible, and refused to expand his father's collection.

In the meantime, he allowed the public and students with their teachers to come in and view the animals in their cages for educational purposes, much like the Duke of Richmond with his statuary.

The sweet-tempered giraffe and the clownish orangutan always delighted the children, but Azrael's personal favorite was the elephant, Henrietta. She had such a wise, calming air about her.

Thank God, the black bear that his father had imported from America had died of natural causes a year or so ago. It had been particularly miserable, but at least with him as owner, it was no longer subjected to the torture of bear-baiting for heartless men's barbaric amusement.

Raja, though…Raja had always been special.

Ever since he'd arrived as a cub, Azrael had treated the leopard more as a pet than a wild animal.

Perhaps that was not wise, but they had a lot in common — and not just because of the leopard rampant on his family coat of arms. It was also because of the world's expectations of them.

People took one look at the leopard and expected him to try to eat them. Likewise, Azrael had the potential for savagery in his blood, but he refused to let it come forth.

Refused.

As the cat tried again to climb the ballroom pillars, the elegant beast's unexpected silliness put a smile on his face, but by God, Azrael thought with a sigh, the poor creature did not belong in this kind of world.

They had that in common, too.

Having helped his pet get some exercise, Azrael finally put Raja away again and retreated to his own chamber.

Glancing out the window, he saw the sky was dark, the fireworks ended by now. He pulled the curtains shut, then drifted over to his dressing table, unbuttoning his waistcoat. He'd already doffed his cravat while playing with the leopard.

When his waistcoat hung open on his chest, he leaned down, planted his hands on the narrow table, and stared hard into the mirror.

I must be as mad as Father was, agreeing to this.

He was beginning to wonder if it was realistic, though, thinking he could "stay out of it" forever. He shook his head and straightened up again with a sigh. Soon he finished undressing and climbed into his large, cold bed, alone as always. Unsurprisingly, considering what awaited him tomorrow, he tossed and turned for most of the night, and when he finally fell asleep, nightmares chased him through the scarlet woods.

CHAPTER 7

Traveling Companions

erena's breath clouded in the damp half-light before dawn as she waited anxiously for Azrael the next morning, as arranged.

Shrugging deeper into her gray woolen mantle, she was but a shadow blending into the gloom beneath the bricked archway of the passage where they'd agreed to meet.

London seemed like another world at this lonely hour.

If it were spring, the sun would've already painted the sky pink and the birds would've been singing, but not now. Night clung on past its welcome, just as it always did this time of year, unwilling to yield to daytime, and then only begrudgingly. Even noontide was gray at best in November.

Serena found the dark, pre-waking world all rather interesting, though.

She had already seen many things that, normally, she and the rest of the fashionables slept right through. The coalman and the milk delivery wagons clattering by. The lamplighter making his rounds to douse the streetlamps.

Some of the shopkeepers had begun arriving, too, yawning as they trudged to unlock their front doors, hurrying into the warmth to ready their establishments for the day's business. She stayed out of sight, like one of Toby's folklore trolls lurking under a bridge, and none of them noticed her.

She watched the first gray hint of sunrise reveal the slippery coat of hoarfrost covering everything, like some strange crystalline mold growing all over the cobbled streets, the buildings, the bare trees. And she smelled the chimney smoke as kitchen servants started their fires to begin making breakfast for their still-drowsing masters across Moonlight Square.

She even heard the horses in the livery stable next to the alley waking in their stalls, whickering for their grain, warm and fuzzy in their thick winter coats.

For her part, she was cold and tired, unaccustomed to rising at such a rude hour. She leaned against the brick wall of the tunnel-like passage between the buildings, still trying to wake up. At least she had managed to arrive on time.

Thankfully, she hadn't had far to walk. The unassuming brick passage in between the livery stable and the tailor's was just around the corner from Moonlight Square.

The tidy row of convenient shops there was where the residents and their servants chiefly went for quick necessities and trifles. She stifled a yawn, her gaze traveling over the quaint storefronts.

Dry goods, grocer's, butcher shop, bakery, florist's, bootmaker, tobacco shop, fine stationery, the milliner's.

They were all still closed, their display windows dark or shuttered beneath their painted signs and hanging placards. Jumpy and a trifle bored with waiting, Serena stared blearily at the shops, pondering how easy it was to take these ordinary folk and their establishments for granted. In fact, she suddenly recalled she'd bought the black velvet bonnet she was wearing at that milliner's.

God, she had agonized over her outfit for today and had stayed up too late last night figuring it out, but she was pleased with the end result. Her black velvet bonnet and gloves matched the black velvet spencer she had donned over a cream-colored carriage dress. Around the bonnet's crown, she'd tied a fetching plaid scarf that matched her gown's burgundy satin trim.

To ensure that her neck and throat stayed warm, she'd tucked a ruffled muslin fichu into the gown's collar, and as an afterthought, had brought along her burgundy cashmere shawl for added warmth. Luxuriously soft, it made her happy.

Of course, her smart traveling costume was still hidden beneath the dull gray mantle that presently kept her from freezing to death, but Azrael would see her in due time.

Hopefully, he would be the *only* one to do so today. She could scarcely imagine the scandal if the world learned she had run off with him unchaperoned for the day. Why, she'd outdo the duke of scandal himself, Netherford.

Gnawing her lip, Serena took a moment to admit to herself that this was without a doubt the maddest thing she'd ever done. She hoped she didn't regret it. It was true that she *did* want to see Owlswick, she needed answers, and was thrilled at the chance to help Azrael look for the papers he believed were hidden at his estate.

But she trembled with more than the cold, for there were also her misgivings to face. *What if he's right? What if I don't like the answer once I know it?* She could still back out—wait for him to arrive and then tell him never mind, that, on second thought, maybe this wasn't a good idea.

It was too risky, and in truth, it didn't matter anyway. She loved her loud, thickheaded, easygoing Papa well enough to consider him her father even if she wasn't his own flesh and blood.

Dunny, as everyone called him, had always been good to her. She had no complaints.

It was just that she'd never really felt like she quite belonged in her family.

Perhaps if she could find out who her *real* father was, then she'd finally learn where she truly fit in. And maybe this hurt she felt over her mother lying to her would fade.

But there was also the small fact that even if she hadn't needed the answers about her own bloodlines, she could not resist the chance to be with Azrael again.

It was time to be honest. He was as much the reason she was here right now as her urgent need for information. Somehow those few short minutes in the Richmonds' statuary hall last night with him, for example, had meant more to her than weeks of needless attention from other gentlemen.

She really couldn't explain why that was. But being with her strange, pale-haired moonlight prince made her feel fully alive. She could not deny how powerfully she was drawn to him. Like they were meant for each other.

Well, someone had apparently once thought they ought to be.

A renegade notion flitted through her head: *I wish he weren't so against the match between us.*

Maybe today would begin to change his mind.

Only time would tell, but she shuddered to think what Mother would say if she could see her there, waiting alone to run off for the day with the forbidden Duke of Rivenwood.

At least now Serena knew that it was not because of anything Azrael had done wrong that her mother had banned him from her circle of acquaintance. It was merely Mama's own dread of him ever telling her the truth.

Well, too bad, she thought, her jaw tautening with simmering rebellion. Perhaps his kiss had put her under a spell, but she could not resist the time with him. In the days between the masked ball and Bonfire Night, she had tried her best to forget about the man.

It should not have been so difficult, considering that, somehow, she'd felt even more rejected by Azrael's refusal to help her than she had at Toby's ending their years-long courtship.

Which didn't make any sense. But then, she supposed the heart never did.

How much longer? Where are you? she thought restlessly. She believed His Grace was now officially late.

Fingers stiff with the chill that bit right through her gloves, Serena managed to dig her locket watch out of her reticule and squinted at it in the steel-gray half-light swiftly replacing the pitch-darkness.

Seven o'clock.

Oh, she thought. Nervousness and perhaps eagerness to see him must've made her impatient.

At that very moment, right on time, a sleek black coach-and-four turned the corner at the end of the lane. Her pulse leaped.

She pressed away from the passage wall. The crunching clatter of the carriage wheels grinding over the cobblestones grew louder as the vehicle approached. The four black horses were impressive—high-stepping, blinkered Frisians with long, flowing manes.

Serena swallowed hard as the carriage approached. She stepped into view and gestured to the driver.

The coach slowed; it stopped for her under the shadowed overhang of the covered passage, and the door opened from within.

Azrael leaned out, offering his hand. Serena's gaze instantly locked on to his, and she placed her gloved fingers in his outstretched palm.

His strong, long fingers curled around her hand as she set her foot on the carriage step, then he pulled her up, and she sprang quickly into the coach.

At once, she dropped into the seat across from him, shivering with the cold and excitement; he immediately pulled the door shut, then rapped on the inside of the rounded carriage wall, signaling to his coachman to drive on.

No doubt working for one of the most eccentric noblemen in London kept his staff's lives interesting, she thought. She heard the reins slap over the horses' rumps, and then they were in motion, continuing on through the passage to emerge on the other side with no one the wiser — hopefully.

Getting her bearings, Serena glanced about at his coach's elegant, beige satin-upholstered interior, and then looked at him.

Azrael was quickly pulling the carriage shades down so they would not be seen riding together. The gleam of the two tiny candles inside the sconces cast a shining halo over his champagne-colored hair. It flowed back from his high forehead and gathered once more into the usual queue at his nape.

Serena couldn't help but notice that the triple-caped box coat he wore over his day clothes made his already wide shoulders look enormous. His Carrick coat was unfastened, so her glance traveled down furtively over his dashing ensemble.

He wore an unfussy snow-white cravat; a pale, muted green waistcoat about the hue of winter pastures; a light brown jacket, barely visible under his charcoal-colored greatcoat; his snug, dark brown breeches disappeared into glossy black riding boots with brown turn-downs.

A black top hat rested on the luxurious seat beside him, along with a pair of black kid gloves. He locked the carriage door and turned to her — and Serena instantly ceased her slightly lustful perusal of him, and smiled.

"Good morning," he said, looking into her eyes with unexpected and disarming warmth.

"Good morning, Your Grace," she replied, sounding slightly breathless, to her dismay.

A wry smile crept across his lips.

"Well then," he said, "here we are."

"Indeed," she whispered.

He sat back, watching her. "Speeding off from Town alone in a carriage together."

"Unchaperoned," she added with a rueful look, since there was no getting around the awkwardness on that particular point.

His smile widened almost to a grin. "Decidedly scandalous behavior, my lady."

She shrugged, blushing as she grinned back at him. "What can I say? I take after my mother."

"You surely do." He laughed, and the twinkle in his pale blue eyes helped to put her at ease.

"It's your fault," she said. "You seem to bring it out in me."

"I noticed that. But never fear. I gave you my word of honor that you would be perfectly safe in my company."

"If I had any doubt of it, I would not be here," she told him.

His small nod suggested he was gratified by her trust. Perhaps finding someone willing to give that to a Rivenwood duke was a rarity.

"I wasn't sure you *would* come, actually," he said as the carriage rolled along. "I thought perhaps I would arrive, and you'd have changed your mind."

"Or lost my nerve? Come to my senses?"

He nodded. "Perhaps."

"No such luck," she said with a smile. "And Your Grace, I appreciate you doing this. Truly."

A low snort escaped him, as if to say, *You're welcome, but you left me no choice.* He did not utter such ungentlemanly sentiments, though.

Instead, he tilted his head, studying her. "You look cold."

She rubbed her arms. "I'm getting warmer."

He held up a finger to signal her to wait, then got up from his seat, turned, and lifted the lid off the padded carriage bench he'd been sitting on. He reached into the storage compartment underneath the seat and pulled out a thick woolen lap blanket, which he gave to her.

"Thank you," she said.

He nodded, reached into the storage bench again, and pulled out a brown clay jug wrapped in a kitchen towel.

"What's that?"

"Mulled cider, still warm—courtesy of one Grimsley, my butler." He took out two tin traveling cups, then closed the bench and sat back down. As she tucked the lap blanket around herself, he uncorked the jug and poured her a bit of warm, steaming apple cider.

Its sweet cinnamon fragrance filled the carriage, and Serena stared at her companion in wonder, stunned by his solicitude.

"Oh, wait—how could I forget?" After carefully handing her the mug, Azrael dug back into the bench and brought out a tin with a boyish glint in his eyes.

Removing the lid, he revealed a sugar-dusted batch of golden Scottish shortbread. She looked at it, then at him with a sense of unreality. *This* was the man some people claimed was evil like his father?

"Take one," he urged her.

"You spoil me," she uttered, trying to hide her astonishment.

"I have a whole hamper of food for us here if you're hungry."

"Er, no. This is lovely for now," she said, taking an offered piece of the crumbly shortbread.

After all, everybody knew it went perfectly with cider.

Serena couldn't take her eyes off her host as he got himself situated with a similar snack.

And, just like that, from the cold and gloom of the morning beyond the curved walls of the coach, inside, it had suddenly grown altogether cozy.

They ate their shortbread, smiling at each other.

"So," she said at length, "where are we going, then?" She did not say so aloud, but this was the most fun she'd had since her world was upended by Toby's revelations.

It almost felt like they were eloping.

Maybe we should. She chased off the rogue thought. "Where is Owlswick, exactly?"

"Buckinghamshire." His tone turned businesslike. "The village of Owlswick lies near West Wycombe, in the Chiltern Hills. It'll take us about four hours to get there. My father's country house is situated a stone's throw west of the village. I figure we'll stop halfway there and let the horses rest. We're sure to come upon a decent coaching inn or some such."

"That sounds fine." She paused, frowning. "What if someone sees us there together?"

He shrugged. "Then we'll have to tell them a Banbury tale of some sort."

She arched a brow. "Such as?"

"You're abducting me?" he suggested, then crunched his biscuit.

She laughed. "Yes, let's use that. I'm carrying you off to Gretna Green against your will. Forcing you to honor our childhood betrothal."

"And using my own carriage to kidnap me! So rude."

"Yes, I am quite diabolical. But you had it coming," she replied.

"Mm," he said skeptically, though his eyes danced, and the color was high in his cheeks.

"We've cleared the city, sir!" his driver called back to them a few minutes later.

"Thank you, Paulson," Azrael shouted back, immediately lifting the blind nearest him.

Serena followed suit. When she looked out the window, she beheld a drab, moody landscape of farms and fields, the spiky branches of bare hedgerows, a distant village and its steeple still veiled in mist.

Nearer the country road along which they rumbled, dingy sheep in thick winter wool grazed in pastures enclosed by brooding stone fences.

It was a contemplative scene, with a pensive beauty, Serena thought.

Not unlike the man across from her. Of course, he hid his nigh-poetic sensitivity fairly well behind his veneer of worldly cynicism. But his house, his reticence, his solitary habits gave him away.

If she had not already loved unusual people, she would've developed a fondness for them after meeting him, Serena decided.

"So," he said. Having finished his snack, he rested his arm along the cushioned back of the seat. "Did you have any trouble getting away this morning?"

"No." She took off her bonnet, since they had a long way to go.

"What did you tell your chaperone?"

"That I'd be spending the day helping my friend Lady Portia Tennesley organize and plan more of her wedding details, along with the other bridesmaids. Do you know her?"

"No."

"She lives on Moonlight Square, Azrael."

"I don't know anybody," he said.

"Well, we shall have to fix that," she declared, and he frowned. "Anyway—my dear Portia is afflicted with a bad case of wedding madness. She's getting married next Season and is quite determined to have the wedding of the decade."

"Oh really?"

"Today, we—the bride and a few close friends, chaperoned by Portia's married elder sister—will supposedly be visiting possible locations for the reception, choosing card stock for the invitations, debating fonts, and possibly Wedgwood patterns for the china, if we can get to it. Then taking supper at a tea shop."

"I see."

"Naturally, Cousin Tamsin wanted no part of this lengthy

excursion."

"I can't imagine why," he drawled. "It sounds positively *riveting*."

She tried to give him a stern look, and failed. "When I asked permission last night, Tamsin declined the invitation to join us, just as I knew she would, and cried off, telling me she needed to spend today reading some novel to get ready for Lady Delphine's book club tonight."

"She's going to read a whole novel in one day?"

"Oh, she does it all the time. She's a famous bookworm. Anyway, the point is, she'll have already left for Lady Delphine's before I get home, so we'll miss each other."

"Crafty girl," he whispered with a half-smile.

"I don't mean to be." Serena sighed. "I do hate lying to Cousin Tamsin. She's such a good, sweet, unsuspecting soul. But alas, as I said, I fear I am my mother's daughter."

Azrael smiled at her. "Your deception would not have been necessary if Lady Dunhaven would've answered your questions, as she ought."

"That's what I keep telling myself." Serena looked away with a nod, thinking. Then she glanced at him again. "Speaking of Mother and all of that unpleasantness, I was wondering, when we reach Owlswick, will we have a chance to see the barrow that started all this? I should like to, if we can."

"It all depends on the time," he said with a shrug. "We should arrive about eleven. Our main objective then will be to find the group's box of records hidden somewhere on my father's estate."

She tilted her head.

He explained: "There is a small trunk of secret books and papers, journals and ledgers and so forth, that should contain information about who was involved in the, er, club—if we're calling it that."

"What would *you* call it?" she asked.

"Cult? Coven? Crime ring?"

"Oh," she said faintly, startled.

He gazed at her for a moment, taking in her uneasy expression. "At the very least, there should be some financial records among these papers that will show indisputably who was involved then. Records of things like illegal business dealings, bribes and extortion payments."

"Good God." Serena shrank down in her seat a bit and pulled her cashmere shawl closer. "Are you saying this was actually all about money?"

"No, power." Azrael fixed her with a probing gaze, his pale eyes wise and secretive as those of the mythical sphinx.

"It all sounds very nasty," she murmured.

"You have no idea." He glanced out the window at the stubbly cornfield where a murder of crows had descended, pecking for scraps. "If we get especially lucky, we might even find some letters they exchanged. That sort of communication, I should think, is more likely to contain the kind of gossip about who was bedding your mothe— Never mind." He looked at her, wincing at his bluntness. "Sorry."

"It's all right," she said with a sigh.

"Anyway, all I have to do once we get there is figure out where Lord Stiver would've hidden their treasure trove of dirty secrets after my father died. I'm sure he'd want easy access to it when necessary, but he would not have risked putting it somewhere that anyone else could possibly stumble across it, God knows."

"Who's Lord Stiver?"

"My father's top toady, or henchman, if you prefer. His right-hand man." Azrael gazed out the window. "I always thought the earl was almost...I don't know, a little in love with my father in some strange way."

She cocked a brow. "You don't say."

"He was fanatically devoted to the blackguard. Believed everything he said, like he was some sort of earthbound god. Naturally, my father trusted him—and my father didn't trust anyone, believe me. That's how Lord Stiver became my legal guardian after Father died."

"Oh," she said.

Azrael fell silent for a moment. "Stiver is their leader now, if they're still up to their old mischief. For all I know, they could be done with all that by now." He paused. "Perhaps they've outgrown it."

"One hopes."

"I sincerely doubt it, though. Because, if there was one rule, as I understand it—once you're in, you never get out."

Serena furrowed her brow. "Yet my parents did. I wonder how."

He shook his head. "I've wondered that, too. But I must warn you: I don't think you'll like the answer to that question, either, if we can ever learn it."

She nodded, chilled with a deepening sense of uneasiness. "It doesn't matter whether I like it or not. All I care about is finally knowing the truth."

"Well, I can certainly respect those sentiments," he murmured.

An awkward silence descended.

"Are you warm now? Comfortable?" he asked.

"Yes, quite, thank you."

He nodded then took off his greatcoat. Between the lap blanket and the hot cider, Serena felt toasty enough in the carriage by now to do the same. She was eager for him to see her carriage dress, after all the trouble she'd gone to choose the blasted thing.

She was gratified when his admiring glance flicked over her body. He turned his gaze out the window once more, as though to stop himself from staring at her.

"Oh, look at that rowdy lot," he said, pointing out a passel of rosy-cheeked peasant children playing in a field, taking turns leaping off the top of a turnstile.

Serena chuckled as she looked out the window. "They seem to be enjoying themselves."

The children noticed their carriage then as it swept along on this flat, lonely stretch of road. Pointing and exclaiming at the beauty of Azrael's magnificent black horses, the children started waving madly to their coach as if Queen Charlotte herself were passing by.

Laughing, Azrael and Serena waved back, but didn't stop.

"Oh, I meant to tell you," he said after they had left the children some distance behind, "I met your ex-suitor."

Serena's eyes widened. "You did?"

"Yes." He paused, gazing wryly at her. "I went to see Lord Toby at his coffee shop."

"Why?" she asked.

"So protective!" he said, his pale, wolfish eyes dancing. "Don't worry, I didn't hurt the dear lad. I just wanted to make sure he understood the need for secrecy about his discoveries."

"Did you terrify him, Azrael?"

"I don't know! Maybe. Well, it wasn't on purpose." He gave an innocent shrug. "You tend to terrify people without even trying when you're named after the archangel of death. But that is hardly my fault."

She sighed. "Very well. Out with it, then, since you must be dying to comment. What did you think of him, the bounder who cast me off like a smelly old shoe?"

"Honestly? I rather liked him. He has an endearing sort of innocent quality about him, hasn't he?"

"Oh, I know!" she exclaimed, clutching her heart with a fond wince.

Azrael stared at her for a beat. "I got my copy of his book signed. I must say, though, now that I've met the man in person, I am all the more perplexed. You really must explain."

"Explain what?"

"Of all your admirers, why on earth *him*?"

"Didn't we already discuss this?" she asked, blushing, though the twinkle in his eyes was hard to resist. "Yes, I'm sure we did. In that bedroom of yours."

"Maybe, but I'm afraid I am still not satisfied with your answer, my lady."

"Oho, Your Grace!" she said, laughing, as he held her in a placid, stubborn gaze.

"All the less so now that I've met him," he added. "Besides, we're stuck in this carriage for the next four—no, three hours now. What else is there to talk about? Politics? Great world events? Mathematics, perhaps?"

"Oh, God no."

"Well then? Confess. Of all the rich and handsome eligible bachelors who follow you around, you chose a silly-headed commoner like Lord Tobias Guilfoyle as your favorite, because…?"

Serena harrumphed. "If I didn't know better, I would think you were jealous, Your Grace."

"Maybe I am," he replied matter-of-factly, and crunched another shortbread.

She held his gaze for a second, unsure how to react. Then she saw the crumbs tumbling down his chest. "Oh, look at you," she mumbled fondly. Leaning across the space between them, she brushed some golden fragments off his warm, muscled chest.

Azrael stopped chewing at her light touch, staring at her.

Her pulse leaped and her blood heated as she saw the quickening interest in his silvery eyes.

But then she remembered her precarious situation, alone with him in a carriage in the middle of nowhere. Unchaperoned. Best not to tempt the tiger. She sat back slowly with a gulp and was suddenly glad to have another topic to distract her from the sudden flapping of the butterflies in her belly.

Toby, she reminded herself. *Ah, yes, right.* He wanted to know about her relationship with her ex-beau.

She shook her head slowly, trying to focus. "I don't know. I suppose I appreciated the fact that he was always kind to me."

"Lots of men are kind to you, I'm sure." His voice had dropped to a low purr.

She faltered. "I suppose that's true enough. As I said, it's hard to explain—" She cast about for words. "He's such a quiz, and I like—I like to feel needed."

He narrowed his eyes. "Very well. The jury will accept that. Still. I think there is more to it. Continue."

"Azrael!"

"Serena."

"What do you want me to say?"

"Merely the truth. You claim that's so important to you, after all."

"Toby loved me."

Azrael said nothing, just crunched his shortbread.

His silence spoke volumes; she realized with astonishment that he didn't believe her. She was almost indignant...

Until she realized perhaps he was right.

If Toby really had loved her, he would not have quit the match over something as absurd as money and some made-up, idiotic curse.

But on the other hand, she realized slowly, if she had really loved *him*, she would not have let her true love walk away.

"Oh hell," Serena mumbled, sitting back in her seat, suddenly morose.

"It's all right," he murmured with a smile. "I understand."

"You do?" she retorted. "Please explain it to me, then."

"You were never in love with him. He was merely safe for you."

She made a small, pouty sound of distress, retreating to lean in the corner of her seat, and scowling at him a bit. But she did not deny it.

Mother had taught her well to marry a man she could manage.

"Come, darling, you think he didn't know?" Azrael asked gently. "We men may be dunces in matters of the heart, especially me, but we're not blind. I daresay our literary friend is clever enough to have realized the deficit in your womanly affections for him. He didn't want to make you unhappy in your marriage. That's probably got more to do with his 'jilt' of you than any so-called curse."

She stared at him, taken aback.

"I hope that helps to soothe any hurt you might still be feeling about the loss." Azrael held her in a caressing gaze. "Frankly, I think he did you a favor, kicking you out of the nest."

"The nest?" His words startled and confused her. "*What*, pray tell, is that supposed to mean?"

"You were too comfortable with him. He didn't challenge you. He didn't excite you," he added, holding her stare, and her pulse leaped.

The way you do, you mean?

She could feel her cheeks heating, and dropped her gaze. "Well," she said, trying to hide her reaction. "Your Grace certainly seems to know a great deal about the mysteries of love. And yet you are not married yourself. Hmm."

"I never claimed to be an expert." He frowned, his chiseled face flushing slightly. "I merely observe humanity…and all its foibles."

"From a safe distance," she said.

He snorted, hesitated, and when she arched a brow at him, he laughed ruefully and said, "Indeed."

He was, she thought, absolutely charming when he smiled like that. It was like the winter sun peeking through the leaden gray clouds.

"*Have* you ever been in love, Azrael?" she asked after a moment.

He lowered his gaze and frowned, silent for a moment, as though dutifully searching his memory. "I'm sure I must've been once or twice, over the years." He shrugged, looking unconvinced.

"So." Serena decided to push her luck. "What about that woman, the actress, from the night of the masked ball? Miss Burns. Has she become your mistress now?"

He looked at her with astonishment. "God, you are impertinent!"

"We are long past the niceties, Your Grace, I daresay," she said, laughing. "Just tell me. Is she yours now, after being Netherford's?" She took another dainty bite of shortbread.

"No."

"And why not?"

"Well, you killed the fun of that with your failed acrobatics, didn't you?" he retorted, and she snickered at the reminder of how she'd interrupted his tryst by nearly falling to her death.

"Besides," he added after a slight hesitation, "I don't like…purchasing people."

"I see." She nodded at him, her esteem of the eccentric duke climbing even higher at that, though the admission, or at least the topic, seemed to have embarrassed him.

He gazed at her with a sardonic half-smile, looking intrigued at her boldness on this topic. "Well, you didn't hear it from me, but the word at my club is that the divine Miss Burns has now moved on to the Marquess of Rushford."

"*What?*" Serena lurched forward. "Are you jesting? Rushford has been paying court to *me!*"

Now it was Azrael's turn to laugh. "Sorry to be the bearer of bad tidings, love. But, really, how do you think *she* feels, having to lower herself to a mere marquess when she'd thought she'd snared herself another duke?"

She shook her head at him. "You are bad."

He flashed a wily grin. "Just a bit cynical, is all."

"Well, I wish them happy," she said with a huff. "But for what it's worth, *I* think you should have another party. A regular one, without masks."

"Would you come if I did? Officially, I mean? No sneaking in the window. You'd send back a proper RSVP then actually show up?"

"Of course I would." She beamed at him, knowing she deserved the ribbing on that point. "If I am invited, after my scandalous behavior at the last one."

"Oh, you will be. How could I have a party and not invite my most agreeable neighbor? As long as you promise not to climb the trellis."

Moved by his gentle confession, she put her hand on her heart. "You have my word as a gentlewoman."

"Said the unchaperoned little kidnapper," he murmured.

She chuckled again, and they lapsed into companionable silence, chatting only now and then of idle things until the end of the second hour, when they stopped to let the horses take a break.

CHAPTER 8

Owlswick

*A*zrael got out of the coach and made sure the place seemed suitable and not too crowded. He did not wish for either himself or Serena to be recognized. He had a look around while assisting Paulson in lining up a place where the horses could stand to rest their legs.

When the innkeeper's boy ran out into the yard to attend them, Azrael made sure that his animals would be watered and given a carrot or two. Then he returned to the coach and handed Serena down.

Though she did not don her mantle, she had put on her bonnet again with the fetching plaid ribbon around it. Azrael found her inexpressibly adorable with the bow tied beneath her chin.

"What is it?" she asked as he stood there smiling doltishly at her again.

"Nothing. Shall we?" He gestured toward the quaint stone inn that awaited them.

She eyed him with playful suspicion, but took his arm, and they went toward the building. It felt good to get out into the fresh air and stretch his legs.

"Another two hours, eh?" she asked.

He nodded. "Do you want a cup of tea or something to eat?"

She shook her head. When they went into the galleried coaching inn, the few people inside turned and glanced at them—the landlord and a couple servants, several other travelers. Serena smiled at them, and Azrael had no doubt they all assumed the two of them were a married couple.

It was increasingly difficult not to let his mind wander down the path of what it would have been like if this beautiful, vibrant young woman were indeed his wife. What it would've been like to share a bed with her every night...

He supposed that would have made him the envy of male London, and more enemies was the last thing he needed. So he told himself.

They parted ways briefly to avail themselves of the water closets, but as soon as the horses had had a break, they were back on the road and, once more, off came the bonnet.

All her little feminine fussings and pattings of her millinery entertained Azrael to no end. Watching her was far better, anyway, than contemplating what awaited him when they reached their destination.

Instead, he let Serena distract them both from their boredom with one of those ridiculous guessing games that people played on Twelfth Night. Normal people, anyway. The game had hardly been part of *his* family's holiday routine.

Soon they were laughing as they tried to get each other to guess the identities of the characters they'd chosen. But when Serena quickly stifled another yawn, Azrael arched a brow.

"Am I boring you?" he asked.

"No! Of course not." She smacked him lightly on the arm. "I had a dreadful night's sleep, is all."

So did I. He flicked away an image from his hideous nightmares like a fly. "You're welcome to make yourself comfortable if you wish."

She glanced around at the coach. "Hmm. Maybe I shall."

He watched her in curious amusement as she tried to fit herself this way and that on the opposite bench. She finally gave up and crossed the carriage to plop down beside him instead.

Without so much as a by-your-leave, she leaned against him, resting her head upon his shoulder.

"Ah, that's better," she declared, snuggling against him, and Azrael had to agree.

Her warm, soft body felt wonderful beside him. He could feel the aura of happiness around her, and it amazed him to think that he could have that effect on the girl. Her hair smelled like honey and flowers.

Soon he put his arm around her to give her a more comfortable resting spot, and they both propped their feet up on the bench across from them. Their guessing game trailed off, and they relaxed together in silence for a while.

Azrael rested his head atop hers, but he should've known that the devious little wheels in her mind were still spinning.

"May I ask you question?" she murmured after a while.

"Aha. As if I have a choice."

"Don't worry, it's nothing too frightening." She glanced up at him and saw his sardonic smile. "I was just wondering what it was like for you, growing up under the administration of a bunch of trustees. What was it like having this Lord Stiver fellow as your guardian?"

"Awful," he said.

She lifted her head off his shoulder and looked at him with concern. "Why? Was he cruel to you?"

Azrael was quiet for a moment. "Not compared to my father."

She winced with compassion, but he did not want that turning into pity, so he turned her questions right back on her. "What was it like for *you* growing up with the infamous temptress Lady Dunhaven for a mum? Did ol' Dunny ever mistreat you, suspecting a cuckoo in the nest?"

"No, never. He doesn't know. Besides, he has his two boys, who are the spitting image of him, but I was always his little girl." She shrugged. "Of course, I bear no physical resemblance to the man, but I've always looked so much like Mama, that that was all anybody ever noticed."

"I see. But how did your mother treat you?" he asked. "Did she like you, or were you just a painful reminder of her wicked past?"

"My mother would've spoiled me rotten if I'd let her," she declared, then paused. "At least now I understand why. Having already lost one daughter, she was happy to give me whatever I wanted. But, Azrael, why did you say it was awful having Lord Stiver as your guardian?"

"So persistent," he whispered, tapping her on the nose with a fingertip and then pushing a lock of her sable hair behind her dainty ear.

She searched his eyes earnestly. "You can tell me, can't you? I would've thought anything would've been better than your sire."

"That is true. I told you, my father was an evil man."

She nodded.

Azrael didn't like the topic, but it seemed he shared Lady Dunhaven's weakness for wanting to give this lovely creature anything she asked.

Very well, he thought. It would be interesting, anyway, to gauge her reaction. He had never attempted to tell anyone about such things before.

"Father put on a good show for outsiders, but everybody close to him lived in dread of the man."

"Why?"

"Occasional fits of rage. Late hours, strange habits. Unpredictable whims. Mind games. And a standard of absolute obedience required." He hesitated. "I had a calico cat once. He killed it when I stood up to him as a boy. He broke her neck right in front of me. Said if I ever crossed him, I'd be next. I think I was ten."

"Oh my God." Serena lifted her fingers to her mouth and stared at him, the color draining from her face.

"She'd had kittens," he said. "I had to feed them with a tiny dropper to keep them alive. But they survived."

"He was a madman."

"Well, yes," he said in a hollow tone. "I thought everybody knew that."

Serena seemed at a loss for words. "My nurse said so, but I...I thought it was just an exaggeration."

He considered this. "Perhaps you've never known anyone truly evil, then. Such people do exist." He managed a slight laugh. "And some of them have children."

She breathed another stunned utterance, then lay back slowly against him. "What else?"

He was silent for a long moment, fighting with himself. Fighting with the law of silence that had been drilled into him from an early age.

He toyed with a lock of her silken hair, unable to fathom why he'd even told her that much. Let alone why he continued. "I wasn't really allowed to have any friends," he said. "Our cook had a son my age. I used to play with him when I was small. Ah, he was a merry little chap, Bobby—loud, brazen. Quite the troublemaker. He never seemed to get caught at his mischief. Unlike me.

"I can't remember what it was that we did wrong on that particular occasion. A lot of my childhood memories are not clear. As if my mind doesn't wish me to recall them. But I believe we broke something, a vase or a lamp or some such." He paused. "Father beat the cook's boy for it to punish me. I didn't want any friends after that."

Serena was quiet for a long moment. "What ever happened to him? The boy, I mean."

"I never heard. The cook left and took her family with her after that. Hardly blame her."

"Was there ever any inquiry into his beating?"

"Are you jesting? Men like my father never face any consequences for what they do. They're quite proud of that, actually."

She made a sound of disgust.

He shook his head. "They chalked it up to *discipline*. I think my mother gave the cook some money to keep silent about the incident. Well, in all fairness, my father hardly invented the idea of a whipping boy. Having some lowborn companion stand in for the punishments earned by a highborn youth is a time-honored tradition among those of our class."

"Yes, I know. But it's a barbaric old practice by any measure—and it's usually a voluntary post, not forced upon the child."

Azrael conceded this with a grim nod.

Serena was quiet for a moment, stroking his chest as she absorbed these things that he probably shouldn't have told her. "So, Bobby went away after that," she said. "What happened next for you?"

"I certainly didn't bother finding a new friend," he said drily. "I'd learned my lesson. What was the point, when my companions would only be used as weapons against me? You cannot imagine how guilty I felt. I made my peace with being alone and just tried to stay out of my father's way."

Serena glanced at him, her face solemn, her eyes misty with tears, then she hugged him without warning.

Azrael liked her embrace a great deal, but he hated the thought that she was feeling sorry for him. So, after a judicious thirty seconds, he politely pushed her away. He was ever so good at pushing people away.

"My nurse told me Mama was afraid of your father," she said in a choked whisper. "Now at least I understand why."

"Everybody was." Azrael poured all his willpower into keeping his tone of voice calm and even. "So," he said with a smile of graveyard humor, "now you know what sort of blood flows in these veins. Rather unnerving to realize that about oneself, frankly."

"I know what you mean." She gave him a grim nod.

"I suppose you do." He gathered himself. "You see, they wanted me to take my father's place when I grew up. Be just like him, only worse. They wanted to mold me into a mighty Promethean leader—that's what they call themselves, Prometheans," he added, "but I'd have rather died."

"Please tell me Lord Stiver did not continue these monstrous cruelties to you after your father was killed."

"No, no. Not to me, anyway. Though I have always suspected he had my tutor killed. And...I understand he forced himself on a few of our maids," he added faintly, still hating the helplessness he'd felt as a young boy, unable to protect the girls under his own roof.

He thrust away a memory of hearing one of the chambermaids sobbing as she dusted the drawing room after a visit from Lord Stiver.

"I, however, was handled with kid gloves. The little prince," he added with a sneer, a razor's edge in his tone. "I was the great one's seed, after all. Stiver's fondest wish was to turn me into a worthy successor to that fiend." Azrael paused. "What a terrible disappointment I have been to them all."

Serena reached out and cupped his face tenderly in her hand.

Unsure what she was about, he captured her wrist, ready to ward her off, because merely talking about this had him feeling cornered. But her soft fingers molded gently to his cheek, and the sense of threat receded.

"I think you are the most remarkable person I have ever met for enduring all this," she whispered. "How did you survive it?"

"By deception, of course. That is the Promethean way."

She searched his eyes, waiting for him to elaborate.

He didn't want to, but he couldn't help himself. "I set out to convince all my father's henchmen that I was broken by what I'd witnessed in those woods—my father's death, I mean. It actually wasn't too difficult to feign." His lips twisted in a bitter half-smile. "I know that doesn't sound terribly heroic or even very honorable, but I was outnumbered and...I was just a boy."

"Oh Azrael, I'm so sorry." She leaned forward and kissed him, much to his surprise.

As Serena pressed her warm, satiny lips to his, his love-starved soul absorbed her tenderness with throbbing need. He was overwhelmed, sensing her desire to kiss away all his hurt and isolation. To be the bridge he needed back to life.

If only he could let her.

But the consequences that could follow were simply too dire, the risk too great. Stiver could use her to pull him back in. And pull Serena in, too, for that matter, after her mother had gone to God-only-knew what lengths to free her from their dark heritage.

Beyond the reach of their wickedness, Serena had had the luxury of growing up innocent. To drag her back into it now would be the lowest form of selfishness on his part. All because he wanted her? No. He wasn't that craven. He couldn't do that to her.

It was true that he hungered for her more than he'd ever yearned for any woman, with a near-agonizing intensity. He savored her innocent kisses, but even as he held her, he knew this could not be.

He had agreed to help her today, but after that, he had to stay away from her. He had no choice.

If he gave in to his craving and made her his bride, the bastards would simply have to threaten her to get control of him again.

And this time, they might finally succeed at making him the monster they'd always wanted him to be. To be sure, with such blood in his veins, he dared not assume that he'd be strong enough to fight the seduction of evil in all its dark power.

No, he swore to himself. If evil men had arranged this match for evil purposes, then surely their love would prove as tainted and corrupt as the sullied ground of the Owlswick estates.

Where, it seemed, they would shortly be arriving, for his driver called back just then that the village had come into sight ahead.

Azrael ended the kiss with regret.

He pulled back a few inches and gazed at his beautiful almost-bride, grateful for the interruption. He licked his lips, willed down his stirring arousal, and set her at arm's length from him once more, though he offered her a taut, reassuring smile.

"Thank you, Paulson," he answered.

It was time to focus on the task before them.

As he took a deep breath, he wondered if she still wanted to know who her own Promethean father was after hearing about his.

She released his hand, still staring at him, her lovely eyes wide and somber.

Feeling acutely self-conscious at her tender scrutiny, Azrael directed her attention out the window. "Here's the village, my lady. Don't blink or you'll miss it."

"Oh...yes." Serena dutifully turned and trained her stricken gaze out the carriage window, but she was dazed by his revelations. She did not know what she had expected Azrael to say when she had asked about his childhood, but it certainly wasn't any of *that*.

She had not expected to hear about violence or mind games.

And given her own cosseted childhood, it had never occurred to her that the person who might've suffered most under the late duke's tyranny should've been his own son.

Staring unseeingly at the hodgepodge of gray stone buildings ahead, her heart broken for the boy he had once been, she still wasn't sure which shocked her more—the horrible acts of cruelty he'd endured as an innocent child, or his casual demeanor about it all now.

How could he, the person that all this had happened to, evince such calm while *she* was on the verge of tears after simply hearing about it?

It was clear, though, that her sorrowful reaction was making him even more uncomfortable.

So she eased off and strove to give him the breathing room that he desperately seemed to crave at the moment.

Owlswick lay ahead.

She did her best to focus on the supposedly cursed village instead of her traveling companion for a bit, and studied the tiny town as they entered it over the humped stone bridge across a wide, babbling brook.

The village looked ordinary enough at first glance: thatched cottages, a few sleepy shops, a plain stone church with a square bell tower, a plaster-beam guildhall of Tudor vintage, the requisite pub.

Farmers' wagons loitered here and there. Townsfolk drifted about, bundled up in their provincial garb. They eyed Azrael's carriage with vague, wary hostility as the fine horses trotted by.

Serena still didn't believe in curses, but she could see why Toby had said the village had made him uneasy.

An indefinable pall hung in the air over the whole place. She could not quite put her finger on it.

But, that quickly, they were through the small village, past a sleepy stagecoach inn on the far end, and out the other side.

She'd furrowed her brow, full of questions, when she spotted the famous barrow in the distance. "Oh, look!" she said, pointing out the carriage window. "There's the barrow Toby described."

The smooth, green, oval mound rose up unnaturally from the mostly flat fields all around it, about as tall as a house. It looked about half a mile west of the village.

"Is that the way we're going?" Serena asked.

"My father's estate does lie in that direction, yes."

Azrael's demeanor was changing, she noticed, as they turned off the main road onto a smaller country lane that twisted off to the left.

He grew quiet—even quieter than normal. The harsh glitter of buried rage she had seen in his eyes when he'd spoken of his father had steadily given way to a deadened, distant expression, hard and cold, as though he were braced for combat.

Perhaps he was, though his battle was an interior one, she gathered, against the demons of his past.

Again, taking care not to crowd him, she fixed her attention on the view outside the carriage window. But privately, she vowed to do whatever she could to help him speed through this task as quickly as possible.

She was already feeling guilty for making him come here and face these awful memories for her sake. The least she could do was keep her own emotions in check, not grow weepy over what he'd suffered—and with that, Serena stiffened her spine.

Out the window, a mossy stone fence flanked one side of the country road, which they followed for another quarter-hour. The road wended its way through the chalk hills until it left the open fields and entered a dense brown wood, where, at last, they reached the gated entrance to the Rivenwood estate, and there the carriage halted.

"We're at the gates, sir," the coachman called.

"Very good," Azrael answered in a loud voice. He glanced at Serena. "Pardon," he said, then he jumped out.

She ducked her head, watching curiously as he walked over to the tall, forbidding wrought-iron gates, taking some keys out of his greatcoat pocket.

His driver offered to see to the task for him, but Azrael waved him off and unlocked them himself. The rusty gates creaked as he pushed them open.

They screeched like damned souls writhing in the flames of hell, she thought, which was exactly where the last Duke of Rivenwood belonged.

As she watched Azrael and thought of him as a towheaded boy feeding orphaned kittens from a dropper, anger at the injustices done to him began replacing her grief on his behalf.

When he'd swung the gates open wide, he walked back to the carriage, saying, "One moment, Paulson," to his driver. He peered through the carriage window at her, resting his long-fingered hands on the door. "I think I'll walk the rest of the way up to the house. It's not very far, and I could use a stretch."

"May I join you? That is—unless you'd rather be alone."

A brief flicker of gratitude brightened the shadows in his eyes.

He opened the carriage door for her and lifted a hand to assist her down without a word.

It meant a great deal to her that he was willing to accept her company at a time like this. She hoped her presence by his side helped him in some small way.

She stepped down from the coach and stretched her back as much as her corset would allow while Azrael shut the door. He told Paulson to drive on, that they'd meet him at the house.

They waited until the carriage had rolled by, then Azrael took hold of one of the gates and hauled it shut. Serena got the other, taking her cue from him.

He seemed surprised she made the effort, but she was determined to be as useful as possible after putting him through this.

Azrael closed but did not lock the gates, just enough to mask the fact that the long-absent master of the estate was paying a discreet visit to his abandoned property.

"I take it you haven't been here in a long time."

"Years," he said.

She nodded, still unsure about his state of mind. He seemed to be retreating ever deeper into his own world. She checked her locket watch and saw that it was just about eleven in the morning now. At least they were on schedule.

They proceeded to walk up the drive as it snaked through the overgrown woods. The wan gray daylight filtered through the sparse branches overhead, and a chill wind rattled the brown weeds and brambles on both sides of the drive.

Serena saw a fallen log swathed in bright green moss; a huge bird nest rested high above in one leafless tree. The trunks of others were slowly being choked by thick, winding vines.

Very well, maybe Toby and the superstitious peasants were onto something, she thought with a nervous gulp. She had to admit the place *felt* cursed, or at least haunted.

She reached instinctively for Azrael's hand, but suddenly jumped, startled at the raucous cry of a bird. She couldn't see it amid the branches, but at least its noisy presence revealed that the estate was not quite as abandoned as it looked.

The animals had taken over.

Indeed, Azrael pointed out a buck moving through the woods

without a sound. The creature stopped and stared at them, fearless, its spread of antlers magnificent. It was followed by three equally silent does.

But despite her fleeting wonder at the woodland animals' beauty, she was reminded anew of that story about his father's death—the one he never talked about—and a terrible suspicion began taking shape in her mind.

According to rumor, Azrael's father had been murdered by a vagrant he'd caught poaching in the woods of his country estate while he and his young son were out taking a walk.

But surely *this* wasn't the estate where that had happened, she thought, suddenly aghast. *Oh, God, please, no.*

It couldn't be! Even aristocrats further down the peerage owned multiple country houses, and dukes owned more than most. But if it was, then that might explain why he had been so reluctant to help her in the first place.

She glanced over at him, wondering what all she was putting the man through. It was bad enough that she'd asked him to revisit the dark memories of his childhood. But was she also forcing him to face the very spot where he'd seen his father killed?

Or maybe even had a hand in it.

Her heart beat faster. As he pulled her gently by the hand, she walked on with a sense of creeping doom toward the white manor house ahead.

A mansion like a Greek temple was becoming visible through the trees. It had broad front steps leading up to a row of white columns, the center block crowned by a dome.

Azrael stopped some distance from the house, his gaze traveling from left to right over the symmetrical wings that flanked the main block. "As you can see, we'll have a lot of ground to cover in searching this place," he said in a taut voice. "It has over sixty rooms."

Serena barely knew what to say, desperately hoping she was wrong about this location.

"But don't worry," he said. "I can think of a few likely spots where the trunk might be hidden. Come—and welcome to my home," he added, a touch of bitterness in his voice.

"Azrael," she said softly as he released her hand and took a few steps ahead of her, his shoulders squared, his strides long and measured, his spine straight with determination.

She had to know. She glanced toward the woods. "Is this the place...?"

He stopped but did not turn around, his posture rigid, his back to her, his stare fixed straight ahead.

"What do you mean?" he asked tensely, as though holding his breath.

She swallowed hard. "Where your father was murdered?"

"Yes," he whispered without turning around. Then his voice grew strong and cool again. "Let's get this over with, shall we?"

Once more he strode forward, but Serena stood in place. She closed her eyes for a second, shocked at the enormity of the gift he was giving her by coming here—and he hadn't even mentioned it.

Repenting of her stubbornness, she flicked her eyes open again, knowing it was too late to turn back now. They'd come this far.

With a pang of regret, she hurried after him into the silent, brooding mansion. The sooner they could find the box and leave this place, the better.

Somehow, she vowed, she would make it up to him for this.

CHAPTER 9

All the Dark Corners

*P*ast the thick, forlorn front columns around the entrance and through the once-grand front doors they walked. Inside, Serena found the furnishings of the late Duke of Rivenwood's estate draped in brown Holland cloth. The tall corners of the opulent saloons were swathed with cobwebs.

The dust was thick, the silence was profound, and she was tempted to run back outside and wait with Paulson and the horses. If the village of Owlswick was eerie, the atmosphere inside the mansion sent a cold serpent of unease slithering down her spine and covered her body in gooseflesh. But when she glanced at Azrael and saw his jaw clenched, she could not let him face this alone, so she followed.

Their footsteps echoed in the hollow space of the entrance hall between the checkerboard marble floor and the lofty painted ceiling far above them.

"Stiver wouldn't have hidden the box on the ground floor. Too public," Azrael murmured, glancing toward the twisting staircase that led up from the entrance hall. "Probably not on the first floor, either, where any outsiders might visit. Follow me."

He jogged up the steps, and Serena lifted the hem of her skirts and hastened after him. Despite its current state of disrepair, the house was lavish. Azrael had truly left a fortune sitting here, but from what she understood, he was so rich he probably wouldn't have missed it.

She caught a brief glimpse of a drawing room on the first floor and a music room across from it, but he continued up to the second floor, the truly private section of the country house, above the public staterooms.

It was dark and shadowy in the upstairs corridor, and the dust made her nose itch.

She kept thinking of how much Toby would've thrilled to the chance to walk through these most likely haunted halls if he were here. She couldn't believe *she* was here, actually.

Just being in this place was enough to make her start believing in ghosts, as much as she had laughed at her ex-beau for his credulous belief in so many foolish superstitions.

Azrael was silent and impassive, striding ahead of her. It was clear he wanted to find what they had come for and get out of here as quickly as possible.

Though she continued to study him discreetly, she could not determine if the ice that had come over his expression was rooted in rage or fear. She followed him down another hallway past doors that she supposed led to various bedchambers.

Since he was clearly unhappy about being here, she felt compelled to say something to acknowledge his unselfishness. "Thank you for doing this for me, Azrael," she offered, but winced at how inadequate it sounded.

He looked askance at her, as though a bit disgusted with himself for agreeing to it.

"Here," he said. As they reached a pair of double doors, he laid hold of both knobs at once, thrust them open, and gusted through. "This was my father's private apartment. The most likely place to start. You check the sitting room, through there." He pointed to an adjoining door. "I'll check the bedchamber."

Serena nodded, glancing around at the room.

It did not look like the private quarters of an elite occultist, but any ordinary upper-class bedchamber. Plush brocaded chairs. Wide windows, though the shutters had been closed. Somehow, though, it felt very wrong being in here.

She got to work, nevertheless, marching into the sitting room. Her first thought was to open the blinds to let enough light in so she could see.

This done, she sneezed from the dust, then started her search for the late duke's small leather case, cask, or trunk, as Azrael had described it, of incriminating papers.

She carefully examined everything in the sitting room, hunting for any possible place that a small leather trunk could be hidden. She opened cabinets, peering inside, scanned bookshelves, knelt to peek beneath the furniture.

Nothing.

"Any luck?" she called to Azrael after a while.

"Not yet."

She decided to check the liquor cabinet again, and reached into it, feeling around. But she let out a shriek and shot backward when a spider dropped clumsily onto her hand. It seemed as alarmed by her as she was by it; she instantly flicked it off and it skittered away.

"What's wrong?" Azrael barked, skidding into the doorway from the other room, rushing to her aid.

"Oh, um, nothing. Spider," she said with a weak laugh, her heart still pounding. "Sorry. It startled me, is all."

He looked relieved, if a bit irked.

"I think I'm done in here, anyway." She closed the cabinet and hurried toward him, gesturing at the windows. "Would it be all right if we leave the blinds open in here after we leave? A little light couldn't hurt."

"Close them," he said in a deadened monotone. "This place is a tomb."

He walked out.

"I really am sorry for putting you through this," she said, rejoining him after dutifully closing and locking the shutters. "I-I didn't know."

"I realize that." Avoiding her gaze as before, he shook his head. "It's of no consequence. Come with me. I think I have an idea."

His own passing use of the word *tomb* had inspired Azrael. Given the cult's preoccupation with death, his father's mausoleum out on the grounds seemed a far more likely place for Stiver to have hidden the cult's secret records.

No one in his right mind would ever look for them there—which seemed the whole point.

It was worth a try, anyway.

Unfortunately, everything in Azrael recoiled from the thought of going into his father's tomb. Not the least because, to get there, he would have to cross through the very woods where...

"What is it?" Serena asked, interrupting his thoughts.

He looked absently at her, found her observing him, and let his hesitation get the better of him. "Let's keep checking more of these rooms. We might as well be thorough."

And so they did.

For the next hour and a half, they scoured the manor house from top to bottom, to no avail.

By the time they had gone through the kitchens, the last room at the back of the house, Serena turned wearily to him, pushing a stray lock of her now messy hair behind her ear.

"I fear we've wasted our time here, Your Grace. I've put you through this for nothing," she said in dismay. She was looking charmingly disheveled after all their efforts, her chignon coming loose, her spencer unbuttoned, her cream-colored skirts wrinkled and dusty.

Likewise, Azrael had taken off his jacket and was down to his waistcoat.

"Any more ideas?" Serena asked with a sigh.

He was silent for a moment. "Only one." It could not be delayed anymore.

"Where?" she asked.

"Follow me." A chill stole into his veins as he turned around and headed back outside.

"Any luck, sir?" Paulson asked cheerfully when they walked back out of the house. The husky, rosy-cheeked coachman was reclining on the driver's box reading a newspaper.

Of course, Paulson had no idea what sort of supposed family heirloom they'd come here to find.

"Not yet," Azrael answered. He could breathe easier in the crisp, cool air free of all that dust—but not for long.

His pulse took up an ominous drumbeat as he crossed the graveled carriage turnaround at the head of the drive, now overgrown with weeds.

Serena followed while Azrael scanned the tree line of the nearby woods until his gaze had picked out the opening of that dire, familiar path to his father's tomb.

Without a word, he reached back and gripped Serena's hand on a pretense of hurrying her along, helping her keep up. But it was just the opposite.

Her touch, the soft, solid warmth of her hand against his freezing-cold flesh steadied him, though he'd never admit it; just having her beside him helped ward off the shivering chill that had gripped his whole body.

"Come," he ordered, pulling her with him into the woods.

He was only doing this for her, after all.

He stared straight ahead as he marched through the overgrown forest, all but dragging Serena with him by her hand. She did not complain, sturdy as she was. Azrael might not have noticed anyway if she had, for hatred and dread and, above all, choking guilt were welling up in his throat.

His chest felt so constricted it was as though iron bands had wrapped around him, squeezing. His pulse pounded, temples throbbing. Perhaps she noticed that his hand gripping hers so tightly was clammy with sweat.

Overwhelming guilt pulsed through him. Guilt for the triumph he had felt to watch his father die.

"Azrael, could you please slow down? Quit dragging me along!" Serena finally exclaimed. "I nearly tripped over my hem back there."

"Sorry," he said. He released her hand from his sweaty clasp and slowed his pace a bit.

He did not want her to notice, after all, that he was trembling, his composure standing on a very knife edge.

Because deep down, in this place, he could well believe he was every bit as evil as his father ever was.

Maybe worse.

For what sort of monster felt joy—even as a child—to watch a parent bleed to death?

Lady Serena apparently noticed his slightly unhinged mental state. "I shouldn't have asked this of you," she said, her breath clouding on the cold air. "Wh-where are we going?"

"Mausoleum. It's just ahead."

She followed the direction of his finger as he pointed, and then she looked at him with surprise. "He built his tomb in the shape of a pyramid?"

"Father liked pyramids," he said through gritted teeth.

"Oh. Is that why he had one in his portrait?"

"Something like that. Come on," he muttered.

"What's so great about pyramids?"

He gave her a look of annoyance for asking questions, but he supposed she probably thought it helped him to talk about it. He shook his head and focused on answering. It was easier, after all, than reliving those bloodied moments over and over again as they walked.

"He went to Egypt on Grand Tour as a young man. Made the pilgrimage. He was obsessed ever after. Swore the shape holds great power. Something to do with immortality, I hardly know. But I can assure you that, like the pharaohs and the Caesars, my father thought he was some sort of self-created god. Turned out he wasn't," he added drily as they arrived at the mausoleum.

There, Azrael took out the key ring again and found the smallest key. It opened the iron grate that barred the black granite door to the third duke's mausoleum.

As he lifted the key to unlock the grate, Serena laid her hand on his forearm. "You don't have to do this," she said.

He turned to her, incredulous. "Now you say that?"

"You're angry. Please—"

"You know nothing about it. Let's just get this over with."

"But I don't want you to hate me. It's not worth it to me."

He looked into her hazel eyes, warm and brownish-green, like the forest around them would've been in any other season.

He managed to soften his demeanor, and touched her gently on the cheek. "I could never hate you, Serena."

"You're scaring me," she whispered.

"I'm sorry." He gathered himself and willed calm. "I've brought you this far, let's check this one last place, and if it's not here, then we'll leave."

She pursed her lips and nodded, but said no more as he unlocked the rusty grate, pushed and heaved with all his might to open the granite slab of a door, then went ahead of her into the charnel house.

Inside the tomb of the would-be pharaoh, the sepulcher sat in the center. On top of it lay a black bronze sculpture of the slain duke, with a perfect likeness of his face cast from his death mask.

The sight of that arrogant nose, the memory of those cold, cruel eyes, the nearness of his bones twisted Azrael's stomach. He tried not to look at the face.

Ignoring the portrait of his father on the library wall in his Moonlight Square house had become habitual. It was easy enough, and, after all, having one's esteemed ancestors on display somewhere in one's dwelling was expected.

Indeed, if he had not memorialized his sire somewhere in his home, it would have looked suspicious to Stiver and company. They thought he'd loved his father as much as they did, and that witnessing the great one's murder was what had skewed his poor, young mind.

If they only knew what really happened in those woods.

He swallowed hard.

Serena came tiptoeing into the tomb behind him. More for the sake of male bravado in front of her than anything else, he propped his fists on his waist.

"Well, you mad old bastard, where are they?" he said, glancing around the inside of the small, dark pyramid. The only light streamed in from the open door.

By its weak illumination, he noticed Serena's frown from the corner of his eye. Yes, that was good, he realized. *Focus on her*, he encouraged himself. That was the only way he was going to get through this.

Then he began to hunt around the tomb.

There wasn't much to see inside the little pyramid. A few shelves for urns full of ashes and coffin niches built into the sides, awaiting future dead Rivenwoods.

But not even Mother had wanted to be buried there.

"What happened," Serena spoke up hesitantly, "when he died?"

Azrael gathered that she was asking about his sire's demise, but he was not discussing that day, ever.

So he deliberately misconstrued the question. "As I told you, I was put in the care of guardians. Trustees. Friends of my father just as bad as him. Maybe worse." He glanced over his shoulder at her. "Maybe one of them your own father."

She sighed and let the mystery go, thank God. Perhaps she sensed it was futile to push him on this point.

"Perhaps we'll never know who my father really was." She paused, glancing around, rubbing her slender arms as though she'd taken a chill. "I am sorry for putting you through this, in any case."

"Would you stop apologizing?" he growled.

"I had no idea I was asking you to come back to the place where your father was killed. I know you never speak of it. How painful that must've been. It must've scarred you for life—"

"Nonsense," he interrupted coolly. "'Twas the day of my liberation. I told you that before, as well. Now, if you don't mind, we are here for a purpose."

Azrael avoided her gaze, perusing the mausoleum.

"Ah," he suddenly said, his gaze homing in on a bit of the carving around the base of his father's sleeping statue atop the sarcophagus. "Why, you canny old bastard," he murmured as he spotted an almost imperceptible seam between the black marble effigy and the smooth, polished teak of the surrounds.

"What is it?" She stepped beside him as he bent down for a closer look.

"Unbelievable," he muttered to himself. A lid within a lid. A lie within a lie. Everything with his father had always been inside out and topsy-turvy.

That was the Promethean way. Black was white, up was down. As above, so below. Life in death.

Azrael took hold of the edge of the black sculpture and began struggling to pry it upward.

Serena gasped. "You're going to open his coffin?"

Before he could answer, the whole sculpture of the duke lifted with a creak, revealing a hidden compartment beneath it, just as he'd suspected.

Secreted away in between the sculpture and the coffin's real lid, there sat the snakeskin box he remembered seeing as a boy in his father's possession, then Stiver's.

"Get it out of there, would you?" he said, straining.

Shaking off her amazement, Serena quickly assisted as he held up the heavy lid, his shoulders and biceps burning as he braced it up with both arms.

She lurched into motion, reaching in and snatching the small leather trunk out of the shallow compartment by the twin handles on its sides.

She set it on the cold flagstone floor at once. Azrael felt a twinge in his back as he lowered the heavy bronze effigy of his father.

Figures his old man would take one last jab at him even in death. A metallic thud rang out as the statue banged back down onto its resting place.

"Go on, open it," he said, dusting off his hands, then stretching his back a bit.

She winced, like she didn't want to touch it a second time. "What is that made of, alligator leather?"

"Snakeskin. Python, I believe. On second thought, best allow me."

"Gladly. I didn't even know they make things out of pythons. How charming." She stepped back from the box with a shudder. "And they say *you're* eccentric."

He looked askance at her, though he was grateful for the comment lightening the mood ever so slightly.

Probably best not to mention he'd once heard about a Promethean grimoire of medieval vintage that had been bound with leather made from the skin of a Benedictine monk. Sickening to be tied in any way to such a heritage.

Azrael crouched down and opened the trunk, taking a moment to confirm that the papers and books he'd seen in Stiver's possession in the past were indeed inside.

He nodded at Serena, pleased. At least the trip had not been in vain. "If we are going to find the identity of your real father, what's in here will be our best hope."

"I can't believe we actually found it." She gave him a wide-eyed look so full of gratitude and admiration that it went a long way toward soothing the pain that being here had reawakened in his soul.

"Let's go." He shut the box and handed it to her. "Hold this while I pull the marble door shut."

She took the sinister box with a grimace, then they both stepped back out of the pyramid. Azrael swept the inside of the tomb with a grim parting glance to make sure they hadn't left any evidence of their intrusion behind.

Satisfied, he pulled the heavy stone slab shut with a resounding boom, then traded Serena the key ring in exchange for the leather box.

"You lock the outer grate," he said. "I'll take this to the carriage. Use the smallest key. Oh, but before you do…" He shifted the box under one arm, reached into his pocket, and handed her his handkerchief. "Wipe the edge of the marble door where I touched it. Shiny as that surface is, I don't want to leave any handprints in case anyone else comes here."

Her eyebrows lifted. "Who else would come here? Your mother?"

"No, she's passed away," he said absently. "I meant Stiver."

"Very well." She nodded. "I will."

"Thanks," he muttered. "Then I'll see you at the carriage, and let's get the hell out of here."

Serena watched him walk away, startled and uneasy to see he was truly leaving her alone beside this horrid tomb. But she supposed he was even more desperate to get away from here than she was.

Well, she thought, laying hold of her courage anew and regrouping with a shrug, *whatever I can do to help.*

With that, she lifted the handkerchief and erased Azrael's handprint from the cold black marble of the mausoleum door. She couldn't help shaking her head, though, still half in shock.

No wonder the poor man never talked about his life and stayed away from people. Who would want to make small talk in Society about a past like his?

Like ours, *you mean,* she corrected herself. For whatever he was connected to, apparently, she was, too—by blood. But at least they were also connected to each other by these secrets and by their childhood betrothal, she thought. That made it somewhat better.

Stepping back out through the small space between the marble door and the wrought-iron grate, Serena pulled the latter shut behind her with a rusty clang.

She searched out the smallest key on the ring, as instructed. Her hand shook slightly as she inserted it into the lock and turned. This done, she gripped two bars of the grate and shook it to ensure it was secure before stepping away, glad to put it behind her.

To be sure, it was her first time tomb-raiding, and her knees still trembled from the unnerving experience. *What a relief to be out of there.*

Obviously, Azrael felt the same. She frowned as she glanced down the path by which he'd gone.

He had already disappeared, obviously eager to start the journey back. For her part, however, Serena still had many unanswered questions.

She was thrilled that they'd found the material they'd come for, but she wasn't ready to go back to London quite yet.

She decided that Azrael probably wanted a few minutes alone after that ordeal. Herself, she was feeling better merely to be free of the claustrophobic space inside the bizarre pyramid.

Indeed, she now felt ready to explore a little further. And though she knew Azrael was anxious to leave, she wanted a closer look at that barrow, just for a few minutes.

She could see it through the trees. The path they had followed to reach the mausoleum continued on through the woods toward the open fields, where the barrow waited.

With a final glance toward the house where Azrael and his carriage waited, she turned away and followed the trail cautiously until she stepped out of the woods and beheld the great green burial mound rising from the flat field.

Her heart beat faster as Toby's account of this ancient site came back to her.

Leaving Azrael to recover from the day's misadventure, she walked out into the field alone, welcoming the tepid warmth of the bleak autumn sun.

Lifting the hem of her carriage gown a bit, she traipsed through the tall, dead grass, and when she reached the base of the mound, she slowly walked around it, searching for an entrance, just like Toby had done.

And just like Toby, Serena did not find one.

As far as she could tell, the barrow appeared to have lain undisturbed for however many centuries it'd been here. Heavens, even a small sapling had grown into a full tree halfway up one side of it.

Shading her eyes with her hand, she tilted her head back and studied the barrow, standing at the foot of it. It looked like nothing more than a small, misplaced mountain. She wondered why the ancient barbarian tribe had chosen this precise spot to build upon, and how many of their ancient dead were buried inside.

What manner of people had they been? she wondered. Vikings? Anglo-Saxons? Celts?

She shook her head, mystified. She was no archaeologist. But the sheer mystery of the mound compelled her to at least try to learn something useful about it.

With that, she decided to climb up on top of it. Lifting her hem out of the way, she began at once, glad that she had worn her ankle-bracing half-boots.

The hill was steep but not impossible to scale. She simply had to lean forward as she hiked up the side, and watch her footing as she went.

Perhaps it was irreverent to be climbing atop a burial place, she mused, but then again, she had just invaded a nobleman's tomb. This seemed a minor violation by comparison.

Several minutes later, she reached the summit of the barrow. The wind was brisker at this elevation. Above her, a flinty gray-blue sky smeared with white clouds spanned the horizon, and as she stood on top of the little mountain, she could see for miles.

She turned slowly, taking in the landscape, the patchwork countryside. As she did so, she counted four additional grand manor houses in the distance, evenly spaced out around the barrow.

How strange.

They all looked as abandoned as this place. The nearest one, a brownstone thing, sat dejected. It had a large stagnant pond out in front of it.

"My lady!"

Serena looked down to see Azrael walking out across the flat field below. "What are you doing up there?" he shouted over the wind. "It's time to go."

Serena didn't answer. He had been acting so strangely here—even strange for him—that she had been glad to have a few minutes away from her traveling companion.

She had been doing her best to remain calm and steady for them both while he struggled against his inner demons, but it wasn't easy, considering she had never encountered such dark things before.

At least being out of the Rivenwood mansion, and certainly, out of the tomb, was a vast improvement.

"Climb up with me!" She beckoned to him as the wind rippled through her skirts.

He only came as close at the base of the barrow, where he stood, hands on hips, squinting up at her against the gray glare of the day. "We need to get going if we're going to make it back to Town by the early evening."

She glanced at her locket watch, which she had taken from her reticule and put around her neck. "It's only half past noon."

Azrael didn't argue.

"Toby said the local folk told him that our parents held certain meetings in the barrow." She shook her head as she went to stand at the edge of the hill. "But I couldn't find an entrance."

His shoulders lifted in a bored shrug. It was very clear the man wanted to go home.

"You should come up. There's a really good view from up here," she said, but His Grace was having none of it.

He shook his head and stayed planted exactly where he was.

She pointed around the horizon. "I can see houses, the village, the river. Farms, lots of farms. London is that way, I should think," she said, gesturing toward the east, but her comments were not enough to lure him up.

"If my brothers were here, they'd want to roll down the side of this like children." She paused, remembering. "Half-brothers, I mean."

"Can we go now, please?"

"Azrael?" Steeling herself, for she feared she already knew the answer to her question, she pointed at the nearest estate. "Whose house is that over there? With the pond out front?"

He glanced in the direction she pointed to, though she was sure he could not have seen the place from down there. He looked up at her again, as though loath to answer the question. But God bless the man, once again, he told her the truth: "That was your parents' estate."

I knew it, she thought, flinching.

That was all she needed to hear to persuade her to start carefully making her way back down the barrow.

The going down was considerably more precarious than the climb up, she soon learned. Thankfully, Azrael caught her in his arms as she came clambering down the steep grade, and slammed into his chest.

"Steady." He stopped her near-tumble and righted her. "You all right?"

"Yes." She let out a breathless laugh of relief at her near-miss, grateful she hadn't fallen down and broken her crown like Jack and Jill. "Thank you."

"That's what I'm here for, dear," he said drily as he secured her in his arms.

She beamed up at him, thrilled by his embrace. "That's the second time now you've rescued me."

"Third by my count. I just got you your papers, didn't I? How soon we forget."

"Azrael?" She scanned his face and noted that he looked a bit better than when they'd first left his father's tomb. "Take me over there, please? I want to see my parents' place."

He studied her with a guarded expression between reluctance and weary resignation. It was clear, however, that her request did not surprise him.

Serena stared at him, unwilling to budge.

Perhaps he was learning how to read her, or at least was now able to recognize when she had set her mind on a thing. He sighed and shook his head while the breeze played with his long hair, then captured her gaze soberly. "Do you really want to do this? I'm sure it won't be pleasant."

"I have to, Azrael. Please, you're not the only one who lost somebody here. I once had a sister."

He dropped his gaze, as though he couldn't argue with that. "Very well," he murmured. Then he took her by the hand and led her back toward the carriage.

CHAPTER 10

Ghosts

On the drive from the Rivenwood mansion to her parents' abandoned estate, Serena stared down at the snake-leather box on the carriage floor beside their now nearly empty picnic hamper.

What mysteries it contained, for now, she could only wonder, but on the journey back to London, she intended to sift through it for any clues about her birth father's identity.

Azrael sat beside her, silent. She looked askance at him, intensely curious about what might be going through his head.

"You know," she said, "I noticed from atop of the barrow that it looked as if the other country houses were arrayed in a circle."

"Not a circle—a star. The five points of a pentagram," he said dully, keeping his gaze fixed straight ahead.

Serena furrowed her brow, not knowing what to make of that.

"Why would you not come up onto the barrow, Your Grace? Do you share Toby's view that it's cursed?"

"I've seen it." He shrugged. "I climbed up there many times as a boy."

He said nothing more, but when they arrived at the Dunhaven estate, the driveway gate was locked, and this time they had no key.

Instead, Azrael got out and Paulson climbed down, and both men followed the fence line in opposite directions, searching for a break.

Serena waited in the coach, musing on how strange it was to think that her parents had a whole property they'd never even mentioned. There had to be something suspicious about their home here, for a tall spiked fence girded the whole property. What exactly were they hiding?

At last, Azrael found a gap in a sagging length of the fence. He beckoned to Serena; she joined him, and there, they squeezed in.

She grimaced as the cold, rusty metal snagged at her clothes.

Meanwhile, Paulson stomped back to the roadside, where he'd pulled the carriage over. Once more, the ruddy-cheeked driver climbed up and waited with the team.

"You all right?" Azrael asked as Serena tugged the ribbon-trimmed hem of her carriage dress through the gapped fencing after her, then dusted off her gloved hands.

She nodded, but mentally berated herself for wearing such a nice dress. If she'd had any idea that she'd be graverobbing and hiking today, she would've dressed differently, but she had so wanted to impress him.

Henwit. It was just as well she'd left her bonnet in the coach—the wide brim wouldn't have fit through the narrow gap in the fence.

"Right," he said, turning. "Let's go."

The dreary russet woods of the Dunhaven estate were as overgrown as those at the duke's house, and there was no path. But since Azrael seemed to know where he was going, she followed him through the tangled forest, picking her way as best she could through leaf mold and mulch, huffing when her skirts caught on some brambles. She yanked them free and nearly tore the hem.

"Everything all right back there?"

"Fine," Serena muttered. She kept her gaze fixed on the wide expanse of his shoulders as he strode ahead of her. She had never noticed before how his flaxen queue curled just a bit at the end, where it lay between his shoulder blades.

He certainly moved like the fey woodland prince she had once fancied him to be, back when she had been his child bride.

It wasn't long before they'd crossed the ring of forest that hid the manor behind a screen of privacy. They stepped out onto the edge of a greensward whose grasses had grown hip-high, and there loomed the house.

She stared, amazed somehow, now that she was here, to see that it was truly real. They had come out of the woods beside the house. Azrael nodded to her to follow him, and they walked around to the front.

It wasn't as grand as the Rivenwoods' abode. Instead of a white Greek temple, the L-shaped Dunhaven manor was a rather ugly, brown, angular thing with three stories and dormer windows leering out from the gabled roof. The design seemed haphazard, unsure; the house looked like it couldn't decide whether it wanted to be a rustic hunting lodge, a cozy cottage, or a faux-Elizabethan manor.

Serena, however, barely paid attention to the ill-favored building, for out in front of it lay the ornamental pond where her lost elder sister had supposedly drowned.

Her steps faltered when she saw it.

Azrael glanced somberly at her. She swallowed hard, steadying herself. He gave her a moment to take it all in and went up to the entrance of the house.

While he jiggled the front door, Serena studied the long-stagnant little lake with chills running down her spine.

What a dismal sight it was. The rusted metal head of a fountain poked up above the bright green algae slime coating the brown water. Dead, dried-out pussy willows ringed the pond's banks. In the summertime, she thought, this place must be thick with frogs and insects, dragonflies…

"I've found a window that's unlocked," Azrael called in the eerie silence. "Do you want to go inside?"

She nodded, pulling her spencer closer around herself as she turned away from the pond and walked numbly toward the house.

He slung his leg over the sill of the ground-floor window, climbed in, then came around a couple minutes later and unlocked the front door for her from the inside.

"Welcome home," he said with guarded irony as he opened it.

She gave him a nod, wordlessly expressing her astonishment at all this. Then she peered into the dim interior, grimacing and shielding her nose from the wave of stale, unhealthy air that poured out and washed over her.

Stepping cautiously over the threshold, she found herself in an oak-paneled entrance hall. Aside from the dank smell, the first two things Serena noticed were the thick, dusty cobwebs that grew like hoary white hair all down the chain of the round iron chandelier above them, and the black crape that had been left draped over the mirror on the wall, a symbol of mourning.

Antlered deer heads stared down from the walls. A dark red and blue Persian rug lay across the cold floor tiles before a ponderous wooden staircase opposite the door.

Azrael started to shut the door behind her, but Serena shook her head. "Leave it open."

The house was in desperate need of fresh air. He did, then they began their wary exploration of the place.

With every step, Serena felt increasingly unsettled.

Where the late Duke of Rivenwood's cold marble palace had held a sinister sensation, the Dunhaven manor seemed utterly forlorn. Instead of the nameless dread she'd felt over there, here, a thick pall of sadness, grief, even despair tinged the atmosphere.

Perhaps servants had cared for the duke's mansion for some years before it had been sealed up for good, but this place appeared to have been simply locked up and left to rot.

Musty smells rose from the carpets and upholstered furniture. Black stains of water damage marred one of the walls all the way down to the wainscoting.

In a dark green dining room whose long table offered seats for twelve, Serena found a portrait of her mother hung over the mantelpiece.

The fireplace below it had been boarded up, but the gilt-framed picture of the countess showed a breathtaking beauty in her prime.

It must've been made when Mama was just a few years older than *she* was now. Serena stared up at it, amazed at the resemblance, but no. Mama had been far more beautiful than she was.

Looking at the smiling, raven-haired vixen, it was easy to believe that Lady Dunhaven would have been pursued by any adulterous-minded lord who saw her.

Which meant that any blasted fool in England might be Serena's father. Her heart sank as she turned away, only to find Azrael glancing from her to the portrait and back again, meaningfully.

She said nothing, but walked on. She climbed the stairs, determined to see the nursery that had been her dead sister's room. With every step, a puff of dust rose beneath her feet from the carpet runner softening the staircase.

She sneezed again, and Azrael murmured, "Bless you."

She mumbled her thanks, absently reminded of how she'd gone exploring in his house on the night of the masked ball.

They peered into the large, once-elegant rooms of the first floor as they went. But when Azrael opened the door to the drawing room, Serena got quite a start.

The upper regions of the drawing room walls were honeycombed with the bulbous, claylike nests of a colony of swallows. The nests were empty at the moment, thank goodness, since the birds had already flown south for the winter. But she winced in disgust to see the once-stately room covered in bird droppings.

Azrael pointed to a hole high up in one of the tall, arched windows through which the feathered tenants must have come and gone for years as they pleased.

That explained why it was so cold on this floor, she thought.

"We're lucky the door was left closed," she muttered as he pulled it shut again.

They moved on.

It was not until they reached the attic level, where the servants' quarters sat, that Serena finally found the nursery, its pink and yellow wallpaper curling in places, the empty white crib sitting starkly beneath the sloped wall of the roof.

The nursery looked practically untouched from the day the two-year-old Lady Georgette had drowned. The moldering blankets in the crib were not made up, left rumpled from the last time the child had lain there.

Toys were strewn about the floor. The blank, staring eyes of a doll propped on a wee rocking chair unsettled her.

Little clothes hung from the wall pegs. Washcloths and towels, a baby-fine hairbrush, a jar of expensive salve, and a soft puff for talcum powder had been abandoned on the dresser.

It was as though the shattered mother of the lost child had somehow believed for a time that it was all just a mistake, that her daughter would somehow be magically returned to her.

Tears welled up in Serena's eyes with a newfound understanding of the raw pain her mother had gone through. She suddenly wanted with all her heart to see her, to hold her in her arms.

And she repented to her soul of all the harsh words she had spoken to her mother these past few months. All the times they'd fought since Toby's revelations…

Now that she was here, she almost couldn't blame her mother for never speaking of this, covering it up. Trying to pretend that this chapter of her life never existed.

Serena felt terrible now about how she'd behaved. But not had she fully understood until now.

To hear that she'd once had a sister whose entire existence had been hidden from her was one thing. But to be here, to see this place for herself, to feel all its ghostly sorrows floating through the dead, abandoned rooms, was something else altogether. Finally, she had some inkling of the true devastation that her mother had survived.

All she wanted to do was put her arms around her and cry with her for what she'd suffered. Not for one second could Serena condemn her anymore for seeking escape from her broken heart in the arms of these lovers, misguided as her actions might have been. Indeed, if not for one of these men, Serena knew she wouldn't have existed.

She crept across the room, loath to disturb anything in it, for this house felt like as much of a tomb as the barrow or the duke's mausoleum.

A floorboard groaned behind her as Azrael arrived in the doorway, but he leaned there, keeping a respectful distance, only offering silent support.

Serena sniffled as she gazed down at the items on the babe's dressing table. A dainty silver rattle rested there atop a bib. She picked it up and shook it, smiling at the sound, tears in her eyes.

She wiped the thick dust off it with her sleeve and turned around.

"I'm taking this as a memento of my sister," she said, more to herself than to him. "Then, someday, when I have a child, I will give it to him to play with in honor of the aunt he never knew."

He gazed at her with a sad, wistful smile.

She very much wanted to leave the house then. She walked toward the door, but when she reached Azrael, still leaning there, he did not move out of her way.

He cupped her face in his hand and tenderly wiped her tear away with his thumb. "I'm sorry for your loss," he whispered.

"And I, yours."

That familiar shadow flickered behind his eyes at her words. Serena didn't know what it meant, but was too shaken up to puzzle it out at the moment.

She stepped past him gently and walked back down the stairs with a sense of unreality.

She was overwhelmed by this tomb of a house and almost felt she couldn't breathe within its cursed walls. She found her way back to the entrance hall and marched outside, chest heaving for air. She left the door open behind her for Azrael, who followed.

As she walked away from the house, at last, she could pull air into her lungs, and the sharp breeze helped to clear her head.

But now she was faced with the ugly, stagnant pond that had

claimed her sister's life.

She stared at it, straight ahead.

Drawn to it for some inexplicable reason, she went closer, mystified by its air of decay. Picking her way around the mud, she found a grassy spot near the edge and stood there in silence for a long moment, trying to wrap her mind around all this day had held for her so far—and it was only midday.

She could not see Azrael behind her, but she could feel him. His quiet, mysterious presence comforted her.

"For what it's worth," he said all of a sudden, "you're not the only one whose whole life has been a lie, Serena."

She turned to him uncertainly. He was staring at the pond.

The skin was drawn taut across his high cheekbones and brow, the corners of his mouth grimly turned down.

He cast her a dark glance. "So has mine."

"What do you mean?" she whispered.

"All through my childhood, people felt sorry for me because my father was murdered." His tone was studied, faraway. "Little did they know his death was my fault."

Her eyes widened, but he returned his gaze to the brown water, the crisp line of his jaw angled down. He stood with hands in pockets, his feet planted wide.

"What are you talking about?" she asked warily.

He was silent for a long moment, as though debating whether to answer.

"The man in the woods that day wasn't a poacher," he said at last in a low tone. "Not some vagrant."

She stood motionless, knowing exactly what day he was referring to—though she could hardly believe he'd broached the subject.

Perhaps, having faced his father's estate, now that he was clear of it, he finally felt able to discuss it.

His gaze was veiled as he met her glance briefly. Then he nodded to himself and forced the words out. "He was only posing as a homeless man camping on our property. In fact, the man was a government agent, sent there to surveil my father."

Serena drew in her breath. "How do you know that?"

"He told me so just before he died. I don't even know how many weeks he'd been there, making observations to report back to his superiors."

"But, Azrael," she said, "why would the government be surveilling your father?"

"Oh, my darling. Can you be so naïve?" He glanced at her. "Surely by now you've realized that the Prometheans' occult fascination is all just a mask to cloak their true purpose—accumulating political power."

She stared at him, shocked.

"They actually mean to run the world in time," he told her with disgust, then laughed. "They very nearly do. It's not just England that harbors their factions, you see. These enclaves, various secret societies exist in most of the countries of Europe; they collude with each other, and their fanatical believers always try to get as close to the seat of power as they can. They love to worm their way into posts as advisers to kings, bosom friends to princes. They make their marks among the aristocracy, court fashionable society...and betray them all in due time."

His words trailed off while she stood there, astonished.

"There is at least one secret division under the Crown that I know of devoted to untangling the Prometheans' international spider web. They're called the Order of St. Michael the Archangel. Few even know they exist, but they answer directly to the sovereign.

"The man in the woods that day was one of their operatives," Azrael continued. "He was collecting information on my father to send back to his superiors when, by merest chance, we discovered him on our property. My father shot him, but he didn't die. Not right away."

Serena stared at him.

Azrael folded his arms across his chest and judiciously studied the pond. She waited, and he continued.

"We went out to do a bit of shooting. It was August, grouse season. I hated killing those birds, so Father sent me ahead to serve as beater. I was always terrified that if I couldn't scare some birds out of the brush, it would be me he shot for sport."

"Oh, God," she whispered.

"We were walking through the woods on our way out to the fields when we happened across our trespasser's makeshift camp. We caught him unawares, and, of course, Father was too shrewd to be fooled by his lowly disguise.

"Guilty as my father was, he immediately suspected why the man was there. Rather than wait for explanations, he fired upon him, just as he would a poacher, since he had a legal right. Only, it wasn't a clean shot. While my father was reloading, the spy attacked him. They fought.

Father dropped his rifle but yelled at me to get it and reload.

"The spy had a knife. He was quite good with it, I recall. The two of them were evenly matched, to my surprise. My father took a few nasty slices before he managed to knock the blade out of the man's hand. So now, they were both disarmed.

"And I stood closest to both weapons. My hands were shaking too badly—I couldn't load the gun. My father cursed me for failing, and ordered me to bring him the knife instead. So I picked it up and suddenly found myself in the unenviable position of having to decide which man to give it to."

Serena could not tear her gaze from his face. His brooding stare seemed a thousand miles away.

"The spy started talking to me. 'Don't do this, boy. You know your father is an evil man. He's a killer and a traitor.' My father punched the man across the face for that, and barked at him about badmouthing a father to his own son. The man went reeling at the unexpected blow, and my father managed then to take him captive. He pinned the agent's arms behind his back, and then he said to me, 'Come and finish him.'"

Azrael shook his head. "I couldn't believe what I'd just heard. 'I gave you an order,' Father said. 'Show some backbone. It's your duty.'"

Azrael shook his head as though he were faced with his tormenter even now. "I refused. 'No sir,' I told him. I was terrified. I already knew I couldn't do it. How could he even ask me such a thing? Then the spy spoke again. 'Give *me* the knife, lad, and I'll set you free of him.'"

"So what did you do?" she asked in a whisper.

"I chose." He looked at her at last. "I gave the spy his knife back and he killed the bastard with it. Just as he had promised."

Serena slowly lowered her gaze, her heart pounding.

"I wanted to run away, but I forced myself to stay there and watch. I had to make sure he'd truly died, because if he didn't, I knew my punishment for this would be unfathomable. Thank God, the agent managed to dispatch him with a stab in the heart. By that time, unfortunately, the spy was also dying. And that's when things got very interesting."

"What do you mean?"

"He made me promise I would not grow up to be like my father. It was he who suggested I tell everyone that he was a poacher. That was his cover story. Before he died, he entrusted me with a signet ring he'd had hidden away, identifying him as a member of the Order of St.

Michael.

"He told me to keep the ring, hide it. Said if I ever needed help or protection, I could take it to a particular house in the Strand and present it as my calling card, and his comrades there would assist me."

"Did you ever go?"

"No," he whispered vehemently, "I didn't dare. Stiver kept too close an eye on me. Everyone believed the vagrant story, but in the care of my new guardians, I was practically a prisoner. Besides," he added after a moment, "once some time had passed, I started doubting everything that happened that day. It was all so confusing…it seemed impossible. I had the ring as proof that I hadn't imagined the whole thing. But for a long time, I wasn't sure my own memories of those events were clear."

He fell silent for a moment. "Mainly, it was just a relief to be rid of him. Stiver and my trustees at least were never cruel to me like he was. Things improved for me and my mother. I didn't feel I needed the Order's help, at least not until my tutor disappeared.

"Mr. Foxham. He ran afoul of my guardian, and I soon suspected Stiver had done something terrible to him. But still, I didn't dare go to that house on the Strand."

"Why not?"

"Ultimately, I decided that I couldn't take the chance of seeking those men's help." He shrugged. "If the Order hunts and kills men like my father, how could I be certain they wouldn't also kill me? Unlike your family, after all, I have a long Promethean bloodline, and it seemed possible that these agents might not even believe me.

"They might've thought my arrival on the doorstep was a ruse devised by their enemies, sending in a child for some nefarious purpose." He shook his head. "For all I knew, they might've suspected I'd had a hand in killing their colleague, like my father wanted me to do."

Serena did not know what to say. She'd never heard such a dreadful account in all her life.

"I've never told anyone this story," Azrael murmured after another long pause. "I don't know why I'm telling it to you now. The truth could get me killed by more people than I even want to think about. But you, at least, can understand, since it's part of your heritage as well, now. Unfortunately."

"I will take it to my grave."

He nodded, but looked so forlorn that she moved closer and put her arm around his waist. Not that she had any idea how to comfort someone who had gone through such a violent ordeal at such a tender age.

After a moment, Azrael put his arm around her shoulders and gingerly rested his head atop hers, both of them facing the dead, stagnant pond.

They stood in silence like that for a long while, leaning on each other in the gray chill of the day, both trying to make sense of it all.

"I know one thing," Serena finally said, breaking the silence that had enfolded them. "You kept your promise to that man. You're nothing like your father. Frightened as you were, a mere child put in an impossible situation, you chose good over evil and refused to shed innocent blood yourself."

"Father mocked me for my hesitation. Called me a coward. Why? Because I couldn't murder an unarmed man in cold blood? I was twelve years old, for God's sake."

Shaking her head, Serena turned so that they faced each other. She rested her hand gently on his chest and gazed up at him. "You're a good man, Azrael."

At her assurance, his pale eyes flickered once more, but with light this time, not shadow in their depths. He took her face between his hands and kissed her gently.

Serena's eyes drifted closed as his lips caressed hers, soft and warm in the day's chill. She parted her lips hungrily, and just for a fleeting moment, he enthralled her with another intoxicating, open-mouthed kiss.

But when she started to slide her arms around his neck, he suddenly stopped her, ending the kiss, and pulling away a bit.

"No. We mustn't," he whispered.

"Why?" She searched his face in confusion. "I want to kiss you."

"Oh, I want to kiss you, too, Serena, more than you know. But this can never be. You've seen it for yourself now—our match was forged in darkness."

"Darkness? Azrael, what I feel for you is not evil."

He looked at her with an aching stare. "Serena, this is folly. You do not understand the price we'd both have to pay."

"I would pay any price to be with you," she said, startling even herself with her sudden declaration, but it was true.

Azrael scoffed and looked away. "You've spent the past couple of weeks ignoring me," he pointed out.

"Surely you can't be that naïve," she said.

He frowned at her again, stubborn, reluctant, but obviously tempted.

She clutched his lapels as she gazed imploringly at him. "What they meant for evil, love can turn to good, if only you'll believe it."

He stared at her for a heartbeat. "You are truly beautiful," he uttered, then he kissed her again.

But only for a moment before pulling away from her, shaking his head. "We cannot travel farther down this path, my lady."

She stepped back, anger flashing amid her disappointment. "I don't understand. You want me. You know it."

"Of course I do. I'm not denying that. But if they see us together, you don't understand what will happen."

"What is your worry, that they'll kill us? My own father, my own flesh and blood, whoever he is?"

"If it were only the threat of murder, I wouldn't be so concerned. But you don't know these people like I do. *Fear not those who can kill the body,* as they say, *but that which can destroy the soul.* They want me under their control, don't you see, Serena?

"I told you, my father was the leader. He molded me from the day I was born to the day he died to follow in his footsteps. They all did. You have no idea what I've done to stay free of all that. The deceptions I've engaged in. But if they see us together, they'll rejoice, thinking *you* the perfect lure to draw me back into the fold—and for all I know, they could be right."

"I wouldn't let that happen to you. Don't you trust me?"

"It's myself I don't trust."

She absorbed this, at a loss. "But, Azrael, you could never be one of them. You're not evil."

"How are you so sure? You barely know me. It's in my blood, after all, and what kind of son is glad to watch his father die?"

"But you're nothing like him."

"I can't take that risk any more than I'd let Raja go roaming free through London. He's a good pet, so long as I keep a tight leash on him. But I never take it for granted that he could switch back to his jungle instincts and tear somebody's throat out in the blink of an eye. And so could I—in a manner of speaking."

"Impossible," she said.

He shrugged. "I'm not willing to take that chance. Especially not with you. You deserve better."

She stared at him, incredulous. "So then you'll be alone."

"'Tis what I prefer."

"You're a liar."

He stiffened. "It's better this way. Then no one gets hurt."

"Don't they?" she whispered, staring at him.

"Please, Serena—find somebody else." He gazed into her eyes. "You don't want this for yourself, and I don't want it for you. I broke off our betrothal for a reason. Your mother found some way to free you from this darkness. I will not drag you back into it for my own selfish pleasure."

She flinched. "So that's the end of it, then? You're simply going to walk away and pretend you don't feel this between us?"

He started to answer, but stopped himself. "It doesn't matter."

"I see." She flinched and looked away, feeling as though he'd just thrust a rapier into her heart.

"Please...try to understand," he said awkwardly. "I cannot get involved."

"Of course," she said, studying the muddied grass. Seeing he would not be moved, all she could do was drop her gaze to hide the hurt and try to retain what was left of her dignity.

It was hardly the first time she'd been rejected, after all.

Thankfully, she managed to keep her outward composure. What else could she do? She'd never beg and plead for any man.

"Very well," she managed at last, her throat straining. "I understand your predicament, I do. And I appreciate your coming here for my sake. I...see now how hard this was for you. Thank you."

"You're welcome," he said.

She swallowed hard. "Could we please go back to the village now and stop at the coaching inn? I'm cold."

Indeed, she felt as though she might never be warm again.

He bowed his head. "As you wish, my lady."

Then they left that dismal place and drove back to the village.

CHAPTER 11

A Change of Plans

Azrael felt like an utter failure as they rode back to Owlswick. There was no conversation in the coach.

His situation felt unwinnable no matter what he chose. He'd ruined this entire day, never mind that he'd delivered on his promise. He'd found the hideous snakeskin box in which they might well discover the identity of her natural father.

Aye, and strained his back for his pains. That damned bronze effigy must've weighed three hundred pounds. The growing cold merely added to his general misery. The temperature was dropping. *That's all we need. Snow for the drive back.*

Serena's unsmiling silence as she huddled alone on the other end of the carriage, staring out the window, made his heart sink lower still.

Maybe I'm being irrational. Maybe the Hamlet routine had started becoming real, and he was losing his wits. God knew his brain felt as tangled and twisted as the gloomy, vine-wrapped woods through which they drove.

By all rights, he should've been feeling rather pleased with himself right now. He had just faced a very difficult thing, setting foot in that place again. He'd waged a battle royal against the demons of his past. He could hardly believe it himself that he had told Serena what had really happened the day his father died.

Having never confessed the true tale before to a soul in his life, he felt bizarre and unsettled to have shared the secret with his should-have-been bride. Uneasy yet relieved about it at the same time.

Which made no sense at all.

He sighed as the carriage rumbled on, while across from him, Serena fingered the baby's rattle she had taken from her sister's nursery. Her soft breaths fogged the carriage window pane where she leaned her head.

He wondered if she felt as wrung out and empty and emotionally drained as he did after that ordeal, grappling with the past. Perhaps. She didn't look it, though. Her haunting beauty fit well with the autumn landscape. The skies were still gray, the countryside beautiful but bleak.

Azrael rested his head back against the squabs and closed his eyes, wishing he could've traded lives with that silly Toby Guilfoyle. What a debacle.

He could not believe one of the most desirable beauties in London had just offered herself to him on a silver tray, and he'd refused.

What the hell was I supposed to do? his stubborn side retorted. *I had to protect her. That's the most important thing.*

Of course you want her. Everybody does. Too bloody bad.

Find another girl. Or just become a bloody monk and be done with it. God knows you're already halfway there.

He lifted his head and flicked his eyes open with a scowl, only to find Serena studying him. She turned away again, but not before he glimpsed the hurt in her soulful, gold-flecked eyes.

It struck him like a blow to the gut from a top pugilist. Bloody hell, if any woman had ever been worth turning evil for…

But even as temptation sent a shiver of desire into his belly, he glanced down at the snakeskin box near his feet on the carriage floor, a sinister presence. He nudged it farther away from him with the toe of his boot.

Serena just looked at him.

They arrived at the edge of the village, where Paulson pulled the team into the yard of the coaching inn, called The Hound and Horn. The inn yard was empty but for Azrael's coach-and-four; they must have been between stagecoach arrivals and departures.

Good. He was in no mood to fight a swarm of loud, jolly travelers.

Paulson brought the team to a halt in front of the pub on the ground floor of the hotel and they got out—to be greeted by the smell of livery stables, smoking chimneys, and, if Azrael was not mistaken, a hint of roast beef with gravy.

And possibly plum pudding.

Why, it was already dinnertime for those keeping country hours, he recalled. His stomach grumbled, much to his surprise. He thought he'd lost his appetite, but the cold must have made him hungry.

Perhaps a good, hot midday meal would restore their flagging spirits and help them both start feeling human again after that experience. With any luck, it might even put them back on speaking terms.

Otherwise, it was going to be a very long, frigid journey back to London.

When they went in, Azrael's eyes had to adjust; it was decidedly dark in the taproom, compared to the brittle pewter glare of the overcast day.

But a welcoming fire blazed in the stone hearth with a snug inglenook around it. The taproom gave an impression of cozy intimacy — a wide, low horizontal box of a space, with heavy beams across the ceiling and slightly wavy flagstone floors covered in woven rushes.

Oil lanterns in sconces hung on the walls at regular intervals, casting dim illumination. There were simple wooden tables and chairs throughout, long tables with benches.

Directly across from the entrance, a husky, mustachioed man, probably the innkeeper, stood behind a weathered oak bar. He was drying and hanging up glasses on a rack, while a bearded man with the look of a yeoman farmer propped an elbow on the bar, nursing a pint as they chatted of local matters.

A plump, curly-haired woman bustled about the dimly lit tavern, straightening chairs and benches around the tables, and bantering with an elderly gent while she worked. The old man, their only customer at the moment, sat smoking a pipe near the mullioned bow window.

In the far corner was a counter set up as a ticket booth for the stagecoach service. There were chalkboards hung behind it, listing an elaborate schedule of arrivals and departures, along with ticket prices and a few maps of the standard routes. The aproned clerk dozed behind the desk, but he blinked awake when the bell above the door jangled.

Azrael closed it behind him. Serena swept into the taproom ahead of him, drawing off her gloves. He removed his hat; the people took one look at him; and all conversation in the pub immediately halted.

The locals seemed to freeze as they stared at him. It was clear that they recognized him as a Rivenwood, probably by the color of his hair.

He dropped his gaze in chagrin.

Serena, however, commandeered their attention.

"Excuse me." The raven-haired beauty in her smart Town garb seemed to take them all aback as she marched in with her usual air of confidence and greeted them, "Good afternoon!"

"Good day, miss. Er, what can we do for you?" asked the barkeep.

"Oh, you have such a lovely establishment here, and we are so glad to find you. It's so cold out! I should love to sit by the fire, if you don't mind—and have a look at your bill of fare. I don't know what you're cooking, but it smells wonderful."

"Oh, um, yes, right away, miss."

They leaped to serve her, and it was only then that it dawned on Azrael that she had deliberately distracted them for his sake. Charming them.

To protect him.

Her questions, her compliments, and her general verve had intercepted the cold, rude stares that otherwise would've been fixed on the dreaded Rivenwood.

It was remarkably kind of her, he thought, startled, especially after the quarrel they'd just had. When he glanced from the innkeeper to her, he saw that she was once again removing her bonnet.

Off it came. And with that, the full revelation of her beauty—the snowy skin, the ruby lips, ebony hair—made them forget all about boring old him.

Azrael was glad. She did have that effect on people, though, he mused. Especially simple country folk, who weren't used to dealing with diamonds of the first water. They treated her as if they had a fairytale princess in their midst.

Or possibly a duchess.

"Shall we?" Serena asked him, gesturing toward the fire.

He bowed his head. "Of course."

Then he escorted her over to a battered armchair in the inglenook and lifted her mantle off her shoulders for her after she'd undone the clasp.

In the next moment, the curly-headed woman—probably the innkeeper's wife—came over to ask if she could get them anything to drink.

"Yes, thank you." Serena smiled at her. "Do you by chance offer a pear brandy? I daresay a wee draught of Alsatian *eau de vie de poire* would be just the thing to warm the blood on a cold afternoon like this."

"I'm not certain, milady, but I'll be very pleased to check and bring it straightaway."

"Any clear fruit brandy would be lovely if you don't, thanks. Otherwise, I'll just take a hard cider."

"The lady knows her own mind," Azrael remarked.

"And for you, sir?" the landlady asked, turning warily to him.

He politely pretended not to notice the flicker of trepidation that passed across the woman's face as he removed his greatcoat. "Er, yes. Kindly bring me a shot of whiskey and a pint of the house ale."

"Right away, sir." She bobbed a curtsy and fled.

"Their food does smell good," he said to Serena. "I'm sure we have plenty of time for a meal. As long as we're back on the road by half past two, that will still put us in London between six and seven."

Without the hotel staff, her expression had cooled. "Very good, Your Grace."

Azrael winced. *Your Grace?* It seemed they were back on formal terms. "Ahem. Think I'll go wash up."

She nodded, and the landlady returned just then, beaming with pride to have found the very bottle Serena had requested.

Azrael left his traveling companion sitting before the hearth fire in the inglenook, sipping her *eau de vie,* while he asked if there was a room where a gentleman might freshen up after the rigors of travel.

Or graverobbing, as the case may be.

The landlady showed him to a small room in the back with a washbasin and commode. Azrael pulled the door shut behind him and took his time refreshing himself, trying to regroup. He washed his hands, splashed his face, and then stared hard into the mirror.

What are you going to do? he silently asked his reflection. But the glass held no answers.

It took him a few minutes longer, but he did not return to the taproom until he'd recovered his usual gift for detachment. No doubt Her Ladyship was glad for a small break from his company.

At length, he sauntered back out, only to spy his shot of whiskey and pint waiting for him in the inglenook, but no Serena.

Her gray mantle and scarlet shawl were draped across the chair where she had been sitting, but as he stepped around one of the thick oak posts holding up the ceiling, he spotted her standing at the ticket counter in the back corner.

He went and got his pint, then drifted over to find out what was afoot.

"What are you doing?" he inquired, hearing some of her exchange with the clerk.

"Oh—Azrael," she said rather awkwardly as he took a sip. "I didn't see you return. I was just sending a letter to Cousin Tamsin. I had to let her know."

"Know what?"

"That I, well, I'm afraid I won't be going back to London with you."

He nearly choked on his pint. "Come again?"

"I want to go and see my mother. Papa's seat is north of here, so there's no point heading back to Town only to traverse the same road again. They don't have postilions for hire, so I'm buying a ticket for the morning stagecoach. I'll stay here tonight. They have rooms available—"

"Stagecoach?" he interrupted, astonished. "No, no, no! It's quite impossible. I cannot allow that."

Her eyebrows lifted. "I beg your pardon?"

Heart pounding at the thought of her latest mad plan, Azrael glanced at the listening clerk.

"Would you excuse us?" He grasped her elbow and pulled her back toward the inglenook to discuss this matter privately.

Insomuch as the staff would let them.

He noticed all of them, including their aged customer, eavesdropping shamelessly on their unfolding exchange.

"Serena, you know quite well you cannot travel by stagecoach. You are a lady. It's public transport, and you're unchaperoned. I won't hear of it. It's not the done thing."

She laughed at such staid words, coming from him. "What does it matter to you?"

"I'm the one who brought you out here today. That makes you my responsibility."

"Azrael, honestly. You're quite chivalrous, I'm sure, but I am a grown woman. You may return to London on your own. I absolve you of any duty toward me. Don't be silly, now. If you'll excuse me—"

"Silly?" he echoed.

She let out a weary exhalation and folded her arms across her chest. He noted that the pear brandy had restored a bit of the roses to her cheeks—and, apparently, much of the usual fire to her spirit. "We accomplished what we set out to do today, Your Grace. Don't worry for my sake. You've done your duty by me. You helped me...gather information," she said with a discreet glance at their audience, "and for that, I am grateful. More than you know. But let's be honest, shall we? I daresay we've both had enough of each other's company for one day."

"You think I want to get rid of you? Is that it?"

"Hmm, something like that."

"Aha," he said, realizing. "You want to get rid of *me*."

She gave him a bland smile.

He winced, though he could not blame her after their exchange outside her parents' abandoned mansion. "All the same, my lady, I cannot let you do this. It's neither safe nor proper. Let me take you back to Town first, then you can make arrangements to go and see your mother—with your chaperone."

She shook her head. "I can't wait any longer. I've left things in a painful state between us for too long. I can't bear thinking what I've put her through. I need to go and fix this, now."

He absorbed her words, at a loss, while she stared implacably at him. What did he know of how normal family bonds were conducted?

He sighed, recalling the rattle she had taken, and the tears in her eyes when she'd stood in her dead sister's nursery.

"Darling, I know how much this situation hurts you. But I cannot in good conscience let the daughter of an earl travel on a stagecoach. If anything happened to you...!" His voice trailed off as he pondered dire possibilities. "Who knows what sort of low company you'd be exposed to, what with all manner of ruffians getting on and off at every stop the whole way? I won't have these strangers pawing at you on the journey," he said while she rolled her eyes. "No, it's quite impossible. And you know it," he added, wagging a finger at her.

"*Fine.*" She heaved a sigh, pivoted, and marched back to the ticket counter. "Excuse me, please. How much would it cost to hire the entire stagecoach to take me by myself where I need to go—as if it were a postilion? I'd only be traveling to the northern border of the county, about half a day's journey—"

"Er, sorry, miss," the clerk interrupted. "We've already sold half the tickets to other folk. Those stages have to run as scheduled, you see, or dozens of passengers all along the route will miss their journeys."

"Oh. Of course. I see." She turned around and gave Azrael a look that seemed to say, *Happy now?* She shrugged as she returned to the inglenook. "At least I tried."

He scowled at her. "Oh, very well, brat. Where is the damned place?

I'll take you there myself."

"I'm not asking you to take me!" she exclaimed. "You've already done more than enough under the circumstances. Do you mind if I take that box of papers to read along the way?"

"Serena."

"You really don't need to be involved in this any further," she said, swirling her pear brandy in the glass before taking another sip. "You've already done enough, as I said. Don't worry, I can manage from here." She sat down again before the crackling fire. "I'll be back in the bosom of my family by tomorrow afternoon."

"No. We'll eat a quick meal and proceed at once. With any luck, we'll get there sometime tonight." Azrael leaned against the mantel, frowning at her. "Although what your parents will say when *I* arrive bringing them their daughter, I shudder to contemplate."

"Which is another reason why we should part ways here." She looked up at him. "I am forbidden to speak to you, remember?"

This time, it was Azrael who laughed. "You should've thought of that before you broke into my house." Then he walked over resolutely to the ticket counter, his heart pounding as he realized what he must do.

"I, too, have a letter I wish to send," he said to the clerk.

The man sold him a piece of foolscap and an envelope, and Azrael wrote his request while Serena came and peeked over his shoulder. He blocked his letter from her view, though she did glimpse the envelope as he was filling it out.

"Who do you know in Canterbury?" she asked.

"Nosy," he muttered, shooing her away. Then he handed the letter to the clerk to add to the box of outgoing mail.

The clerk arched a brow when he read the address. But Azrael gave him a look demanding discretion. Then he paid for the postage and returned to the inglenook, where he and Serena ate a hasty repast.

Half an hour later, they were on the road again. Heading north, Lord help them, instead of back to Town.

Serena didn't understand why Azrael seemed to feel so strongly about escorting her to her family's country house. He didn't have to do this.

But...even she could admit it was probably best that he did.

Still, it was extremely awkward being confined together in the carriage after he had rejected her. She found it hard to be near him, feeling for him the way she did.

Do you care for me or don't you? she wondered. He was such a confusing man. All that talk about chivalry had sounded convincing enough, but she had given him a way out. If he was so keen to escape her company, why hadn't he taken it?

She supposed he was merely being gallant.

In any case, once more they rolled along inside Azrael's well-cushioned carriage. The horses had had a chance to rest and a bite to eat.

By tonight, they should reach Dunhaven Manor. She wondered how her parents would react when she walked in unannounced.

With Azrael.

There was sure to be a row of some sort, but since the country house was forty miles away and they would not arrive until eight or nine o'clock tonight, she did not intend to torture herself with dread over it for the next five to six hours.

She'd start worrying once they got closer.

For now, she had her work cut out for her sifting through the contents of the snakeskin box before the daylight faded.

As she began slowly going through the papers, she was surprised that Azrael did not want to participate. He eyed the papers with distaste, as if they were the sloughed-off skins of rattlesnakes.

Sometimes she thought he must be as superstitious as Toby, but when she remarked upon his indifference, he merely mumbled that reading in a moving carriage made him queasy.

The deeper Serena got into the stack of papers, what she found actually started making her queasy, too.

She started wishing that the box had only held financial papers. What she found inside was worse.

Far worse.

There was a man named Lord Jarvis that she sincerely hoped was not her real father. He was particularly bad, and fancied very young girls.

Her mouth went dry as she read of kidnappings of random young women of various ages, procured for particular "events."

What happened to them, Serena couldn't bring herself to ask.

Thank God, these things were dated in recent years, meaning that the Dunhavens had not been involved.

She moved on and discovered that Lord Falk had been in charge of arranging bribes, and then making sure the compromised individuals carried through on their promises. Those who didn't were disposed of promptly, according to the records.

She came across the minutes, of all things, from some of their meetings, which they conducted like an ordinary club, it seemed. Lord Stiver had kept up the late Duke of Rivenwood's habit of keeping detailed notes on his supposedly faithful underlings.

The deeper into the box she ventured, the worse it got.

There were also drawings, diagrams, strange shapes, alchemical symbols. A black candle with runes or something carved into the side of the wax, and a necklace with a large pentagram medallion. There were three small books labeled as grimoires that contained vile recipes for spells and supposed enchantments, hexes, curses, and rituals for summonsing demons.

All of which called for blood.

She felt Azrael studying her, and lifted her gaze to his, her fear and bewilderment no doubt written all over her face.

He somehow managed not to say *I told you so.*

His gaze—deep, calm, and knowing—helped to steady her.

He had removed the length of leather cord binding his hair at his nape. It now flowed long and silky over his shoulders. He'd lain back in his seat, his hands idly clasped across his middle.

"Find anything interesting?" he asked in a cynical tone.

He'd barely spoken until now.

She did not even know what to say. She just shook her head and read on by the feeble glow of the carriage sconces.

Finally, her eyes grew bleary as the world beyond the windows turned black. Trying to read with so little light was giving her a headache.

No doubt the alarming contents of the box had contributed to that.

She slowly placed them back inside and shut the lid. "I think that's enough for today," she said, dazed.

Then she cracked the carriage window, needing air.

"Are you all right?" Azrael asked as she sucked in a few deep breaths of brisk air through the crack in the window.

She nodded at him, but immediately noticed that the temperature had fallen dramatically. She was surprised, moreover, to find that full darkness had engulfed the world beyond the glass.

She shut the window again and leaned back against her seat. But before pulling her shawl closer around herself for warmth, she lifted the locket watch that hung around her neck and squinted to read the time.

"It's almost six o'clock."

"Good. Halfway there."

"We should be coming upon Aylesbury quite soon, I should think."

He nodded. "The horses are past due their break. We should have our choice of coaching inns as we approach the outskirts of the town."

"Wake me up when we get there," she said, then settled into a lounging position on her seat and managed to doze off.

Her rest was fitful after the sinister materials she had consumed for the past three hours. Drifting in her sleep, she dreamed she heard devils howling around her, buffeting the carriage and attacking them. Attacking Azrael. They wanted him dead, and they were clawing at the horses.

She awoke with a start, shaken, only to realize it wasn't demons.

It was wind.

Good God, they were in the middle of a blizzard! Gales shook the coach, wailing through the wheel spokes; blinding white snow raced past the windows.

Her breath clouded inside the coach as she sat up, disoriented, frightened by the ferocity of the weather, and rather ashamed at herself for having left the two men and the horses to deal with it while she loitered in dreamland.

The inside of the coach had gone dark except for the lurid glow of the snowstorm. But when she glanced at her fellow traveler for reassurance, she was astonished to discover it was Paulson, the coachman, seated across from her rather than the duke.

"Where's Azrael?"

"N-n-no worries, miss," said the cheerful driver, teeth chattering. His tricorn hat was coated with ice. "His Grace fancied a turn at the r-r-ribbons."

Her jaw dropped. She craned her neck around and looked toward the driver's box. "He's out there?"

"He t-told me to tell you that, on account of the weather, we won't m-make it to your p-parents' house till m-morning."

"Of course," she murmured, finally starting to feel fully awake. She glanced again toward the front of the coach, amazed at Azrael's concern for his servant. "Will he be all right out there?"

"It's a bad night, t-to be sure. We'll be pulling over at the first inn we come to. The t-team's spent."

One of the horses whinnied in protest at the gale. Serena could just make out Azrael's deep voice over the storm, reassuring his animals.

The snow swirled about the black, bare trees, and had painted the fields and squat stone fences on both sides of the road in a thick layer of gray-white.

"Oh God," she whispered, cringing to know she was the one responsible for putting them all in danger by insisting on her chosen course of action. If she had simply gone back to London with Azrael as planned, this could have been avoided.

But none of this was supposed to happen!

They'd have been back to Town by now. Besides, the weather in London was usually milder, since it lay farther south and was better moderated by its closer proximity to the sea.

Lord, what else can go wrong?

The poor Frisians had now spent twelve hours under harness, and as for Paulson, this whole trip was no doubt turning out to be much more than the poor driver had signed on for.

As the coach struggled forward at a crawl, they'd be lucky if they didn't all freeze to death.

"I am so sorry about this, Paulson," Serena said with a wince. "I know this was not how you were expecting to spend your evening."

"Ah, no need to apologize, milady. It's my duty," he said, his teeth no longer chattering as he warmed up, though his round cheeks were still red with the cold. "An early snow is not unusual up in these hills. Besides, the weather's been mad all year."

"I suppose. You're kind to say so. This day really hasn't gone quite as planned."

He smiled. "Sometimes it just doesn't, to be sure."

"Would you like a blanket? His Grace keeps a lap blanket under the bench you're sitting on."

"No, I think I'm ready to go back out—I can feel my face again!" With a chuckle, Paulson opened the carriage door a crack, mumbling that the window was frozen shut.

At once the wind gusted in, flinging a load of flurries into the coach.

"I'm ready whenever you want me to come back up there, sir," the coachman hollered to his master.

"No need," Azrael shouted back from the box. "There's an inn ahead. I'll see if they can take us. We'll be there in a few minutes."

"Oh, thank goodness," Serena said as Paulson pulled the door shut.

The large, hardy man sat there looking uncomfortable at this reversal of roles.

"His Grace was always a dab hand with a coach-and-four," he said after a moment. "Understands animals. You could swear he reads the horses' minds."

Smoothly and surely, Azrael guided the no-doubt-exhausted Frisians under the archway over the entrance to the cobbled yard.

Within the stone walls, the enclosed space was coated with a few inches of snow and crowded with numerous stagecoaches whose passengers, drivers, and horses alike, she surmised, were all stranded there for the night, just like them.

"I do hope they can take us," Serena murmured.

"I must go assist His Grace," Paulson said, and jumped out. He shut the door firmly behind him.

Serena waited, peering out the window, unsure if it would be worth her while getting out into snow up to her ankles.

Stable boys ran out carrying lanterns; Paulson checked on the horses while Azrael sought to secure accommodations for their party, though what sort of bribe he offered them, Serena did not know.

She saw a sum discreetly change hands.

Then Azrael marched back to the carriage and opened the door, peering in at her, his cheeks red with cold, his pale hair blowing and tossing in the snow-embroidered wind.

"Good news. They can squeeze the horses in. Let's hope they can fit us, too."

Serena quickly grabbed her reticule, pulled her mantle more tightly around her, and moved toward the carriage door.

"Here. You needn't get your feet wet." Azrael swept her up in his arms off the edge of the coach where she stood, shoved the door with his elbow, and carried her toward the entrance of the inn.

She held on to his neck, startled but pleased at his gallantry.

His grip was firm, his strides sure. The snow crunched under his feet as he carried her across the yard to the double doors beneath a wooden sign that read *The Rose and Crown*.

The hanging placard swung in the wind, creaking on its hinges.

The last thing Serena saw over Azrael's shoulder was the stable boys helping Paulson unhitch the team and lead the spent horses into the stable.

The coachman went with them.

Then Azrael asked her to get the door latch. Their eyes met briefly and held as she reached down to open the door. With that, he stepped over the threshold and into the crowded, chaotic madhouse that was the Rose and Crown.

CHAPTER 12

First Snow

*W*hen they stepped inside, Azrael set Serena down on her feet, blinking against the warm light after the wintry darkness outside. His face was still numb from the cold, but he was relieved to have delivered the lady as well as his driver and horses to the safety of the inn.

Unfortunately, one glance around the thronged, noisy taproom dimmed his hopes of finding a room for the night.

The passengers of several stagecoaches, which must've been loaded to capacity, had all been stranded there. Azrael wanted to plug his ears against the clamor, and stiffened at the crush of so many bodies jammed into one room.

Everyone seemed grumpy and disheveled. Nearby was a large family with fighting children, a screaming baby, and a harried mother snapping at everyone around her.

An itinerant linen-draper clutched his case of samples, eyeing the baby like he was worried it might throw up all over his wares.

A rotund man nearby had apparently eaten something unpleasant for dinner, judging by the cloud of awful smell around him. The people nearby looked thoroughly disgusted.

At least the half-dozen soldiers loitering in the corner were jolly, though, loud and boisterous, as their breed tended to be. He overheard them telling the serving wench that they were from a Northamptonshire regiment and were on their way home.

Apparently accustomed to the chaos of war, the veterans took the delay in their homecoming in stride and used the opportunity to start getting drunk together.

And who could blame them? They had much to celebrate. Azrael stared a few of them down from across the room, however, when he noted the men eyeing Serena.

"Come along," he murmured, taking her by the elbow.

The two of them began weaving through the taproom, hoping to find somebody in charge.

The innkeeper's servants, potboys and serving maids alike, made their way through the crowd of stranded travelers like galley cooks on a ship in the high seas, buffeted about by countless questions, complaints, and requests tossed at them from all directions.

Azrael was beginning to wonder if he and Serena would end up sharing a stall with the horses, a la Mary and Joseph, when he finally managed to capture one of the innkeeper's lads. "I say, there, young man."

"Can I 'elp you, sir?" The boy's tone was polite, but he looked overwhelmed, his eyes rather frantic. He was only about ten, delivering drinks and such to customers.

Azrael rested a steadying hand on the potboy's shoulder. "Would you kindly point me toward your employer?"

"There's Mrs. Marney, the landlady." The lad gestured at a stout woman in an apron, directing traffic near the kitchen door.

"Thank you. Do you know if there are any rooms left in the house?"

"No idea, sir." The lad shook his head and darted off to see to his duties again.

Azrael took Serena's hand. She held fast to it as they traversed the crowded taproom. He couldn't help wondering how she felt now about her earlier notion of taking the stagecoach by herself, for she clung to his hand in a manner that gave him the distinct impression she was desperately glad he was there.

For his part, he couldn't help taking command of the situation. It was instinctive. Unlike Serena, he was taller than most people in the room, which made it a good deal easier for him to lead the way over to the landlady.

In short order, he managed to get her attention, and inquired about getting a room for the night.

Mrs. Marney knew members of the Quality when she saw them. In a heartbeat, her gaze had skimmed Azrael's expensive greatcoat, tidy cravat, and gentlemanly bearing, then darted behind him to note

Serena's luxurious cashmere shawl, satin reticule, and velvet bonnet.

"You're in luck, sir. I've just one room left. You and your wife are welcome to it, but I'm afraid it's the most costly room we 'ave. The only one that ain't been taken."

"Of course," Azrael said. "We'll take it."

"Your name, please?"

"Er, Dane. Mr. and Mrs. Dane."

Serena glanced up quizzically at him, no doubt confused by the oblique Hamlet reference. It was the first thing that had popped into his mind.

"Let me send my girl up to make sure it's all ready for you, Mr. Dane. Would you and Mrs. Dane like a cup of warm negus while you wait?"

"Yes, please." Azrael nodded. But as Mrs. Marney turned to order one of her maids to go prepare the room, he felt a tug on his sleeve.

He glanced down at his "wife."

"Yes, dear?" he said with a sardonic smile.

"We can't take their last room," she said softly.

He stared at her. "Why ever not?"

"There are women here with small children. Babies. That one hasn't stopped crying. He probably has to nurse, but the mother can't feed him in front of all these people. Let them take the room."

Azrael stared at her, startled. "Darling, they can't afford it."

"Well?" she said. "Surely neither of us could sleep in comfort knowing these little ones are down here spending the night on hard benches, surrounded by men getting drunk."

Uncomfortable with crowds as he was, Azrael was flabbergasted by her request. *Bloody hell.*

Just then, Mrs. Marney returned, beaming. "We're all ready for you now, Mr. and Mrs. Dane. If you'd like to follow Constance, she'll show you to your chamber." The woman gestured at a waiting maid with frizzed blond hair and a frazzled expression.

"Er," he said, frowning as he hesitated, torn.

"Something wrong, sir?" Mrs. Marney asked.

"My, er, *wife* would like to offer the room to the women over there who are traveling with small children."

The landlady's eyes grew as round as saucers, and frankly, Azrael couldn't believe he was saying it himself.

"But sir—"

"I'll pay for it," he grumbled.

The smile Serena bestowed on him for his begrudging compliance almost made up for it all.

Almost.

He harrumphed while Serena stepped around him to confer with the landlady and Constance the maid, who was as shocked by this change of plans as Azrael was.

"I daresay it will be more peaceful in here for everyone once the children are settled," Serena said.

"Why, that is remarkably kind of you, Mrs. Dane, both of you." Mrs. Marney looked stunned. "But if you're sure, I'll see right to it."

"We're sure." Serena nodded firmly.

Constance was sent to go and discreetly gather up the two or three women with small children present to advise them that a room had been made available for them.

Azrael watched their expressions. The mothers looked exhausted, and the children were beyond tired, thus the infant's angry squalling and the two young siblings' grappling over a toy.

They were obviously poor. Saving up money for a stagecoach trip had probably taken the women weeks. This delay due to bad weather must've put them in a position to have to choose between food and shelter while they waited to continue their journey.

The serving maid explained the situation, and the women looked over at him and Serena in shock. One got tears in her eyes. Azrael was too late to tell the maid that he didn't want any credit for it; he just bowed his head.

The women gathered up their broods and followed the maid out of the taproom, which instantly got a great deal quieter, to everyone's relief.

When Azrael glanced at Serena, her gaze glowing with pride in him warmed him more than any roaring fire. He could feel the color rising in his cheeks, but he rolled his eyes and shrugged off his good deed, feeling self-conscious.

People all around the taproom were lifting their glasses to him and thanking him for all their sakes.

Where that left him and Serena for the night, Azrael did not know. The two of them glanced at each other and shrugged. What more could he do but gesture at one of the long wooden tables near the hearth? He spotted one whose benches had a few open seats.

"I had no idea you were such a do-gooder," he murmured wryly as they trudged over and sat down across from each other.

"I'm full of surprises, Mr. Dane. I'm proud of you. See how much calmer it is in here now?"

The soldiers sat down to play cards a few tables away. The linen-draper finally put down his case of samples, and the stinky fellow stepped outside to dispel his gases in the fresh night air, much to the relief of everyone around him.

Paulson came in to inform them the horses were settled in for the night and none the worse for wear. The coachman reported that he had been given a comfortable cot in the long, snug dormitory above the stables for the drivers, footmen, and grooms traveling with their employers. Meals were also brought out to the carriage staff, so he would soon have some supper.

Paulson seemed startled and concerned, however, to hear that Azrael and Serena would have to make do with a bench in the taproom. They assured him they'd be fine. Indeed, it was probably for the best, Azrael reflected.

Spending the night in a bedchamber together could be highly dangerous, as much as the notion appealed.

They told Paulson to get a good night's rest. Weather permitting, they'd press on in the morning. The remainder of their journey should take no more than two or three hours, provided the roads weren't covered in ice and snow.

It seemed to take a very long time for Constance to return with their refreshments, but when she finally came over to their table carrying two cups of negus on a tray, she leaned down to whisper some news. "Mr. and Mrs. Dane, my mistress bade me tell you another room's just become available, if you'd like to have it."

They looked at each other in surprise, having already resigned themselves to spending the night on the hard bench.

"Yes, that's excellent news," Azrael said, then they took their drinks and followed her.

They left the taproom, climbing a creaky staircase all the way up to the top floor of the galleried coaching inn.

"This way," said Constance.

"If you don't mind my asking, how did this come about?" Azrael inquired.

"Mrs. Marney forgot about the old master chamber until you arrived. We've been using it for storage," Constance explained. "We never get so crowded as we are tonight. Usually, it's the last room to be let, because it's our grandest—and most expensive. But you did such a nice thing for those poor women in the taproom, it dawned on her we could ready it up for you two right quick and push some of the boxes out of the way. She wanted me to tell you we apologize for the dust. Me and one of the other girls were just up here giving it a quick tidyin'. It'll be better than those hard benches downstairs, anyway."

"We appreciate this," Serena told her.

"Yes, please give your mistress our thanks."

"I will, Mr. Dane." Then Constance opened the door at the end of the hallway and stepped in, holding up her candle to show them into the large chamber with green walls and heavy plum-colored draperies. "I just made the bed up fresh and got the fire started. We should've had the room ready before, in truth, but no one ever takes it on account of the price. If you don't mind ignoring those boxes and crates by the wall there, they're nothing but extra dishes and table linens and so forth."

"We don't mind a bit," Serena assured her.

Constance smiled shyly and used her candle to light a few tapers in the room. "Can I bring you anything? Busy as we are, I'm not sure the servant bell will bring service right away, but I'd be happy to take your order if you want something to eat."

"Yes, please," Azrael said, "your house bill of fare for two will do nicely. And a couple of bottles of wine."

"Very good, Mr. Dane."

"Would it be possible to get a bucket of warm water?" Serena asked. "I am desperate to wash up."

"Aye, ma'am. I'll let the kitchens know about your supper and then bring you hot water right away."

Constance curtsied at the door, but Azrael gave her a shilling before she left. Her eyes widened as she glanced at the coin in her hand.

Azrael caught Serena smiling at him as the girl hurried out.

Slowly, he closed the door after the maid had gone, and they looked at each other, incredulous at their good fortune.

"You see?" Serena teased. "Your kindness was rewarded."

"*My* kindness? I wouldn't have even thought of it if you hadn't said something about those little screamers."

Serena chuckled at his quip, but once Constance had left them alone, acute awareness sparked to life between them, making her self-conscious.

Azrael slipped off his greatcoat and hung it on a wall peg. Serena set her bonnet down on the chest of drawers and took off her loose gray mantle with a weary sigh.

They glanced at each other uncertainly. An awkward silence dropped like a cloak over the room and filled the space between them.

Serena gulped and forced her gaze downward, trying not to stare.

Azrael also lowered his head and turned away, and then seemed inspired to busy himself by taking action. "Perhaps I can coax the fire a bit."

He marched over to the fireplace and picked up the poker, giving the blaze a few purposeful pokes, pumping the bellows a few times. Then he nodded at the hearthstone. "They've left water bottles here to help warm...the bed."

They exchanged a searing glance at that word.

Serena felt her cheeks redden and did not know where to look. "Perhaps we should figure out where we're each sleeping?"

He looked startled at the question. "Yes. Yes, of course. You must take the bed, obviously." He cleared his throat and swept to his feet again. "I'll arrange myself on this armchair. It looks comfortable enough."

He proceeded to take hold of the cushioned chair and drag it closer to the fire's warmth.

Serena bit her lip, since this hardly seemed fair, given that none of this was his fault. "What if you wake me up halfway through the night and we could trade places?"

"Don't be silly. I don't mind. As long as I have a pillow and some sort of blanket, I'm sure I'll be quite comfortable."

She cast about, desperate for some way to dissolve the awkwardness. She suddenly seized upon the footstool next to the canopy bed. "Here!" She hurried over and got it, then set it down before his chair near the fireplace. "You could put your feet up."

He rested his hands on his hips and inspected his sleeping place, nodding. "Yes, this should suit quite well."

She gazed at him wistfully for a moment. *You are altogether gallant,* she thought, and a pang clenched her heart.

How she wished he had not refused her today. Otherwise, the prospect of tonight would've been very different.

"Well!" Azrael said, putting the fire poker back on its holder and dusting off his hands. "We might as well get comfortable."

A hapless laugh escaped her. "Yes, there's not much point standing on ceremony by now, is there?"

He sent her a winning little smile.

Then he retreated to his side of the room, keeping a safe distance over by the window alcove with a view that overlooked the road. Chivalrously, he left her with the half of the room containing both the fireplace and the bed.

Serena slowly took off her black velvet spencer, drawing her arms out of the long, tight sleeves. While she sat down to unlace her half-boots, Azrael unbuttoned his waistcoat and rolled up his loose white shirtsleeves. Then he, too, sat down wearily and pulled off his boots.

A minute later, she happened to glance over and see him sliding his untied cravat from around his neck. There was something so sensuous about the motion that her heart skipped a beat.

She had to look away and force herself to think of something else.

Cousin Tamsin, for example.

The letter she'd dispatched from the Owlswick inn to her family home in Moonlight Square should've arrived by now. Cousin Tamsin had probably received it and headed out to join her book club.

A sudden knock at the door broke into her thoughts. It was Constance bringing the warm water Serena had requested. The girl told them that their meal would be right along. Azrael opened the door wider for her as Constance carried in a pail of warm water draped with a hand towel.

Azrael took the heavy pail from her, then Constance went on her way. He divided the hot water into the two washbasins the room contained.

Serena thanked him and carried her bowl of water over to her half of the room, along with one each of the towels, washcloths, and bars of soap that had been provided for them.

It felt absolutely wonderful to press the warm, wet washcloth to her face, splashing away the wearisome grime of road dust and travel, and all the traces of spider webs and barrows and tombs that she'd dealt with today.

She washed behind her neck and ears, and when she happened to glance across the room at Azrael, she saw him doing the same, the water trickling through his elegant fingers as he cupped them to his chiseled face.

She got distracted watching him drag the washcloth down his throat to the top of his chest, visible now that he had removed his cravat and unfastened the top button of his shirt.

She looked away with a slight shiver.

Relaxed and rejuvenated after the chance to refresh herself, she felt emboldened enough to loosen her elegant carriage gown, but not in front of him, to be sure.

He glanced over and arched a brow as she went around the canopy bed, closing its curtains, boxing it in. He looked on curiously as she then climbed onto the bed, grinned at him, and pulled the curtains shut.

"What is going on in there?" he inquired.

"Wouldn't you like to know," she said in a saucy tone. "You said we should get comfortable, Your Grace, so I am."

"Hmm. And will you be coming out again?"

"Well, I certainly don't intend to miss out on the food."

She smiled behind the curtains when she heard him chortle at her reply.

Within the rectangle of the bed hangings, Serena unfastened her cream-colored carriage gown, loosened the long sleeves, peeled the bodice down to her waist with a shiver, and then, joyfully, removed her corset.

She placed her hand on her stomach, slumping with relief for a moment to be free of the restrictive garment. How she wished she could have taken a full bath tonight and changed into her night rail and fresh wool stockings.

No polite person of any breeding wore the same linens for twenty-four hours, but her white chemise would have to do until tomorrow midmorning, when they arrived at Dunhaven Manor, Lord willing.

She hoped the snow did not cause this night's sojourn to grow into an extended delay.

When she emerged from between the long, plum-colored bed curtains, the mattress creaked under her. She crawled back to the edge of the bed on her knees, then sprang back down onto the floor in her stockinged feet.

Azrael sent her a curious glance. "Everything all right?"

"Better now, thanks. Be glad you're not a woman. Sometimes a lady's wardrobe is altogether complicated."

He chuckled. "I'm sure."

She wondered if he could tell she was no longer wearing her corset as she sauntered over to the fireplace and stood on the toasty bricks to warm her frozen feet. "Oh, that feels wonderful. It was so cold in the taproom." She drew up her hem to keep it out of the fire.

Azrael watched her as she wriggled her toes happily atop the heated bricks.

"That was incredibly kind of you to trade places with Paulson."

He lifted his eyebrows and glanced up from her feet to her face. "I didn't mind. I like handling a coach-and-four. Besides, they're my horses, and I didn't want a frozen driver."

"I fell asleep."

"I know," he murmured. Then he stood up and drifted over to read the labels on the boxes that the hotel staff had pushed off to the side of the room.

He seemed restless, and it was no mystery why. This was quite an awkward situation, and would only become more so once they bedded down for the night.

She wasn't even sure about what modesty dictated that she ought to wear for sleeping tonight. Her tight-sleeved, formfitting carriage gown, she decided, would be too restrictive to sleep in.

She supposed that once they said goodnight, she'd take it off behind the bed curtains, strip down to her chemise, and then wrap herself in her mantle like a banyan robe for added modesty and warmth.

That way, her gown could air out a bit overnight. It only had to get her through half of one more day. By tomorrow noon, she'd be back at Dunhaven Manor, where she had plenty of clothes to wear and could languish to her heart's content in a long, hot, rose-scented bath.

Provided, of course, that her parents did not disown her the moment they saw her in the company of the forbidden Duke of Rivenwood.

Somehow she'd have to make them understand that Azrael had been a perfect gentleman toward her for the duration of their trip. Indeed, His Grace had acted with the utmost chivalry.

Which is rather a shame, really, she thought, casting him a wicked glance.

"What did you find?" Serena asked, since he was still moving about like a caged leopard, halfheartedly inspecting the boxes.

"Extra dishes, like she said." He shrugged. "Old pots and pans. Linens, extra candleholders."

"Fascinating," Serena said with a yawn. The fire's warmth was making her sleepy. "Mind if I try your chair?"

"Help yourself." He rejoined her by the fire, hefting the poker again and giving the logs another restive jab. "Do you think it'll be much longer? I'm starved."

Even as he spoke, there was another knock at the door, and Serena smiled at him, rising from the comfortable armchair.

"There's your answer, Mr. Dane," she said as she went to open it.

Sure enough, it was Constance bringing their food, with the assistance of two of the young potboys from downstairs.

She hurried in to set the table for them while the lads stood by with two covered trays they'd carried up from the kitchens and set on a wheeled cart upon reaching the upper story.

Azrael enlisted the larger boy to help him carry the small, square table in the room over to the fireside rather than leaving it pushed against the drafty wall.

As Constance whipped out a tablecloth and set their places, Azrael carried over a second chair for Serena. Then the cart was wheeled in, and dinner was served.

They looked over the table, making sure they had everything they needed—salt, pepper, silverware, napkins, a pitcher of drinking water—and Constance offered to leave one of the potboys behind to serve as their waiter, but they declined.

It wasn't necessary, and given their masquerade as a married couple, they did not need the audience on hand reporting any gossip back to the kitchens.

So they sent the potboys and the efficient, hardworking maid on their way.

"Something smells delicious," Azrael said as he closed the door behind the trio and locked it.

He returned to the table while Serena lifted the lids.

"This looks wonderful." The food was incredibly hearty, not perhaps the most elegant meal she'd ever taken, but perfect for a cold, blustery night.

They began with bowls of piping-hot cod and oyster chowder, alongside a warm loaf of fresh brown bread. The two small roasted woodcocks with gravy, one for each of them, would have been filling enough, but there was also a lovely shepherd's pie to share, as well as two bowls of vegetables—one containing boiled broccoli drizzled with butter, the other a mix of green peas and carrots.

The wines provided were burgundy for the red and hock for the white. Azrael poured glasses of the latter for both of them to start with, while Serena peeked at the sweets course waiting for them afterward.

Half a dozen festive biscuits of varied types and flavors were arrayed on a painted dish. But there was also chestnut pudding and two slices of a crumbly, soft golden apple cake, fragrant with cinnamon.

As a finisher, a hunk of white cheddar, pears and a knife to slice them with, and a pewter cup of spiced, roasted almonds. Even an after-dinner glass of port had been provided for Mr. Dane, in a small decanter.

"All they forgot was your cigar," she teased.

"I don't smoke," he answered with a twinkle in his eyes.

"I'm glad to hear it, Mr. Dane. Dreadful habit." She lifted her glass. "To safe travels?"

"Safe travels, Mrs. Dane," he said, and clinked his glass to hers as they sat before the crackling fire.

Their situation seemed so intimate that Serena found herself feeling awkward and starting to grow nervous again, though Azrael could not have been more of a gentleman about all this. She took a sip of the rather too sweet white wine, trying to still the butterflies that had begun fluttering in her belly again, while the snow tapped against the windowpanes.

She set her glass down and looked at him. He was eating his soup and clearly enjoying it, but he paused in the middle of lifting a bite of bread to his mouth when he noted her stare.

"What?" he asked.

The nervousness eased at his disarming manner. "I just wanted to say that I really am sorry for inconveniencing you like this. And poor Paulson, and your horses, too. I've put you through too much today, and I feel awful about it."

"Eh, don't bother." He smiled and shrugged it off. "It's not as though I had anything important to go home to." He slowly scooped another spoonful of soup. "I'm just glad I was with you when the storm hit."

"Oh?" she asked with a glow of pleasure at his concern for her.

"I'd have been beside myself if I had let you go off on your own and then it started snowing."

"You're very kind," she said.

"No, I'm not. It's just you. I daresay you are my Achilles heel, Mrs. Dane."

Serena furrowed her brow, her spoon poised over her bowl. She couldn't tell if that was an insult or a compliment, but he said no more.

The silence dragged on until she felt she simply must make some attempt at conversation, however stilted it might seem. There was still so much about him that she wanted to know. But not for the world would she ask him any more *difficult* questions today, after he had already shared so much with her.

Casting about for a topic, she seized upon the safe and easy subject of food, inspired by the fact that they were in the middle of a meal.

"So, Your Grace," she attempted, "do you usually eat at home or dine at your club? You are a member of the Grand Albion, I presume? I've heard the food is very good. I've only been there myself during the Season for the weekly subscription balls upstairs."

"Yes, I am a member. It just depends. I don't have fixed habits. One of the luxuries of bachelordom. You?"

"Oh, I usually eat at home with Cousin Tamsin."

"What is her connection to your family, exactly?"

"She's my mother's spinster cousin. She's always been devoted to Mama." Serena refrained from saying that she'd always suspected the mousy, timid woman lived vicariously through her bold, beautiful countess cousin, Mariah.

In Tamsin's eyes, Mama could do no wrong.

"Well, she should've received your letter by now," Azrael remarked.

Serena nodded, still wondering about the one he'd sent to Canterbury. But she swore to herself she would ask no more nosy questions. She'd already put the man through enough.

Instead, she glanced at her locket watch. "Lady Delphine's book club would've started by now, too. I say, do you know Lady Delphine?"

"Yes, she's quite an interesting woman."

"Yes."

Another lag stretched.

Serena tapped her foot under the table, worried she was boring him. Not that it really mattered. It wasn't as though she needed to charm him. What good would it do her? He'd already declined her interest in furthering their newfound friendship, which had been humiliating enough. She understood his reasons, but his rejection still stung.

She continued eating, furtively watching him finish his soup. Setting his bowl aside, he put some vegetables on his plate beside the gravy-covered poultry.

It was only then she realized that maybe Azrael had been feeling as awkward about all this as she did, for he suddenly seemed to tire of both the silence and her attempts at small talk. "So," he said, resting his forearms on the edge of the table, "should I expect ol' Dunny to try and shoot me when we arrive at your country house tomorrow?"

Startled by the question, Serena considered and took a measured sip of wine. "Oh, I don't think so. He's not the best shot, anyway."

His eyebrow shot up. "Not the most encouraging answer, my lady."

She smiled. "Don't worry, Your Grace, I won't let anybody shoot you. The neighborhood would be so much duller without you. The eccentric of Moonlight Square."

He snorted. "I thought Lady Delphine held that honor."

"Er, no. It's you. And I, for one, wouldn't have it any other way," she teased, lifting her glass to toast him with a warm smile.

Azrael smiled back at her almost shyly and drank with her, looking a little self-conscious.

Whether it was from food and wine, the nearness of the fire, or her fond tone as she tried to be pleasant company, a flush of color had stolen into his light complexion.

Well, my, my.

The intimidating Duke of Rivenwood was blushing—just a bit—and it was the most adorable thing she'd ever seen.

From then on, all she could think about was kissing him again.

CHAPTER 13

Destined

ortunately, she warded off temptation like a good girl. But by the time they finished eating, fatigue from the long day's travels had overtaken Serena.

She figured Azrael must've been even more tired than she was, after driving through the snowstorm, so she helped him get his sleeping place set up with pillows and a blanket.

She rested one of the hot-water bottles warming on the hearth on the footstool, which was also draped under the blanket, to help keep him warm.

When he was all settled, she bade him an awkward goodnight, climbed up onto the bed still fully dressed, and shut the bed curtains so they could both have some privacy.

Even through the draperies, though, her awareness of him was intense as she undressed. Finally stripped down to her chemise, she slid down under the coverlet.

Staring up at the ceiling, she kept recalling his kiss this afternoon, and throbbed with a futile pang of yearning.

Ah well. The decision was his.

After the nightmare of his past as he'd described it to her today, it was not her place to pressure him about a future for the two of them. He had been through so much—what could she do but respect his wishes?

And yet she knew in her heart they could've been happy together.

Wondering how he was doing out there, whether he'd managed to get comfortable on his armchair, if he was warm enough, if he needed anything, she peeked out from the bed hangings to check on him, but he was not sitting by the fire.

She scanned the room and spotted him sitting, shirtless, in the window nook, watching the snow whirl over the bay window, and drinking his port.

She stared at him, riveted.

Never had he looked so purely magical before. Her fey woodland prince, with his silvery eyes, moonlight-colored hair, and fine patrician face.

How beautiful he was...and she longed for Azrael as she'd never wished for any man before.

The realization gripped her. She couldn't say when exactly the strange, secretive, and quietly wonderful man had stolen her heart.

Perhaps it had been signed over to him when she was just a child. But she knew in that moment that she was in love with him.

She wondered if she should speak or even go to him. But he'd made his wishes plain earlier today.

Even if he felt the same about her, and she dared to believe he did, he refused to act on it.

Now that she knew some of what he'd been through, she had to accept that, for his sake.

Gazing at him, she reflected on the fact that Mama was wrong; the last thing a woman needed was to marry a man she could rule, like she'd always taught her. Indeed, Serena knew deep down that being indulged and cosseted all her life had in some ways made her selfish.

But this time, she refused to be so, no matter what.

Azrael was too important to her to try to force getting her own way. She wanted to be better than that for him. If all he would be was her friend, she'd take that and be happy.

In any case, he looked so lost in his solitude that she did not want to bother him.

He seemed troubled again, brooding. He was probably wondering what he was even doing here. Indeed, she rather wondered that herself.

He looked so lonely and faraway sitting there that she debated for a moment if she ought to say something to him. Reach out. Offer a willing ear to listen if he wished to talk. It was the least she could do, after all he'd done for her.

But in the end, she decided not to intrude. *Leave him alone.* She feared she pestered him too much as it was.

Reluctantly, she left him to his brooding and lay back down again in silence. She closed her eyes, still seeing his face and the smooth, pale angle of his muscled shoulder in the cold, bluish-white illumination of the snow. Yearning filled her body.

But her libido must've simply given up, for the tension began easing from her. The bed was comfortable, the hot-water bottle had made a warm, toasty spot for her feet, and she was utterly worn out.

Her muscles felt sore all over from bumping along in a carriage all day, and so it was inevitable.

She drifted off to sleep.

Sitting in the bay window, Azrael was cold but didn't care. Frost spun lace across the diamond-shaped windowpanes; he watched it grow while the snow coated the world like a fresh start.

It was beautiful, whispering against the glass, whirling by the light of the lantern somewhere in the yard below. The snowfall spun all around him there in the jut of the bay window, like dancing, which he so rarely did. A sweet, lovely dizziness and a lightness like Serena made him feel.

Whether the armchair was comfortable or not, he knew he would not be able to fall asleep in this state of mind. All he wanted to do was spend the night making love to her.

Frankly, he was ashamed of his unmanly hesitation on this front—and others.

Refusing her hopeful attempt to strengthen this connection between them had seemed like the right thing to do at the time, but it had felt increasingly wrong to him all day.

Damn it, he had worked at deceiving his enemies for so long that, somewhere along the way, he had begun deceiving himself.

This life he had limned out so carefully suddenly didn't fit him anymore. The isolation of it shocked and overwhelmed him.

He might as well have walked out half-naked and shoeless in the snow right now, he was so alone, so frozen inside.

The worst part was knowing he had done this to himself. And now he had frozen out Serena, as well.

All he could do was call himself a fool. For she made him truly happy. He loved taking care of her, and the small ways in which he'd done so today—and, indeed, ever since the masked ball—had filled him with a sense of meaning that his life otherwise completely lacked.

He loved being with her. Yet he feared he had surely lost her respect today. He'd lost a great deal of his own for his cowardice.

Unfortunately, the only way he could have what they both wanted was dire to contemplate.

Contemplate it he did, however.

Dark shadows were stirring in his mind like the shifting snow outside as it blew and gathered in piles, changing shape.

He was not a helpless boy anymore. He was a man. With power, wealth, resources. Wits.

Such a man had no excuse for possessing full knowledge of such evil at work and doing nothing about it.

It had all suddenly become crystal clear. Azrael felt as though he had been asleep all these years, nodding off behind his impenetrable shield of detachment. But the boy's helpless paralysis was leaving him. Strength and feeling had returned with Serena.

The battle, he was beginning to see, was no longer avoidable.

The fact was, he *was* involved in the Promethean underworld, whether he liked it or not. He had been born into this, and by God, if he did not take action and do something about this hidden cancer in his country, who could?

Earlier today, he had refused Serena's artless offer of her love because he had dreaded the specter of taking her as his wife and then the two of them and any future children of theirs being claimed by and having to live under the dark shadow of this evil.

How his enemies could use a wife and family against him, he had always shuddered to think. But in actuality…

It didn't have to be that way.

Not if he lived up to his name.

Not if he drew upon his father's own expert treachery flowing in his veins and turned it all against them. Began taking steps to rid the world of their foulness.

After all, he was one of them, though he had kept his distance. They trusted him. That could be their fatal mistake.

God knew if he succeeded, the most luscious prize he'd ever beheld waited for him. Serena could be his. They could live in peace. She would be free of this dark heritage—they both would.

He'd have swept the earth clean of their satanic filth and broken the curse, if there was one.

True, if he did this thing, the chances were good that someday one of their foreign assassins might show up on his doorstep to punish him for the betrayal he was contemplating, for the Prometheans lurked in courts across the world.

But God, he thought, even spineless bloody Hamlet had eventually picked up his sword.

Azrael supposed he had merely needed the proper motivation.

And she was that. Sweet Christ, she was that.

He looked over his shoulder hungrily toward the canopy bed where his should've-been bride slept on behind the curtains.

His heart was pounding, but his mind was made up; he would not be deterred. *You are mine and we both know it.* Yes, their match had been his enemies' plan, but he no longer cared. What was it she had said this afternoon?

"What they meant for evil, love can turn to good."

I hope you're right, my darling. Azrael swung his feet down from the window nook and rose silently.

His body tingled with awareness of her, this beauty whose voluptuous appeal he had been striving all day not to notice.

Now all he wanted was to taste her mouth, feel her soft body beneath him, and make it so that there could be no backing out.

For either of them.

He felt the warmth of the fire as he passed it, reaching out to take hold of the edge of one of the bed hangings. With no more hesitation, he slid the curtain aside. It rasped quietly on its rings.

Her beauty overwhelmed him as he gazed down at her sleeping on her side, facing him.

She was like a rose in winter, so perfect and pure. Her black lashes fanned against her skin as white as the snow, her lips crimson. The luxurious black silk of her wavy hair flowed across the white pillow where she had laid her lovely head.

Dry-mouthed with need, Azrael wetted his lips with a hungry pass of his tongue as his gaze traveled down her creamy chest to the scoop neck of her chemise. Her full, round breasts strained against the paper-thin linen, and his stomach tightened with growing, desperate want.

So beautiful…

He gazed at her arms, bared by the sleeveless garment.

Unable to resist, he touched her, resting burning fingertips on the curve of her hip, barely able to hold himself back.

"Serena?" he called in a deep, husky whisper. "Wake up."

❖

Serena thought at first that she might be dreaming when she opened her eyes to find Azrael standing by the bed.

The firelight flickering behind him shone around his pale hair like a halo and outlined his dark, imposing silhouette with an orange glow — tall and taut, his wide shoulders tapering down to a lean waist.

Bleary and confused, she pushed up onto her elbow. "Is something wrong?

"I need to ask you something." He leaned down toward her, solid and real.

"What is it?" she mumbled, raking her fingers through her hair as she sat up uncertainly.

He stared at her with a gaze that pierced into her very soul. "When you said you would pay any price to be with me," he whispered, "did you really mean it?"

His question took her aback. Suddenly, her heart lurched, a new realization entering her fuzzy mind. "Yes," she said breathlessly. "Why do you ask?"

"Because..." He licked his lips, his stare locked on hers. "I feel the same."

"You do?"

"Remember that letter I sent to Canterbury?"

She nodded.

"It was a request to the Archbishop for a special license."

Her eyes widened, and she came fully awake.

He sat very still on the edge of the bed. "I initially sent it in case anything went awry with our travel plans. I would not leave you ruined. But once I'd sent it off, I realized...it is what I want."

She blinked. "Are you sure about this?"

"I am," he whispered. "Will you have me?"

She lifted her hand to her head. The room was suddenly spinning. "But—you said it was impossible."

"I was wrong. No—I was not being entirely truthful," he admitted. "There is *one* way."

"How?"

He took her hand but evaded the question. "You must trust me."

"I do."

"Do you?" He trailed his gaze over her face, her lips, her body. "How much?"

She stared at him, and thought of all the months of watching him. Learning him. Wanting him, if she were truly honest. God help her, she wanted him still. More than anything.

"Completely," she finally answered, and to prove it, she pulled back the coverlet, offering him the warmth of her bed.

Offering much more than that, to be sure.

His eyes narrowed, lightning in their depths. She bit her lip with anticipation as he accepted, joining her in the bed.

"You're cold," she murmured as she touched his smooth, muscled shoulder.

"You're warm."

"Yes, come, I'll warm you up," she promised, and he immediately kissed her. She welcomed him under the covers, lay back on the pillows strewn against the headboard, and wrapped her arms around him, kissing him back for all she was worth.

Her heart was pounding. She'd been dreaming of this, and now his weight atop of her felt lovely.

"You really want to marry me?" she whispered after a moment, joy welling up within her.

"So badly," he said in a husky murmur.

"What made you change your mind?"

"You did, my darling." He leaned on his elbow and cupped her face in his palm. "You gave me hope that perhaps things really can change. You gave me a reason to fight. I don't want to lose this chance with you. I need you, Serena. I want you with me, and I want to take care of you always."

"Oh Azrael," she said tenderly, melting at his words. Then she kissed him with redoubled enthusiasm.

His lips slanting over hers, his port-flavored tongue sweet and deep within her mouth, he pressed up smoothly onto all fours over her body, freeing his hand to caress her.

She sighed anew, restlessly, as his caresses moved up and down the middle of her body, gliding between her breasts, down her belly, and back up again, through the thin cloth of her chemise.

Her limbs grew heavy with desire, but she found the will to lift her hands and explore him in return. She felt his chest, his pulse pounding underneath her fingertips, and lower, the splendid carved muscles of his abdomen. She caressed his arms and neck.

Molding her palms over his shoulders, she marveled at the gathered power of sleek, rugged sinew and bone beneath the velveteen warmth of his skin. As promised, she had heated him up quickly, she thought with a giddy smile as he went on kissing her.

"I love the way your skin feels," she whispered when he let her up for air moments later.

"I'm all yours."

"You're not going to change your mind, are you?" she asked, feeling vulnerable to realize how easily he could wound her—or worse.

"Not a chance," he said. "I want to make you happy, sweet Serena." Then he lowered his head into the crook of her neck and intoxicated her with warm, nibbling kisses there, all the way up to her earlobe, and then stronger ones, lightly nipping her flesh.

Soon he had her gasping with delight. His fingers curled around the sleeve of her chemise, and he inched it down, kissing as he went.

As his lips skimmed the upper curve of her breast, she was suddenly desperate to be rid of the garment. She wanted nothing, nothing at all between them.

He obliged her in this as if he'd read her mind, moving back to wait while she lifted it off eagerly over her head, her body trembling.

His ravenous stare sank from her flushed face to her now-naked body with an almost pained look of admiration, and a low moan escaped him.

He pressed her back onto the pillows, and she watched him take her nipple in his mouth, stroking his blond head at her breast. It gave her the most exquisite thrill, feeling him stoke her arousal to fever pitch. He moved to her other breast, and she savored the sensation, arching her back.

Never could she have allowed any other man to do these things to her. But he would be her husband, as she'd known somehow he had to be. And so it was easy to cast aside any maiden shyness and put herself in his hands completely.

She lifted her arms above her head and clutched the edge of the pillow as he explored her body with his lips, skimming kisses down her stomach, nibbling at her hip. Limp with desire, she wondered if she ought to worry that he now lay between her legs.

Her chest heaving, she barely noticed as he tickled and tormented her with sweet, maddening kisses everywhere, that he was unfastening his breeches.

She dragged her eyes open when the lovely torture of his attentions stopped. At once, she saw the reason. He had moved back to shed the remainder of his clothes.

This is real, she thought. It seemed like a dream, but he really meant to deflower her. She registered hesitation, uncertainty, and even though she wanted him, she was a little afraid.

When he tossed his drawers and breeches onto the floor, Serena cast an awestruck glance down at his oh-so-masculine splendor, his sleek hips, his rigid member standing forth, tall and proud.

"Like what you see, madam?" he teased in a silken whisper. Then he returned and took control.

She moaned as he kissed her with patient, lavish seduction. He slid his arms firmly around her, cradling her in his embrace as he eased her back down onto her back and atop her, pressing against her in all the right places.

As she ran her hands over his sculpted body, she felt a gathering frenzy in her blood the likes of which she'd never experienced before.

He seemed to know exactly what she craved. He trailed his hand down the front of her bare thigh, and Serena squirmed with tantalized desire as he walked his fingers delicately across her mound, then lower.

She shuddered and let out a soft groan as he slipped a finger into the petaled folds of her wet, swollen passage. "Oh, Azrael…" She licked her lips with anticipation.

"Patience, my love."

He was driving her mad with his soft, satin touch. She dug her fingertips into his shoulders, then ran her hand through his long hair.

"So passionate." His whisper had turned to a fevered rasp. He moved atop her. Her heart flamed with sudden joy to realize he would join himself to her now.

There was suddenly nothing in the world she wanted more.

"Will it hurt?" she asked with a fleeting pulse of not quite fear, but uncertainty.

"I've heard it may, but don't be afraid. Just tell me if it does, and I'll stop. You do want this, don't you, Serena?"

"Oh, Azrael, I'll die if I can't have you." She pulled him down to kiss him with stormy tenderness. "I half wished you had done to this to me on the night of the masked ball."

"God, I wished that, too." He kissed her heartily. "Instead, I had to barter with you. Kisses in exchange for information, you lovely little minx?"

"Yes, and you told me the price would be too high for me, Your Grace." She nestled her nose against his. "You have no idea how eager I was to pay it."

"How you delight me," he uttered with a haze of doting softness in his eyes.

"Likewise, my darling." She molded her hand to his cheek. "Now, Azrael, give yourself to me."

He obeyed with a low, hungry moan, and neither of them knew anymore who was seducing whom. He covered her with his body and lay between her legs, spreading them wider with a calm, masterful press of his hand.

Serena's chest pitched with excitement as he guided himself to her threshold, her womanhood opened to him like a flower. She closed her eyes, mesmerized by the feel of his hardness there—and suddenly, he was inside her, and she was no longer a virgin.

The soft cry dwindled on her tongue as she panted with the knowledge that she was now his woman, as destiny had set forth so many years ago. He cradled her in his arms, waiting until she was ready to continue. She held him to her heart, dizzied with the sweet fulfillment of their oddly sacred joining.

Her restless sigh a moment later urged him back into motion.

He moved so gently with her, stroking her body with elegant hands to soothe her, but there was no pain. Serena opened her eyes. Azrael's were closed. He looked lost in dreamy, intimate ecstasy, gliding back and forth between her thighs with sensuous and total giving.

I cannot believe how lucky I am. She skimmed her fingertips along his high cheekbone, then captured a length of his hair where it hung down like a flaxen veil beside her face.

His lashes swept upward, and he gazed into her eyes as he continued making love to her. He did not require words to tell her in that moment that this was the closest he'd ever felt to anyone.

She lifted her head from the pillow to press a sensuous kiss to his cheek, and made a private vow that he'd never be lonely again. Then she wrapped her legs cautiously around him, and he pressed up onto his hands, his skin hot, his muscular arms and chest flexing with his supple undulations.

His eyes gleamed like silver flames as he quickened his pace, taking her at a gallop now, until her body burned. The bed rocked, her wits whirled like the scattering snow, and the Duke of Rivenwood had his way with her entirely, his body damp with sweat, slick between her thighs.

She gasped with awkward suddenness at the wave of astonishing pleasure that washed over her out of nowhere. It took her so off guard that she nearly shrieked with her first full release.

Azrael growled—he actually growled like a wild animal—thrilling her to the core as he stiffened and slammed atop her, two, three times, roughly—delicious roughness. Panting, jaw clenched, he clutched her to him, gripping her by her buttocks. In the glimmer of firelight, she saw his face etched with untamed passion. Fierce and beautiful, he surrendered at last.

She felt his wrenching pulsations within her as pleasure exploded from him. Fascinated, she was intensely aware of him, his every move and shift and nuance, everything. Her own shocking spasms of bliss receded as his violent climax also passed, slowly easing.

He was left breathing heavily, his face flushed. He looked as incredulous as she felt about it all, maybe even more so.

"Oh my God," he whispered fervently, finally withdrawing from her body. He rolled off her onto the mattress beside her, spent and panting.

She looked over at him, dazzled. "Oh Azrael," she purred.

He lifted her hand to his lips and kissed it, still panting. After a moment, he rallied himself to pull the covers back up over them.

She smiled, more deeply touched than ever by his solicitude. What a splendid husband he would make.

"Come here, my beauty." He swept her into his arms and pulled her down.

Serena rested her head on his muscled chest, still beaming at the feeling of his naked skin against her. He wrapped his arms tighter around her. She snuggled against him, ridiculously happy.

"Did you like that?" he murmured, as though he couldn't resist asking.

Serena gave him a dubious smile, still glowing from his lovemaking.

Like was so drastic an understatement for her reaction to the earth-shattering thing she'd just experienced that all she could do was laugh. "You might say that. Did you?"

His answer was a low, very wicked, sensual groan.

Serena grinned, though, in truth, she was relieved to hear it. "Good. I wasn't sure if I was doing it right."

"You were perfect," he whispered. He kissed her on the forehead, and she sighed with contentment.

Then they fell into a contemplative silence, holding each other while the wind whistled through the eaves of the old coaching inn.

"When do you want to get married?" he asked after a while.

"Soon. So we can continue doing plenty of *this*."

He laughed. "Naughty girl."

"Sorry," she said, flashing a saucy grin.

"Don't be. It's one of your best qualities."

"Mm." She rested her head on him again. He spun a lock of her hair around his finger. "Azrael?" she said after a moment.

"Yes, my love?"

"You said you found one way that we could be together. Well?" she asked. "Aren't you going to tell me what it is?"

He was silent for a long moment.

She furrowed her brow. "At least tell me what it entails."

"Very well." He glanced at her, and his eyes gleamed like silver blades. "The people mentioned in that box. I am going to destroy them."

Serena sat bolt upright and turned to him in shock. "What do you mean?"

"Exactly what I said. Don't worry, sweet," he murmured. "I can be a much nastier fellow than you know when the occasion calls. It's in the blood, don't you know."

"But—that sounds so dangerous. And one of them is my father."

"Yes." He considered this. "I suppose everything has its price." He captured a length of her hair again and twirled it around his finger, gazing at her. "I'm sorry, but you saw what was in the box. You know what manner of men they are."

She gazed at him, at a loss.

"I won't let them control us or threaten you, or our children, or our future together. And they're not going to pull me back in," he whispered with ice-cold steel in his eyes, "because they're going to be dead."

Then he tugged her back down gently into his arms, but even after Azrael had fallen asleep, Serena lay wide-awake with dread over what he intended.

CHAPTER 14

Origins

*E*verything was so clear in Azrael's mind the next morning. Crystal sharp, like the glint of sunlight on the snow that was already melting. How had he ever been confused over the right thing to do?

The answer seemed so obvious now. There was good and there was evil; having been born to the latter, perhaps his confusion was understandable. But this morning, he knew exactly where he stood.

No more hiding in the safe, dull, shadow realms of gray. No more staying out of it.

He would end this nest of vipers, for he alone was in a perfect position to do so. And it was not just for Serena, her safety, and the freedom and happiness of their future family.

It was for his mother, too. And old Mr. Foxham. It was for Bobby the cook's boy and Lady Dunhaven, and the maids his guardian had raped and paid to keep silent. Hell, it was even for his poor dead cat, murdered by that demon whose seed had given him life.

Azrael was *not* one of them, and it was time to prove it.

If he did not take action, then he did not deserve Serena.

But first he had to see his fair betrothed home—*and* figure out what to say to Dunny at this juncture, having just deflowered his daughter.

Perhaps that part did not bear mentioning quite yet.

In any case, they set out at midmorning. The Frisians had grown playful in the snow after a good night's rest and a generous serving of grain. Nickering in the harness, the team was raring to go, and Paulson was as cheerful as ever, though he sneezed twice within the first mile.

Serena and Azrael exchanged a rather guilty look, riding in the carriage.

"I fear your poor coachman has caught cold," she said.

"A hazard of his trade, my dear. It's not your fault." Azrael did not mention the dubious look his driver had sent him this morning.

Paulson was no fool, nor was he blind.

Of course, Azrael did not make a habit of worrying what his servants thought about his morals, but Paulson seemed slightly scandalized to draw his own conclusions about what happened between Serena and Azrael last night.

They didn't hide it very well. Nor did they try to, at least not at the Rose and Crown. After all, the staff there still believed they were Mr. and Mrs. Dane.

They had complimented Mrs. Marney on the hospitality of her establishment, and once they were well fortified with a hot breakfast and an extra jug of hot tea for the road, they set out for the northern border of the county, where the Earl of Dunhaven's ancestral pile straddled the border of Buckinghamshire and Northamptonshire.

Serena and Azrael sat side by side, arms linked. She had a bright, well-ravished glow in her cheeks this morning, and her hazel eyes shone.

The sight of her enchanted him.

As the morning wore on, the sky grew gray again, bringing back more normal temperatures for November, but Azrael did not mind the gloom. She lit up for him with a warmth to rival any cozy fireside.

Azrael could not remember when he'd been so happy.

Every time he thought of making love to her last night, he wanted to do it again immediately. He was no rakehell like Netherford used to be.

He'd always been a choosier and more discriminating lover, and it was true that she had been a neophyte in his arms last night, but God, she had satisfied him to his very soul.

He could not stop touching her, caressing her this morning, possessively, perhaps. He kissed her often and put his arm around her, and laid his hand on her thigh through her skirts as she sat beside him.

And why should he not? She'd soon be his forever. This time by choice, nobody forcing them.

Serena doted on him, smiling as they traveled along. Satisfaction and complete absorption with him shone in the gold-flecked depths of her eyes.

He noticed, however, that she grew more nervous the farther north they went across the county. Finally, it seemed, she was beginning to worry what her parents would have to say about all this.

Sardonically, Azrael found her belated concern about their reaction rather amusing. At least his impetuous little minx hadn't worried her pretty head prematurely, he thought, looking askance at her with a smitten smile.

At length, she decided to distract herself from her dread by getting back to the business of perusing the contents of the snakeskin box.

It still sat on the floor of the carriage, surrounded by its invisible aura of evil. Sometimes Azrael almost fancied that it was a live thing, with a wicked consciousness of some sort. That it was listening to them, no doubt disgusted by their newfound love.

Serena was undeterred by its serpentine nastiness. Moving her bonnet out of the way—he decided to count how many times she took it off and put it on again today—she opened the lid and reached in to start on another stack of its unsavory contents.

"Might as well keep myself busy," she announced.

Azrael smiled softly at her. "You needn't be so skittish, my darling. What we did last night is nothing compared to the sort of things your parents did when they were our age, remember?"

"An excellent point, Your Grace." She nodded. "Thank you, that actually helps."

"Don't you think they'll be at least somewhat happy that their daughter is going to be a duchess?"

Serena laughed. "One would hope so, but we'll see."

"Well, I think you're going to make the most beautiful Duchess of Rivenwood there's ever been." He paused, cupping her cheek. "We'll change the entire meaning of what this title signifies, you and I."

Visibly touched by his words, she leaned closer and kissed him. "You say the loveliest things."

Then she got down to business, and he decided to help.

"Where shall I start?"

Her slender eyebrows lifted. "You're going to assist?"

"Might as well." He drew off his gloves and reached into the box, pulling out one of the bound ledgers to review.

"I thought it made you queasy reading in a coach."

"Not exactly." He gave her a penitent look, uneager to admit that he just hadn't wanted to get involved, as per usual. He supposed he hadn't wanted to face the past any more than her mother did. But he had seen the error of his ways.

Serena gave him a fond, forgiving smile, then they got to work.

"You know, darling," she said at length as the carriage rolled along a road that wound through the slushy fields, "it was hard to fall asleep last night after what you told me."

She looked over at him with concern. It was only then that Azrael suddenly realized she was worried about more than just her parents' reaction today—she was worried about *him*.

"What exactly do you mean to do?"

His first instinct was to stay silent. Keep everything a secret—again, as per usual.

But he reminded himself that, last night, he had violently overturned all his old assumptions, all his old ways of doing things. So that he could be with her. And though it still felt strange to him to be so open with someone, Serena was a part of this, and she deserved to know.

Besides which, he loved her and could deny her nothing, though he hadn't said *that* aloud yet, either.

"Remember back at Owlswick, when I told you about the man in the woods, the agent?"

"Of course."

"He'd informed me about a house in London, where I could call on the Order of St. Michael if I ever got into serious trouble with my father's companions."

"Yes. You told me you decided not to contact them for fear they might think it was a trick and target you, like they did your father."

"Right. Well, it's time to take that chance." He nodded grimly to the box. "I'm going to give this to them as a token of goodwill and proof of my sincerity, and hopefully, they'll work with me to eradicate this problem."

Her eyes had grown round at his explanation. "But, Azrael, what if they don't believe you? What if they think it's a trick?"

Then you'll probably never see me again, he thought, but he just smiled at her. In fact, the Order agents had a reputation for making those associated with the occult brotherhood mysteriously vanish.

"They'll believe me," he assured her. She was already worried enough. "I'll give them the ring—I still have it—and they'll know I'm telling the truth."

She stared at him, looking frightened and pale.

Her stricken expression convinced him not to tell her the rest right now. She had enough to manage in the coming confrontation with her parents.

But the truth was that Azrael very much suspected that, provided the Order *did* believe him, he would have to be personally involved in seeing the thing through.

Hidden as the group was, he predicted that he would have to lure the villains to some particular location, where they could be taken into custody.

Unfortunately, to justify their arrests, they would probably have to be caught doing something horrible red-handed.

Azrael had a feeling that he would have to be at the middle of it. But if that was what it took to bring all this to an end, to exorcise the evils of his dark heritage, then so be it.

All he wanted was a clean slate and a fresh start without all this ugliness lurking in the corners of his life.

Serena shifted in her seat, looking unsettled, but said nothing. He appreciated the fact that she did not argue with him about it.

Having to persuade her every step of the way about his dicey undertaking would only complicate matters. Her stoic silence about his intentions relieved him, as it showed she was truly on his side. For the first time, it gave him the sense of having a real partner in life.

She chewed her lower lip while she continued scanning the papers. "Azrael?" she said. "If you give all this material to the Order, how will I find out who my real father is?" She glanced over at him, her lovely eyes troubled beneath her thick black lashes.

"Your mother is going to tell you."

"Oh? What makes you think she'll reveal it now?"

"Because I'm going to *insist*. You have a right to know."

She frowned. "Azrael, you're not going to yell at her, are you? She's already been through so much, and I honestly forgive her for lying, now that I've seen the place where my sister died for myself. It made it...so much more real."

"Darling, haven't you noticed yet that I never yell?"

"Hmm, now that you mention it, you don't, do you?"

"No. Don't worry. I'm simply going to remind Her Ladyship of what's at stake and make her understand we can't afford to spare her modesty any longer. If she knows who your real father is—and she might not—then I will prevail upon her—tactfully, I promise—to reveal the answer to you. I just hope you don't regret it once you know."

He noted the doubt on her face, the puzzled knitting of her brow, the frown on her lips.

"What?" he murmured.

"If you were confident that you had the power to make my mother reveal this information all along, then why didn't we just do that from the start?"

"Because," he said, irked at himself, "I was determined not to get involved, remember?"

At that moment, they turned in at the long, flat drive of Dunhaven Manor. It was wet with mud and lined with bare-branched trees.

Serena promptly began smoothing her hair and fussing with her clothing, making sure she was in good order to face her parents.

Azrael returned the papers and ledger book to the snakeskin box and closed it, then he sat unyielding and still.

Ahead lay the Earl of Dunhaven's ancestral pile, a dull, unimaginative mansion exactly like a hundred others across England. It was built of gray stone, with the requisite four pillars out front and symmetrical wings off the main block.

It was the second stolid, unexciting house of his that Azrael had seen, so perhaps this gave some hint of the owner's nature.

Well, that could explain why his daughter fancied eccentrics, he mused.

In fact, the dreary sameness of the house also gave him a sharper hint of the boredom that must've overtaken the former temptress, Lady Dunhaven, so many years ago. Was it ennui that had driven the countess to seek her thrills by dabbling in a form of decadence that had surely led to a darker place than the woman had ever imagined?

No doubt, the young Lady Dunhaven had soon discovered she was in over her head with the likes of his father and Stiver and the whole demented lot.

He would wager it was her beauty alone that had saved her. Like Serena, that lovely face probably had let her get away with anything in her youth.

Ah well, he thought. Whatever their faults, his future in-laws had escaped the Prometheans' clutches somehow, and Azrael respected them for that.

As the carriage rolled to a halt, he noticed Serena looking ashen, dread stamped across her face. Now that they were here, her nervousness had turned to terror.

He touched her cheek gently. "Don't worry," he said, "it'll be all right. You're of age. They can't forbid us."

"Y-yes. I know. Still. This is sure to be difficult."

"I'll be with you every step of the way."

With an adoring look, she captured his hand where he had pressed it to her face, and gripped his fingers, giving them a squeeze.

He winked at her for encouragement, then she squared her shoulders and they both got out of the coach.

The manor's front door opened even before they reached it, and there stood a short, stout butler, gaping in amazement.

"Lady Serena! Come in!"

"Hullo, Bosworth. I'll bet you weren't expecting me."

"Heavens no! Sir." Bosworth nodded politely to Azrael as he opened the door wider for them both. "Welcome," he added, already looking troubled that there was no maid and no chaperone with the young lady.

Azrael followed her into a simple entrance hall painted a predictable green, with an oaken staircase built on strong but uninspired lines.

Serena's smile was tense as the butler closed the door behind them. "Is Mama at home?"

Caught studying Azrael with a look of increasing alarm, Bosworth turned to her again. "Wh-why, yes, milady," he said. "Upstairs in the drawing room. Shall I—"

"And Papa?" she interrupted while Azrael remained near the door, hat in hand.

He was rather wondering that himself.

"His Lordship has gone out shooting with your brothers, milady."

Azrael and she exchanged a glance.

On the one hand, he was glad to hear they had a temporary reprieve. Unfortunately, it also meant that when the Dunhaven males returned home, they would be armed.

Perhaps he should worry.

Bosworth hastily took their hats and Serena's mantle and went to hang them up on the coat tree in the corner.

"I'll go tell Her Ladyship you've come," he said, but this proved unnecessary, for at that moment, Lady Dunhaven herself appeared at the top of the staircase.

"Serena!"

They heard her gasp, and looked up.

"Serena, what are you doing here? Is everything all right?" Her mother came running down the stairs in a flurry of footsteps, scanning her daughter with a panicked look.

Damned if Serena didn't look exactly like her mother, thought Azrael. Only the original copy, now in her forties, carried an extra stone of weight on her more statuesque frame, and silver streaks sparkled in her coal-black hair.

Even so, there was such a striking resemblance between them that it was no surprise the countess had got away with her deception since Serena's birth. The daughter looked so much like her dam that it would probably never occur to most people to question the identity of her sire.

The countess had not yet noticed Azrael, standing by the door. "Darling, what are you doing here? Is something wrong?"

"No, Mama, I'm fine." Serena strode to the foot of the staircase, her skirts whisking over the marble floor. "I...I just had to see you."

Clearly taken aback, her mother approached more slowly.

"Mama, I don't want to fight with you anymore," Serena wrenched out.

He could hear the flutter of tears in her voice, and saw an answering look on her mother's face.

The butler took that as his cue to bow out.

"Oh, darling," Lady Dunhaven murmured, her stare locked on her daughter's face. "I don't either."

Azrael hung back, holding his breath at the strangely intimate reunion of two women who obviously loved each other very much.

Their only problem, he suspected, was that maybe they were too much alike. Clashes would've been inevitable.

"Oh, Mama, how I've missed you!" Serena suddenly said, and ran to her.

"Sweeting."

Azrael didn't know where to look when her mother sobbed in answer and reached the bottom step, where she caught her daughter up in a fierce embrace.

They hugged each other hard for a long moment.

Though she'd squeezed her eyes shut, twin tears rolled down Lady Dunhaven's face, an older mirror of her daughter's.

"I'm so sorry, Mama, for fighting with you and for everything you went through," Serena said. "I didn't understand till now. You've suffered so terribly. But I love you. I only want to help."

"My darling girl." Her mother hugged her for all she was worth, then captured her face between her hands. "All that matters is you're here now. I love you so much."

"But, Mama, we really have to talk."

Lady Dunhaven sniffled and nodded. "Yes. You're right, of course. I know."

Azrael waited discreetly, awash in awkwardness.

Lady Dunhaven drew back a bit from her daughter, but kept an arm around her waist. "Come up to the drawing room, darling. We'll take refreshments. This calls for a celebration. I can't believe you're here!"

"Um, Mama, I haven't come alone."

"Is Tamsin here?"

"Er, no." Serena sent a meaningful nod in Azrael's direction.

He lifted his head and took a step forward, offering the countess a wary nod. "Lady Dunhaven."

Her eyes widened. She reached for the banister and steadied herself as the blood drained from her face.

"Rivenwood!" she whispered, staring at Azrael as though a large serpent had just slithered into her house. "What are you doing here?"

"Azrael's the reason I came home to you, Mama," Serena said calmly, hesitating. "I have a lot to tell you."

"But—he can't be here. You shouldn't be here!" Lady Dunhaven cried in fearful tones of reproach.

Serena laid her hand on her mother's forearm. "It's all right, Mama. Azrael is not like his father. Surely you know that. That's why he broke off our betrothal."

"You know about that?" Her mother glanced in shock from her to Azrael. "How much have you told her?"

"Everything I know," he replied.

She gasped. "How could you?"

"She deserves the truth," he said.

"Mama, Azrael's got nothing to do with—the things his father was involved in. He's as much against it as you are, I swear."

Again, her mother glared at him, looking slightly panicked. He took a step closer.

"My lady, I mean you no harm," he said, choosing his words with care. "Your daughter and I have been working together to sort out some unanswered questions from the past. However, there is one piece of information that only you can provide. You know of what I speak," he added in a hard tone, "and on this, you will give my future bride an answer."

Lady Dunhaven looked swiftly at her daughter. *"Bride?"*

He saw Serena brace herself. "Yes, Mother," she said. "We are going to be married."

The countess recoiled. "No!"

"*Yes*, Mama. Yes," Serena said in a softer tone. "I love Azrael, and he loves me." Then she glanced at him, for they had not actually exchanged *I love yous* yet.

But it was true for him, and he rejoiced inwardly to hear her say it. From across the entrance hall, he offered his future wife a tender smile, aware of nothing in that moment but her.

Her lashes fluttered as she read the meaning in his heartfelt gaze, and her lips trembled, then she turned back to her mother.

"We want to be together," she said, "and no one can prevent us. It is already done."

Azrael stood unmoving in the entrance hall, his expression humble but in full accord with Serena's statement.

Glancing from one to the other and back again, at last, the countess seemed to absorb what they were saying.

That they'd already made love.

To his relief, the countess looked more confused than angry about it.

Well, he thought, at least she was no hypocrite. Lady Dunhaven licked her lips and finally gathered her thoughts.

"Both of you, upstairs," she ordered. "It won't do for Papa to see Azrael here first thing when he gets back. Bosworth! Bring us tea in the drawing room," she instructed when the butler came scurrying.

"Yes, Your Ladyship." The little fellow bowed and withdrew.

Serena gave Azrael a reassuring look and beckoned him upstairs, where all three of them repaired to the drawing room.

The countess closed the door behind them, a leery eye fixed on her daughter. "I told you that you were forbidden to go near him."

"Yes, and that was the *only* thing you told me, Mama. If you would've simply shared the rest of the story... But your refusal to talk to me is what sent me seeking answers from Azrael in the first place. He, at least, has been honest with me."

"You're deluded, Serena. You can't trust these people!" Lady Dunhaven cried with an angry gesture at him. "You have no idea how hard I fought to keep you away from all that, and now you've walked right back into the trap. Well, it won't work." She turned to Azrael, her hazel eyes blazing with defiance, the color finally returning to her cheeks. "You cannot have my daughter. I am not going to let you drag her back into that unspeakable—"

"Mother, Azrael wants out, too. He's not one of them," Serena insisted. "Don't you see? That's why he's here. In fact"—she glanced at him—"he means to bring an end to their activities."

"That's part of why we need your help," Azrael added, unmoved by the countess's tirade.

Lady Dunhaven lowered her head and rested her fingers atop the Bible sitting on the table by the couch. Her touchstone seemed to calm her down a bit, though she still trembled visibly.

Serena went over and laid a reassuring hand on her arm. "You can trust him, Mother. Azrael's going to help us. He's a good man, and I love him."

The countess studied him with a dubious frown.

Just then, Bosworth knocked and brought in the tea. No one made any move to touch it or said a word as the servant hurried out, obviously noting the tension.

When he had gone, Azrael looked at the countess. "It's time to come clean, my lady. The more forthcoming you choose to be with information, the better my chances of removing any future threat of danger from these men to you or your family."

She sat down slowly on the sofa but turned her gaze away. "You want to know about Serena's natural father?"

"Yes, Mother." Serena lowered herself to perch tensely on the edge of the sofa. "Please tell us who it was."

The countess was silent, staring out the window at the bleak landscape.

Azrael frowned. "At least explain how it was that you and your husband were permitted to leave the organization."

A low, bitter scoff escaped her.

For a long moment, the countess looked wistfully at Serena, then at him. Then she dropped her gaze to the floor.

"There was only one reason we were allowed to leave," she said in a low tone of disgust. "Because I finally gave Stiver what he wanted."

Serena's eyes widened—and Azrael's heart sank.

"It wasn't just once. That's how I know he was the one." She looked at Serena. "I'm sorry, darling. The Earl of Stiver, he's your father. I had no choice."

Serena laid a comforting hand on her shoulder as the countess forced herself to continue.

"He'd been after me for years, ever since I was a girl and he was but a young man. But I always refused. He made my skin crawl. But once your father died," she said with a grim glance at Azrael, "he only chased me harder. He loved the power he'd come into after taking Rivenwood's place as the leader."

She paused, closing her eyes. "After losing my firstborn because of those people, because of what we all did, I would've paid any price to escape their cursed company, believe me. So I let him have his way." She shuddered. "I dreaded it every time I heard his footsteps on the cellar stairs in the dead of night. I could hear them from my room."

"From the cellar?" Azrael asked.

"He'd use the secret tunnels that connect the five houses through the barrow."

Tunnels? He made a mental note of that while the countess turned to Serena.

"Darling, you must never tell Papa of this. They'd have killed him if they ever thought that he'd become a problem. I promised he would not."

"I won't, Mama," Serena promised, looking overwhelmed.

Lady Dunhaven collected her frayed composure, gazing at her daughter with regret. "You were one of the main reasons Stiver left me alone. When he found out I was carrying his child, he was quite happy about it."

"And you, Mama?"

"I didn't expect to have another baby so soon after losing Georgette. And as I said, I despised him. But, you know, I forgot all my shame at his hands from the moment I beheld your face. So perfect, so strong a babe." She took Serena's hand. "You gripped my finger so hard when you were just a newborn, I used to think you'd pull it off."

Tears in her eyes, Serena clung to her mother's hand.

Lady Dunhaven shook her head. "I did not want to be Stiver's mistress, but I had to pay for my sins. And it was the only way he'd let us go, both me and your papa. I was fortunate that was all he asked." She paused with a shudder. "It could've been worse. Much worse. He took pity on me...because of you, my dear. He was terribly proud of you. That's why he wanted you pledged to the next Duke of Rivenwood. By then, you see, Azrael was also under his control."

Lady Dunhaven glanced at him, perhaps realizing, as he did, the kinship they shared as two of Stiver's former victims.

"He yearned to blend his bloodline with Rivenwood's. Said there'd be no higher honor for the daughter we had made than to pledge her to the next duke. What could I do but agree?

"He held all the power. If I refused, he would've killed Dunny. The only one who ever really loved me. I was not a good wife, but I loved my husband in my own fashion."

The countess blinked away tears. "And so Stiver had me right where he wanted me. Under his thumb." She shrugged. "I went along with the betrothal at the time. However, since I assumed that Azrael would grow up to be just like his father, I always planned to spirit you away somewhere, Serena, before you came of age. Someplace they'd never find you."

She glanced at Azrael again. "Then one day, out of the blue, you came here seeking to dissolve the betrothal, and there was nothing Stiver could do about it. I was never so relieved in all my life.

"Yet I always feared, deep down, that when you saw the beauty she'd grown into, you'd change your mind." The countess shook her head, blotting away a tear. "I knew this would happen. It's the curse again."

"It's not a curse, Mama. We love each other."

"Is a Rivenwood even capable of love?"

Azrael could not hide his wince at her question. He looked away, but Serena frowned at her mother.

"Very much so. Azrael is kind and honorable and gentle with me. You must give him a chance. He only wants to help. Nobody suffered more under the late duke's cruelty than he did."

Her mother glanced over at him uncertainly.

"Come, doesn't the Bible say we must forgive if we wish to be forgiven?" Serena reminded her. "It wasn't Azrael who wronged you, anyway. He was just a child himself then. He had nothing to do with it." She shook her head. "He was just a pawn."

"Yes. I suppose that is true," the countess said quietly, then took a deep breath and looked at Azrael again. "I'm sorry if I misjudged you. My daughter is quite right. You showed honor in releasing her years ago from the arrangement. And even if fate has played its hand, you don't deserve to be held accountable for your father's misdeeds, or your guardian's.

"And if my daughter loves you, then you must have a good heart, whatever your origins, for she's always been much cleverer than me."

Serena hugged her mother after that. At least now she had the answer she'd wanted so badly.

He wondered if she already regretted it. She seemed dazed by the news, not just of her father's identity, but of the price her mother had paid for her freedom.

Mingling their tears, the two women barely seemed aware of him now. Azrael murmured his thanks for Lady Dunhaven's willingness to at least give him a chance, but then stepped out of the room, leaving the pair to mend their bond.

No wonder it had bothered Serena so much to realize her mother had been lying to her all her life, when the countess was practically her best friend, by the look of it.

Himself, he'd never had any sort of intimate family connection like that, but maybe someday he would. Maybe he'd have children of his own to love and get the chance to be a proper sort of father.

All he knew was that, whatever sort of hussy the beautiful Mariah had been in her youth, she seemed to be a doting mother.

He got the feeling that the way she had survived the crushing loss of her firstborn daughter all those years ago was by devoting herself all the more to raising her subsequent children.

As for his former guardian, Azrael was deeply disgusted to hear that Stiver had extorted the woman for sex.

Disgusted, but not surprised. The man had his appetites.

At least now he knew where Serena got her passionate nature.

There were other similarities, as well, now that he reflected on it. Stiver was an intelligent man, handsome for his age, with dapper tastes, and quite healthy, as far as Azrael knew. Physically, at least.

Pondering this new information, Azrael wandered down the stairs to the entrance hall.

He glanced around for the butler, thinking he'd inquire if there was a particular room nearby where he should remove himself to sit and wait for his lady like a good fiancé. What was the little chap's name again?

"Er, Bosworth?" he called down the corridor leading off the entrance hall.

All of a sudden, behind him, the front door barreled open.

"Mariah!" a loud, jovial voice boomed. "Whose carriage is outside? Have we got visitors?"

Azrael spun around and found himself face to face with a large, stout bear of a man—the Earl of Dunhaven.

And his hunting rifle.

The ruddiness instantly drained from Dunny's beefy face. He slammed the door behind him, staring at Azrael like he'd seen a ghost.

"*You!*"

CHAPTER 15

The Past Catches Up

*U*p in the drawing room, Serena and her mother gasped simultaneously at the sound of the door slamming below. They both knew in an instant who it was, and shot to their feet. They were already rushing out of the room as Papa's roar reverberated up from the entrance hall.

"What are you doing here, you demon? You have no further claim on this family! I'll not let another Rivenwood drag us all back down to hell!"

"Papa, no!" Serena cried from the railing of the upstairs hallway, then bolted down the stairs, appalled by what she saw.

With her two hefty younger brothers flanking him, Papa had shoved Azrael against the wall. Dunny had drawn back his meaty fist to strike, but Azrael made no move to defend himself.

The brawny, russet-haired earl looked over his shoulder at the sound of her voice. "Serena? What are you doing home?"

"I'll tell you, but first let him go." She rushed over to her fiancé's side against the wall, ready to protect him however she could.

Azrael cast her a grim look askance.

"George, let His Grace be," Mama ordered, joining them.

"What is going on here, Mariah?" he demanded.

"I will explain, but there is no need for violence. Please, George."

Clearly confused, his bushy reddish eyebrows drawn into a line, Dunhaven released Azrael, stepping back from him with a scowl.

Meanwhile, Serena's two chunky younger brothers, George Jr. and Tom, looked surprised to find their sister home unannounced.

As she stood by Azrael's side, it seemed that even the two boys began to realize there was some sort of mischief afoot. They glanced from her to Azrael with confused suspicion on their round, freckled faces.

Papa also seemed to be putting two and two together. "Someone had better start talking," he growled.

Mama sighed wearily. "They've found each other, George," was all she said.

Incredulity scrunching up his face, Papa looked from Serena to Azrael, and then back at his wife.

"No," he suddenly said. "Absolutely not. You can't have her, you hear me? You gave her up. It's too late."

"Papa!"

"Sir, I love your daughter—"

"You shut your bloody mouth, Rivenwood! I want none of your lies under my roof."

"Papa, I think you're getting Azrael confused with his father. He's not like that. Please—I'm marrying him, and there's nothing you can do to stop us."

"You listen here, cheeky, I am your father!" he bellowed, but Azrael, staring at him in defiance, laid a hand gently—possessively—on Serena's shoulder.

The wordless statement of his protection only enraged Papa more. His broad face reddened. "How dare you touch her?"

"George," Mama said as Azrael removed his hand from her shoulder, his point made.

Serena sent her dam a pleading look. Only her mother could control the old brawler when he lost his temper.

"Listen to me," the countess said in a steady tone, gliding over to his side. "He is not the villain we assumed, my love. They won't be dissuaded."

"Over my dead body," Dunny said.

"Darling," the countess said quietly to her husband, "they have to marry now."

"*What?*"

Her brothers' eyes popped open wide, the puppyish seventeen-year-old, George Jr., with a start of indignation, understanding. But Tom, age fourteen, looked bewildered.

"Why?" he mumbled.

No one answered.

George Jr. growled. Serena gave him a quick sisterly glare that said *shut up*.

Papa, however, let out a curse word that Serena had never heard him use before, then called Azrael the son of Lucifer.

But when he lifted his rifle and aimed it at him, she shrieked in terror, Azrael drew back against the wall, and Mama stepped in the way, pushing the barrel toward the ceiling.

"Stop it," she commanded in a steely tone. "They are in love. We will not destroy our daughter's happiness."

"He's ruined her, he's stolen her, and happiness is what you call it?" Dunny retorted. "This is your doing, Mariah. You're the one who spoiled her."

Mama stared fearlessly at him, though her mate towered over her. "Give him a chance."

Something in her stare brought Papa to heel, just as it always had.

He lowered his weapon with a growl.

Serena's pulse pounded and her stomach churned, but although Papa glared at his wife, he did not try to prevent her from lifting his gun out of his grasp.

Lady Dunhaven handed the hunting rifle off to Tom with a look that needed no words, ordering him to take it away, and to get his brother's gun, as well.

The milder-tempered fourteen-year-old went over to ask for his elder brother's rifle, to return to the gun case.

George Jr. tried to resist being disarmed, but Mama hissed at him, and the big, husky seventeen-year-old handed his gun over to his younger brother with a sulk, then glared at Azrael.

Tom marched off to put their weapons in the gun case.

Papa just shook his head at Serena, disappointment stamped all over his face.

She struggled for something to say. "I'm sorry, Papa," she said, scarlet-faced over her willing role in her own seduction.

The big man simply scoffed, glowered once more at his future son-in-law, then stomped out of the entrance hall to disappear into his study down the hallway.

Serena shut her eyes for a second, then turned to make sure Azrael was all right.

"I think I'd better leave," he murmured.

"Please do!" George Jr. huffed.

"Junior, for heaven's sake, go take off your muddy boots!" Mama said.

The lad gave Azrael a parting glower just like Papa's, but he obeyed Mama as surely as his father had.

Serena sent her mother a look of thanks, then touched Azrael's arm gently. "Don't go anywhere yet," she murmured. "Let me talk to him first. I'm sure he'll come around. Just give us a few minutes."

"Perhaps I should come with you."

"God, no. Stay back—just don't leave." As she hurried after Papa, her mother and Azrael stood in the entrance hall gazing awkwardly at each other. She could hear their exchange.

"Thanks for saving my life," he said drily.

"He wouldn't have done it," Mama assured him.

Serena paused outside the open door to Lord Dunhaven's study. It was officially a library, but she was fairly sure he had never read a single book in there.

She closed her eyes to steady herself before going in, embarrassed at having to own up to her seduction. Yet she was not ashamed of what they'd done last night, and felt no regret whatsoever.

They were going to marry, anyway. She reminded herself of what Azrael had said in the coach—their becoming lovers was nothing compared to some of her parents' antics when they were their age.

Bolstered by these thoughts, she flicked her eyes open and stepped cautiously over the threshold.

Lord Dunhaven was sitting on a leather ottoman with his back to her, staring into the unlit fireplace, and holding a small glass of scotch.

"Papa?"

He huffed but did not turn around, grumbling something under his breath about beautiful women being too damned difficult to manage.

Serena stopped just inside the doorway, twisting her clasped fingers together. As angry as he was—rightfully so, in hindsight—she agreed with Mama. He would not really have pulled the trigger on Azrael.

Punched him, yes. Shot him, no.

He didn't have it in him.

Indeed, now that she had the answer she'd sought for so long about the identity of her natural father, all the evidence she'd read about Lord Stiver from the snakeskin box, and both Mama and Azrael's accounts of what sort of man he was, she appreciated Papa all the more.

"I'm sorry I upset you, Papa." She hung back near the door. "But I beg you to understand. Azrael and I have fallen in love."

"Cursed," he ground out with a scoff. He shook his head and kept his back to her. "Fool girl! All I ever wanted was to protect your mother and this family—but off you go, headstrong as she was, dancin' with your own destruction. You have no idea what you're dealing with."

"Actually, Papa, I do. Azrael is not a part of his father's cult. He never was. Unlike you and Mama."

He turned around at last, looking stunned not merely by her impertinent reproach, but to hear that she'd found out about her parents' wild youth.

"Did you two think you could hide it from me forever? I know about my sister, too."

He flinched and lowered his head.

Serena held her ground. "I'm sorry for everything you both went through, but there was no need to hide her existence from me."

"It was too painful," he said. "Your mother feared even to speak of it. As if talking about it would make it happen again. To you. Or the boys."

"Well, just so you know, Azrael has nothing to do with his father's group. He hates it," she said. "He's always hated everything about it. In fact"—she hesitated—"he means to destroy it."

"Is that so?" He raised his head to eye her skeptically.

She nodded. "All those wicked men you used to know, his father's friends, he's going to fight them."

"How?"

"I don't know. But he means to see them brought to justice, and I believe in him."

"Huh." The big, gruff earl lurched up from the ottoman and came over to her, lifting her chin with his fingertips. He stared into her eyes. "Just one question, Serena, and you tell your papa the truth. Did he force himself on you?"

"What? No!"

"Did he trick you? Manipulate you? Scare you into it?"

"No, Papa!" she exclaimed, shaking her head. "Azrael would never do such a thing! He's a good man. That's why I chose him. Come, Papa, you always said I was a down-to-earth, sensible girl. Do you not trust my judgment?"

He studied her, debating this with himself, and she could fairly see the wheels turning in his mind. "Fight them, you say?"

She nodded.

He snorted all of a sudden. "Well, I want in on that." Without warning, he marched back out to the entrance hall.

Baffled, Serena scrambled after him in a rustle of skirts.

When he strode back out to the entrance hall, Azrael came to attention.

"She says you're going to fight 'em," Dunny declared as he came to stand before the duke, feet planted wide, arms akimbo.

Azrael nodded.

"You swear this is true?"

"Yes, my lord."

"Good. But you'll need help. Junior! Pack your bags!" he bellowed.

"Sir, no!" Azrael exclaimed, as aghast at this prospect as both Dunhaven women were.

"George, what are you thinking?" Mama said, going ashen. "You cannot be involved in this, and neither can my son. He's just a boy! I can't lose my child, or you."

"I owe those sons o' bitches, Mariah, and you know why." He slanted her a hard look. "Especially Stiver."

Utter silence dropped.

For the three of them—Serena, Azrael, and the countess—all knew what thickheaded old Dunny was saying in that moment.

He knew.

He'd known all this time that Serena wasn't his.

"I'm not quite as dense as you think, love," he said softly to his horrified wife.

Lady Dunhaven covered her mouth with both hands and fled the entrance hall in tears.

Serena and Azrael glanced at each other in shock.

Papa watched her go, making no move to follow.

Just then, Junior peered over the edge of the railing above. "Did you call me, sir?"

"Pack your things, lad. We're going to London."

Tom flung eagerly up to the railing beside his elder brother. "Can I come, too?"

"No."

"Aww, why does he get to do everything?" the youngest whined.

"Sir," Azrael broke in, "I appreciate the offer, truly, but I most assuredly do not need your help, or your boy's. Any information you can share that I might not know about would be welcome, but leave the battle to me, I implore you. Once things are set in motion, you'll be needed here to protect your family."

"Papa, Azrael has a plan," Serena said, barely recovered from learning that her mother's "secret" had been no secret from her husband after all.

"Oh really? Let's hear it." Dunny propped his giant fists on his waist. "Must be quite ingenious if you think you can take these bleeders on yourself. Or maybe you command the spirits like your sire did, eh? Got an army of devils to come and assist you?"

"On the contrary, sir. I'm taking my case to the Order of St. Michael the Archangel."

Papa fell silent for a moment, and the grim way he looked at Azrael worried Serena. "You sure about that? You go callin' on those boys, mate, you might never come back. Far as I know, those chaps make men with your kind of bloodlines disappear. Permanently."

"Azrael?" Serena asked with mounting alarm.

"It'll be all right," he said, then addressed the earl again. "Our paths have crossed before. I was approached when I was just a lad by one of their agents. He offered me the Order's help if I ever wished to turn informant. Well, now's the time. It may be over twenty years after the fact, but better late than never."

Papa sized him up. "You pull this off and, aye, I'll let you marry my daughter."

Behind him, Serena rolled her eyes. She was legally old enough to wed whoever she wanted, and Papa knew it. It was just bluster.

She looked at Azrael, who sent her a discreet look of amusement.

"Well then, in that case, sir, I'd best be about my task." He cleared his throat a bit. "I bid you a good day, sir. Gentlemen." He nodded to the boys still standing at the top of the stairs, listening to everything. "Lady Serena. Please give the countess my regards."

With that, he gave her family a formal bow, then headed for the door.

"Where are you going?" Papa asked when Serena hurried after him.

"To see him out."

"Humph. Don't take too long. And no kissing!"

Tom feigned a gagging noise at that.

Azrael let himself out without further comment, and Serena cringed at how he'd been treated as she stepped outside after him, pulling the door shut behind her.

"Must you go?"

"Oh, I think it's advisable," he said drily. "I've already intruded enough."

She winced, turning to him. "I'm so sorry."

He smiled. "I don't think it went too badly, do you?"

She gave him an arch look, wishing she had grabbed her mantle. It was cold out. "Where will you go?"

He took both her hands in his. "I'm heading back to London before he insists on 'helping' me and gets us both killed. Don't mistake me, he's a good man. But I'm afraid His Lordship has got all the subtlety of a bulldog with a blunderbuss, and I'm sure this will be a very delicate operation, requiring finesse. I don't want the boy involved, either."

She nodded. "I understand. Still, I hate to see you go." She paused. "Maybe I could come with you."

"No, darling, you stay here and smooth things over with your family. I daresay we've given everyone enough of a shock with our announcement. Besides, it appears your parents have a few personal matters to sort out privately. They don't need me here, getting in the way." He glanced at her, reading her face. "At least now you finally got your answer."

"Ugh." She shook her head, still at a loss over the price her mother had paid to gain her freedom. "Well, you might as well say it, Azrael."

"Say what?"

"*I told you so.* You warned me I wouldn't like the answer I would find, and you were right."

He smiled ruefully. "I'm not going to say it. But I did."

Laughing softly, she slipped her arms around his waist, then gazed up at him for a moment. "I hope I didn't overstep my bounds with what I said to Mama in the drawing room. I didn't mean to put words in your mouth. Mainly, I just wanted to put her mind at ease about the two of us."

His gaze caressed her. "You mean when you told her you love me and that I love you?"

She nodded shyly. "It's true for me, I know that much. But if it's too soon, it's all right, you don't have to say it—"

"Serena," he interrupted in a silken whisper, capturing her face between his hands. He stared into her eyes. "*I love you.*"

Then he lowered his head and gave her a deep, slow, luscious kiss, gathering her into his arms. Serena's heart soared at his ardent answer.

She lifted her arms around his neck and returned his kisses with breathless abandon.

At length, their kiss ended, and he rested his forehead against hers.

"I never thought I'd ever feel this way about anyone," he breathed. "Thank you for loving me."

"Oh, sweeting." Standing on her toes, she hugged him tenderly, then closed her eyes and rested her head on his broad shoulder.

One arm around her waist, Azrael caressed her hair with his other hand. "Listen, it's cold out here. You should get back inside, and I really should go," he murmured after a moment. "Once all this is over, then our lives together can really begin."

She conceded this with a pensive nod and somehow found the strength to let him go. "Promise me you'll be careful."

"I promise." He stepped back, but held on to her hands, his gaze locked on hers.

"Write to me and let me know you're safe, or I'll go mad with worry."

"I will, and no you won't." He smiled with gentle affection. "You'll be too busy planning our wedding."

She beamed at that.

"Which reminds me. I've got to find you a ring when I get back to Town."

"In due time, Your Grace. I think you'll have your hands full enough as it is."

"I'll send for you as soon as it's safe."

"I love you," she told him.

"And I adore you." He leaned down and pressed another firm kiss to her lips, then tore himself away.

She winced, watching him stride toward his carriage.

Paulson saw him coming, and got the door.

"Get back inside before you catch your death."

She ignored her fiancé's command, but folded her arms across her chest to ward off the chill. Worry for him still plagued her.

"Azrael, if it's really as dangerous for you to go to the Order as Papa said, maybe it isn't a good idea."

"I'll be fine. I still have that fellow's signet ring, remember? It's back at my house in Moonlight Square. That and the box of unpleasantness will be sure to make a fine peace offering for them. I'm not worried."

Liar. You're very brave, she thought with an ache as she stood outside the manor's front door. The hard truth, she suspected, was simply that there was no other way.

"Come back to me unscathed, do you understand?"

"Yes, ma'am. I'll miss you."

"I'll miss you more."

"Well, we'll have to make up for it next time we're together."

A flirtatious, blushing laugh escaped her at his innuendo. "I'm game, Your Grace."

He stopped, staring at her. "God, look at you. How am I to leave when you smile at me like that? Hold on, Paulson. Just one more."

Azrael jogged back and swept her up in his arms, lifting her off her feet as he claimed one last, urgent kiss, hurried and hungry.

It sent her world spinning and heated her blood from the bleak day's chill. She kissed him back for all she was worth, loath to ever let him go.

"Mm, that'll inspire me," he murmured, releasing her again. Then he tapped her on the nose. "I'll see you as soon as it's safe, my love."

She heaved a sigh, pained as he pulled away again. "Oh very well. Go, then! Before I tie you up and keep you here."

"That could be fun," he said, flashing a roguish smile over his shoulder. "Homeward, Paulson!" he called as he marched away, his step light.

"Very good, Your Grace." Paulson held the coach door.

"Send for me if there's any way I can assist," Serena called. "You know I'm not afraid."

"Indeed I do, my daring lady. You never shrink from a challenge, do you? I like that." Then he blew her a kiss and sprang up into the coach.

Serena flinched a little when his driver shut the door, separating them.

"Achoo!"

"Bless you, Paulson. And thanks for everything. I hope you feel better soon."

"Thank ye, milady." The cheerful coachman bowed to her, but sneezed loudly again before swinging back up onto the driver's box.

Serena winced. She still felt guilty about the man's cold.

Then she waved as the coach rolled into motion, and somehow kept the smile plastered on her face. She refused to give in to the shadow that their parting had cast across her heart.

Through the window, Azrael blew her a seductive kiss full of patient promise as the carriage circled the turnaround, with its center fountain, before trundling off down the tree-lined drive.

She offered up a silent prayer for his protection, remaining outside with her arms wrapped around herself until his coach had disappeared.

CHAPTER 16

Angels & Demons

zrael made it back to his house in Moonlight Square late the next afternoon.

"Well done, Paulson," he said to his driver, who was blowing his nose into a large handkerchief. "I've imposed on you enough since we left. Feel free to take a couple of days off, and do get well."

"Dat's very gederous of you, sir. Achoo!"

"Bless you. God's sakes, man, you should be in bed."

"Aye, sir." Paulson chuckled, his jovial nature none the worse for wear.

Azrael ordered his grooms to take care of the horses and put the coach away, then sent a footman to draw a hot bath for his ailing driver and to look after him.

When he went inside, missing Serena but glad to be in his cozy home, he was startled to find Grimsley beside himself with worry.

"Your Grace!" the old man burst out with an unprecedented display of feeling. The butler's bony face was drawn into an expression of alarm fit to rival the wee gargoyles perched atop the fluted pilasters as he rushed forward to take the snakeskin box out of Azrael's arms for him. "Is everything all right, sir? You were gone three days! I was beginning to fear something dreadful had befallen you."

"I'm fine, Grimsley," Azrael said. He immediately reproached himself for worrying his staff. It was easy to forget that his longtime servants were well aware of the enemies he had out there in the world. "We had a slight change of plans on the road, that is all. Sorry to have worried you. I trust everything is in order here at home?"

"Well, yes, sir—of course, Master Raja requires your attention. He's been rather bored."

"Ah." Azrael slipped off his greatcoat.

"And there's an abundance of mail for you, as well. Including a letter from the Archbishop of Canterbury's offices," Grimsley added, raising an eyebrow.

"Yes?" Azrael couldn't help but grin. "Bring it to me at once."

Grimsley hurried off to set the snakeskin box in the library and find His Excellency's reply among the many letters on the mail tray on Azrael's desk.

When he returned with the envelope, Azrael took it nervously, braced himself, and cracked the holy man's letter open.

He read it and looked up slowly from the paper a moment later, wonderstruck.

Grimsley was staring at him. "Good news or ill, Your Grace?" he asked.

The question snapped Azrael back to reality. He blinked off his daze. "The best news possible, Grimsley." He suddenly laughed, which in itself was enough to shock his butler. "I'm getting married."

He held up the letter as proof, and Grimsley's jaw dropped.

The letter contained the Archbishop's blessing on the match, along with instructions on how to collect the special license—and where to pay the exorbitant fee for the convenience it secured.

"Don't tell the rest of the staff yet, though," he instructed. "Only Paulson knows so far. But the girl I drove out to the country with, she will soon become the lady of the house."

"You found your duchess," Grimsley said, amazed.

"I have. And she is...magnificent." He clapped his butler heartily on the shoulder, shocking him anew with the simple contact.

"Er, c-congratulations, sir!"

"Thank you very much, Grimsley. I can hardly believe it myself. Well! Much to do. Have them draw me a bath, would you? I haven't changed my clothes in three bloody days. His Grace stinks." He began marching away to go and reassure the leopard he was home. "Oh—and Grimsley?"

"Yes, sir?" the ordinarily gloomy fellow asked, blinking out of his daze.

"Do make sure to have the staff look after Paulson. It snowed, and the poor man caught a dreadful cold."

Gaelen Foley

"Should I send for the physician, sir?"

He shrugged. "That's up to him."

The butler bowed, then Azrael jogged up the ornate wooden staircase, his mood buoyant, his steps light. It was good to be back, and he couldn't wait to share his home with Serena.

After he had paid his respects to the lonely and disgruntled leopard, who was quite cross at him for his absence, Azrael retired to his chamber to find the steaming bath waiting for him, set up next to the crackling fire.

He quickly stripped, noting the dried copper trace of Serena's maiden blood that had lightly brushed the inside of his drawers when he'd dressed again after making love to her. The memory of that night filled him with anticipation, and he sank down into the hot bath with a sigh of pleasure.

As he rested his head back against the tub, he still couldn't believe that he had seduced her, or for that matter, all that had transpired between them. It stunned him to contemplate how that little vixen had sneaked into his masked ball and proceeded to upend his quiet, orderly existence altogether.

He'd tried, God knew he'd tried to fight the attraction. But he'd failed completely.

And he'd never been happier.

Good thing I didn't accidentally drop her off the balcony that first night, he thought, chuckling to himself, and savoring the memories of all that had occurred between them.

To be sure, dwelling on the joy she brought him was better than brooding on the uncertainty of his venture tonight.

Unfortunately, the reprieve did not last long.

For within an hour, he had dug out the dead agent's signet ring from its hiding place in the jewelry box with his cufflinks and cravat pins; he ordered his phaeton made ready with fresh horses under harness; and for a driver, he secured the assistance of his wily footman, Jenkins—the same discreet fellow he had previously sent to spy on Lord Toby.

Going out in a carriage again was the last thing he felt like doing, but he was eager to get this mission underway, the sooner to have it over with.

And so, with the Order signet ring tucked into his waistcoat pocket and the snakeskin box of his father's papers on the seat beside him, Azrael set out for Dante House. The agent had insisted the eerie old

Tudor mansion on the Strand, believed by the world at large to house the notorious Inferno Club, was actually the Order's headquarters.

What mattered was that this was the place where he'd been told he might find allies against his father's henchmen.

He only hoped it wasn't too late.

Before long, Jenkins drew the phaeton to a halt outside of the decrepit-looking black mansion on the Strand. Its twisty spires rose like devil horns reaching for the stars, and Azrael mused on the irony of it—how all the members of the exclusive Inferno Club posed as decadent rakehells of the most godforsaken stripe to keep prying eyes away, while his father's Promethean brethren usually presented themselves as pillars of society. They pooh-poohed the gossip about them as malicious rumors.

Of course, the previous Duke of Rivenwood had refused to hide behind such masks. He had been insolently open about his fascination with the occult. No wonder the Order had sent that agent to investigate him, but Father's untimely death must've brought their interest in him to a halt.

No doubt they wondered what had happened to their agent. No one had ever come inquiring, though, so maybe the "vagrant" had been working independently and his superiors hadn't even known he had gone there.

Azrael had heard these gentlemen were given a great deal of latitude on how they operated. The fact that they answered directly to the sovereign without a complicated chain of command, as with military intelligence units, no doubt proved a boon.

At any rate, his answers on the tragic fate of their agent was only one of the many riches he could share with them tonight, if they were willing to help him in return.

For a moment, nervously drumming his fingers atop the snakeskin box on the seat beside him, Azrael studied Dante House. The Thames ran behind it, slick and glimmering with oily reflections.

As he waited for Jenkins to come and get the door, he noted that the broad avenue was quite deserted at this late hour. It worried him that Dante House looked forsaken, too. What in the world was he going to do if the Order was no longer here or had disbanded?

The question left him floundering. He had staked everything—his future with Serena—on these fellows helping him. If they refused, or worse, if they were all gone, he truly did not know what else to try.

Dread skittered through him, but he shunted it aside, grabbed the box, and alighted from the phaeton. He turned to his trusty servant, shifting the leather cask under one arm.

Jenkins looked uneasy, his breath clouding around him in the windy chill along the river. "Are you sure you don't want me to go to the door for you, sir?"

"No—and I do not wish you to tell anyone else on the staff that I came here, either."

"Understood, sir," Jenkins said with a nod.

Azrael glanced up at the spiked wrought-iron fence that girded in the property. If this place indeed housed a nest of spies for the Crown, then those gates were more than just a remnant of centuries-old fortifications. And if that represented the place's first line of its defenses, then any sort of traps might wait for him inside.

He looked again grimly at his man. "Wait for me for half an hour. If I do not reappear by that time, you may go. And, er, if I have not come home by morning... Well, I do not know what to suggest in that case, actually. Because it probably means I'm dead or in a dungeon somewhere."

The footman's eyes widened. "Shall I go to the authorities in that case, sir? Lead them here? The Bow Street boys could storm the property—"

"Ah, there would be no point." Azrael sighed, for after all, these men were the heroes of the play, while he was of the villains' party, at least by birth. "This place, you see, is not what it appears, Jenkins." He gave him a taut half-smile. "Let's just hope for the best."

With that, Azrael strode toward the spear-tipped gate, hauled it open, and winced when it let out an earsplitting metallic creak.

"Right," he whispered to himself, squaring his shoulders. "Wish me luck, Jenkins."

"Good luck, Your Grace." Jenkins squinted at his fob watch to mark the time, then stood by the horses, worriedly clutching his hat.

With the snakeskin box under one arm, Azrael marched up to the house and gave a confident rap on the door. He arched a brow as a clamor of vicious canine barking immediately assaulted the other side.

"Egads," he murmured, then quickly took the dead agent's ring out of his waistcoat pocket. He'd better have it ready, if that was any indication of the welcome he was likely to receive.

He heard shouts in some foreign tongue from behind the door, and eventually, the pack of dogs quieted. Azrael braced himself and lifted his chin when the portal swung open with an eerie moan.

"Good evening," rasped an old, gray butler who resembled a reanimated skeleton. He was a small man; the heads of the half-dozen thickly muscled black-and-tan guard dogs seated in a deadly arc behind him were nearly up to his waist.

Azrael hid his blanch.

The butler narrowed his eyes at Azrael in disapproval, as though he had been woken from the grave to answer the bloody door. "May I help you?"

Azrael steeled himself. The moment had come to see if that agent twenty-two years ago had been telling the truth. *God help me if he wasn't.*

With a crisp, precise motion, Azrael lifted the dead agent's ring and showed its insignia to the butler. "I am the Duke of Rivenwood," he said. "I've come to see the Order of St. Michael."

The butler cocked a bushy pewter eyebrow at the ring, then gave him a deadened look. "I'm sorry, sir. I fear you have the wrong address. This place houses the Inferno Club. Members only."

"Yes, I've heard. Nevertheless, do me the honor of presenting that trinket to your master. And then we'll see if I have the right place."

The dogs growled behind the old man.

Who looked exceedingly annoyed. "Your name again?" he grumbled.

"Rivenwood," Azrael replied, all the more convinced the Order of St. Michael was indeed here, for this was not how a normal butler behaved.

This old chap had obviously been paid for many years to keep visitors away. "You may tell your masters that I have some rather interesting information for the...gentlemen of the club."

The butler scrutinized him. "As you wish. Perhaps you should step in, sir. It is a ghastly night." He opened the door wider after taking a wary glance at the ring.

It was a curious thing to say, for the weather seemed the only normal thing about this night, at least in his estimation. But while Azrael appreciated the invitation to enter, he looked at the white-fanged, panting dogs and couldn't help but hesitate.

The butler gave the pack another order in what Azrael now identified as German, then glanced expectantly at Azrael, who took a wary step over the threshold. "May I tell my master what is in the box, sir?"

Azrael duly lifted the lid to show it contained no weapon, merely papers and books.

"A peace offering of sorts. I'm sure they will find its contents most enlightening." Then he closed it again and offered the cask to the strange old man, his heart pounding.

He could feel that they were being watched all the while, and not by just the dogs, whose black eyes shone with eagerness to tear him limb from limb.

Someone unseen was sizing him up, and had no doubt heard their whole exchange.

To be sure, a visitor here must be a rarity.

Azrael glanced around to see if he could spot the unseen watcher's hiding place. Unfortunately, the florid décor concealed it too well.

The inside of Dante House was as gaudy as one would expect for a gentlemen's club that was said to be comprised of London's worst scoundrels. From its red velvet furniture to its sticky floors, the place had the feel of a decadent brothel.

It smelled of mustiness, which was why he'd left the door open behind him, but the butler reached past him and shoved in closed. Azrael heard it automatically lock.

"Remain here, please. I will take these items to my master." The ancient guardian of the house then gave the dogs an order that Azrael very much hoped meant *Heel!*

Instead, the command apparently meant *Stay*, for the dogs sat planted, keeping him pinned against the wall where he stood.

"I shall alert the master you are here." Having taken the snakeskin box and the ring, the butler pulled on a bell rope, but large as the hulking mansion was, Azrael did not hear the clang at the other end. The old man started to walk away, but paused. "For your own safety, I very much suggest you stay exactly where you are—Your Grace," he added skeptically, as though he did not entirely believe that Azrael was who he claimed to be.

Azrael frowned.

Then the butler marched away slowly into the depths of the house, leaving Azrael cornered by the half-dozen slavering beasts.

The seconds ticked by like hours while he waited, and a bead of sweat gathered on his brow. He was besieged by gory visions of being eaten.

But Azrael soon discovered that it wasn't really the dogs who were the dangerous ones here, as three large men came sauntering out of the shadows, approaching from the hallway down which the butler had gone.

Astonished, Azrael recognized them from Parliament—they were all his fellow peers. Good God, the Marquess of Rotherstone!

He wasn't much for ton gossip, but the last he'd heard, Rotherstone had been making a drunken nuisance of himself on a highly inappropriate Grand Tour of Europe, never mind the war in progress. He watched the battles like a tourist, according to rumor.

Black-haired and gray-eyed, the marquess's presence was tolerated by the officers because the man was said to be as rich as Croesus.

Meanwhile, in the center of the trio towered the rugged and fearsome Duke of Warrington, who usually stayed at his castle in Cornwall, having his way with the local wenches, so Azrael had heard.

To Warrington's left was the more quietly lethal and urbane Earl of Falconridge, a highly clever man by repute. He was supposed to be some sort of diplomat to Russia.

But Azrael stood there astonished to realize that the stories of where these highborn fellows had been for the past few years, and what they'd supposedly been doing, were utter cock-and-bull tales.

Or rather, cover stories.

At the moment, to be sure, not a one of them looked like rakehells in the slightest.

They looked like trained killers.

Closing in on him.

From an adjoining room stepped a hearty-framed fellow of about sixty, with fierce eyes, bushy auburn hair streaked with gray, and a short red beard. Azrael did not know him, but the older man had the snakeskin box in his grasp now, as well as the agent's ring.

The master of the house, Azrael concluded at once. *Spymaster is more like it.*

Clearly, the older fellow was in charge here, and had probably been the one eavesdropping on his conversation with the butler.

"I'm Virgil," he said with a strong Scottish brogue. "And ye're probably a dead man, comin' here. What is the meaning of this?"

"I've come in peace and in the hopes that we might be of mutual benefit to each other."

Rotherstone scoffed, while Falconridge shook his head, looking amazed. "Rivenwood, of all people," the blond diplomat murmured.

"Promethean scum," mumbled Warrington. Azrael then noticed a black cloth hood dangling from his fellow duke's massive clenched fist.

"Son of a bitch! I don't believe this," Rotherstone said to his colleagues. "We're off risking our bloody necks to fight them in Europe, and he's operating a bloody Prome cell right here at home?"

"No, you're wrong," Azrael said, but the marquess drew a knife, his wolfish stare fixed on him.

"Virgil, let me do the honors."

"Gut him, Max," growled Warrington.

"Wait," the Scot ordered, holding up his hand, much to Azrael's relief. "Let him explain himself first."

"My lords," Azrael forced out, nodding at the box, "I'm not operating anything. But you're right, there is a coven here, and I know who's involved. I want them gone as much as you do."

"Lies. Never trust one of their kind," Warrington said, glowering at him.

"But this is unheard of," Falconridge murmured to his colleagues. "A Promethean simply waltzing up to our front door and popping in for a visit? What game are you playing, Rivenwood?"

"This is no game. I have information. Lots of it," Azrael said, losing patience with their doubt, though it had probably been drilled into them from the same age Azrael had been when his father and company had started loading up his brain with hatred of the light.

Only, their training had never quite taken.

He hoped to God these people at least gave him a chance. "I've brought you this cache of their records. I'm sure you'll find it useful."

"We'll see about that," Virgil said, then glanced at his agents. "Bag him, lads, and take him to the Pit."

The three moved on him at once, and the next thing Azrael knew, the black cloth hood was over his head, blinding him and stifling his breath. Good God, Dunny wasn't jesting. They seemed quite expert in abduction.

Shoved and jostled about, Azrael lifted his hands and offered no resistance. But fear of their intentions spurted cold in his veins, and his heart pounded with the question: *What the hell is the Pit?*

❖

Serena sat by the window in her bedchamber, staring out anxiously at the black night.

Worry clawed at her insides, for she knew that by now, Azrael would have reached London. He might be knocking on the Order's door at this very moment.

And she might never see him again.

Her bedroom door creaked, and in the reflection of the windowpane, like a black mirror, she saw her mother peek into her chamber. "May I come in?"

"Of course, Mama." She managed a fond smile, feeling closer than ever to her mother now that she understood her so much more.

"My, you are in love with him, aren't you?" the countess teased upon finding her daughter brooding.

But knowing Azrael had changed Serena. Everything she'd been through these past few months had. To think now she'd be his duchess, his wife...

"I'm so worried about him, Mama. Do you think he's safe?" she whispered as her mother came into her bedchamber.

As she approached, Serena noticed that the countess looked weary and drained from the emotional tumult of the past two days.

Yesterday, through the walls of Dunhaven Manor, Serena and her brothers had heard the muffled sounds of their parents' tearful exchange as they faced the reckoning of their past.

From what she'd overheard—certainly without trying to—Papa had made up his mind early on to love his beautiful Mariah in spite of her unfaithfulness, and to accept Stiver's by-blow as his own. He'd never said a word about it to spare his wife's pride and his own, because he knew why she had done it.

All these years, he'd been as ashamed about his powerlessness to free them from the Prometheans' clutches as Mama had been about the exploitation she'd endured as payment for their safe exit.

Serena was already learning to despise Lord Stiver for what he'd put her parents through.

At least now, thank God, all their family secrets and lies were coming out into the light, where they could be resolved. But one thing was certain. Whatever may have happened in the past between her parents, it was plain that they loved each other very much now.

Serena found it very touching. She just hoped she'd get the chance to grow old with Azrael like her parents were doing.

"Try to have a little faith, my love." As Mama sat down in the window seat beside Serena, she seemed different, worn out but more peaceful. The countess offered a smile and shivered a bit. "It's drafty over here. Are you warm enough?"

Serena just shrugged. Even if she had a hundred blankets on her, she'd have still been cold with fear, not knowing Azrael's fate.

Mama laid her hand on Serena's forearm. "He's kept himself alive so far, hasn't he?"

Serena nodded tensely. "He's very intelligent. And courageous. He's had to be, to outwit these people ever since he was a boy."

"Considering his influences, it's a wonder he has a soul at all."

"Oh, he does," Serena said with a pang in her heart. "What was he like as a boy, Mama? Did you know him then?"

"Yes, but not very well. From a distance, mainly. Especially after Stiver chose him for your husband. You were just a newborn and Azrael was a lad of thirteen. For his part, he had no idea about the match for years, by the way. But I knew. So I kept something of an eye on him, since I assumed he would eventually be your husband. Lo and behold, now he will."

Serena searched her mother's eyes anxiously, craving more details. It helped take her mind off the danger she just knew in her heart that he was in. "How did he seem to you then?"

"Quiet, a bit shy, *very* self-controlled. Wary of everybody. He always seemed very deliberate and careful to me. Well, except when he was around all those silly animals. Then he lit up and acted like a normal child. Animated, laughing, relaxed. His father collected exotic animals, you see—I have no idea why; he probably liked having things in cages. The Rivenwoods had a menagerie at one of their estates at one point."

Mama shrugged. "I just remember being relieved to see that side of him and to notice how kind he was to the creatures. Given his father's cruelty, I was worried how he'd treat you. But you know, I thought even then that those poor animals seemed to be his only friends. I daresay they probably saved his life."

Serena fought back tears. To think of how people called him eccentric and a recluse back in London infuriated her.

They had no idea what he'd been through. What had made him that way. She repented that she'd ever thought the same.

She shook her head and made a private vow that once they were married, she would fill his life with joy and all the love that he'd missed out on in his youth.

If he survived this.

She glanced out the window again, worried sick about him.

Mama caressed her hair. "It's in God's hands, my love."

Serena was in no mood for her mother's religiosity right now, and bit her lip against a flash of impatience.

Faith was the evidence of things not seen, and she was desperate for solid proof that the man she loved was safe.

"I will pray for him," Mama said softly. "I suggest you do the same."

Serena nodded, a lump in her throat. There didn't seem much *else* that she could do for him right now. She hated the helplessness she felt, simply waiting for word.

Gazing out restlessly into the darkness on the other side of the glass, Serena tried to take heart. But it seemed like she'd lose either way.

If anything happened to Azrael, she'd be shattered.

Of course, if his quest succeeded, then her real father would probably die at the hands of the Order before she ever got to meet him.

She had no idea how to feel about that.

The worst part was this deep-down, gnawing fear that had taken hold of her tonight. It whispered that the so-called curse on their families—the one she didn't believe in—might yet rise up somehow to wreck their newfound happiness.

"Mama?" She looked at her mother, eager to hear her say that it was all nonsense. "You and the others back then didn't *really* think you had been cursed, did you?"

"Oh, I know we were," the countess said, a shadow passing behind her eyes.

Serena furrowed her brow. "So you really believe in that stuff, then? Just like Toby?"

The countess considered for a moment. "Let me ask you a question. Do you believe in angels, Serena? Guardian angels and such?"

The question surprised her, but she shrugged. "Actually, I do, I suppose."

"Well, if they're real, wouldn't that mean the other kind exist as well? Evil spirits, demons. Not as strong as the good side, but just as real."

Serena eyed her uncertainly. "You really do sound like Toby now."

"All I know is that curse took its toll. Misfortune struck everyone involved. We should never have opened that barrow." She shuddered and lowered her gaze, obviously loath to say more. "But if there can be tangible blessings in life, like a beautiful daughter or good health, then why not curses, too? I know there are demons," she added. "I've met them."

A chill ran down Serena's spine; she sat stock-still, pondering this.

Her mother fell silent and looked away with a small sigh. "I should like to meet an angel someday."

I already have. Serena wrapped her arms more tightly around herself, missing Azrael with every fiber of her being.

It struck her then that that was what he really looked like, with his shining hair and pale blue eyes—not a fey prince, but a beautiful angel, celestial and strange.

Perhaps his father hadn't been so far off the mark when he had named his son after the archangel of death.

And given Azrael's vow to wreak destruction on his enemies, it seemed the time had come for her beloved to live up to his dark and terrible name.

Azrael was scowling when a rough, unseen hand pulled the sack serving as a blindfold off his head. He'd been transported to he knew not where, though he did not believe they had left the building.

Immediately after they'd seized him, shackling his hands behind his back as though he were some common criminal, he'd been marched across the entrance hall. He knew because he'd heard the clicking nails of the dogs hurrying out of the way.

After that, stepping clumsily, unable to see, he'd heard creaking pulleys similar to the cables on a dumbwaiter. Then he'd felt his stomach lurch with a drop of downward motion.

Somehow he kept his mouth shut, though he was incensed at such treatment—for a duke, no less—when he'd come here in good faith, and by invitation of one of their own.

He'd arrived twenty-two years late, true. But still.

God, if they killed him, who'd take care of Serena?

Downward the dumbwaiter took him and his captors, finally lurching, scraping to a halt. He'd sensed the air turn clammy and damp as somebody hauled open what sounded like a sort of stall door; he noted at once that the sounds around them had taken on a hollow, echoing quality.

Then he was marched across what felt like a stone floor underfoot, and shoved into a hard wooden chair.

"What was the point of all that?" he muttered, blowing a stray lock of his hair out of his eyes when they yanked the hood off his head. "I've already seen your blasted faces. I've voted with you in the Lords, for God's sake."

Rotherstone sat down slowly before him. "How did you know about Dante House?"

"And where," Virgil growled, staring at him, "did you get that ring?"

Azrael drew a deep breath and let it out slowly, while his quick glance around established they were in a subterranean cave of some sort. Probably built right under the old house.

Warrington gave him a warning poke in the shoulder. "Answer the question, mate."

"Untie my hands. Oh, for heaven's sake, if I meant you any harm, would I have arrived alone, unarmed, knocking on the front door, as Falconridge pointed out? Would I have brought you the secret records from my father's group?"

"Who sent you?" Falconridge demanded.

"Nobody! In fact," Azrael said with a huff, "there are those who'd gladly kill me—slowly and painfully—if they knew I was here."

Virgil narrowed his eyes then sent Rotherstone a terse nod.

The marquess rose from the wooden bench where he sat, looking disappointed. "You try anything unfriendly, Rivenwood, and we'll stop being so polite."

Azrael harrumphed, but once Rotherstone had freed his wrists from the manacles, he rubbed them in relief, straightening up in his chair. He had to admit that seeing the three spies staring at him like that was a little unnerving.

Fortunately, his father had hardened him early to fear. He stared right back at them.

"Why are you here?" Warrington asked.

"How many times do you want me to say it? I have information for you. Whole troves of it, actually."

Falconridge laughed at his offer. "And why should we ever trust a bloody Promethean?"

"I am not a Promethean! My *father* was. He also happened to be a raving lunatic." Azrael glared at them. "I, however, am sane." Then he glanced around at the men uncertainly and mumbled, "Which is why I need your help. And frankly, you need mine."

"*Your* help?" Virgil echoed.

"Aren't you still in the business of routing out Promethean cells? If so, then yes, you need me as much as I need you. I want rid of them. They've been trying to control me all my life. I'm set on marriage now, and I won't have them threatening my wife or trying to lay claim to my children in the future. Surely you can understand that. But I can't take them on alone, which is why I came to you, and I can see now it's a good thing I did, because you obviously have no idea who the hell they are!"

They glanced around at each other.

Then Rotherstone nodded. "We're listening."

"Start at the beginning," Falconridge added.

And after rubbing his wrists where the shackles had chafed him, Azrael obliged.

It was going to be a long night.

CHAPTER 17

Coming Home

*E*xactly eight days later, Serena heard hoofbeats and the rumble of carriage wheels coming up the drive to Dunhaven Manor. It was a sound her ears had strained to detect from the moment she had kissed Azrael goodbye.

He had written a few days ago, thank God, to let her know he was still alive, but his message had been cryptic, ending with the promise that there'd be more news to come shortly. Though she had rejoiced to receive his promised letter, it was torture that he had not said when they would see each other again.

She knew she had to be patient. At least the Order hadn't harmed him. Her prayer had been answered.

But that morning, in mid-conversation with her family at the breakfast table, hearing someone coming up the drive, Serena jumped to her feet and raced to the front door, barreling past Bosworth on his way to answer it.

She flung it open and looked out, heart pounding, eagerly expecting to see Azrael's team of magnificent black Frisians, Paulson, and her love coming up the drive.

Instead, it was a strange carriage, brown and weather-beaten, pulled by four chestnut horses, with four riders flanking it, moving along at a businesslike trot. She studied them in wonder as they stormed up the drive.

They were dressed in ordinary clothes, but as this mysterious cavalcade arrived at the house, she thought they had the rugged, sun-leathered look of military men, as did the driver and the armed groom riding beside him up on the box.

She stood in the doorway, heart pounding, ignoring the fact that she was letting the cold in as she wondered what all this was about. Her father followed but commanded the rest of the family to stay back.

"Do you know these people, Papa?" she asked as the earl marched up beside her.

"No. Do you?"

She shook her head in confusion.

"You should get back inside."

"No, please—I'm sure this must have something to do with Azrael."

"That's what I'm afraid of," he grumbled.

As soon as the carriage halted in front of Dunhaven Manor, the door opened and out jumped an extremely handsome young man with golden hair and bright blue eyes.

"Good morning!" he called, striding toward them, his greatcoat trailing out behind him, tapping his hat cheerfully against a muscled thigh.

Neither answered, staring at him.

Serena felt sure she knew the fellow—she could've sworn she had danced with him at a ball or two at some point, but she couldn't place him. Surely he was a member of the ton, though. He had a gentlemanly bearing and moved with the grace of an expert swordsman.

"I'm terribly sorry for the intrusion at such an early hour," he said with easy charm while his comrades waited on their horses. He came up to the door and bowed to them.

"Lord Dunhaven, Lady Serena. Please do not be alarmed. We've been sent to assist you. And I made a solemn vow to your fiancé that I'd deliver this as soon as I saw you." He reached into his waistcoat and pulled out a letter, presenting it to Serena with a flourish.

"Thank you!" She snatched it gleefully out of his hand, but paused, wrinkling her forehead. "Don't I know you?"

"What? You don't remember? My lady, you wound me," he said with a wicked little laugh.

"Viscount Beauchamp!" she exclaimed, remembering all of a sudden. "Of course. Oh my goodness. *You're* with the Order?"

"What Order?" he said meaningfully.

"I see." She could only shake her head. "I can't believe it. You always seemed like such a scoundrel."

"Merely doing my duty, mademoiselle. And yet it does seem to come rather naturally to me." He winked.

She couldn't help but chuckle. No doubt his skill at putting people at ease with humor probably helped him a great deal as a spy. Serena stepped back out of the doorway, gesturing at the entrance. "Would you like to come in?"

Papa growled, however. "I'd rather you explain your visit first."

"Of course, my lord." Beauchamp looked from one to the other, the playfulness vanishing at once from his cobalt eyes. "Things are about to get very interesting in London, and it has been determined that Lady Serena's participation in the mission is essential."

Her eyebrows shot upward.

Beauchamp addressed Papa. "My superiors request that you bring your daughter to Town, sir. Two of my men will remain here to protect your family. The rest will escort you and Lady Serena safely to London."

Her heart lifted the moment he said she'd be going back to Azrael.

With that, she broke the wax seal on his letter and eagerly read the few lines he'd written. It merely contained a simple assurance that she could trust these men and that the plan was in motion.

"We've provided the young lady with a new chaperone until all this is over," Beauchamp continued. "A Mrs. Fisher. She is thoroughly respectable, and also quite deadly with a knife. Once you leave your daughter in her care, we strongly encourage you to remove your kinswoman from Town and bring her back here with you."

"You want me to leave my daughter by herself with you people?"

Beauchamp blinked at Papa's hostile tone. "And her future husband."

The spy renewed his efforts to put them at ease: "I assure you, sir, many measures have already been put into place to keep your daughter safe for the duration. You won't see us, but we've got Moonlight Square locked down like a fortress, especially your house and your future son-in-law's.

"In any case, this should all be over soon. Rivenwood is helping us see to that. As soon as Lady Serena has played her part, she may either return here, or you and your family may join her in Town. Until then, it wouldn't be safe for you all to be there. It's not entirely clear yet what the enemy's current numbers are, and we don't wish to dilute our protective detail trying to cover you all, when the rest of you don't need to be there."

"I don't like this," Mama said, arriving at the doorway.

Beauchamp nodded to her. "My lady. You needn't fear, truly. The

Order's accustomed to protecting kings and all manner of important persons under threat, both here at home and on the Continent."

"You see, Papa?" Serena said, then nodded at Lord Beauchamp. "I'll go fetch my things." In truth, she'd been packed to return to London for days.

But the earl had still said nothing.

"Are you willing, my lord?"

"Humph. If you need her to help bring that blackguard Stiver and his cronies to justice, of course. You've got my help, too, if you want it."

"George, no!" the countess said. "I will not permit this—for either of you! I've already lost one daughter."

"Mama, they need my help," Serena said.

"Hmm." Papa glanced at his lady, then turned back to Lord Beauchamp. "My wife is right. We can't go through that again. What if something goes wrong?"

"Papa, it won't. I'm not afraid!"

"Er, not to put too fine a point on it, sir, I do suggest you comply," Beauchamp said. "You see, the only reason the Order's overlooking *your* past participation in this group, and your wife's, is because it was one of Rivenwood's conditions for working with us, and because of your daughter's unique ability to help bring the matter to a close.

"I'm afraid that some in my organization wished to see you prosecuted, but your family being left alone was one of the points on which Rivenwood would not budge. I, er, regret to inform you that if you refuse to allow your daughter to assist us—given your own past dealings with this group—it would be viewed as obstructing the investigation, and we would need to look more closely at you. And your wife."

Papa growled, but that was all he needed to hear. Nobody would interrogate his Mariah.

"Fine. She'll do it. Go fetch your things, girl."

"George!" the countess said.

"Please, Mama. Don't fret. I want to help. Of course we'll come," Serena told Lord Beauchamp.

His sunny smile returned. "Excellent."

"Would you like to come inside?" Serena asked, gesturing to the entrance hall.

"Thank you, don't mind if I do." Beauchamp turned and signaled to his men before stepping over the threshold.

Three of the riders dismounted, while the armed groom climbed down from the coach.

Papa closed the door behind the viscount.

"Can't I help instead of my daughter?" Mama said.

"Mariah!" the earl said.

"No, ma'am," Beauchamp replied. "It's Rivenwood himself who is their chief interest. They seem to think he's some sort of chosen one. Lady Serena's role is essential, since the duke is betrothed to her. There's also the fact that she is the current leader's natural daughter. Lord Stiver wants to meet the young lady."

"No!" cried the countess.

"I'm not afraid, Mama," Serena said. "I'm his daughter; he's not going to hurt me. Believe me, if there's some way I can help to bring these blackguards down, then I will do it. Azrael needs me. And besides," she touched her mother's arm as she passed her on the way to the staircase, "I owe that monster for what he did to you."

Her mother said nothing more, seeing Serena would not be deterred in spite of any danger. Serena pounded up the steps to go and fetch her things. She didn't care if any army of giants awaited her in London.

Nothing could have prevented her from flying back to Azrael.

Many weary hours later, after yet another long, tedious carriage ride, the outline of London seeped into view in the distance, materializing out of the drizzly afternoon fog.

Serena sat up and peered eagerly as the spires and St. Paul's famous dome emerged from the gray autumnal gloom. The tiny orange lights of Town glowed like welcoming beacons, and Serena started fixing her hair and freshening her mouth with a mint confectionary drop, knowing she would soon see her favorite neighbor again.

In actuality, though, it took the better part of another hour before they pulled into Moonlight Square.

His letter had instructed them to come to his house first, since it was now well protected by the Order. There, he would apprise them of the latest developments.

Beauchamp had parted ways with them halfway through the journey to embark on some task he was not at liberty to explain, but Serena wondered if she'd get to meet more of the Order agents when they arrived. Would they be mean to her, she wondered, because of her

Promethean connections?

It wasn't her fault Lord Stiver was her natural father. She was just barely getting used to that fact herself. But however the Order's people might treat her, it didn't really matter.

There was only one man in this whole city of a million souls that she cared about seeing, and the moment she got out of the coach, she ran straight into his arms.

He embraced her, standing on the pavement outside his house in Moonlight Square.

They hugged each other hard for a long moment. She gloried in the solidity of him, safe and sound, the smell of him.

"I missed you," Azrael whispered, then gave her a quick kiss—but only on the forehead, since Papa climbed out of the coach just a step behind her.

Azrael greeted his future father-in-law stiffly, looking braced for another possible attack. "Sir," he greeted him, offering a bow.

"Rivenwood," Papa grumbled.

Azrael gestured toward his front door. "Won't you both come in?"

Serena took hold of her fiancé's arm and did not let go as he led them into his house. Papa glanced around, brow furrowed, at its gothic interior, but if he thought that was strange, she wondered what he would've said about the leopard.

All business, Azrael presented several more of the military-looking foot soldiers of the Order, who he said would be posing as his servants until this matter was settled. They would also be protecting Serena.

She gathered these were not the elite agents, like Lord Beauchamp, that his letter had hinted were assisting him behind the scenes, but the Order's hired muscle.

Whoever they were, she was glad to have them on hand, for after perusing the contents of that snakeskin box, she no longer doubted the extent of the Six's wickedness.

He then introduced her new chaperone—a tall, slim lady who appeared in her mid-thirties and claimed her name was Mrs. Fisher.

The silent, eagle-eyed woman was an impressive personage; the Order's henchmen treated her with deference, but Serena doubted she would ever know the real identity of the lady spy.

"Are you an agent of the Order of St. Michael, too?" she whispered, rather in awe of the woman as Azrael led them all upstairs to the drawing room across from the ballroom.

"No, darling," the tall, worldly-looking Mrs. Fisher replied. "The lads are colleagues of mine, but their charter doesn't allow women, you see. I belong to another service." Mrs. Fisher gave her a sly wink, and Serena knew at once they would get along famously.

Papa studied the lady spy, looking puzzled, as they all sat down in the faux-medieval drawing room.

"May I offer you refreshments after your journey, Lord Dunhaven, Lady Serena?" Azrael asked, then turned to his butler, lurking near the doorway, apparently eager to be of service. "Grimsley?"

"Oh, no thank you, I don't want anything just now." Serena caught the old fellow studying her with a doting look, which amused her greatly, since he had such a dour face. Aha, she thought, apparently the master had informed his top servant that she would soon be lady of the house.

Serena sent Grimsley a smile, but when Papa and she declined the offer of food and drink, the butler bowed out, pulling the door shut after him.

Then Azrael began explaining the plan as it now stood.

Serena found it difficult to focus on the details he laid out when all she wanted to do was throw everyone out of the room and kiss him senseless on the couch. Indeed, aside from worrying about him, she'd thought of little else since they'd parted.

Being near him now, seeing him unscathed, as promised, filled her with giddy joy. And other sensations—decidedly more carnal. She couldn't stop staring at him; when he glanced over at her, as though feeling her lustful gaze, he seemed to lose his train of thought. His words trailed off.

"You were saying?" Mrs. Fisher prompted.

"Er, right." Azrael gave Serena a quick, sternly playful glance that seemed to say *Behave yourself,* then refused to look at her again.

Hmm, do I break your concentration, Your Grace? She hid her grin, but butterflies crashed about in her belly, and she could not stop her wayward imaginings as she envisioned undressing him piece by piece...

Shifting in her chair, she forced herself to pay attention to the matter at hand as best she could. The long and short of it was that preliminary steps had already been taken.

Azrael had been in contact with Lord Stiver and procured an invitation to bring Serena to his house so he could introduce her at last to her natural father. He had told him that they'd both found out about her true parentage. Stiver had merely chuckled over his years-long deception.

"When he sees us together," her lovely duke explained, "he'll believe that I've come back to the fold in order to claim the bride who was to have been mine. The whole ton knows how beautiful Lady Serena is, after all." He glanced at her, and she sat up straighter, beaming at his compliment.

Gentlemen often said flattering things about her, but now only the words of one mattered.

"Stiver will easily believe I returned to my heritage because of Serena," Azrael continued, looking around at his audience.

Papa listened, taking it all in, while the lady spy inspected her nails, as though she considered this child's play. The Order's foot soldiers stood against the walls dressed as footmen, their hands folded behind their backs, feet planted wide.

"When I tell him that Lady Serena and I are to be married, that will make Lord Stiver very happy. It will help restore his trust in me, since I have ignored the lot of them for years. Once he lets his guard down, I'll make sure he reveals his guilt to the Order in a way that leaves him hoisted by his own petard. Any questions?"

Dunny held up a finger.

"Yes, my lord?"

"Not sure I like you lot using my daughter for bait."

"Neither do I," Azrael admitted. "But her role in this will be minimal—"

"I'm not afraid," she interrupted.

Azrael's eyes glowed silver as he sent her a brief smile. "I knew you wouldn't be, my lady. If I had any doubt in your mettle, I would never have agreed to it myself.

"Unfortunately, Lord Dunhaven," Azrael continued, "your daughter is the key to my getting back into Stiver's good graces. Only by doing so can I get close enough to the blackguard and his current group of henchmen so we can take them down."

"That sounds dangerous," Serena murmured.

"It is, dear," Mrs. Fisher said with a smile. "That's what makes it *fun.*"

"Well, don't go getting yourself killed and breakin' her heart before the wedding," Dunny grumbled at his future son-in-law.

"Ah, don't worry, Lord Dunhaven," Mrs. Fisher assured him in a breezy tone. "My associates and I will keep them both safe as houses. Now then, if we're quite through here?" She rose in her tight black gown, and, politely, the men did the same.

"I have nothing further at the moment," Azrael said with a shrug.

Papa nodded, satisfied with the plan they had concocted. "In that case, think I'll pop across the square to take my leisure for an hour or two at home before I'm back out on the road again with Tamsin."

On Lord Beauchamp's advice, Papa had already decided not to stay the night in London, but to turn right around again and start the journey back to Mama and the boys, post-haste. After making sure Serena was settled in with her temporary chaperone and army of protectors, he wanted to get back to his wife and sons, who could also come under threat once the plot was fully in motion.

In any case, it was not unusual to travel overnight; the stagecoach lines did it all the time so that passengers could doze on the way and wake up in the morning at their destinations.

Papa headed for the dark oaken door of Azrael's sitting room. "Come along, Serena."

Mrs. Fisher and two of the no-nonsense Order guards duly followed Papa down to the entrance, but Serena lingered in the drawing room, glancing at Azrael in raw frustration at having to leave him again so soon.

They hadn't even been given a moment alone.

He took her hands in that brief moment while her father and their new entourage waited for her in the entrance hall.

"I'll see you later this evening," he whispered, and gave her a chaste peck on the cheek. Even so, she quivered when he leaned near.

She gripped his hands harder, wanting them on her. "I can hardly wait," she said, giving him a meaningful look.

"Serena!" Papa boomed from the entrance hall.

"Coming!" She hurried off to join them.

Then Papa and she, along with their trio of discreetly armed protectors, went across Moonlight Square to the Dunhaven residence, where Serena was reunited with Cousin Tamsin. Mama had written to her a week ago to let her know that Serena had made it to Dunhaven Manor without incident, but, of course, she had not yet told her cousin the whole story. Only a fool would entrust such scandalous secrets to the mail. Besides, Serena wasn't sure her kinswoman's nerves could've handled it, so that was no doubt for the best.

The timid, homely creature was all aflutter to see Serena again, and to know that she herself would soon be reunited with her idol, Mama.

While Papa went to make himself comfortable, Serena picked up Wesley the cat and introduced Mrs. Fisher to Cousin Tamsin. The lady spy proceeded to charm her mousy cousin with a skill as practiced as Lord Beauchamp's.

At last, after about two hours, Papa and Cousin Tamsin traipsed out toward the carriage. Lord Dunhaven had braced himself for the long trip back, while Tamsin fluttered along haplessly with an armful of books and papers, muttering that she was sure she was forgetting ten things.

"If you remember something you forgot, just write to me, and I will send it to you," said Serena. By then, she was ready to kick them both out the door so she could be free to run back to Azrael at top speed.

Papa had thought of one more thing he wanted to tell her fiancé before he left Town, so Serena and Mrs. Fisher rode back across the square with them in the coach.

It was no secret that Serena intended to spend more time with him this evening, after their painful separation. She assumed they would have dinner together. Papa frowned but did not object.

"And, um, why are we going here?" Cousin Tamsin asked, looking at Mrs. Fisher. "We don't even know this gentleman."

"Serena's marrying him," Papa grunted.

"What?" Tamsin's eyes bulged behind her spectacles.

Mrs. Fisher chuckled.

Serena shrugged and gave her kinswoman a sheepish smile. "Mama will tell you all about it." She kept as innocent a look on her face as she could manage until they reached the other side of the square.

Papa got out and handed her and Mrs. Fisher down, while Cousin Tamsin waited in the coach, peering out the window in confusion. The two Order "footmen" jumped down off the back of the coach where they'd ridden, marching over to stick close by Serena.

They'd been introduced to her as Brody and Porter, and both were charged with defending her with their lives, if necessary. Quite impressive for two people she didn't even know, she thought.

Azrael came out to the front of Rivenwood House again to see the travelers off. Papa marched ahead of the ladies to have a private word with the duke; Serena did not hear what was said.

She stared at their exchange, though, worried that Papa might be threatening her fiancé again, but to her surprise, Azrael pulled a piece of paper out of his waistcoat pocket and showed it to him with a smile.

Papa glanced at the paper for a moment by the light of the front lanterns—daylight was fading fast—then he nodded, gave the paper back to Azrael, and offered him a handshake.

Azrael shook his hand, and the sight of the two men officially reconciling after their row at the manor warmed the cockles of her heart.

Tamsin looked completely baffled, but the private exchange between future father- and son-in-law was brief. Then the two men returned to the waiting vehicle, where Serena and her new chaperone stood, waiting to see them off.

Azrael hung back at a polite distance to let her say goodbye to her father.

"How do the new horses seem?" Dunny called to his fresh driver, another Order man, who'd be making the return trip to the manor, along with another armed groom.

"Sound and ready to go, my lord," the driver called back.

They'd replaced the four hired horses and added two more, for extra speed and power.

"Right. Well then, I'm off. Come here, you." Papa hooked an arm around her shoulders and pulled Serena near to kiss her on the forehead. "I'm proud o' you, poppet."

"What did I do?" she asked. After surrendering her virginity to the duke across the street, the last thing she expected was to hear that Papa was *proud* of her.

He shrugged. "I just am. You'll always be my little girl, you know that, don't you?"

Serena nodded and hugged him, choked up. "And you'll always be my papa."

She knew in that moment exactly why Mama had chosen Lord Dunhaven, when she could've married anyone with her beauty. He was a good man, and he truly loved her and her children.

Even the cuckoo in his nest.

"Anyway, you were right." He cleared his throat. "The lad's nothing like his father, thank God."

"What were the two of you talking about?"

"He got the special license. He was asking me officially for your hand. A bit late for that, so what else could I say? It's all right, though. I know a man in love when I see one."

She beamed.

Then Dunny turned to the unsmiling, square-jawed footmen. "You lot, look after her for me."

Brody and Porter nodded. Serena wondered if these fellows ever spoke. Papa tapped her on the nose. "And *you* be good."

She flashed a grin. "I'll try. Thank you—for everything, Papa. Truly." Then she stood on her tiptoes and kissed his cheek. "Safe travels. I'm sure we'll all be together again soon. Give Mama and the boys my love."

He nodded, and Azrael came over to stand beside her as Lord Dunhaven lumbered up into the coach. The whole thing tilted, and the springs groaned a bit under his bulk.

"Take me home, driver!" the earl boomed cheerfully through the window, which he'd let down a crack. "Let's get this journey over with."

"Hear, hear!" Tamsin squeaked.

"Goodbye." Serena and Azrael stood waving in front of Rivenwood House as the carriage rolled off down the street toward a sunset the color of a bruise.

Tamsin waved through the back window, but even before the coach had disappeared, Azrael leaned down toward Serena.

His warm lips brushed the curve of her ear with a whisper that sent a thrill through her entire body: "I want you in my bed. *Right now.*"

CHAPTER 18

Wild at Heart

$\mathcal{T}$he needy little groan that escaped her at his mere proposition stoked Azrael's blood. She bit her plump lower lip and gave him a smoldering, sidelong glance that admitted she'd been as desperate for him as he'd been for her over the past week.

He started getting hard where he stood right there on the pavement. Now that would get the neighbors talking, he thought as he captured her hand.

"Come with me," he whispered, pulling her inside.

She pattered after him with an eager skip in her step. He sent her a doting smile and got the door, already undressing her with his eyes.

His heart pounded as they strode back into the entrance hall followed by Mrs. Fisher, whoever the hell she really was.

"Ahem, er, yes, I say," Azrael attempted, turning to the spy, "Lady Serena and I need to discuss a few particulars of our wedding…privately, if you don't mind—"

"Oh please," Mrs. Fisher drawled, while Brody and Porter exchanged a cynical glance. "I am not some Patroness of Almack's, darlings. Help us rout out this nasty cell, and I don't give a damn what you do."

"In that case, see you in the morning." Azrael hurried Serena ahead of him, his hands on her waist.

Giggling wickedly, she picked up the hem of her long skirts in both hands and pounded up the stairs ahead of him.

He captured her on the landing above and pinned his luscious prize against the wall, claiming her mouth fiercely. She clung to him, kissing him back just as heartily, her dainty fingers already plucking at his clothes.

Her chest heaved against his. Unable to resist, he cupped her breast. "I've been wanting you *sooo* badly," he admitted in a ragged murmur. But that was no doubt obvious when he leaned against her body, demonstrating the truth of his claim by letting his hardness throb between the juncture of her thighs.

She groaned, visibly enjoying the randy caress of his pelvis against hers. Serena captured his face between her trembling hands and kissed him with drowning depth. "Oh, God, Azrael, I need you," she panted. "I missed you so much." She slid her hand down between their bodies and squeezed his rigid member through his clothes.

Azrael closed his eyes with a shudder. His world was spinning. At this rate, they'd never even make it to his chamber. He laughed breathlessly. "Oh, my angel, you have no idea how much I've missed *you.*"

"Why don't you show me, then, Your Grace?" The little hellion pulled back to entice him with a sultry stare. The golden chips in her eyes burned, and her ruby lips were already swollen with his kisses.

He needed no further invitation, and lifted her off her feet and carried her into the nearest chamber. The hell with waiting. He had to have her now. He had brought her into the music room. Indeed, it would serve, for the instrument he intended to play was her enchanting young body. By God, he'd make her sing, he vowed as he nudged the door shut behind him.

The room was all but dark with the last glimmer of daylight fading beyond the windows. The curtains were still open, swooped back in their holders, but since no candle burned in the room, nobody would see them.

Azrael laid her down on a luxurious divan of green brocade near the tall harp and stool. Reaching out her fingertips, Serena could just skim the strings, and they trilled gently through the room.

He smiled, then kissed her again.

The music room connected by pocket doors—currently closed—with the drawing room, where he had just explained the plan to everyone.

At least, as much of it as he was willing to share at this point. He did not want to worry his future bride unduly, but things could get more dangerous than she yet understood. Azrael could not think about such things at the moment.

He was desperate to be inside of her. He knelt over her, unfastening his trousers. Serena licked her lips beneath him and loosened the bodice of her gown.

Belatedly remembering the rest of his clothes, he tore away his cravat. She helped him peel his tailcoat off his shoulders, and his waistcoat, too.

His skin burned, flushed with fevered longing as he lifted his shirt off over his head.

She murmured that he was beautiful. It was a strange thing for a man to hear, but he knew she had meant it with earnest innocence as she curled up to a sitting position and kissed his chest softly, again and again, while her hands caressed him.

Her touch told him she knew he was all hers. Not an atom of his body could have denied it. He jolted with a thrill of anticipation when he felt the exploratory brush of dainty fingers at his waist; she proceeded unfastening the placket of his trousers the rest of the way, and he caught his breath when she thrust her hand daringly inside.

He rested his palm on her hair, a breathy whisper of relief escaping him as her hand curled around his throbbing cock. *"Yes."*

He bared her shoulders, tugging at her gown, while she went on kissing his stomach and chest. He forced himself to be gentle, though he wanted to rip the damned thing off her, half ready to spend in her hand simply from her touch. He could not remember any woman in the past ever making him feel so out of control. It was all he could do to rein himself in, let alone her, the little wild thing.

He captured her hand, stilling her ardent stroking, lest she make an adolescent fool of him. Determined to hold himself back, he pressed a fingertip softly under her chin to lift her gaze to his and bring the rain of her sweet kisses all over his torso to an end.

With his entire being focused on her, he pressed her down gently onto her back once more. Then he moved downward over her body, tugged her bodice just a bit lower, and captured a plump, straining nipple in his mouth.

He moaned with his mouth full. She gripped his hair in both hands, squirming with pleasure beneath him. As her body undulated with still-innocent demand, he was consumed by the fire he'd awakened in her. So ripe, this flower he had plucked.

He needed more of her. So much more.

He could feel her heartbeat thumping under his palm as he caressed her chest and throat with his right hand, swirled his tongue around the swollen nipple in his mouth, while his left hand crept down her thigh to gather the hem of her skirts in his clutch.

He pulled the crumpled fabric upward slowly until he found the shapely stockinged leg beneath her skirts. He quivered as he molded his hand against her calf. *So perfect.* The white stocking under his skimming touch was soft, but the flesh beneath the thin silk was even softer, as he rediscovered when he reached the lace garter around her thigh and found bare skin above it.

He lifted his head to attend to the other nipple, pausing only to say, "You are truly exquisite."

She whimpered with need and arched beneath him, and he sucked longer on that sweet pink candy while his fingertips explored and played with the regions above the pretty garter. Serena groaned and bit her lip when he slipped a finger into the pearlescent dew that dripped from the folds of her quivering passage.

Feeling her teeming wetness for him was more than he could bear. Much as he wanted to drink it all up, his cock had other, very firm ideas. He couldn't wait a moment more. He needed her at once.

Keeping his finger sliding within her, teasing her with a little hors d'oeuvre ahead of the main course, he raised his face from her breast, licked his lips, and then lifted her skirts the rest of the way.

Her eyes glazed, frantic with want, she clutched at his waist, pulling him to her. He withdrew his hand from between her legs and braced himself over her, plunging deep into her core, unable to hold back a second longer.

Serena yielded to his taking with wanton abandon. To his delight, she simply lay back and enjoyed it. Probably not as much as he did, though, thrusting between her silken thighs as he willed.

Soon, she was writhing beneath him, lifting her heels onto the edge of the divan, so that her knees embraced his sides. His hair fell forward amid his lusty exertions, veiling them both as he lowered his head and kissed her again.

His tongue swirling in the warm, welcoming depths of her mouth, his cock surging deeper in her body with every needy lunge, he took her with all he was, all he had. And he'd never give her back.

She ran her hands up and down his arms, scratched at his chest with her fingernails with just enough pressure to arouse him all the more. She touched his face and petted his hair, making him feel so loved, so very loved, as she lifted her hips to take him in as far as her soft supple body would allow.

They were both frenzied with desire; Azrael was out among the stars. She had intoxicated him entirely. He was shaking as he braced himself on his hands over her. God, he had tried to fight this, but it was no use. If he failed, if his enemies won and destroyed him rather than the other way around, this moment made everything worth it.

Yet even as she satisfied him, he only wanted more of this woman. Everything, forever.

"Oh, Azrael, I love you," she said against his mouth.

"I love you so much, Serena," he whispered. He slowed in his rhythm, moved by her breathless confession. Half of him wanted to explode with release, but the other half yearned to make this moment last forever.

Above all, he wanted to please her as she pleased him. And so he made an effort to help her savor every sensation, kissing her more tenderly, gliding back and forth between her thighs with deep, leisurely thrusts.

Ah, but the lady was impatient.

She gripped his shoulders with an anguished moan. "You are a cruel man," she panted. "In the *best* sense."

He stopped kissing her and pulled back a bit to give her a very wicked smile.

"Do you like this?" he asked, lifting his hips and inching into her again from a steeper angle with tantalizing slowness.

"*Unh,* I'll get you back for this, I swear. Next time."

"You promise?" he whispered.

"Oh, darling, make me come," she begged him, her chest heaving.

"I love to hear you say that." He bent his head and brushed his lips featherlight atop hers.

"Make me come," she repeated in the most seductive murmur he'd ever heard.

A violent ripple of need flamed through him — and it was time.

"As you wish, my lady," he growled, gripping her.

Then he obeyed.

Afterward, Serena was left languishing, enervated, in a mindless state of bliss as he withdrew from her body. After a long moment, catching his breath, Azrael rose and pulled up his trousers, then dragged a hand through his long hair and went to close the curtains.

"Mm. Truly," she said, laughing with satisfaction, "you are a talented man, sir."

"You don't say." He lit a candle, and Serena could only stare helplessly at his handsome face as the light rose, sculpting his high cheekbones and seductive mouth in its faint glow.

The most delicious feelings, both of body and soul, enveloped her every time she looked at the man. With a great heave of strength, she managed to sit up, idly brushing her skirts back down where they belonged, straightening her bodice.

"It was terribly agreeable of my new chaperone to leave us alone, don't you think?"

"She's an interesting woman," he murmured as he sauntered back to her in all his shirtless glory. He sat down beside her on the divan as she swung her feet down to the floor, her core still throbbing.

All she wanted to do was lie back in his arms, but merely being with him was just too exciting. She put her arm around him, then ran her hand back and forth lovingly along the line of his smooth, solid shoulders.

She played with his hair for a moment, then, overcome by the need to dote on him as much as he would let her, she rose and went to stand right in front of him while he sat.

She stepped between his legs, still caressing his shoulders and neck.

"That was fun," he purred.

"There's that wonderful gift you have for understatement again," she teased, leaning down to steal a kiss.

He pulled her down unceremoniously onto his lap. She sat down on his thigh and rested her head against his, simply adoring her fiancé. He linked his fingers through hers and ran his thumb along the side of her hand. The tender sensation pleased her.

"So what do we do now?" she asked. "I'm afraid you may have to explain the entire plan to me again, now that I can think."

A husky laugh escaped him. "It's simple. Next I introduce you to your father."

"Oh." She nodded, marveling to think of how far they had come. From his initial refusal to get involved at all in her search, now he would be doing the introductions.

"However," he said, "there's someone else I want you to meet first."

"Oh? Who? Azrael, I only want to be with you right now."

"Trust me. Wait here. It's a surprise." He spilled her off his lap and then pulled his shirt on over his head, tucking it into the waistband of his trousers as he headed for the door.

"Azrael, who is it and where are you going?"

"Just be patient for once. And for heaven's sake, fix your clothes." He sent her a mock leer. "You look like you were just ravished out of your mind."

"Because I was," she said, laughing.

He sent her a roguish little smile and left the room.

A happy sigh escaped her. Dutifully, she sauntered over to a mirror on the wall and attempted to recover her modesty. It was easy enough to pull her bodice back up, though her skirts were wrinkly. Well, that could be blamed on a long day's travel, couldn't it?

Not so easy to fix was her mussed hair, and only time would subdue the glowing blush in her cheeks. She looked thoroughly relaxed, which a person probably shouldn't be in their situation.

The telltale signs of their tryst were abundant. Her lips were still swollen with his kisses...

She shuddered, shocked to realize she could've done that again with him already. What on earth had the man done to her, turning her into some sort of wanton hussy?

Yet she'd never been happier.

By the time Azrael returned a few minutes later, she had redone her hair into a simple knot, refastened her dress, and splashed a bit of the drinking water she had found in a pitcher on the sideboard on her face to try to cool the flames in her cheeks and revive herself from her blissful drowsiness.

She also took the candle Azrael had lit and used it to light a few more around the room. It was growing quite dark out now. Indeed, she was suddenly quite hungry for supper.

But the torpor he had lulled her into by drowning her senses in complete, overwhelming pleasure fell away when the door opened and Azrael returned—with a leopard on a leash.

Serena gasped and braced herself against the pianoforte behind her. "Azrael?"

"Now, now, don't worry," he soothed, "it's quite safe. I wanted you to meet Raja."

Serena glanced from Azrael to his gorgeous but terrifying pet. "We've met, remember? He nearly ate me."

"And whose fault was that?" he replied with amusement. "Don't worry, he's friendly, at least when I'm around. Come, I want you to be friends."

Serena stayed exactly where she was, but she watched the animal with deepening fascination.

Raja prowled silently alongside his master—if such a princely creature could truly be said to have a master. Raja leaped up onto the couch near the fireplace and sat there, at eye level with her.

Thankfully, the leopard was still six or seven feet away from her, but as they studied each other, she noted that the big cat's collar of white kid leather was made to look like a cravat.

"I see he's dressed for the occasion."

"Yes, I had to make sure he had a proper Town wardrobe."

A nervous laugh escaped her. "I don't know about this, Azrael."

"Darling, you trust me, don't you?"

"You, yes. The wild animal, not entirely. But...he is a magnificent creature."

Azrael scratched the leopard's head between his ears. "He's a good boy. It's all right, come closer. I promise you he won't bite you. Can't you see he's in a good mood?"

Serena cocked a glance at her future husband, but, not wishing to look like a coward, she finally pressed away from the pianoforte and approached, one small step at a time.

Raja did not look entirely impressed with her. He lifted his paw like an ordinary house cat and nibbled one of the leathery black pads as though it itched.

She gazed at the creature's fine head, solid chest, and velveteen ears.

Azrael was stroking Raja's back, which was good, Serena thought. It seemed to make the monster calm.

"He's happy to be out of his room," he said. "This is his waking-up time. He sleeps during the day for the most part."

Raja set his paw, which was as big as her hand, down on the couch again and looked straight at Serena.

She froze momentarily, but the expression in those greenish-yellow eyes was placid. Raja had white whiskers, and he twitched them at her, his rounded ears perking up.

She glanced at Azrael, hesitating. "Are you sure about this?"

"Absolutely certain. It's only right that you should be great chums. Until you came along, after all, I could say with confidence this was my closest friend."

That offhand confession sounded so innocent, almost boyish, that she did not have the heart to refuse. If this animal mattered so much to her beloved, then she would do her best to befriend the beast.

Warily, she closed the distance between herself and Raja, praying the big cat would not grab her by the throat. But her eyes widened, for she'd just stepped close enough to hear the big brute purring.

"He's purring!" she said, pointing at the leopard.

"He's happy, I told you. Hold your hand out flat and let him sniff you."

Serena decided to offer the beast her *left* hand, just in case. The right one was considerably more important to her. She stretched out her palm, her heart thumping, and Raja stretched his flat nose toward her fingers.

She held her breath, but a smile of sheer wonder crooked across her face as she felt the long, snowy whiskers tickle her fingers and palm. She felt a short, warm puff of breath on her skin, then Raja lost interest and sat up straight again.

"Oh my goodness," she said, pulling her hand back and tucking it against her chest.

Azrael smiled from ear to ear with approval. "He likes you."

She looked at him in doubt.

"Here, touch his fur. I guarantee you, you've never felt anything like it."

Still hesitant, she went around to the cat's side, keeping Azrael between herself and Raja. Finally, she worked up her courage to reach out and touch the leopard's withers and, at once, she drew in her breath.

Raja's sleek, shiny fur was softer than the richest velvet.

He chewed his paw again, as supremely indifferent as Beau Brummel to the universal admiration he inspired.

Serena began petting the animal, barely daring to breathe. At this close range, she could see faint rosettes typical of an ordinary-colored leopard. They were just visible beneath the ebony fur around his belly.

Her eyebrows shot up when Raja's large pink tongue flapped up and licked his nose. She caught a glimpse of a white fang as long as her index finger, and nearly lost her courage then, but she held her ground because Azrael did not react in any manner that signaled a warning.

He scratched Raja behind one of his ears, and the big cat tilted his head into the caress just like Wesley would've done.

Charmed as she was, Serena did not ask what Azrael would do with the animal once the two of them had small children running around the house. It would hardly be safe. But the moment was too magical to speak and break the spell.

"What do you think?" Azrael murmured.

"He's beautiful," she said, "and so are you." She left off petting the cat and leaned near to press a soft kiss to Azrael's temple.

He turned and gazed at her, as mysterious and untamed in his own way as his large, deadly companion.

Just then, Raja decided to jump down off the couch.

Though still on his leash, he lay down on the floor for a moment, then rolled onto his back and began playing with his own tail, biting the tip of it like a giant black kitten.

Serena laughed in delight at his antics.

Azrael grinned and leaned down to scratch the big cat's belly. Raja seem to love the attention, and bit his master's wrist gently.

"Oh my God, he'll take your hand off."

"No, he'd never hurt me. He thinks I'm his brother. Or possibly his mother, I'm not sure," he added with a chuckle.

Watching him, Serena shook her head and fell in love with her eccentric duke all over again, even more deeply than before.

She could not believe her good fortune. She was tickled, just thinking about what sort of interesting life they would have together.

Provided, of course, they both survived the coming days.

CHAPTER 19

Blood Ties

*A*zrael despised the task that brought him out the next day, introducing Serena to her natural father.

He knew she was nervous, as well she should be, as he escorted her into Lord Stiver's mansion in St. James's the next afternoon.

The stalwart Brody and Porter attended them as far as the front door, but it would have been irregular to bring one's own footmen inside. It would only draw suspicion, so after seeing them to the entrance, the formidable pair returned to wait with the coach.

Azrael did not expect any problems with this first visit, in any case. He knew Stiver was excited to meet his grown daughter at last.

As a reflection of himself, Serena's very existence, not to mention her beauty, appealed to the man's narcissism.

On Azrael's prior visit here, he had told his former guardian that he'd heeded his advice from the night of the Bonfire Ball and sought to rekindle their childhood match. That he'd found he couldn't resist her.

At least that much was true.

Stiver had been delighted to hear that destiny had overruled Lady Dunhaven's efforts to keep Serena away from her Promethean heritage, as he called it.

Azrael let the devil assume whatever he liked. But perhaps destiny did have a hand of some sort in this.

As they walked up to the front door of the earl's stately mansion, right on time for their agreed-upon appointment, Serena clung to Azrael's forearm, her face pale beneath the brim of her satin bonnet. He gave her gloved hand a reassuring squeeze.

He could certainly understand why she was nervous, but she need not be, he thought. To be sure, she would dazzle Stiver or anyone, arrayed in the especially elegant finery she had donned in honor of the occasion.

The future Duchess of Rivenwood looked gorgeous in what she called a very special gown, with small amber flowers on a white ground. The flowers had a subtle golden luster that shimmered softly when she walked.

With this she wore an open spencer of amber silk that brought out the gold in her eyes. But just to keep things interesting—she being Serena—she had chosen red shoes, tied a red ribbon around her bonnet, and draped an India shawl with red and gold in it across her shoulders with such picturesque ease.

He didn't usually think about it much, but she was the sort of aristocratic lady the fashion writers followed religiously in their detailed explanations to their readers each month about what the ton was wearing.

Azrael still couldn't believe that she was his.

He noticed she had a strange look on her face. "What's wrong?"

"Never mind. It's absurd."

"What is it, darling?" he whispered.

She glanced up at him, hesitating, and he could see in her soulful eyes how conflicted she was about this meeting.

He knew she already despised Stiver for using her mother as he had, but he realized then that, tenderhearted as she was, a small part of her sincerely wanted to know the earl.

For all his faults, the man *was* her father, after all.

Azrael's heart sank at the hope in her eyes, but there was no time for more discussion, for at that moment, the door opened. Stiver's musclebound brute of a butler ushered them in right away.

They were on time and expected.

As they stepped over the threshold, Azrael just hoped Serena did not grow too fond of the earl—let herself be deceived by his surface charm. Because by now, he knew what the Order had planned for Lord Stiver and his henchmen. The three agents and the big, gruff Highlander had been making their arrangements behind the scenes.

Frustration welled in him. He hated having to involve her in this deception and risk her getting hurt either physically or in her affections, but what choice did they have?

She was the only person who could do this. The Prometheans had intended to use Serena as the lure to cement Azrael to their cause, but instead, she would be the lure for Stiver that would bring them all down.

Shoving their true, dark motives out of his mind, Azrael escorted Serena through the earl's residence, keeping a pleasant smile on his face.

The butler led them across the black-and-white checkerboard floor of the entrance hall and up the sinuously curved marble staircase of Stiver's palatial house.

The rooms they passed were painted in pastel hues and decorated in the spidery Etruscan style, one of the ancient classical forms. Like so many of their homes, the interior mimicked a pagan temple—a temple dedicated to self.

Which was exactly why Azrael had not chosen it for his own. He did not share their desire to become a god.

If anything, he figured he needed the churchlike trappings of the gothic style as a constant warning against his bloodline's tendency toward evil. He could only figure the gargoyles must be doing their job.

Serena released his arm as they mounted the stairs. Besotted as he was, his heart clenched when she carefully took off her bonnet. Why this little ritual of hers touched him every time, he could not put into words.

He simply found her adorable.

She caught him gazing at her, and smiled. He winked at her to cheer her up, because she still looked slightly terrified.

Hell, even *his* heart was pounding over how this meeting would go. The stakes could not be higher. Stiver could not be permitted to catch any whiff of deception.

Earlier, Azrael had done his best to prepare Serena about what to expect, but, as for her sire, it turned out that Stiver already knew a lot about her. Well aware that this raven-haired belle of the ton was his offspring, he had monitored her from a distance for years.

Indeed, he was quite proud of her, and had admitted to Azrael with a chuckle that he hated not being able to brag to all the world that she was his.

"Who in his right mind would ever believe that muttonhead Dunny could've ever fathered such a splendid creature, anyway?" Stiver had said when Azrael called on him a few days ago to share their happy news.

Presently, His Lordship received them in the drawing room. After a quick knock, the butler went in, swung the door open wide, and announced them: "His Grace, the Duke of Rivenwood, and Lady Serena Parker."

"Come in, come in, both of you!" Stiver said warmly, walking toward them with a smile.

It was easy to see where she got her fashion sense—not just from her mother, but from Stiver as well. The earl was as impeccably dressed and groomed as ever, from his slicked-back salt-and-pepper hair to his smart daytime attire. He'd always had a bit of the dandy in him.

The butler bowed out behind them, and Stiver stood beaming as Serena ventured toward him.

"So. You are she," he greeted her with real warmth. He couldn't take his eyes off her, practically ignoring Azrael.

"Yes, my lord." Serena dropped a quick curtsy. He had never seen his bold lady looking so meek and unsure.

"Lord Stiver, allow me to present Lady Serena Parker, my fiancée, and your natural daughter."

"I am so very pleased to meet you at long last, my dear." Stiver took both her hands gently, leaned down, and kissed Serena on the cheek. "You are most welcome in my home."

She stared at him with wonder.

They stood in silent recognition for a long moment, studying each other, holding hands. Azrael dropped his gaze to the floor, feeling sick about the loss that he was setting her up for.

"I'm very pleased to meet you, sir," she said at last, barely audible.

"You may call me Father if you like while we're alone."

She said nothing, but Azrael gathered she was slightly bowled over by his elegance.

Stiver gestured at the seating nearby. "Come, let us have a chat and get to know each other. Would you care for refreshments?"

She shook her head, declining with a smile, but walked across the room, the flowers on her dress glistening, and lowered herself with regal elegance to the dainty armchair.

"She is even lovelier up close, and so charming," Stiver remarked with a proud glance at Azrael.

"Thank you, sir," Serena murmured.

"My, but the two of you make a very handsome couple." He glanced at Azrael. "You, light as your father; she with her ebony locks, so like Mariah in her youth. You are like the day and the night come together. It's very powerful."

Serena sent Azrael a discreet, startled glance at the earl's flowery language.

Stiver moved to the chair beside her, but gestured to Azrael. "Won't you sit, Your Grace?"

"I'm fine here, thanks." Azrael folded his arms across his chest and leaned a hip on the arm of the couch nearby.

Just in case Stiver asked, he had already made up his mind he was not leaving her alone with the man under any circumstances. They would have to throw him out bodily.

"So, my dear, you are how old now?"

"Twenty-one. I'll be twenty-two next month."

"Ah, that's right, you were born in December."

She smiled, though Azrael could sense her awkwardness. "Yes, my lord. Not quite a Christmas babe, but close."

"Ah, there are far more interesting holidays in December than Christmas, as Azrael can tell you. But you'll learn all about that in due time, my lovely Serena. I'm the one who chose that name for you, did you know that?"

"No." She shook her head, wide-eyed.

He sighed. "I only wish it would've been possible for me to be a larger part of your life. But...other parties would not have understood."

"It's all right," she said. "I have been well looked after, I assure you—Father."

He smiled with genuine delight when she tried out the title. "And you will no doubt *continue* to be well looked after by your future husband."

Stiver glanced approvingly at Azrael. "If he takes half as good care of you as he does his silly animals, you'll be in very good hands."

"To be sure," she agreed with a grin while Azrael chuckled ruefully.

"He is a fine man—prone to surprises, as I'm learning—and I know you will be very happy together. Which is all I ever wanted."

Serena clasped her father's hand, looking a little misty-eyed at his touching words. Unfortunately, Azrael knew they were lies.

The whole point of pledging them to each other was so that one day they'd create a child, some horrid future demon spawn, infused with dark power from his Promethean bloodlines on both sides.

And, secondly, of course, to satisfy Stiver's unnatural obsession with his friend, Azrael's father. Never mind that the previous Rivenwood had abused him horribly from their Eton days onward, Azrael had heard.

Made him run and fetch for him and do God knew what else.

"Come, a toast!" Stiver suddenly stood. "Your union represents a whole new beginning for us all." He marched over to a liquor cabinet and poured them all a drink.

While his back was turned, Serena sent Azrael an alarmed glance, wordlessly asking if it was safe to drink from the glasses he brought them.

He gave her a discreet nod of reassurance.

Stiver had swallowed their story whole. Having studied his guardian carefully since childhood, he could read the man well, and knew that Stiver's elation about all this was genuine.

Just then, a champagne cork popped. Azrael saw Serena jump.

Returning a moment later, Stiver gave them each a fizzing champagne flute. Serena rose to take her glass. "I have had this bottle chilling in the icehouse ever since Rivenwood told me how my beautiful daughter had brought him to his senses. I should've known I could count on you, my lad. Both of you."

Stiver lifted his drink. "To destiny."

"Destiny," they both echoed, and with a chill down his spine, Azrael clinked glasses with his innocent bride and her treacherous father.

The fine crystal tinkled with a melodious ding. The champagne itself was exquisite, the best money could buy.

Azrael watched Serena as she took a sip.

"My dear." Stiver turned to her. "I know you must continue your charade as Dunhaven's daughter, but you must promise me we will always be friends. And when you have a child, I want to be the first to know. Or at least the second," he added, glancing at Azrael with a chuckle.

"The second, perhaps," Azrael agreed, smiling.

Stiver clapped him on the arm. "Your father would be so proud, my lad. I wish he were here to see this day. By Jove, the prospect of the future fills me with boundless optimism now. So many of our hopes were dashed upon the Continent in recent years, but a well-built plan must stand ready to weather the centuries if need be, no?"

"Just like the pyramids," Azrael said softly.

Stiver snorted with a knowing look. "Indeed."

Serena furrowed her brow, puzzled by their cryptic exchange, but they all drank.

Azrael swallowed a mouthful of champagne, but it could not wash the taste of his own lies out of his mouth. Unfortunately, deception and betrayal were evil necessities in this. His and Serena's eventual freedom hinged on beating the Prometheans at their own game.

As the Bard had once written, *The play's the thing*.

They took leave of Lord Stiver before too long to avoid raising any suspicions with a misstep. Things had gone well for their first meeting, and Azrael didn't want to push their luck.

But on the way out of the drawing room door, Stiver asked him for a private moment. "A word, Your Grace. I'll only keep him from you for a moment, my dear."

"As you wish," Serena said with a smile.

"I'll be right with you," Azrael told her.

She nodded to him, then gathered up the hem of her skirts and followed the butler, who showed her out and pulled the door closed. Azrael could hear their footsteps heading back down the stairs toward the entrance hall.

He turned to Stiver. "What is it, my lord?"

"Have you been studying the materials I gave you?"

"Oh yes." *And so has the Order.*

"If you have questions at any time, I am always glad to elaborate on the teachings."

He nodded. "It seems to come fairly naturally to me."

Stiver crooked a smile. "I'm not surprised. I am glad to hear it, though. There is so much to learn. You're years behind in your studies. Above all, you must be ready for your initiation. I won't have you embarrassing the memory of your father by fumbling your responses during the ceremony."

Azrael said nothing. His formal initiation as a Promethean had been Stiver's one requirement before he'd "permit" him to marry his daughter.

Not that they could've stopped him. But since this was the game that he and the Order were playing with the bastards, he'd pretended to agree to this stipulation.

Stiver and his cronies wanted Azrael bound to the brethren and sealed by blood for once and for all. Besides, he apparently had to be an Initiate first before he and Serena could be joined in what they termed a black wedding.

Stiver wanted *that* to be held in December, on the night of the winter solstice.

Azrael's initiation, therefore, was duly scheduled much sooner—indeed, just a week away—on the night of the November full moon.

The whole coven would gather for the occasion.

Then the Order would strike.

"Don't worry, sir, I will be ready. If there's nothing further?" Azrael turned with a casual air toward the door, assuming that was all.

"Actually," said Stiver, "there is one more thing I have not yet mentioned that you'll need to prepare in advance for what will happen in the barrow. A decision you shall have to make. A difficult one."

Azrael paused. "What's that?"

"I told you there must be a blood sacrifice, as with all the great rituals."

"Yes." It was such a strange, primal, and barbaric term to hear a man in fine Bond Street tailoring use in the midst of such civilized surroundings.

And yet Azrael knew the term would've been quite ordinary to him by now if he had handed the knife to his father instead of the Order agent all those years ago.

He'd have been hardened by now to the whimpers and screams of sacrificial victims begging for their lives.

"You explained how you will have to pierce my chest with a dagger when I take the oath."

"Well, yes. But that is not the blood sacrifice I mean," Stiver said, and stared at him hard.

When Azrael joined her in the entrance hall, Serena instantly detected by his expression that something had upset him. His face looked tense, perhaps a trifle pale, and there was a stiff set to his shoulders, but he walked her out quickly to his carriage waiting under the portico as if nothing was wrong.

A light, steady rain had started falling while they were inside. Serena took her seat inside the carriage and waited while Azrael had a word with the Order footmen and the burly Order driver, who'd replaced the jovial Paulson for the time being.

Azrael gave the trio some instructions, then joined her in the coach.

"What did Stiver say to you in there?" she asked as soon as they were in motion.

"Nothing I'd care to discuss right now."

"Oh." His answer startled her. "Was it something bad? Was it about me?"

"No, darling. Just some details concerning the night we enter the barrow. I'll tell you later, I promise. Right now I need to think."

She fell silent, well aware that the once solitary duke still needed his own space sometimes. It was simply how his mind worked.

"I'll gladly listen once you sort it out."

He gave her a grateful glance, then paused. "What did you think of your sire?"

She shrugged. "He's a pleasant man. On the surface, anyway."

For a few minutes, they both fell into brooding on their own private questions and cares.

"What will happen to him, Azrael?"

"Stiver? He'll be arrested for his crimes and taken into custody."

"Will there be a scandal?"

"No. He'll be disappeared," he said wryly. "They all will. The public will be told some fairytale, like the one about the vagrant caught poaching on my father's property. The Order's working on an explanation for how their collective demise will be reported. Shipwreck or fire, most likely."

Serena shuddered and gazed out the window at the rain coursing down the windows of the buildings they passed.

Lost in her thoughts, it was only then that she noticed they had not gone back to Moonlight Square.

"There's the British Museum," she said in surprise. "Where are we going?"

"Killigrew's Coffeehouse."

"Toby's grubby writing haven?" She searched his face. "Why?"

"I need a brief word with our ol' friend."

"Whatever for? Azrael, what is going on? What did Stiver say to you?"

He huffed with frustration but said nothing as the coach turned the corner onto the side street where Killigrew's was situated.

"Azrael?"

"Your dress is too nice to spoil by chancing the rain," he said as the coach glided to a halt in front of the coffee shop. "Just wait here. This won't take long."

He jumped out without answering her questions and dashed into

Toby's pokey little hideaway, ducking his head in the rain.

What is going on? Serena wondered, miffed. *This can't be good.*

She was tempted to follow in defiance of his wishes to find out what was afoot. But he would be her husband. She supposed she had to trust him.

Besides, he was right—the rain would probably ruin the fine crape of her gown, and she'd spent such a ridiculous amount of money on it. Not even a future duchess could justify throwing away a gown that cost nearly a guinea a yard in a pique of impatience.

Still, she couldn't help thinking that this shift in his attitude did not bode well. *What in the world could he want with Toby?*

"Just the man I've come to see." Azrael spotted Lord Toby as soon as he ducked into Killigrew's, escaping the rain.

At once, the familiar smells of pipe smoke and coffee grinds washed over him. The fire was crackling in the big hearth, as before, and the writer was working at the same round table by the bay window where he'd sat last time, his notes and papers chaotically arrayed before him.

"Rivenwood?" Toby said, looking up as Azrael strode over to him. He peered at him through his spectacles. "What are you doing here again?"

Azrael brushed the cool, refreshing mist of rain off his face as he went over to his table. He hadn't really minded getting wet. The light dousing helped to clear his head after those disconcerting final minutes with Lord Stiver.

He braced his hands on the wooden chair back next to Toby. "I've come to ask you for a favor."

"Me?"

He nodded. "I need you to do something for me. And for Serena."

Toby gave him a dubious look, then gestured to the chair. "Care to sit?"

With a nod of thanks, Azrael pulled the chair out and slumped down onto it, struggling for a moment with how to begin.

Toby pushed his glasses up onto his nose, looking concerned. "What is it, Your Grace? Something wrong?"

"You might say that." Azrael sighed. "Well, you already know too much, so I might as well tell you the rest. The group you learned about, at Owlswick. I'm taking measures to halt their activities for good."

Toby's eyebrows shot up. He put his pen down and listened intently.

"Obviously, crossing such people can be dangerous." Azrael faltered, feeling awkward. "To be frank, I've fallen in love with Serena—I'm sure you can relate—and for some strange reason, I trust you. You seem a good man, and I know she is still quite fond of you."

"Wait—you're in love with Serena?"

"Terribly," he admitted. "She's agreed to marry me—"

"I say!" Toby breathed.

"But the fact is, these people I mentioned, well, things will soon reach a head with them, and I need to know she'll be all right if anything happens to me. That's why I'm here." Azrael stared at her former suitor. "If anything happens to me, I want you to marry Serena yourself—and promptly."

Toby's jaw dropped.

"I know that, as a younger son, your current financial footing depends on your parents' largess, but that is of no consequence. I have put aside most of my fortune in trust for her and, er, any children she may have. If you take my meaning."

"Good God, man." Toby sat back and folded his arms across his chest, giving Azrael a disapproving scowl.

Azrael frowned. "Look, I don't like it much either. But a week from now, I may be dead, and that could leave her in serious danger. If it goes the wrong way, you may need to get her out of England." He glanced around to make sure no one was listening. The place was nearly empty. He returned his attention to Toby.

"Half a million pounds in the bank should make you very comfortable wherever you may land," he continued in a low tone. "The United States should be safest. These people have not yet infiltrated there, to the best of my knowledge, but God knows they're working on it. For a secondary choice, I'd suggest the West Indies, but stay on your guard. It's easy to be caught unawares on an island."

"Let me see if I have this right. You want me to just pick up my life and run away to the other side of the earth a week from now with Serena—who may be carrying your child?" he whispered.

"Well, only if I'm dead," Azrael shot back. "I would marry her myself before the danger starts, because then at least she'd have full legal control of all my holdings, but it's too risky. They're watching me. And it's desperately important to them that she and I wait until December to marry."

"Why?"

"Trust me, you don't want to know." He waved off the unsavory details about the supposed magical energy of the winter solstice. "The point is, if they found out I went behind their backs and wed her sooner, that could expose the fact that I'm deceiving them and jeopardize our one chance to bring the bastards to justice."

"Who's we? You and Serena?"

"The authorities are involved, but it's extremely confidential, do you understand? That's as much as I can say." He glanced over his shoulder again and then out the window, leaning closer. "The point is, if I die fighting these people, I need to know she will have someone on hand who truly cares about her, someone she trusts. Her family may also come under threat, so I can't rely on them. That's where you come in."

Toby looked dazed, taking it all in.

"Now, if you agree to this, the first thing you'll have to do is use a part of my fortune to hire guards and make sure she stays protected around the clock for at least six months. The forces currently helping us will guard her for the short term. I'll consult with them to make sure they give you the names of a few trusted men… Say something, Guilfoyle," Azrael said in a low, urgent tone when the young man just sat there, amazed. "Will you do this or not?"

"Of course," Toby said, blinking. "I would do anything for Serena."

Relief flooded Azrael. He nodded. "I had a feeling you'd say that. You have my deepest thanks. Truly."

"I must say, this is a great deal of trust to place in someone you barely know."

Azrael smiled. "Serena was ready to marry you. Her judgment of your character is good enough for me. That aside, I'm fairly good at reading people, and I believe you have a kind heart. That quality is important to me for her sake and…" His voice faded away at the thought of leaving his child to be raised by some other man. "If there is a child, you will be kind to him, won't you, even though he's not your own?"

"You have my word," Toby said solemnly.

Azrael managed a taut nod and looked away, clearing his throat. "Mind you, it's only if I fail, and I'm not planning to. It's just that things have taken a very serious turn, so I am making provisions for all eventualities."

"Of course." Toby looked worried behind his spectacles. "Is there anything more I can do?"

"No, just what you've agreed to. I've already asked plenty of you."

"You can count on me," Toby said with a nod.

"Good." Azrael rose from his chair, greatly relieved, but still restless over what lay ahead. "Thank you once again. Even if it all goes smoothly, I shall be in your debt. If not, I'll have my man Jenkins contact you at once. This, er, event is to take place on the night of the full moon. So, that's when you can expect news either way."

"I'll be ready."

"Good. Well! I'd best not keep her waiting."

Toby rose as well, and put out his hand. "Godspeed, Your Grace."

Azrael clasped the man's hand and shook it.

They stared gravely at each other.

"You know," Azrael said, releasing his grip, "perhaps you should write their story. Perhaps the world deserves to know."

"I'm not sure I'm that brave. I hope you can defeat them—and break that curse."

"So do I, Toby," he said, nodding as he turned to go. "So do I."

CHAPTER 20

The Duke's Revenge

*H*er first trip to Owlswick had been an experience of sorrow and gloom. The second filled Serena with a pervading sense of dread.

What the local peasants must've thought to see the cavalcade of aristocratic carriages pounding past the village, dispersing through the surrounding roads to return to their own country houses so long abandoned, she could not imagine.

But, no doubt, their confusion was nothing compared to what poor Raja must be feeling.

The leopard was confined in a cage tied down in the back of the wagon behind the coach in which she and Azrael rode.

Serena now knew why her betrothed had been so quiet and grim when he had come out of his private meeting with Lord Stiver a week ago. It sickened her to think that these evil men needed him to prove their loyalty to them and to their twisted cause by personally offering up a sacrifice, taking the life of some innocent being he loved.

Even worse, he was expected to murder Raja himself. Slit the throat of the creature that trusted him so much.

She knew as he sat beside her in silence that he was infuriated by all this with a rage he could not show. He had mumbled that at least he was glad they hadn't suggested he kill a human being.

Yet.

That likely would've come later in his "training" as the future leader of the Prometheans, if any of this were true rather than a masquerade.

As their carriage barreled through the village and on into the night, the full moon of late November leered down on them. Azrael sat stiffly beside her, his spine ramrod straight, his face resolute, his hands rested on his knees, his stare fixed straight ahead.

Frankly, he looked rather convincing as an evil Promethean magnate in this icy silence he'd been keeping since they'd left London. Indeed, he almost looked like his father in the portrait.

But she knew he was keeping himself in check for all that he must do tonight. She just wished, for her part, that she could've stopped shaking.

She hoped he didn't notice. She was trying to keep a brave face for him. She even managed a faint smile when he glanced at her, determined to let him think she was merely shivering due to the plunge in temperature, for the night had turned somewhat frosty. But it was merely fear.

Have courage, she kept telling herself, but it was no use. She was terrified of what might happen tonight. To him. To their future.

She felt sick with foreboding that the curse that had robbed her of her sister could still rise and snuff out their fragile, newfound happiness.

If there was one boon to all this, it was that Lord Stiver and his men seemed to have no inkling whatsoever that the Order of St. Michael was behind this, that tonight was all a grand charade, and that the clock was ticking on those devils' final moments of freedom.

Thank God, they had taken no notice of the footmen and driver, Order-trained soldiers all. Brody and Porter would attend Serena while Azrael went into the barrow to participate in the night's arcane ceremonies.

She would've appreciated the sardonic presence of Mrs. Fisher to keep her company this evening, but the spy's skills would be needed closer to the action. Instead, Serena had the responsibility of watching over the caged leopard.

Azrael's large, exotic pet had become somewhat used to her over the past week, so much so that Serena had managed to pet him a few times by herself. She was still afraid of him, but they were becoming friends.

Raja would wait with her in her forlorn family house, supposedly until it was time for him to die in the rite. But it would never come to that.

The animal's presence here was all for show, merely part of the ruse, signaling Azrael's willingness to do what the villains asked of him.

In reality, the Order was not going to let things go that far. Serena couldn't see them, but she knew they were out there somewhere.

They'd arrived several days ago, according to Mrs. Fisher, getting into position, making their preparations.

Once all of the members of Stiver's current cell had assembled in the barrow for Azrael's initiation, only then would the Order strike, trapping the Prometheans inside.

Serena could not bear to admit it to herself, but her fiancé's chances of getting out of that mound alive seemed extremely slim. At least to her.

She could not believe Azrael had offered himself up as the bait for this entire operation, setting the trap to draw in scores of these Promethean villains.

How could they resist? The son of the great Rivenwood, returned to their sinister fold at last? They would come from miles around to witness that, Azrael had told her.

All of this meant that, for a time tonight, he'd have to stand practically defenseless, surrounded by enemies who would realize as soon as the Order unleashed its attack that Azrael had betrayed them.

He was so brave that she couldn't even speak, and it made her want to weep to know in her heart that he was doing this all for her. So they could have a future together.

That was why she had insisted on coming along tonight. Not for the world would she leave him to face this alone. She would go with him as far as they'd permit her.

Besides, as she had told him, she'd be well protected. And Stiver had no objections to her waiting nearby.

Being the devil's daughter apparently had its privileges.

Of course, she was not supposed to know much of anything yet about what was really going on.

On their second father-daughter visit a few days ago, Stiver had dropped a few hints about his secret life and how his line—including her—shared a certain ancient heritage with the Rivenwood dukes, among others.

The earl was unaware that Serena already knew a great deal more about it than she was letting on, thanks to the contents of the snakeskin box. She had played along, nodding, feigning admiration, and pretending to be intrigued, a skill she'd honed with her deadly-dull suitors.

God, she looked forward to the day when they wouldn't have to lie anymore.

At last, the carriage stopped, as did the wagon behind it. Lord Stiver had provided Azrael with a key to the gates of the Dunhaven mansion. Brody and Porter promptly jumped down to get them open.

Ahead, she heard the rusted gates creak with a pained moan. She shivered again. Azrael glanced over at her, then laid his hand over hers as the carriage proceeded up the overgrown drive.

The ugly house loomed before them with the full moon perched atop one of the chimney pots.

At last, they got out. It was almost time to part ways. The wagon carrying Raja pulled up behind them.

As Azrael walked up to the front door and opened it, glancing around inside to make sure the house was clear, the footmen slid long poles similar to those used to carry sedan chairs into the rings atop the animal's cage.

Working together, the two brawny men hefted the metal cage off the back of the wagon and set it on the ground. Azrael returned while Serena stood there, too scared to speak now that the moment of their parting was nearly at hand.

Azrael went over and checked on his pet. Serena's eyes filled with tears, seeing his solicitude toward the animal. She could hear Raja's unhappy yowls from where she stood, mingled with Azrael's reassuring murmurs.

Stiver's instructions regarding the leopard were to keep him elsewhere, inside his cage, until it was time. Apparently, the cage was too wide and cumbersome to fit through the narrow opening into the barrow.

Given the dangerous nature of the animal, Stiver had said that Azrael would be sent out to bring Raja in on his leash once they reached the appropriate moment.

This was to happen in the second part of their horrendous rite; there were other steps in their occult mumbo-jumbo that supposedly had to take place first. Azrael hadn't talked much about it, and Serena didn't want to know.

Finding out that her natural father relished such things had made the man all the more repulsive in her eyes.

Admittedly, there was a part of her that felt the pull of kinship toward Lord Stiver, especially after she had sought him for so long. Even she could detect similarities between herself and him. But after much pondering, she decided she did not feel sorry at all about his looming fate.

He'd brought it on himself, just like Azrael's father.

Besides, after the way the earl had cruelly used, terrified, and manipulated her mother, and all the other twisted wrongs he'd done, Serena had concluded that she cared more what happened to the leopard than to him.

Above all, though, she cared what happened to Azrael.

As she watched him, he straightened up again, the moonlight gleaming on his pale hair. He walked away from Raja's cage and marched past her into the house, beckoning to her to follow.

She hurried after him, blinking her tears away, while the footmen lifted the poles up onto their brawny shoulders and carried Raja inside.

The musty smell of the abandoned estate invaded her nostrils. It was very dark inside, and she could only wonder how many spiders were lurking in the corners just now, studying her with their beady little eyes.

At least the birds that had taken up residence were somewhere hundreds of miles away, in a sunny clime. She envied them at the moment.

Tonight, it felt like the light would never return.

"Where do you want this, sir?" Brody asked as the two men carried the cage inside.

Azrael turned to Serena. "Where would you like to wait?"

"Not here," she said, glancing around at the entrance hall, with its dead animal heads—no doubt Papa's hunting trophies—staring down at her. She gestured toward the sitting room to the right. "In there will do."

The footmen carried Raja's cage through the wide, open doorway and into the adjacent room she'd specified. They set it on the floor while Raja hissed, then marched back outside and fetched a few extra lanterns from the coach, lit them, and set them around.

The dim glow of illumination seemed to help drive the gloom back a bit. Cold as it was, it would not have been wise to start a fire in any of the fireplaces without it first being cleaned after years of disuse, or they could burn the whole house down.

"Well," said Azrael, with a note of finality.

She steadied herself as he turned to her.

"How long do you think this will take?" she asked, striving for a casual tone as she pulled her gray woolen mantle closer around her shoulders.

"I have no idea." Azrael shook his head. "Just stay put. You should be quite safe here. Try not to worry. It will all be over soon." He glanced toward her guards when the two returned from clearing the premises, and asked them if they had everything they needed.

They nodded and checked their weapons, and Azrael looked again at Serena. Her heart was pounding, her stomach in knots.

"I can't stay," he said. "They're waiting for me. I have to get over to Stiver's house."

"I know." Serena embraced him. While the wind whistled around the house, she clutched him to her like she'd never let him go.

He wrapped his arms around her shoulders and held her close. He rested his head atop hers, and she needed him so much in that moment that she almost begged him not to go. But she knew he had no choice if they were ever going to be free of this dark heritage they shared.

What else could it really be called other than a curse?

She looked up and captured his beautiful face between her hands. "Come back to me," she whispered, tears filling her eyes.

He gazed down at her with the utmost tenderness, and cupped her cheek for a moment in his palm. His finely chiseled countenance seemed ghostly and celestial in the beam of moonlight streaming through the window. "You are my light, Serena," he breathed. Then he leaned down again and kissed her passionately.

She gripped his arms in anguish, for it tasted like goodbye. *No!* She choked back a sob when he ended the kiss somehow and turned away.

She clung to his arm. "I will see you when all this is over," she whispered, savoring the words like a prayer.

He nodded slightly. "And then our lives can start." His face flooded with emotion, and he returned to kiss her fiercely once more, clutching her to him. "I love you, my darling."

"I love you, too." At last she found the strength to let him go. "And always remember, Azrael. You were never one of them."

You have no idea how much I needed to hear that, he thought, gazing at her in torment.

He kissed her one last time on her smooth white forehead, then took leave of her with a small but heartfelt bow before turning away and stalking out the door.

As he headed back toward the carriage to go to Stiver's mansion, he scanned the dark, moon-silvered landscape with a restless glance around.

You bastards had better be out there, he thought. Because if the Order agents failed him this night, he might well walk out of that cursed barrow as the embodiment of everything he loathed, pledged to evil. Everything he had sworn he would never become.

It would be his father's greatest victory.

Indeed, it would be the last Rivenwood's revenge on the son who had betrayed him.

An hour later, blindfolded, Azrael felt rough hands jostle, shove, and guide him through a dank, narrow space where all sound seemed muffled. He stumbled but caught himself as the weight of earth and stone loomed above him. He could feel it pressing down on the air beneath the ground, in this tomb to which they were taking him.

He could hear the rustle of the robes they had donned, the chants and jeering abuses. He could see nothing through the black cloth, but the image of their masks was imprinted on his mind.

Not even he knew yet who they all were, nor would he be permitted to know, until he'd satisfied them of his sincerity. His lineage only got him so far among these skeptical fiends.

They had cause to be paranoid. The Order had been wiping out their numbers on the Continent of late. Certainly, the agents he had met wanted blood all the more, upon learning that the foes they had fought abroad had burrowed like parasites into the very bosom of their homeland, while they had been off fighting the elite conspirators elsewhere.

More and more, Azrael felt split off from the moment at hand. A part of him pulled back, went numb, in a sense, while his body went through the motions.

Memories of his childhood began emerging from the dark vault of his mind, where it had stored some of his own secrets even from him. They flooded back in, sharper than he'd ever let them before.

In the teeth of this evil, he could no longer hold them back. Robed men, torches in the distance, the sound of chanting in strange languages.

A goblet filled with blood. Things glimpsed from the corner of his eye, studiously ignored, in his terror. The nightmarish future that had waited for him when he grew up.

Father had let him see glimpses of it as a child, but that was all.

As he was led into the cult's midst, he heard shuffling feet around him on all sides, a distant cough. The smell of clay, the dank and damp of the barrow. He felt the pressure of the black cloth around his eyes.

Somehow he thrust away the horror and played his part in the task at hand.

Stiver's voice went through the rehearsed series of questions, subjecting him to their little inquisition. Making him swear secrecy on pain of a slow and horrible death. Questioning him to test his fealty to the prince of the air, the light bearer who they said brought men wisdom and shared forbidden knowledge with the worthy few.

For a price.

Each response tasted foul on his tongue, but Azrael gave the answers that he'd memorized, yet even as he stood there in their midst, he felt like it was all happening to someone else.

It was enough to stave off panic, for in that moment, he knew he was as much in a cage as the leopard. How could they wish to make him kill such a magnificent creature, such a true friend? What was wrong with these people?

But he could not ponder the endless questions racing through his mind. If he was ever going to be free of this, of them, he just had to get through this.

They chanted around him, and he smelled strange smoke of some sort. Incense, perhaps opium smoke, hashish.

It was hideous. He felt like insects were crawling all over him merely being in their presence.

"And now," said Stiver, "the Initiate will swear. Put out your hands," the earl ordered. "What is this object you feel?"

On his knees in their midst, blind, helpless and surrounded, Azrael reached forward with his palms up and felt an object that he knew at once was a sword. Perhaps a rapier. He said as much.

"Correct. You will now be pierced and make your blood oath."

The loose white shirt he was wearing was moved aside, baring his chest. He had no idea who was touching him. He just knew that he hated them.

He braced himself as someone, Stiver, probably, pressed just the tip of the sword to the left side of Azrael's chest, near his heart.

He held perfectly still, but barely even felt it, much to his surprise.

He was so far removed from himself. Perhaps that was just as well.

In accordance with the ritual, Stiver thrust the blade in no more than half an inch. "Let this serve as a warning and reminder that your life is forfeit should you ever reveal our secrets to any other outside of ourselves. Do you understand this? Do you agree? Speak now or this blade will pierce your heart."

"I solemnly swear it," Azrael said. He repeated more hollow vows after Stiver, and the earl withdrew the tip of the blade from his chest.

Only then did Azrael feel the hot trickle of blood down his chest.

"Now you may rise."

He did so, climbing to his feet, listening acutely all the while for the sound of the Order making their move—a moment that he both dreaded and craved.

He wondered how long it would take Stiver and the rest to realize it was he who'd brought them here. Seconds? A minute, maybe two?

The heart they had very nearly pierced was pounding as he waited for the next step.

"Now, brothers," Stiver said with a note of pride in his voice, "let him be enlightened."

With a tug of someone's fingers, the blindfold was removed. The cloth was damp with the cold sweat that had been pouring down Azrael's face and all over his whole body.

He blinked rapidly to clear his vision after the pressure on his eyes, but Azrael's stomach lurched when he saw the number of men crowded into the barrow.

God, help me. Dry-mouthed, blood running down his chest, he glanced around the inside of the ancient chambered tomb.

He did his best not to think about the unlikelihood of his getting out alive. Instead, he distracted himself from the fear by focusing on the barrow.

Since his boyhood, he had always wondered what it was like inside. *Wouldn't Toby love to see this?* he tried joking to himself while Stiver consulted with Jarvis.

At least, he suspected it was Stiver and Jarvis. Robed and masked as they were, it was impossible to be entirely certain.

In any case, Azrael had to admit he could feel the profound and mysterious power resonating in this place. A womb of stone arced overhead, but there was the smell of death and a claustrophobic closeness. It was rounded and dark, though lit by torches.

Meanwhile, Stiver's followers, some three or four dozen cloaked figures, stared at him from behind their masks, silent.

It was one of the most unnerving moments in his frequently unnerving life.

Jesus.

"Brothers," Stiver said, the first to remove his expressionless black mask, "I present to you our newest member. Know, all of you, that our seers predicted at Azrael's birth that he was destined to be great among our number, touched by the gods. Behold, I give you the Duke of Rivenwood."

Azrael lifted his chin and looked around, acknowledging them with a nod, acutely aware of the dagger in his boot. How would he ever fend off so many?

Suddenly, the moment was at hand. A muffled shout echoed down one of the subterranean passages into the barrow: *"Masters, the tunnel's been discovered!"*

"What's this?"

"What did he say?" Confusion, alarm, and murmurs of uncertainty rippled through the crowd.

Azrael was already reaching for the knife hidden in his boot.

"How can this be?" someone uttered.

"Run, my lords!" the watchman bellowed down the tunnel. *"It's a trap!"*

In the next moment, chaos broke out everywhere.

With a roar, Rotherstone and his forces attacked, blasting out of three of the tunnels simultaneously, their faces covered. They barreled forth into the gathering, knocking men down, pursuing others, wreaking havoc on the crowd. Or rather, putting the fear of God in them.

The agents were armed, but Azrael knew their goal was not to kill unless they had to.

Instead, they were driving the Prometheans as a herd into the fourth tunnel, on the other end of which Lord Falconridge and Mrs. Fisher waited with more men stationed there to capture the conspirators as they came pouring out.

The fifth tunnel—leading to the Dunhaven house—had been sealed off long ago, as Serena's mother had explained. Both sides knew this by now, so no one attempted either to enter or to flee by that route.

The barrow had now turned into the scene of a riot. Mere seconds had passed, and Azrael had to plant his feet wide to keep from being swept along in the stampede.

Across from him, Stiver also stood firm against the rushing of the panicked occultists.

Azrael looked over at the earl and found him staring at him with shock and utter hatred.

Stiver still clenched the ceremonial dagger in his hand, and across the mass of fleeing men between them, Azrael saw the earl's eyes turn black with rage.

"*You* did this. Traitor!" Stiver said through gritted teeth. "Oh, but you'll pay. Kill him," he ordered his followers, then he moved toward the narrow mouth into the fifth tunnel.

"Not that way, my lord. It's sealed!" Jarvis cried.

"My daughter will let me in. Just like her mother," Stiver said with a bone-chilling sneer.

Azrael's heart skipped a beat as he realized the sickening double meaning, the vile threat.

Hearing that Stiver thought they could penetrate the blockade at the end of the tunnel, Jarvis and a few others rushed in ahead of him, while Stiver lingered just long enough to send Azrael a look that brimmed with vengeance. "Goodbye, Rivenwood. I intend to disappear, and I'm taking my daughter with me. You'll never see her again."

"*No!*" Azrael bellowed.

"Follow me and she dies," Stiver added. Casting off his robes, he vanished into the blackness of the tunnel.

The next thing Azrael knew, he was fighting for his life. On the earl's orders, half a dozen men hemmed him in and attacked.

Azrael fought like a demon, besieged on all sides.

All he could think about was going after Stiver and stopping him before he got anywhere near Serena, but he was detained by a ring of bastards out for his blood, now that they knew he'd betrayed them.

He punched one in the face, sent another sprawling into his fellows with a kick to the side, then slashed at a third who came at him from the left. He was pummeled several times, thrown into a cluster of men, bleeding all the while from the ritual wound on his chest.

Soon, thankfully, even his most determined opponents fled before the onslaught of the Order.

The agents were clearly in their glory, loving the melee, and relishing the chance to strike terror in the hearts of their enemies.

Obviously, the big one was Warrington, but, damn, Azrael thought,

Rotherstone was fast, and the one laughing in the middle of the fight, mocking the haughty Prometheans to their faces must be Beauchamp.

The agents were making their way toward him, trying to come to his aid, but by now, it was no longer necessary. He had matters in hand.

"You all right?" Rotherstone shouted.

Azrael waved and gave him a nod, then blocked a blow and struck back at his next attacker with a sharp jab to the bastard's throat. He collapsed with a garbled cough, clutching his neck.

Azrael didn't wait to speak to his new chums, as they were still engaged managing the flow of angry occultists into the tunnel, unaware that on the other end, Falconridge and company waited to take them into custody.

Instead, he finally extricated himself from the fray. Several minutes had passed, but at last, he was able to pursue Stiver into the fifth passageway.

He grabbed a torch off the wall, his heart pounding, and left the chaos behind, ducking into the pitch-black tunnel to go to Serena.

He vowed that he'd burn down the world if he got there too late.

CHAPTER 21

Unleashed

"*I* know, Raja, I'm worried about him, too."

The dim, flickering glow of three small lanterns sent shadows writhing over the walls of the musty parlor, where Serena had determined to wait with her two large guards.

Brody and Porter stood watch at the wide threshold where the sitting room joined the dark, spacious entrance hall beyond, with all its staring deer heads.

Her parents' abandoned hunting lodge was ten times eerier at night than in the daytime, Serena decided as she perched tensely on the Holland-covered couch near Raja's cage.

She'd been trying to soothe the animal with soft-toned words, but it wasn't working.

The leopard could not sit still, trying to pace in his cage, though there was scarcely room in it for him to turn around.

Raja was understandably agitated, snarling and hissing by turns—but his ears perked up when a deep, muffled banging started.

Serena froze at the sound.

It was coming from somewhere in the house.

Terror speared down her spine at the ominous rhythm, reverberating up to them from somewhere deep in the bowels of the house. She glanced at her guards in alarm.

"What the hell is that?" Porter murmured.

"Sounds like they're trying to get in through the tunnel," Brody said in a grim tone.

Serena shot to her feet and looked at them anxiously. "But my mother said it's all boarded up!"

Both hard-eyed men sent her skeptical glances, and she realized that, to some degree, they didn't really trust her because of her Promethean bloodlines.

"Milady, where does the tunnel come out inside the house?" They drew their weapons and both began stalking out into the entrance hall.

"I don't know." She shook her head, heart pounding. "My mother said it's in the cellar. Where that even is, I've no idea. I never lived here."

"Probably accessed through the kitchens. Get Roy in here. Tell him to stay with her, then follow me," ordered Brody.

While he strode off toward the kitchens to investigate, Porter jogged to the front door and called in their equally intimidating driver to assist.

Apparently this was Roy.

Still in his greatcoat, the big coachman hurried in carrying a shotgun and got into position by the sitting room doorway. This left only the driver of the wagon outside to mind both teams of horses, but Serena didn't know his name.

Once Roy marched in, Porter ran off to assist Brody in finding the entrance to the tunnel—and to bar the door, if need be.

Serena was still standing there, trembling. "This was not supposed to happen," she said in a small voice. The words escaped her by accident, but hearing them, Roy laughed softly.

"Ah, milady, if I had a penny for every time I 'eard that."

His quip put her slightly at ease. "What should I do?" she asked, needing some way to contribute to take her mind off her dread.

"Just be patient. It'll be all right," he said, never taking his stare off the corridor at the back of the entrance hall leading toward the kitchens. He did spare a glance at Raja when he hissed, though. "That thing can't get out of there, can it?"

"No."

"Whew. That's all we need," he muttered. "A damn tiger on the loose."

She didn't bother pointing out the absence of stripes, but perhaps it would help if she could keep Raja calm. Of course, she could hardly keep *herself* calm right now, but it couldn't hurt to try.

She lowered herself gingerly onto the dust-filled sofa near the leopard's cage and spoke soothingly to the animal. "There, there, boy."

Raja wanted her to know how unhappy he was about all this, though, baring his fangs and letting out a wild roar that made her gasp.

"Sheezus!" Roy glanced at the beast, then chuckled again.

His graveyard humor was so at odds with his bristling stance and the deadly loaded weapon in his hands that Serena found it all less than reassuring.

The banging from below seemed to be getting louder.

"What do we do if they break through?" she asked.

"Those two fight. You and I leave."

"I can't leave Raja. They'll kill him just for spite if they get this far."

"They won't." Roy paused, staring into the corridor. "Anyway, it's just a cat, ma'am. And I have my orders."

She frowned at his back. "Well, His Grace raised Raja from a cub. This *cat* means a great deal to him."

"Not as much as you do, I warrant. Your safety is our first—"

Gunfire erupted from somewhere below. Shouts, more banging. Serena jumped to her feet again, wide-eyed, and Roy brought up his weapon immediately.

They heard a man scream downstairs, obviously wounded.

But which side was he on?

It was impossible to tell.

The front door suddenly opened and a fourth figure appeared, a long gun in his hand. The wagon driver. "What's going on?" he exclaimed.

Roy waved him out again. "Hold your position! Get back to the horses. We may need to go!"

The man nodded and dashed out again, pulling the door shut behind him.

Roy turned to Serena. "Go outside and get in the coach, ma'am," the big man said calmly, his shotgun aimed at the kitchens. "We'll be leavin' in a moment. I'm goin' to block the cellar door, then I'll be right with you."

"But you can't lock Brody and Porter down there with the Prometheans!" she said. "We don't know how many they may have to fight. Roy—you have to help them."

He glanced back at her, wavering.

"Go!" she urged him. "I'll stay out of sight, I promise."

He nodded. "Be right back. But you're right. I'll see what I can do." He ran off in the direction of the clamor.

Serena cast about for a way to conceal Raja's presence just in case the intruders made it past her guards.

Glancing around, she whisked the dust cloth off the couch she had been sitting on, draping the large brown span of plain fabric over the leopard's cage.

Then she quickly doused the lanterns, ran to the front door, and opened it, waving to the wagon driver.

"Go get the gates open!" she called as loudly as she dared.

He snapped into motion, leaving both teams of horses in place, presumably, with the brakes of both vehicles set.

Serena turned around and glanced at the corridor on the other side of the entrance hall, leading toward the kitchens.

She could not see Roy coming back yet, but at least, in the now darkened sitting room, Raja's cage could easily be mistaken for a large table covered in a tablecloth.

If only its occupant would be still.

Leaving the front door open behind her to admit the moonlight, she hurried over to the cage. "Raja, you have to be quiet, please," she murmured through the Holland cloth.

Perhaps the leopard somehow understood the urgency in her voice, or maybe he just felt calmer underneath the fabric barrier closing him in, for he went silent.

Serena swallowed hard. She was sure her three formidable guards would stop any incursion into the house by Prometheans who might've somehow escaped the barrow, but she hurried to find a hiding place, just in case.

She ducked out of sight behind the couch, just a few feet away from Raja's cage.

Maybe Roy was right. It probably *was* better to leave in one piece, if it came to that, rather than stay with the cat. Azrael would be *most* displeased if she got herself into a scrape on account of the animal.

Suddenly remembering the weapon Mrs. Fisher had given her, she reached into her reticule and pulled out the small, one-shot pistol. She desperately hoped she didn't have to use it.

Her chaperone had showed her how it worked, but her knowledge was strictly theoretical. She had never fired a gun in her life—and wasn't even entirely clear on how to reload it, though the lady spy had also given her a small, dainty case of extra ammunition. This, too, was in her reticule.

Serena's pulse pounded and her mouth was dry as she listened to the distant sound of a fight taking place somewhere within the house.

Roy seemed to be taking a very long time. He must've gone down into the basement to help his mates after all, she thought, her heart in her throat.

A few minutes passed. It was impossible to tell how many. Time had lost all meaning in her fear. Her limbs tingling with the pins and needles that heralded a nearing state of panic, she crouched out of sight, waiting, and striving to be calm.

She heard more gunfire and nearly jumped out of her skin—what if the bullets could come through the floor? There was another scream or two, as well.

Then silence.

She didn't know which was worse, the fight sounds or the ominous quiet.

She waited, motionless, straining her ears for any hint of her guards returning.

After an interminable pause, she heard stealthy footfalls coming across the entrance hall. One set. No, two. Or was it three? It was hard to tell.

They moved softly, then the moldy old Persian rug that covered part of the hardwood floor muffled their steps. Her hands shook, slick with sweat as she clutched the pistol.

She closed her eyes to focus on her sense of hearing. She tried with all her might to determine who was out there by the way they walked. If it was her guards, then why didn't they say anything?

What if they were tracking Prometheans who had entered the house?

Or, God, what if it was Azrael? Order agents?

Blast it, she had to know. Unable to bear the suspense, she inched upward silently, cautiously, and ventured a peek over the back of the couch.

Stiver!

Terror spilled down her spine at what this might mean. But it was him, all right.

She saw him clearly in the shaft of moonlight pouring in through the open front door. And the panic she'd been just barely holding back crashed through the barriers of her composure.

Her mind went blank. *Oh my God, what do I do?*

As though he could feel her gaze on him, he turned and spotted her at once. "Serena! There you are. Darling, hurry. Come with me. We have to go at once."

There was no point hiding anymore. She stood up slowly from behind the couch, her legs wobbly beneath her. But she set her reticule on the floor and tucked her hand behind her back, hiding the pistol behind the drape of her skirts.

"Wh-what's happened, my lord?" she asked with a gulp, trying to look innocent.

"We've been most foully betrayed. Hurry!" He beckoned her impatiently and then held out his left hand to her. "I know you don't understand any of this, but we must go at once. I'll explain on the way. You have to trust me."

"But Azrael—"

"Darling, I'm sorry to tell you Azrael's been captured."

The moment he said it, she knew that he was lying. It was possible the Order had betrayed Azrael, but she doubted it.

In the next heartbeat, she noticed the knife in his right hand.

He'd been trying to hide it behind his leg—like father, like daughter, it seemed—but a moonbeam streaming in from the fanlight over the front door caught the silver of the hilt.

The blade glistened with blood.

The sight of it, along with his obvious lie about Azrael, jolted her wits back into operation after their momentary paralysis.

All in a rush, she remembered what sort of man her real father was.

The sense of kinship she felt toward him, along with his pleasant surface charm, sometimes blurred her awareness of how evil he was at his core.

There was no way she was going anywhere with him. But she had to be clever about this. He was dangerous.

She swallowed hard.

"Father," she ventured, playing for time, "whose blood is that?" With her free hand, she gestured at his knife.

The other tightly clutched her pistol.

"Oh—er, I had to defend myself, I'm afraid. Azrael told you he has enemies. Well, they've found us tonight. Which is why we must go. Those men you thought were your servants, they were with them. But they won't be a problem anymore. Now, let's go."

He quickly wiped the blade clean on the arm of the couch. The careless smearing of crimson all over the upholstery made her queasy.

"Oh my God," she whispered, feeling faint.

Was that Brody's blood, Porter's? Roy's?

"It's all right, darling. Don't be afraid. I am your father and I'll protect you." He headed toward her, rounding the coach, closing in. "Take my hand and come with me. It's what Azrael wants you to do."

She backed away from him.

He lost patience and reached for her. "Damn it, Serena—"

"Stay back!" she yelped, lifting the pistol and aiming it at him. "Don't touch me. I know you're lying."

He stopped, staring at her as realization dawned.

"Aha," he said slowly. "So. You're in on this charade." He shook his head. "Betrayed by my own flesh and blood. Figures."

"Stiver!" Just then, two more strangers jogged into the entrance hall, a short man with spectacles and a beard, and a tall, gawky one with a reddish moustache.

"Did you finish them?" her father demanded.

"They're either dead or unconscious. We didn't wait to find out," the smaller one said.

Serena gulped, assuming they were referring to Roy and her two guards.

"Who's this bit o' muslin?" asked the tall one, nodding at Serena, and wiping the sweat off his brow with a pass of his forearm.

"Be polite, now, this is my little girl. Unfortunately, gentlemen, Lady Serena has decided to disobey her father." He nodded to them to surround her.

At once, his companions approached on either side of the couch.

"Stay away from me, all of you!" she said, sweeping her weapon across the arc of men closing in on her.

They blocked her escape in either direction.

"Serena," Stiver said with a knowing smile, moving closer, "you're not going to shoot me. I'm your father. Come, we must away."

"I'm not going anywhere with you! In fact, you're not going anywhere either. You're all staying where you are until the Order gets here to take you into custody. Roy!" she shouted in rising desperation, hoping against hope.

Stiver laughed darkly. "Spirited filly, eh, boys?"

His bearded henchman scowled, but the moustache man chuckled, leering at her.

"Demmed spitting image of Mariah," the tall one remarked.

"Yes. I wonder if she likes to play like her mother did," Stiver whispered, licking his lips at her.

Serena recoiled, astounded. "You are *vile!*"

"Take her," Stiver commanded his henchmen.

They both lunged at her; she didn't know which one to aim the gun at. In the blink of an eye, the bearded one had driven her arm skyward.

Knocked off balance, she squeezed the trigger by accident and fired into the ceiling in her fright. Stiver and the tall one laughed as plaster dust rained down on them.

As if all this was a game.

But the bearded man wrenched the weapon impatiently out of her grasp and tucked it into his waistband. "Can you two stop fooling around so we can get the hell out of here before the Order catches up?"

"Relax, Falk," said the moustache man. "They haven't caught us yet and they never will."

"Humph," said the bearded one, Falk. "A little assistance if you don't mind, Jarvis. Or do I have to do everything myself?"

Jarvis? Serena quaked at the name, glancing at the moustache man.

She remembered it well from the papers inside the snakeskin box. Lord Jarvis was the one who had a penchant for twelve-year-old girls.

"Bring her," Stiver said through gritted teeth, then started toward the door.

When Jarvis grasped her other arm, Serena planted her feet and began fighting them for all she was worth. "Let me go! Azrael will never let you get away with this!"

"Azrael is dead, my dear. That's whose blood it was, if you must know. I didn't want to tell you, but there it is."

She froze, drawing in her breath, then snapped out of her moment's fleeting horror, rejecting his claim with every ounce of her will.

"I don't believe you. Take your filthy hands off me!"

She began fighting twice as hard as before, thrashing as they dragged her toward the doorway of the sitting room.

"Quit struggling!" Jarvis said.

She brought her heel down hard on his toe.

"Ow!" He cursed several times. "You take her, Stiver. She's your damned problem, anyway." When Jarvis stepped back, limping slightly, Serena all but hissed at him.

This was not much of an improvement, though, as Stiver grabbed her arm and wrenched it to get her full attention.

She cried out, but he ignored her discomfort. "Behave yourself! I don't want to hurt you, Serena, but if you don't come quietly, I will."

"Likewise." She started to kick him in the groin, but he blocked the blow, quickly turning aside.

Enraged by the attempt, he struck back, punching her.

The unexpected blow snapped her head back; pain exploded through her face, so sharp it stole her breath.

No girl who had grown up with two roughhousing brothers could've escaped childhood without being punched once or twice. But never in the face, and never with such sharp, controlled skill.

He'd meant to knock her out so she'd quit struggling, and it seemed to have worked. Her eyes watered, a trickle of blood dripped from her nose, and the world turned woozy.

Seeing stars, she went limp in her captors' grasp, but her father caught her.

She was only dimly aware of Stiver heaving her up onto his shoulder.

"Cheeky little bitch. Just like your mother," he muttered, shifting her weight a bit, then heading for the entrance hall. "Come on, you blackguards. Let's get out of here. We'll take their carriage."

Serena's head and arms hung down behind her father's back as they trooped out of the sitting room toward the entrance hall.

Unfortunately, when they passed Raja's covered cage, a distinct feline snarl came out from underneath what appeared to be a mere table.

"Did you hear that?" Jarvis whispered.

"I did," Falk said.

"What the hell?" Stiver murmured.

Serena was dimly aware of her captors stopping, turning toward the cage.

Falk approached it warily, then whipped the cloth away.

"It's Rivenwood's animal!" Jarvis exclaimed. "By Jove, look at that thing."

"Shoot it," Stiver ordered.

"No, please...leave him alone," Serena protested weakly, half conscious, but they ignored her.

Falk pulled the pistol he'd taken off her out of his waistband. "Bullets?"

"Try her reticule. She dropped it behind the couch," Stiver said, motioning.

"We really don't have time for this, Stiver," Falk said, trudging back to find it.

"Nonsense; it'll only take a moment," Stiver replied. "Besides, Rivenwood needs to suffer for what he's done."

I thought you said he was dead.

"You two finish here while I go put her in the coach, then we'll be underway." Stiver shifted her weight on his shoulder and marched on toward the front door, crossing the entrance hall.

Struggling back toward consciousness, Serena saw Falk hand the gun to Jarvis with a look of distaste. "You do the honors."

"What, you don't like big game hunting?" Jarvis quipped with a cruel smile, aiming the pistol at Raja.

Suddenly, before Stiver reached the door, a tall, pale-haired figured exploded out of the shadows, ducking his head and barreling into Jarvis with the force of a battering ram. Through her groggy state, Serena saw that it was Azrael—his blond hair flying, his white shirt stained with blood.

His elegant face had turned to a mask of savagery as he attacked, and when his shoulder slammed into Lord Jarvis, the hit threw the man across the room.

Jarvis stumbled and fell onto his back.

A sickening crack sounded when his head smashed against the floor. Lord Jarvis did not move again.

A pool of crimson began spreading under his head as he stared up at the ceiling, stone dead.

"He's killed him!" Falk said to Stiver, peering down at his dead comrade. Then he backed away, suddenly diving for the loaded pistol Jarvis hadn't got the chance to fire.

He picked it up, looking unnerved, and aimed it at Azrael, who stalked inexorably toward him.

Hands shaking visibly, Falk squeezed the trigger.

And missed.

Azrael hurled his knife in answer, his movements smooth and lethal; in the blink of an eye, the hilt of his dagger was sticking out of the bearded man's chest.

The blade was sunk somewhere in his heart and left lung. Falk looked down in disbelief at the knife sticking out of his chest and then fell with a garbled groan.

Stiver let out an angry snarl, tumbling Serena off his shoulder onto a nearby armchair. "Well! If it isn't the traitor. You're a disgrace to your father's memory, do you know that?"

"Good," Azrael replied. "I hate the lot of you. I'll see you all burn in hell."

"You think you're so pure?" Stiver taunted, circling with Azrael. "Look at your handiwork here tonight. Most impressive, Your Grace." He gestured at the two corpses in the room. "I daresay you're more like your ol' man than you care to admit."

Azrael charged him with a muttered oath for that remark.

They clashed, brawling right there in the entrance with the gusto of two opponents who had secretly longed for a go at each other for years.

Now all that bottled-up rage on both sides was coming out.

They'll kill each other. Serena righted herself slowly on the chair, head pounding. The room was still a bit fuzzy, and her nose was throbbing, but somehow she fought her way back to full consciousness while the two men battled.

Stiver, though in his fifties, seemed filled with the superhuman strength of some demonic rage as he warded off the younger, taller man.

He somehow anticipated Azrael's every move as he swung at him again and again, growing ever more furious.

Stiver continually ducked, mocking him. "You ungrateful little shit. After all I've done for you, this is the thanks I get?"

"You only ever cared about yourself." With that, Azrael knocked Stiver's feet out from under him with a sweeping motion of his leg, and Stiver lost his balance, landing on the floor.

Azrael dropped down to punch him again and again.

God, does he mean to beat him to death? Serena wondered, stunned by his ferocity. He'd already killed two men—probably more—and judging by the blood seeping through the front of his shirt, Azrael himself was wounded.

He did not seem to feel it. But surely this had gone far enough.

Thinking she should say something to try to calm him down, Serena tried to stand up, but the effort made her queasy. The fiery pain throbbing in her face nearly made her throw up. She leaned forward and saw a drop of blood fall onto her skirts from her nose.

She could taste the blood, too. When she'd hung head-down over her father's shoulder, it had run to the back of her throat.

The taste of it was sharp and metallic, like biting down on a dirty penny.

She closed her eyes until the queasiness had passed, but what she saw when she opened them again appalled her.

The two men were now locked in a death match. Her father and her fiancé.

Somehow Stiver had got the better of Azrael. He was kneeling atop him, trying with all his strength to drive the blade he'd wielded earlier down into Azrael's throat.

Azrael was on his back on the floor, his arms braced upward, keeping Stiver's knife at bay.

Serena rose, willing away the nausea and holding back a whimper. She knew Azrael was already hurt and losing blood. She had seen his red-stained shirt when he'd arrived. Cold terror gripped her. If his strength ebbed or his arms buckled for one moment, Stiver's blade would cut through his windpipe.

Stop it, both of you! she wanted to scream. But she dared not even speak for fear of breaking his concentration.

Damn it, she felt as helpless and frustrated as the caged leopard.

Raja was moving about restlessly behind the iron bars, snarling like he was dying to get out.

Maybe he should, she thought suddenly.

Dire inspiration filled her. Heart pounding, Serena went over to the cage.

Driven by the blind, instinctual need to do something, anything, to save the man she loved, she did not stop to think about the consequences.

She just wanted that knife pointed anywhere else but at Azrael's throat.

She looked at the leopard, hesitating only for a heartbeat.

She understood the choice she was making, but if the leopard killed her father, then by God, she would be Azrael's true bride in a deeper sense than either of them had ever anticipated.

She gripped the latch on the cage door, aware she risked losing a finger or even a whole hand with the wild state the leopard was in at the moment.

"Help him, Raja," she whispered.

Then she unlocked the cage.

"Father," she said slowly, calmly, "I would run if I were you."

Actually, running was the worst thing a person could do around a wild animal, so Azrael had told her.

But Stiver took the bait, looking over just as she opened the cage door. Horror flooded his face. He jumped to his feet with a stifled cry, then bolted out the front door, abandoning Azrael.

He didn't get far.

Raja was after him like a streak of black lightning, rocketing out into the night.

Serena ran to help Azrael, but he was already getting up. He sprang to his feet, and they both raced to the doorway.

They arrived just in time to see Raja leap off the small front terrace and pounce on Lord Stiver, landing on him with graceful ease, flattening the earl onto his stomach.

"Raja, no!" Azrael roared as the snarling leopard began biting Stiver about the shoulder and neck, tearing into him, his ebony tail whipping back and forth, his razor claws out slashing at the man's back.

Azrael ran outside, but Serena took a step back in horror as the reality of what she had done played out before her eyes. Her heart thumped like it would jump right out of her chest.

Stiver was on the ground being mauled, letting out bloodcurdling screams, kicking his feet, flailing.

Meanwhile, with the wagon driver off opening the gates, as Serena had ordered, the unsupervised horses hitched to the coach got spooked enough to overpower the brake and bolted off, taking the carriage with them. The wagon's team of larger, more docile workhorses reacted with terror as well, but only dragged their burden twenty feet or so away.

Much closer, Stiver managed to knock Raja briefly off his back, but the leopard merely caught the arm he'd swung at him between his jaws.

"Help me!" the earl begged while Raja started dragging him by the arm across the overgrown drive.

Instinct had taken over, and Raja seemed inclined to carry his prey off into the bush so he could devour him in privacy.

At that moment, the wagon driver returned from opening the driveway gates, saw what was happening, and aimed his rifle at Raja.

"Don't shoot!" Serena cried at the same time Azrael bellowed at the man, *"Don't you dare!"*

The roar of his master also managed somehow to get the leopard's attention, penetrating Raja's fury.

Years of training seemed to override the predator's instincts momentarily.

The big cat hesitated, but did not let go of his quarry.

At that moment, Stiver stopped screaming. His body went limp.

Whether he was dead or had simply passed out from blood loss or pure horror, there was no way to tell.

Azrael moved toward the leopard, keeping eye contact now that he'd finally captured the animal's notice. "Raja. *No.*"

The beast hissed at him as if to say, *Don't come near my prey.*

Serena watched with her heart in her throat.

The Order man looked terrified but held his fire; he kept his rifle trained on the big cat in case it made any move toward his horses—or them.

"Come, Raja, you are not a monster…" As Azrael began speaking in a low tone to his pet, Serena heard footsteps behind her.

She turned, stunned to find Roy and the two Order footmen limping back into the entrance hall.

Roy and Brody had Porter between them, holding him up. She gathered he was the most seriously injured. They'd tied a bandage around his thigh.

"What's happening?" Roy asked.

"Bring the cage!" Azrael said, hearing them arrive, but he did not look over, never taking his eyes off Raja.

The two abler men quickly deposited Porter on a chair and picked up the cage by its metal bars, not bothering with the poles, in their haste.

Serena stepped aside as they carried it out. They set the cage on the ground a safe distance from Azrael and quickly backed away.

It was then that Serena and everyone there witnessed something extraordinary.

While the two Order men hurried back toward the house, Azrael kept his stare fixed on the beast he had raised since it was a cub.

There was no question in this moment that Raja was a wild and fearsome force of nature.

But so, it seemed, was the Duke of Rivenwood.

Azrael loomed over the deadly predator, making sure the leopard understood who was larger, who was really to be feared here. He all but hissed back at the beast.

Raja's tail thrashed back and forth, challenging his master. His ebony ears were flattened. He shone like liquid darkness in the brilliance of the full moon.

The light glimmered over Azrael's pale hair as he willed the animal into submission, never breaking his stare.

Serena scarcely dared breathe, watching the primal battle of wills unfold before her eyes. Her hands clutched to her chest, she did not even blink, half convinced that Raja would leap on Azrael next and continue his rampage.

If that happened, she knew what fate awaited the leopard.

A swift bullet—and it would be all her fault.

"Raja. *No*," Azrael commanded one last time, and suddenly, something barely perceptible in the big cat's demeanor changed.

He seemed to remember who he was. He still hissed with princely displeasure, but took a slinking step toward Azrael, abandoning his prey.

Fearlessly, Azrael reached down and grabbed the beast's collar.

He only had to walk the animal four or five steps toward the house to reach the waiting cage.

Raja went willingly, padding into his familiar confinement. The big cat seemed confused by the attack he had just launched.

It was not until Serena heard the cage door slam back into place and the latch drop that she finally exhaled.

Crouching down next to the leopard's cage to catch his breath, Azrael closed his eyes, his shoulders drooping with exhausted relief.

He lowered his head, still panting from his many battles of this night. With the deadened pond beyond him, the moonlight glowed in the clouding halo of warm breath surrounding his head.

Serena ran to him, though she slowed down a few paces from Raja's cage, approaching more warily.

Azrael lifted his head and met her gaze, his eyes silver in the night, the traces of savagery still gleaming in their depths.

But whatever wild streak of mayhem and darkness was in him by birth, they both knew now that he had mastered it, as surely as he'd tamed the black leopard.

She reached out and laid a tentative hand on his shoulder.

He covered it at once with his own.

"How did you do that?" she whispered.

"I have no idea."

"Are you hurt? Your shirt's all bloody."

He shook his head. "Nothing serious. You?"

When he glanced up to scan her face, his gaze suddenly homed in on the dried blood beneath her nose.

Shock flooded his eyes. He swept to his feet. "Who did this to you? What happened?" he demanded, capturing her chin gently and lifting her face to the moonlight.

"He hit me."

"Stiver?"

She nodded. "He tried to abduct me. He threatened…unspeakable things." She shook her head with a shudder, then grimaced as she glanced toward her sire's prone, mangled body. "Is he—dead?"

Azrael motioned to the wagon driver to go and check.

Serena held her breath as the Order man walked over for a closer look at the earl. He felt for a pulse, then shook his head at Azrael.

"He's gone," Azrael whispered.

A sob tore from her. "Oh God, what have I done?"

"Shh. I've got you." Azrael wrapped his arms around her, steadying her as she broke down, though he himself was bloodied and cut.

"He was my father. I know he was a terrible man but—I didn't really mean for this to happen."

"I know, sweeting. Believe me, I know." He cradled her in his arms.

She clung to him, ignoring the blood on his shirt smearing onto her clothes. She curled her hands around his hard biceps; his strength was all that was holding her up as it sank in that she had killed a man, though indirectly.

She had killed her own father. "I-I didn't know what else to do. I thought he was going to kill you," she said tearfully.

"He would've. He tried to. But you saved my life."

She shook her head. "Raja saved you, not me."

"No, it was your quick thinking, Serena. You saved me, and I am in your debt. Shh, sweeting, I know."

He did know, she thought. Now they both did.

Azrael held her, caressed her back, and gently strove to calm her down while the Order reinforcements finally arrived.

Two riders and a carriage came barreling up the drive, but she paid them no mind, and Azrael just waved them on about their business.

Thankfully, they'd brought a pair of medics with them—military-trained surgeons, most likely. The medics jumped out and got to work tending the injured at once. Their assistants covered Stiver's body with a cloth while the wagon driver calmed down his team, while others went to help recapture the runaway coach horses.

All around them, the Order's operation continued with a bustling air of controlled chaos, but Serena hid her face against the less bloody side of Azrael's chest, wanting the world to go away.

Roy limped out to brief his colleagues. "Two dead in the entrance hall and four more in the cellar," he told them. "Porter got shot in the leg.

He's inside."

One surgeon ran in to start working on Porter. The other jogged over to Azrael and Serena. "Do either of you require medical atten—"

"I'm fine," Azrael interrupted, "but my lady might."

"No, please, see to the others first," Serena said.

The medic looked skeptical, noting both of their bloodied appearances. "If you're both quite sure…"

Azrael waved the man off.

"I'll check back in a bit." The medic hurried off to seek another patient.

The excitement around them soon moved inside, leaving the two of them standing there, more or less alone.

The night suddenly grew very quiet.

"Maybe we really are cursed," Serena said at last in a dull, weary tone.

"*No.* Not anymore. Darling, listen to me." He set his hands on her shoulders.

She gazed up at him with tears in her eyes, unsure.

"The curse is broken now. We did it," he said softly. "For the first time, we're finally free. Can't you feel it? Everything's changed. Even this place." He glanced around at the dismal setting, then looked at her again.

She gazed up at him, longing to believe.

At that moment, the night sky released a delicate sprinkling of snowflakes.

Serena looked up as the snow swirled and wafted down around them. Azrael lifted his head and stared at it, too.

Silently, the snowfall began painting over the black landscape and the dead pond before them, covering the jagged, thorny branches of autumn with its clean blanket of white. Erasing all the ugly memories, like they were nothing but a mere bad dream…

In minutes, the snow began collecting on the grass, the trees, and everywhere, brightening the forlorn darkness of this place with its pearly glow. It turned the shadows blue, until, soon, its pristine brilliance glistened magically in the light of the full moon.

The whole landscape was transformed.

"Maybe you're right," Serena finally whispered. "It does feel different here."

Azrael nodded.

It was as though a great darkness had lifted, an immovable weight dissolved, unburdening them. Serena leaned her head against Azrael's warm chest and listened to the peaceful silence.

She remembered her mother's words back at Dunhaven Manor, and could've sworn she sensed blessings falling down on them in between the snowflakes.

Azrael leaned down and pressed a kiss to her brow. "I love you, my angel," he whispered.

Then he lifted his palm and offered his hand with a wary gaze, as though he feared she might not wish to take it any longer, after watching him so ruthlessly dispatch those evil men.

Seeing for herself what he was capable of.

But she grasped it without hesitation, lacing her fingers gently through his.

Relief and gratitude flickered in the silvery depths of his eyes as he tightened his grip.

"I love you, too, Azrael," she said. "Never doubt it."

He smiled wearily. "We should go inside."

"In a moment." The cold air felt good.

Hand in hand, they stood watching the snow in wonder.

At last, they looked at each other as it started sinking in that the nightmare truly was over.

The ghosts of the past and all their families' dark secrets had, at last, been laid to rest.

Which meant the two of them had finally reached their new beginning. Indeed, thought Serena as she held his tender gaze.

They had earned it.

EPILOGUE

Snowfall

Four Weeks Later

He was the perfect birthday present, Serena mused as she lay on her side watching Azrael sleep, her head propped on her hand.

The gold canopy of his bed made a cozy swoop of fabric above them, but where they lay, the satin duvet was luxuriously rumpled, and the tousled sheets wound around their naked bodies.

Her entire being was filled with the warm, deep satisfaction of her new life as his duchess. Just feeling his bare leg next to hers under the covers made her happy.

How beautiful he was, she thought with a small sigh as he slept on, his muscled chest rising and falling with each slow, peaceful breath.

He looked different somehow since all of this was over, she mused. Younger, his color better, not as pale. It was like he was coming more fully to life.

Of course, there was also his charming new haircut.

His flax-blond hair no longer reached past his shoulders, barely even touching the back of his neck. She loved the way the front part hung down coltishly over his forehead.

She was filled with the tender urge to brush that silky forelock gently out of his face.

Their sudden wedding had caused quite a stir in Society. But what else could the ton expect from such an unpredictable man?

His secrets, however, had turned to surprises, she thought with a fond smile.

Then her gaze wandered past him, through the ornately carved bedposts, to the French doors that led to the snowy balcony.

The sky was pale blue. It must be nearly eight o'clock, she thought. They really should get up. It was just so sublimely cozy to lie abed together on a snowy winter morning.

Through the glass panes of the French doors, Serena could see the black, lacy treetops in the garden park of Moonlight Square across from Rivenwood House, all newly lined with crisp white snow.

The snow lay thick and dreamlike on the ground outside, promising a perfect setting for their Christmas party this evening.

It would be their first time hosting a gathering as a married couple, but they had much to celebrate.

Her birthday tomorrow, their twelfth day of marriage, the Yuletide right around the corner, and, of course, their survival.

Serena had insisted on inviting whole families for the holiday occasion. Her parents and brothers and, of course, Cousin Tamsin would all be there. The Netherfords would be bringing their two small children, as well as Felicity's brother, Major Peter Carvel.

All her husband's friends from the gentlemen's club at the Grand Albion would be coming, including Sidney and Gable.

Serena had invited not only Trinny, Lady Gable, but *her* whole clan of red-haired sisters and their parents, Lord and Lady Beresford, as well. After all, they were neighbors. In short, the whole square had been invited. Oh, and even Toby.

He and Azrael seemed to have hit it off well, much to her amusement. That pair of eccentrics, she thought with affection.

She could hardly wait. It would be wonderful having Azrael's medieval-ish house garlanded with evergreen boughs and sprigs of holly, wreaths and ribbons, bright lanterns, and music.

He needed that sort of thing, she thought. Healing all the scars of his past could take a lifetime, but she had devoted herself to that mission from the moment she had said *"I do"* at the little church of St. Andrew's across the square.

Her sweet husband had never had a normal family life of any kind, but Serena considered it her duty and privilege to shower him with all the joys he had never known.

Wonderful holidays full of family and friends were just the beginning of the home she would make for him, brimming with love and laughter.

She was grateful for the task before her. Reflecting on her own life, she knew how easily she could've gone down a very selfish track, indulged and cosseted as she'd been from her childhood.

But meeting Azrael and sharing some small part of all the pain he'd known had opened her eyes to the preciousness and fragility of existence. She looked forward to devoting herself to taking away his cares and loading up his life with every happiness she could think of. For, truly, he had only just begun to live since their ordeal at Owlswick had ended.

She thrust those dark memories out of her mind, however, beginning to wish her husband would wake up.

Blissful as this moment was, their busy day was wasting. Besides, she had a present for him this morning, and was getting impatient for him to open it.

"Are you staring at me?" he mumbled just then, his eyes still closed, but a drowsy smile tugging at his lips.

She grinned and rested her chin on his warm shoulder. "Wake up, lazy. Anyway, who could blame me, handsome as you are?" At last, she gave in to the urge to brush the forelock gently out of his eyes.

He opened them, a distinct silver twinkle in their ice-blue depths as he looked at her.

Without warning, he grabbed her around the waist and pulled her atop him. She went willingly, laughing.

"How did you know I was watching you?"

"I could feel it," he whispered playfully. "We have a very powerful bond, remember?"

"Oh my," she said, startled by the rigid length against her. "I feel something, too, Your Grace!"

"Who could blame me, luscious as you are?" he said, then gave her a lingering kiss. "Good morning, wife."

"Good morning, husband. Oh my! It's growing." She giggled at his insistent hardness throbbing against her belly. "It is a good morning indeed, I see."

"It's about to get even better." He rolled her onto her back and moved atop her.

"Azrael!" She stopped him with a breathless laugh and a halfhearted hand on his chest. "Not today, darling. There's too much to do!"

"But look at you," he protested, his voice still scratchy and seductive with sleep, "in my bed, so gorgeous, without a stitch of clothing on. There's always time for *that*." He kissed her neck. "I may not be evil incarnate, my love, but I am not a saint."

"No, you're not." Her toes curled with delight at his warm nibbling at her neck. "Nevertheless!" She planted her hands on his shoulders to keep him at bay, and attempted to take a firm tone with him. "Behave yourself, sir. Our Christmas party is tonight, have you forgotten? There is so much to do." She gave him a playful little slap on his lean bottom. "Now, move."

He gave her a mock pout but allowed her to sit up.

"Besides, as it happens," she said, "I have an early Christmas present for you."

"Another one?" he asked, perking up and looking adorable, she thought, all rumpled and flushed.

"Yes, and this one's much better than a cravat pin."

For a moment, she thought he would argue. He was not used to getting presents, and for the first few she'd given him, he hadn't known how to react.

But he must be adapting to being doted on and spoiled, for today he merely shrugged.

"All right, then. Bring it forth. All presents from *you* are most heartily accepted here."

She smiled at him over her bare shoulder as she bounced out of bed. They were making progress.

"I wonder what it is," he said, folding his hands behind his head as he leaned back against the headboard.

"You'll soon found out." He eyed her naked body as she quickly slipped on her dressing gown, tying the cloth belt around her waist. "I think you're going to like it."

She crossed their bedchamber, opened the door, and beckoned to the footman stationed in the upstairs hallway. "We'll take our breakfast now. Tell Grimsley to bring the present up, too."

The footman bowed and hurried off.

Serena shut the door and turned around again. "This could take a few minutes. I'm not sure it's…wrapped yet."

"Hmm," he said, fixing her with a piercing stare, as though trying to read her mind. She moved onto the bed again on her knees and caressed his leg through the covers.

"Any nightmares last night, sweeting?" she asked softly. "It seemed like you slept well."

He captured her hand and held it. "None for me. You?"

"No, they seem to have gone away. Thank God."

"Toby was right when he told me how strong you are," he murmured. "You're very resilient."

"Love makes me so," she whispered, holding his gaze. Then she smiled ruefully. "I'm just glad to have my old nose back instead of that hideous eggplant I had on my face for a few days."

He shook his head, lifting his fingertips to her chin to inspect her face. "You're lucky your nose wasn't broken." A shadow passed behind his eyes, but he must've willed his wrath away, for his voice stayed gentle. "It would be such a shame to mar that lovely face."

Serena snorted. "I looked so ugly for a while there that I marvel that you still saw fit to marry me. Good thing we had a tiny wedding."

"You could never be ugly," he said. "But even if your nose was smashed as flat as a pugilist's, you'd still be the most beautiful woman in the world to me."

"Ohh! You say the sweetest things." She moved forward on her knees and kissed him, caressing his head and laying her palm next to the scar above his heart, where he'd told her Stiver had pierced his breast in their horrid ceremony.

All those men had got what they deserved in her view.

A shipwreck, according to the newspapers, had tragically claimed the lives of several dozen prominent men. A late November squall, it was reported, had sent their bark to the bottom of the Channel when the group of jolly club mates had been traveling for an annual social event on the Isle of Man.

Where the Prometheans actually were, only the Order knew.

Mrs. Fisher had also vanished, and the elite agents who'd been working with Azrael had likewise withdrawn from their lives for secrecy's sake. Azrael had told them that if he could ever be of help to the Order on Promethean matters, they had only to call on him.

Serena dearly hoped they never did.

As for her erstwhile Order footmen, Porter was still recovering from being shot in the leg, but Brody and the big driver, Roy, had been left behind to guard her and Azrael for a while longer, in case of any possible retaliation by unseen enemies connected to Stiver's group. This was only a precaution, however.

From what she understood, any other Promethean cells operating in

England had gone to ground. She suspected that the many who'd been captured that night were providing the Crown's secret warriors with all sorts of useful information.

Azrael suddenly glanced toward the door. "Sounds like our breakfast is coming. I'm hungry."

"Well, we must feed you, then. *After* you open your present."

Hearing the service cart rolling down the hallway, Serena was already on her feet and crossing to the door when the footman knocked. She answered it and nodded cheerfully to him.

The servant rolled the breakfast cart as far as the doorway. Serena pulled it the rest of the way into the room herself, but was far more interested in the gaily decorated box Grimsley was holding.

It was about the size of a hatbox, and the lid was tied on with a big red bow.

"Thank you, Grimsley. I'll be with you soon to talk about how the staff's preparations are going for tonight. But first, I must give His Grace this wee trifle."

"Good luck, Your Grace," Grimsley whispered.

She gave the old butler a conspiratorial wink, then nudged the door shut with a bare toe and hurried back to their bed, carefully concealing the shifting weight inside the box by the steady way she carried it.

"You got me a hat?"

"Maybe."

"What are you up to, woman?" Azrael inquired, scanning her face with his most piercing gaze.

"Trust me, you're going to love it."

And more importantly, it's going to love you back, she thought, but didn't say so aloud. She had to surprise him.

She set the box on the bed and slid it toward him. "I really didn't mean to give it to you quite yet, but it was delivered yesterday, and there was no way to conceal it from you for long."

"Hmm. I am altogether intrigued."

"Just—leave the box on the bed when you open it. I don't want you to get any advance clues."

He furrowed his brow. "Very well."

Playing along, he sat up with the gold satin coverlet swathed around his waist.

As he slowly untied the bow, a strange sound came from inside the box.

A muffled yip.

Azrael glanced at her, perplexed.

Serena stifled a laugh, waiting with bated breath for him to lift the lid.

Uncertainly, he moved the ends of the ribbon aside, but before he could open the box, the lid started nudging itself upward.

And a little black nose poked out.

"Serena…?"

She burst out laughing as he took off the lid, then reached into the box, and discovered that the fuzzy, wriggling gift inside required both hands to lift.

With a look on his face that she'd never forget, Azrael pulled his present out of the tissue paper lining the box and held it up by its furry, wriggling waist, staring at it.

"You got me a *puppy*?"

He started laughing in disbelief.

She lifted her hand and let the puppy prop its hind paws on her palm. "Isn't he precious? This is Franklin! He's a Westie."

"I can't believe it."

He stared at the cheerful white puppy dangling from his grasp.

All of ten weeks old, Franklin panted as he stared back at Azrael, his fuzzy hair sticking out in all directions, his little wisp of a tail wagging at top speed, his tiny paws kicking with eagerness to get down and play.

Azrael cradled the pup against his chest. "How do you do, Franklin?"

Serena tried to read his reaction, but Azrael's head was down as he held the tiny terrier in his arms.

She couldn't hold back. "When you told me you never had a puppy in your whole life… Well, I know how sad you've been since Raja had to go back to the menagerie after what happened. And I just thought, since everything is new in your life now—since it's time to try new things— why not give him a normal pet? One we don't have to worry about. One that will actually fetch, with the proper training."

He looked up. "It fetches?"

She gave his shoulder a shove. "Not yet, silly, he's just a baby. And he's not an *it*, he's a he. But he's smart. I'll bet you can easily train him to fetch when he's older. Isn't he darling?"

He nodded, head down, his gaze fixed on the pup.

"Well? What do you think?"

He scratched Franklin under the chin for a moment, then gave Serena a besotted grin. "I love him."

"Me too!" She clapped her hands triumphantly at his response. "You can take him everywhere with you, little as he is. He won't get much bigger than my cat, Wesley. You can walk him in the park and bring him to the country whenever we go. And when we have children, he'll be perfectly safe with them. For all we know, he might even be a good little guard dog, too."

"He's perfect, and you are the most thoughtful, precious, kind, lovely, caring wife that any man could ever hope to win." He gazed at her as he held the new arrival. "Serena, every day I'm grateful and stunned to wake up and discover it wasn't a dream—that this is our life now, and you're really mine."

"Oh Azrael, I am. And I always will be." She reached out and cupped his face. "It's easy to love you. You're more than my husband. You are my best friend."

He released the puppy to pull Serena into his embrace and began to kiss her, easing her back onto the mattress. As she wrapped her arms around his neck and returned his tender kisses, she felt him tugging open the cloth belt of her dressing gown. He slipped a warm, smooth hand inside the silk, caressing her curves.

But the puppy, who had been digging in the blankets and attacking the tassels adorning the headboard pillows, decided then to wage a merry war on the duvet.

Grabbing the edge of Azrael's blanket between his teeth, Franklin started backing up with it, shaking his head, letting out adorable little growls, until suddenly, he tugged the blanket off Azrael entirely, displaying the Duke of Rivenwood in all his naked splendor.

"Excuse me!" His Grace exclaimed, laughing.

"Good boy!" Serena cheered, blocking the pup with her arm from falling off the bed.

Azrael sighed and covered himself from the waist down again. "I suppose that's Franklin's way of telling us it's time to wake up."

"And quite right he is. We've got a very busy day ahead, getting ready for our gathering."

Azrael smiled at her and raked his fingers through his hair. Serena rose and scooped Franklin into her arms, gave him a kiss on his fuzzy head, then put the wee pup down on the floor.

At once, he went scampering off to investigate his new

surroundings. Azrael rose and pulled on his blue silk dressing gown.

Serena's heart was aglow as she went over to the breakfast cart. She could not have been more pleased by the success of her gift. "Chocolate or tea this morning, love?"

They looked at each other and both said: "Chocolate."

She smiled at him, removed the lid from the ceramic decanter, stirred it with a knife, and then poured them each a steaming mug of hot chocolate.

While she put the lid back on, she glanced over and watched her husband playing with his ankle-high puppy like the boy he'd never been allowed to be in his childhood, and her heart clenched with love.

When the pup made a mad dash toward the French doors, where some unknown trifle had captured his attention, Azrael followed.

"Hey, you little nutter, come back here." He captured the dog and picked him up. "You want to see the view?"

He paused to look out at the glistening winter's day.

Serena was captivated, admiring his elegantly muscled silhouette against the French doors, with the snowy world beyond.

"Look at that." He pointed out the window. "Someone's moving in down the street. Appears we're getting a new neighbor."

"Oh? Which house?"

"On the corner."

"Really? One of the ducal mansions?" Intrigued, she joined him there, bringing him his chocolate as well as her own.

"Thank you, my dear," he said, puppy in one hand, hot chocolate in the other. He gestured with his cup out the window toward the right.

"Aha," she said, peering out at the busy prospect of servants unloading furniture from a wagon. "Well, they must've finally tracked down the old duke's next heir."

Azrael looked at her in question, and she remembered that he still didn't know many of the neighbors around the square, nor did he follow the local gossip.

"The old Duke of Amberley died…I should think it's been five years ago now. But the title's changed hands two or three times since. Dreadful bad luck. The heirs keep dying." She shrugged, then looked out the window. "I wonder who it went to this time. Probably a distant relative by now."

"Well, whoever the chap is, perhaps we should invite him to the party. 'Tis the neighborly thing to do, right?"

Serena turned to him. "Why, that's a splendid idea, darling. Thank you for suggesting it. I will send a servant over with an invitation. He might not come, but yes, we'll let the new duke know he's welcome to join us if he likes. That's very thoughtful of you."

He looked pleased that she'd praised his idea, but privately, Serena couldn't help smiling with affection. *Whatever happened to my loner?*

"What?" he asked.

"Nothing." She caressed him. "Come. Eat your breakfast before it gets cold." She bustled away to fix their plates.

"You heard the lady, little fellow." Azrael set the puppy down, and Franklin immediately scampered after Serena, trying to catch the hem of her dressing gown wafting out behind her.

"Naughty!" she scolded, laughing.

"He takes after you, I see," Azrael said.

"Ha!"

He collected the puppy so she could ready their plates, but he continued to tease her, as was his wont.

No matter.

She teased him right back, and neither of them minded a bit, for any day that started with kisses and banter was a good day indeed.

Author Note

Weird stories were told of the fabulously rich and brilliant Sir Francis Dashwood. He'd had a vast system of caves dug in a cliff near his estate at West Wycombe, some thirty-three miles northwest of London, and villagers passing the entrance late at night told of seeing strange figures dressed in red robes dragging screaming girls into the black entrance. But no one liked to complain, because Sir Francis was such a pleasant gentleman.

~ Daniel P. Mannix, *The Hellfire Club*

Evil in high places was as much a feature of bygone eras as it so often is today.

As Daniel P. Mannix writes in his 1961 classic, *The Hellfire Club* (reissued in 2001 by ibooks, inc.) was "an association dedicated to Black Magic, sexual orgies, and political conspiracies. The club included among its members the Prime Minister of England, the Chancellor of the Exchequer, the Lord Mayor of London, the first Lord of the Admiralty, the son of the Archbishop of Canterbury, several of England's greatest artist and poets, the Prince of Wales, and even Benjamin Franklin."

The implications are rather terrifying once you start digging into it, past the familiar protestations that it was all in good fun. If you are interested in researching historical secret societies and the world of elite conspiracies—insofar as they *can* be researched—I definitely recommend the Mannix book.

I should mention while touching upon this topic that the original inspiration for this book came about as an offshoot from my Inferno Club series. A few of the Inferno Club agents put in cameo appearances in the story you just read, so by now, you know the gist of what they're all about.

When they're not falling madly in love with their heroines, they are hunting "Promethean" bad guys for the Crown. (If you missed this series, you may like to check out the first Inferno Club book, *My Wicked Marquess*.)

My original intention in devising the Prometheans was to concoct a set of villains worthy of taking on heroes who are at the top of the food chain in Regency England's pecking order.

A story, in some ways, is only as strong as its villain, and you need a VERY strong villain to seriously challenge a hero who's already got everything going for him: rank, power, fortune, the best education money can buy, physical strength, loyal friends and connections, etc. So I came up with the Private Prometheans as worthy opponents for my tumultuous Inferno boys.

The Prometheans, in turn, are modeled after the infamous "Illuminati." Yes, the pyramid-obsessed, left-eye covering Luciferian freemason sect who were first exposed to the world when one of their couriers was struck dead by a lightning-bolt. Although it is said that both horse and rider were charred, oddly enough, the saddle bags were unscathed; inside them were found secret messages and papers detailing the conspirators' plans for world domination, starting with an uprising against the Hapsburgs.

Arrests followed and warnings were sent out to world leaders, including George Washington, who discussed his worries about the Illuminati's infiltration in his letters (available online, thanks to the Library of Congress. See Washington's letter to G.W. Snyder, 1798).

So. That is how the Prometheans came about. Although the Inferno Club series was completed in 2014, somewhere along the way, one of my readers put the darnedest idea into my head. She remarked (with an embarrassed giggle) that she found one of the Promethean assassins sexy. "Is that wrong?" she teased.

Hey, whatever floats your boat. *g* But it got me thinking. Wow, wouldn't it be cool if there was one good guy who'd had the great misfortune of being born into a sinister Promethean family?

Duke of Secrets finally gave me the chance to let Azrael out of his cage.

Moving on, one extremely interesting research topic that I wanted to mention for the history buffs out there with regard to this story is the fascinating, prehistoric barrows all over the British Isles.

These are so abundant that I marvel we don't run across them more often in Regency romances. There are over 6000 of them in the West Country alone, according to an article on Britain Express that I'm sure you'll enjoy.

(See www.britainexpress.com/history/prehistoric_monuments.)

Different types of barrows and earthworks (and of course, henges) were built across Great Britain by a succession of prehistoric peoples from as early as 3500 B.C. The type of barrow mound I envisioned for Owlswick was most commonly built during the Bronze and Iron Ages, but then began to reappear during the Dark Ages, which ranged from 410 A.D., the end of Roman Britain, till 1066, the Norman invasion.

Regency people were as fascinated by the mysterious mounds in their midst as we are today. Many mounds were broken into during the centuries, but intact sites are still regularly found. Indeed, one of the most spectacular of them all was not opened until 1939, Sutton Hoo in Suffolk. When archeologists finally peeked inside, they discovered the tomb, treasure—and buried ship!—of an Anglo-Saxon king, Redwald of East Anglia, who died in about 625 A.D.

(If you're interested, do an image search for Sutton Hoo, and prepare to be dazzled by the artistry of these ancient Anglo-Saxons.)

One final historical note concerns Richmond House, overlooking the Thames. The gentle reader, I hope, will forgive me for taking a slight liberty (twenty-five years long, to be exact) with Richmond House, the location of the Bonfire Night ball in this story.

Richmond House existed exactly as described up until 1791, when it was destroyed by a fire. Rebuilding commenced in 1822. The reason I decided to include it *anyway* and pretend, just between us, that it was still there in 1816 is because Regency fans have so often run across references to the famous Waterloo ball given by the Duchess of Richmond in Brussels.

You know the one—where half the gentleman had to run out of the ballroom oh-so-dramatically to go and fight Napoleon's approaching forces. Yet we never hear much about the 4th Duke and Duchess of Richmond themselves beyond that one historical footnote, despite them being quite interesting people.

Well, now you've gotten the chance to see at least a little glimpse of what had been the London house of the Richmond dukes before it burned down. (If you'd like a recap of what happened at this famous ball, I recommend this great article with pictures at www.historic-uk.com/HistoryUK/HistoryofBritain/The-Duchess-of-Richmonds-Ball/)

Another reason I chose this location was because of its association with fireworks. FYI, London fireworks often happen on the river. Richmond House, overlooking the Thames, was famous for the fireworks display given by His Grace, the second Duke of Richmond, to celebrate the Treaty of Aix-la-Chapelle in 1749. Classical music buffs will be tickled to hear that this fireworks extravaganza was accompanied by one of the first performances of Handel's *Music for the Royal Fireworks*.

Well! I am always amazed at the fun facts I get to learn as I'm writing my novels, and I hope you enjoy my passing them along to you. In closing, let me say thank you once more for reading my books, and I hope you'll join me again on my next excursion back to Moonlight Square.

Sincerely,

Gaelen

One Moonlit Night
(Moonlight Square: A Prequel Novella)

At the ripe old age of two-and-twenty, Lady Katrina Glendon just can't seem to snare a husband. Whether her frank tongue or slightly eccentric ways bear the blame, she faces a houseful of younger sisters clamoring for her, the eldest, to marry and move aside before they all end up as spinsters. When her latest suitor defects and proposes to another girl, Trinny throws up her hands in despair of ever finding a fiancé. But sometimes destiny waits just around the corner...and love lives right across the square!

Duke of Scandal
(Moonlight Square, Book 1)

Jason Hawthorne, the Duke of Netherford, made it clear to the young, lovesick Felicity Carvel long ago that nothing could ever happen between them. He has *earned* his reputation as the Duke of Scandal—and she's his best friend's little sister. For honor's sake, he vows to stay away from the lovely innocent. But even now, all grown up, Felicity still wants Jason for her own. And after getting her heart broken once before by Naughty Netherford, does she dare attempt to play with fire again—and this time, can Jason resist?

"Enchanting, intriguing, fun."
~Stephanie Laurens, #1 *New York Times* Bestseller

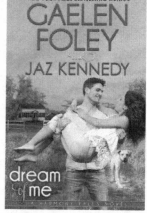
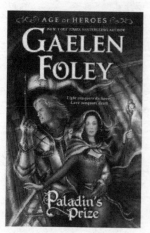

Enter a world of wonder & whimsy, adventure & peril in the Middle Grade/YA series that's as much fun for grownups as it is for kids!

Gaelen Foley writing as E.G. Foley
THE LOST HEIR: The Gryphon Chronicles, Book 1

Jake is a scrappy orphaned pickpocket living by his wits on the streets of Victorian London. Lately he's started seeing ghosts and can move solid objects with his mind! He has no idea why. Next thing he knows, a Sinister Gentleman and his minions come hunting him, and Jake is plunged headlong into a mysterious world of magic and deadly peril. A world that holds the secret of who he really is: the long-lost heir of an aristocratic family with magical powers.

But with treacherous enemies closing in, it will take all of his wily street instincts and the help of his friends—both human and magical—to solve the mystery of what happened to his parents and defeat the foes who never wanted the Lost Heir of Griffon to be found...

"A wonderful novel in the same vein as Harry Potter, full of nonstop action, magical creatures, and the reality that was Queen Victoria's England." ~The Reading Café

About the Author

 Noted for her "complex, subtly shaded characters, richly sensual love scenes, and elegantly fluid prose" (Booklist), New York Times, USA Today, and Publisher's Weekly Bestselling author Gaelen Foley has written over twenty (and counting!) rich, bold historical romances set in Regency England and Napoleonic Europe. Since her debut in 1998, her books have been published in seventeen languages worldwide and have won numerous awards, including the National Readers' Choice Award, the Booksellers' Best, the Golden Leaf, the Award of Excellence, and the HOLT Medallion.

A versatile and hardworking writer, Gaelen's passion for the craft of fiction keeps her exploring new creative ground. While continuing to entertain her Regency fans, she has branched out into contemporary small-town romance as well as fantasy romance. Since 2012, Gaelen has also been co-writing fantasy middle grade/children's novels with her husband, a former teacher, under the penname E.G. Foley. The Lost Heir, Book 1 in their Gryphon Chronicles series, was a #1 Amazon Children's Bestseller (and was optioned for a movie!).

To learn more about Gaelen and her books, visit her at GaelenFoley.com.

Made in the USA
San Bernardino, CA
07 March 2018